THE
EDGE
OF
EVERYTHING

JEFF GILES

BLOOMSBURY

LONDON   OXFORD   NEW YORK   NEW DELHI   SYDNEY

For Jenny

BLOOMSBURY YA
Bloomsbury Publishing Plc
50 Bedford Square, London, WC1B 3DP, UK

BLOOMSBURY, BLOOMSBURY YA and the Diana logo
are trademarks of Bloomsbury Publishing Plc

First published in the USA in 2017 by Bloomsbury Children's Books
This edition published in Great Britain in 2018 by Bloomsbury Publishing Plc

A catalogue record for this book is available from the British Library

ISBN: PB: 978-1-4088-9732-4; eBook: 978-1-4088-6908-6;

2 4 6 8 10 9 7 5 3 1

Typeset by RefineCatch Limited, Bungay, Suffolk

Printed and bound in Great Britain by CPI Group (UK) Ltd, Croydon, CR0 4YY

MIX
Paper from
responsible sources
FSC® C020471
www.fsc.org

To find out more about our authors and books visit www.bloomsbury.com
and sign up for our newsletters

From the beginning of time,
in childhood, I thought
that pain meant
I was not loved.
It meant I loved.

—Louise Glück, "First Memory"

Prologue

SHE NAMED HIM HERSELF, so it felt like he belonged to her.

He said that where he was from, which he called the Lowlands, they strip your name away like a husk the moment you arrive—to remind you that you're *no one* and *nothing*. When he told her this, she moved a little closer. She should have been scared after what she'd seen him do to Stan, but she wasn't. Stan deserved everything he got and worse.

The lake was frozen, and they were standing way out in the middle. The ice was shifting, settling. It made booming sounds beneath them, as if it might give way. Stan was gone, but drops of his blood had seeped into the lake. There was a dark constellation at their feet.

She refused to look at it. She suggested some names, and he listened in silence, his eyes shy and wounded-looking. She wanted

1

to step even closer, but she was afraid she'd startle him. She teased him instead.

She told him he seemed like either an Aragorn—or a Fred. He tilted his head, confused. She'd have to work on his sense of humor.

Otherwise, there was nothing about him she'd have changed. He had tangled black hair that fell near his eyes like vines. His face was pale, except for bruises high up on both cheeks. It looked like someone had grabbed his face and dug their fingernails in. Over and over. For *years*. She didn't ask who had been hurting him—or why he'd been sent to whatever the Lowlands were in the first place. It was too soon for questions like that.

He told her that even if she gave him a name, the lords of the Lowlands wouldn't let him use it. She'd heard him shout so fiercely at Stan. But with her, he was quiet and unsure. He said he didn't think he even deserved a name after all the things he'd done. Been *forced* to do.

If that didn't break her heart, it definitely tore a little bit off.

He was staring at her now—looking *into* her, like he thought she was the answer to something.

She gave him a playful look.

"Dude, seriously," she said, "*enough* with the eyes."

She told him everybody deserved a name—and that "the lords" should shut up.

She said hers was Zoe Bissell.

He nodded. He already knew. She couldn't figure out how.

She told him she'd call him X until she knew what sort of person he was. X for an *unknown variable*. Zoe was 17, and so many crappy, lonely things had already happened to her that she knew it

2

was insane to get close to even one more person. But maybe X's pain, whatever it was, would help her put aside her own.

She told him that if the Lowlands took *this* name away, she'd just give him another one.

"Such as Fred," he said, and attempted a smile.

He was learning.

PART ONE

A Rescue

ONE

ZOE MET X ON A SUNDAY IN FEBRUARY, when there was a storm on its way from Canada and the sky was so dark it looked like someone was closing a giant coffin lid over Montana.

The blizzard wasn't supposed to hit the mountain for an hour, and her mom had gone to get groceries to tide them over. Zoe had wanted to go, too, because her mother couldn't be trusted to choose food. Not ever. Her mom was a badass in many ways. Still, the woman was a hard-core vegan and her idea of dinner was tofu or seitan, which, as Zoe had stated repeatedly, tasted like the flesh of aliens.

Her mother had insisted she and her brother, Jonah, stay home where they'd be safe. She said she was pretty sure she could get down the mountain and back up again before the storm ripped through. Zoe had driven in blizzards herself. She was pretty sure she couldn't.

Zoe wasn't thrilled to be in charge. It was partly because Jonah was a spaz, though she was not allowed to call him that, according to a sign her mother had posted above the gargantuan juicer in the

7

kitchen: Uncool Words That I Cannot, in Good Conscience, Tolerate. More than that, though, it was because the place she'd lived her whole life suddenly seemed menacing and strange. In November, Zoe's father had died while exploring a cave called Black Teardrop. Then, in January, two of the people she loved most in the world, a couple of elderly neighbors named Bert and Betty Wallace, were dragged out of their home by an intruder and never seen again. The grief was like a cold stone on Zoe's heart. She couldn't imagine how bad it was for Jonah.

She could hear her brother outside now, chasing Spock and Uhura around like the ADHD maniac that he was. She'd let him go out because he'd begged to play with the dogs, and, honestly, she couldn't stand being with him one more second. He was eight. If she'd said no, he would have whined till her ears bled ("Just let me go out for ten minutes, Zoe! Okay, five minutes! Okay, *two* minutes! I can have two minutes? Okay, what about five minutes?"). Even if she'd managed to shut him up, she'd have been stuck with his crazy energy in a small house on an isolated mountain with a blizzard coming their way like a pissed-off army.

She went online and checked WeatherBug. With the windchill, it was 10 degrees below zero.

Zoe knew she should call Jonah inside, but kept putting it off. She couldn't deal with him yet. At least she'd wrapped every inch of him up tight: a green skater-boy hoodie, a down jacket, and black gloves decorated with skulls that glowed in the dark. She had insisted that he wear snowshoes so he wouldn't sink into a snow-drift and disappear. Then she'd spent five minutes forcing them onto his feet while he twitched and writhed like he was being elec-trocuted. He really could be ridiculous.

8

She checked her phone. It was five o'clock, and there were two texts waiting for her.

The first was from her friend Dallas, who she'd been seeing off and on before her dad died.

It said: *Blizzards be awesome, dawg! You doing OK??*

Dallas was a good guy. He was muscly and dimply in a baseball-player kind of way—cute, but not exactly Zoe's type. Also, he had a tattoo that used to kill the mood whenever he took his shirt off. He'd apparently gone back and forth between *Never Stop!* and *Don't Ever Stop!*, and the tattoo artist had gotten confused and the tat wound up reading, *Never Don't Stop!* Dallas, being Dallas, loved it and high-fived the guy on the spot.

Zoe texted him back in Dallas-speak: *I'm solid, dawg! Thx for checking. You rock on the reg. (Did I say that right?)*

The second text was from her best friend, Val: *This blizzard sucks ass. ASS! I'm gonna take a nap with Gloria and ignore it. I'm VERY serious about this nap. Do you need ANYTHING AT ALL before nap begins?? Once nap is in progress, I will be UNAVAILABLE to you.*

Val's girlfriend was extremely shy. Val was . . . *not.* She'd been crazy in love with Gloria for a year, and was always doing beautiful, slightly psycho things, like making a Tumblr devoted entirely to Gloria's feet.

Zoe texted back: *Why is everyone worried about me? I'm FINE! Go take your nap, Nap Goddess! I will be soooo quiet!!!!*

Smiling to herself, she added emojis of an alarm clock, a hammer, and a bomb.

Val wrote back one more time: *Love you too, freak!*

ZOE FOUND DUCT TAPE in a kitchen drawer and taped up the downstairs windows so they wouldn't shatter in the storm. Her mother had told her that doing this in a blizzard was dumb and possibly dangerous. Still, it made Zoe feel safer somehow, and gave her something to do. She peered outside, and saw Jonah and the black Labs jumping back and forth across the frozen river at the bottom of their yard. Their mom had prohibited this activity on another sign she had made: Uncool Behavior That I Cannot, in Good Conscience, Tolerate. Zoe pretended she hadn't noticed what her brother was doing. Then she stopped watching so she wouldn't see him do anything worse. She went upstairs and taped *X*'s on the second-story windows. She threw in a few *O*'s, too, so that when her mother finally drove up it'd look like giants were playing tic-tac-toe.

She finished taping the windows at 5:30, just as the storm finally found the mountain. She made herself a cup of coffee—black, because her mother only bought soy milk, which tasted like the *tears* of aliens—and drifted into the living room, so she could sip it at the window. Zoe stared out at the forest, which started up at the bottom of their yard and ran all the way down to the lake. Her family's land was a mostly bald patch of the mountain, but there was a stand of larch up against the house to give them shade in the summer. The wind had agitated them. Branches were stabbing and scratching the glass. It was like the trees were trying to get in.

Her mom had been gone two hours. By now, the police would have barricaded the roads and, though her mother was not usually someone who took no for an answer, the cops would never let her back up the mountain tonight. Zoe pushed the thought down into a box at the back of her brain labeled Do Not Open. She shouted out the front door for Jonah. She'd been an idiot to leave him out there so long. She pushed that thought down, too.

Jonah didn't answer. She hadn't really expected him to. She loved the little bug, but most days it seemed like his sole purpose in life was to make everything harder for her. She knew he could hear her. He just wasn't ready to stop romping around with the dogs. They weren't allowed in the house, even during storms, which Jonah thought was mean. He once protested with an actual picket sign.

Zoe shouted for her brother three more times: loud, louder, loudest.

No answer.

She checked WeatherBug again. It was 15 below.

All she could see out the window was a riot of white. Everything was shapeless and heavy with snow: her spectacularly crappy red car, the compost bin, even the big wooden bear that her mom's hippie-dippy artist friend, Rufus, had carved for the driveway. The thought of having to bundle up and trudge around in the storm just to drag Jonah's butt inside made Zoe so angry that her face started to get hot. And she wouldn't be able to complain to her mom because she shouldn't have let him outside in the first place. Jonah always found a way to win. He was nuts, but he was clever.

She yelled for Spock and Uhura. No answer. Spock was two years younger and a big-time coward. Zoe figured he was hiding under the tractor in the pole barn, quivering. But Uhura was a daredevil and scared of nothing. She should have come running.

Zoe sighed. She had to go find Jonah. She had no choice.

She threw on a scarf, gloves, boots, a puffy blue coat, and a tasseled hat that Jonah had knitted for her when their dad died (actually, Uhura had eaten the tassel and in its place there was just a hole that kept getting bigger and bigger). Zoe didn't bother with snowshoes because she was only going to be out as long as it took to march Jonah back inside. Five minutes. Maybe ten. Tops.

Zoe knew it was pointless to wish that her dad were around to help her track down Jonah. She wished it anyway. Memories of her father swept over her so suddenly it made her whole body clench.

ZOE'S DAD HAD BEEN goofy, excitable—and completely, infuriatingly unreliable. He was obsessed with everything about caves, down to bats and flatworms. He was even bizarrely into cave mud, which he insisted held the secret to a great complexion. He used to bring Ziploc bags of it home and try to dab it on Zoe's mother's face. Her mom would shriek with laughter and run away in mock horror. Then her dad would smear it all over his own cheeks, and chase Jonah and Zoe around the house, making monster noises.

So, yes: her dad was weird, as you pretty much have to be to go caving in the first place. But he was weird in a good way. In fact, he was kind of amazingly weird. He was superskinny and flexible, and if he put his arms over his head like Superman, he could crawl through incredibly narrow passageways. He used to practice by bending a wire hanger into an oval and wriggling through—or by crawling back and forth under the car. Literally, he'd be doing this stuff in plain sight when Val or Dallas came over. Dallas was a caver, too, and thought it was all deeply awesome. Val would avert her eyes from whatever bizarre thing Zoe's father was doing and say, "I'm not even noticing—this is me *not noticing*."

Zoe started caving with her dad when she turned 15. (Nobody called it "spelunking"—because why *would* they?) They caved religiously every summer and fall, until the snow blocked the entrances and ice made the tunnels treacherous. Zoe was only semi into it at first, but she needed time with her father that she knew she could count on. Unless you were going caving, you just couldn't trust the guy to show up.

Zoe had gotten used to his disappearances, just as she'd gotten used to the fact that there were things he never talked about. (His parents, his hometown in Virginia, anything at all that happened when he was young: those parts of the map were never colored in.) Her father specialized in grand gestures—he'd changed his last name to Bissell instead of asking Zoe's mom to change hers—and he could be the coolest dad in the world for weeks on end. He'd make her feel warm and watched-over, like there was a candle or a lantern by her bed. But then the air in the house would change somehow. It'd lose its charge. Her dad's SUV would disappear, and for weeks she wouldn't even get a text.

Zoe eventually stopped listening to her father's excuses. They usually had to do with some weird business he was trying to get off the ground—something about "drumming up the freakin' financing." When she was younger, Zoe blamed herself for the fact that her dad never stuck around for more than a few months at a time. Maybe she wasn't interesting enough. Maybe she wasn't *lovable* enough. Jonah was still so young that he worshipped their father unconditionally. He called him Daddy Man, and treated every glimpse of him like a celebrity sighting.

Zoe knew that she and her dad would always have their treks up to the caves, and she stopped expecting anything else. So that day in November when she'd woken to find that he'd gone caving without her felt like a betrayal.

The cops led the search for his body. Zoe had invented the Do Not Open box to hold back the memories.

* * *

ZOE CURSED JONAH UNDER her breath the minute she got outdoors and started hunting for him and the dogs. She couldn't see more than a couple of feet in front of her or walk more than a few steps without stopping to catch her breath. The wind, the snow: it was like being punched in the stomach.

The light, meanwhile, was dying fast. The coffin lid over Montana was getting ready to snap shut.

Zoe felt inside her pockets, and had a surprise bit of good luck. She found a flashlight—and it actually worked.

It took her five minutes just to zigzag down to the river where she'd seen Jonah playing. There was no sign of him or the dogs, except for a snow angel already partly filled in by the storm and two weird, blurry indentations nearby, where Jonah had apparently tried to get Spock and Uhura to make *dog* snow angels.

She screamed Jonah's name but her voice didn't travel. The wind pushed it right back to her.

For the first time, she felt dread crawl up into her throat. She imagined telling her mom that she'd lost Jonah, and she pictured her mother's heart blasting apart, like the Death Star in *Star Wars*. If something happened to that kid, her mother would never recover. Zoe tried to push that thought down, too. But the box at the back of her brain could only hold so much, and everything began seeping out.

Zoe finally found Jonah's footprints and followed them around the house. It was slow going because she had to bend down low to the ground, like a hunchback, to see the trail. Branches were breaking off trees and blowing across the yard. Every step exhausted her. Sweat was trickling down her back even though she was freezing. She knew that sweating in the frigid cold was bad news. Her body heat was evaporating. She had to pick up the pace, find

14

Jonah, and get inside. But if she moved any quicker, she'd sweat even more and freeze even faster.

Another thought the box didn't have room for.

Maybe Jonah was back in the house already. Yes. He definitely was. Zoe pictured him, his face and hands all puffy and pink as he spilled cocoa powder across the kitchen floor. She told herself that all this was for nothing. She followed his tracks, sure they'd lead right to their door.

But ten feet from the front steps, they veered down the hill and got swallowed up by the woods.

Zoe took a few cautious steps into the trees and shouted, but she knew it was pointless. She'd have to go in after Jonah and the Labs. Her cheeks and ears stung like they were sunburned. Her hands, even in gloves, were frozen into little sculptures of fists.

SHE USED TO WORSHIP the forest. She'd grown up running through the trees, sunlight splashing down around her feet. The trees led to the lake, where Bert and Betty Wallace had lived. They'd been like grandparents to Zoe and Jonah. They'd been there for them even when their dad was off on one of his mysterious trips, and they were a continual source of kindness when he died. But Bert and Betty had been going senile for years. This past fall, Zoe had kept Bert company as he cut photographs of animals out of the newspaper and barked random stuff like, "Gimme a break, I'm just a crazy old codger!" (When she asked him what a "codger" was, he rolled his eyes and said, "Gimme a break, same thing as a coot!") Jonah had sat crisscross-applesauce on the floor and knitted with Betty. She'd taught him how, and it turned out to be one of the few things, besides chewing his fingernails, that eased his ADHD and stopped his brain from whirring like an out-of-control blender. Toward the end, though, Betty couldn't keep her hands from shaking, and she'd forgotten everything she knew about knitting. Now Jonah had to teach *her* how.

Then, last month, the Wallaces had disappeared. Betty, the less senile of the pair, apparently got away from the intruder for a moment and rushed Bert into their truck. That was the police's theory, based on the blood on the steering wheel. The truck was found smashed into a tree a hundred yards from the house. Its engine was still running. Its doors were flung open and there was no sign of the Wallaces, except for more blood. Imagining the confused look on Bert and Betty's faces as someone scowled murderously down at them hurt Zoe's heart so much she could hardly breathe.

The Wallaces' house was left just the way it was, lonely as a museum, while their lawyers looked for the most recent version of their will. Zoe had promised herself that she'd never go near it again. It was too painful. The lake outside Bert and Betty's house was frozen over with cloudy gray ice now. Even the forest seemed scary—dense and forbidding, like somewhere your evil stepmother takes you in a fairy tale.

Yet here she was on the edge of the trees, being pulled down toward the Wallaces' place. Jonah knew better than to walk through the trees in a storm. If the dogs had gone into the forest, though, he'd have followed them. Spock and Uhura had lived with Zoe's family for a month, but they used to belong to Bert and Betty. They might have plunged into the icy trees, thinking they were going home.

THERE WAS LESS THAN a mile of woods between the Bissells' land and Bert and Betty's house. Ordinarily, it was a 15-minute walk, and it was impossible to get lost because Betty had made hatchet marks in the trees for the kids to follow. Also, the woods were divided into three sections, so you could always tell if you'd gotten spun around somehow. The first section of forest had been harvested for timber a while back—Zoe's mom preferred the term "raped and pillaged"—so the trees closest to the Bissells' house were new growth. They were mostly flaky gray lodgepole pines. They were planted so close together that they seemed to be huddling for warmth.

The second section was Zoe's favorite: giant larches and Douglas firs. They were Montana's version of skyscrapers. They were only a hundred years old, but looked dinosaur-old, like they'd come with the planet.

The trees closest to the lake had burned in an unexplained fire before Zoe was born. They'd never fallen, though, so there was a quarter-mile's worth of charred snags just standing there dead. It was a spooky place—and Jonah's favorite part of the woods, of course. It was where he played all his soldier-of-the-apocalypse games.

Walking to Bert and Betty's house meant following the path through new trees, then old trees, then dead ones. Zoe and Jonah had made the trip a thousand times. There was no such thing as getting lost—not for long. Not in decent weather or in daylight.

After Zoe had walked 20 feet or so into the young part of the forest, the world became quiet. There was just a low hum in the air, like somebody blowing across the top of a bottle. She felt sheltered and the tiniest bit warmer. She aimed the flashlight at the treetops and then at the surly sky above them, and she had a weird, dreamy impulse to plop down in the snow. She shook her head to erase the thought. The cold was already gumming up her brain. If she sat down, she'd never get up.

Zoe shone the flashlight in a wide arc along the ground, looking to pick up Jonah's tracks again. The beam was weak, either because of the batteries or the cold, but eventually she found them. Jonah probably had a ten-minute head start on her and because he was wearing snowshoes he'd be covering ground faster. It was like a math problem: If Train A leaves the station at 4:30 p.m. traveling 90 miles an hour, and Train B leaves ten minutes later traveling 70 miles an hour ... Zoe's brain was too numb to solve it, but it seemed like she was screwed.

Jonah knew the path to the lake but he must have been following the dogs. Their paw prints were messy and wild. Maybe they were being playful. Maybe they were chasing grouse or wild turkeys, which sometimes rode out storms beneath the skirts of the trees. Maybe they were just flipping out because it was so cold.

Zoe could see Jonah's snowshoe tracks chasing the dogs every which way. She couldn't tell if he had been playing along happily or if he had been terrified and begging them to turn back. In her head, she repeated over and over: *Just go home, Jonah. This is insane. Just leave the dogs. Just walk away.* But she knew he wouldn't abandon the dogs no matter how scary things got, which made her angry— and made her love him, too.

So she just kept slogging through the woods. Which sucked. *Drag right foot out of snow, lift it up, stick it in again. Drag left foot out, repeat. And repeat and repeat and repeat.* Zoe was losing track of time. It took forever to go even a couple hundred feet—and much longer when she had to hike herself up and over a fallen tree. Her legs and knees began to ache, then her shoulders and neck. And she became obsessed with the hole at the top of her hat where the tassel used to be. She imagined it yawning wider and wider, and could feel the wind's bony fingers in her hair.

After Zoe had been in the woods for 20 minutes or so, her cheeks, which were partly exposed to the air, were scalding hot. She thought about taking her gloves off and somehow peeling the skin off her face—and then she realized that that was completely crazy. She and her brain had stopped playing on the same team. Which scared the hell out of her.

The ground started to level off and Zoe saw an enormous old fir tree up ahead. *New trees, old trees, dead trees.* She was almost a third of the way through the woods. She told herself to keep walking, not to stop for anything, until she could touch that first giant tree. That would make everything feel real again.

About ten feet from the fir, Zoe stumbled on something under the snow and belly flopped onto the ground. A bolt of pain tore through her head. She'd hit it against a rock or a stump, and could feel a bruise blooming on her forehead. She took off a glove and touched it. When she pulled her hand away, her fingers were dark with blood.

She decided it wasn't that bad.

She forced herself up onto her knees, then her feet. And, using that first fir tree as her goalpost, she walked the next few yards. When she got to the tree, she leaned against it and felt a wave of relief because, no matter how heinous things are, you gotta love a Christmas tree.

Zoe was in the second part of the woods now, with maybe half a mile to go. The trees were massive—they roared up toward the sky—and set far enough apart that what daylight was left trickled down to her. Here, Jonah and the dogs' tracks were clean and clear. They seemed to be sticking to the path now. She started off again, trying to think of nothing but the rhythm of her steps.

She imagined finding Jonah and marching him home. She imagined wrapping him in blankets till he laughed and shouted, "I! Am! Not! A! Burrito!"

Zoe had been outside for 30 or 40 minutes, and it had to be 25 below. She was shaking like she'd been hit by an electric current. By the time she'd made it halfway through the fir trees, every part of her ached and shivered like a tuning fork. And the storm seemed stronger now. The forest itself was breaking apart all around her. The wind stripped off branches and flung them in every direction. Whole trees had toppled over and lay blocking the path.

She stopped to rest against a tree. She had to. She swung the flashlight around, trying to figure out how far she was from the lake. But her hands were weak and she fumbled and dropped it in the snow.

The light went out.

She sank to her knees to search for the flashlight. It was getting dark so she had to root around in the snow. The shivering had gotten worse—at first it'd felt like she'd touched an electric fence, but now her nerves were so fully on fire that it felt like she *was* an electric fence—but she didn't care. And she didn't care about the bruise or the cut or whatever it was that was pulsing on her forehead. She didn't care that there were thorns and branches hiding under the snow and that they were tearing at the skin beneath her gloves. She could barely feel anything anyway. After a few minutes on her knees—it could have been two, it could have been ten, she had no idea anymore—her hand found something in the snow. She let out a yelp of happiness, or as much of one as she could manage, and she pulled it out. But it wasn't the flashlight.

It was one of Jonah's gloves.

The skull on the back glowed up at her, the empty eye sockets like tunnels.

She pictured Jonah stumbling through the woods, sobbing loudly. She pictured his hand frozen and raw and beating with pain. She pictured him pleading with the dogs to go home. (He *must* have started pleading by now.) His face came to her for a second. He had their father's looks, which still made her wince: the messy brown hair, the eyes you assumed would be blue but were actually a cool, weird green. The only difference was that Jonah had slightly chubby cheeks. *Thank god for baby fat*, Zoe thought. Because, tonight, it might keep Jonah alive.

She found the flashlight, and—miraculously—there was some life left in it. She got to her feet and started out again.

A few feet from the first glove, she found the second one.

Ten feet later, she found Jonah's coat.

It was a puffy black down jacket, patched with electrical tape—and he'd left it draped over the jagged stump of a tree.

Now Zoe imagined her brother dazed and wandering, his skin itchy and hot, like it was crawling all over him. She imagined him pulling off his clothes and dropping them in the snow.

Zoe was exhausted. And freaked out. And so unbelievably mad at those idiot dogs who didn't know enough to stay close to the house—who didn't realize that her beautiful brother would follow them and follow them and follow them through the snow. Until it killed him.

She had to erase that awful image of Jonah. She cast around for a happy thought. She remembered how Jonah used to hide in the exact same place every time they played hide-and-seek with their dad—the old meat freezer in the basement, which hadn't been used in years. She remembered how they'd act like they had no idea where Jonah was, even though they could see his little fingers propping the lid open for air. And she pictured the ecstatic look on Jonah's face when she and their dad pretended to give up and Jonah thrust the freezer open and revealed himself, like a magician at the end of a death-defying trick.

"It's me!" he'd shout happily. "It's me! It's me! It's me!"

For a few seconds that image of Jonah warmed her. Then it disappeared, like a star snuffed out forever.

ZOE MADE IT TO the edge of the fir trees—right up to where the forest died suddenly and gave way to fire-charred stumps and snags. She was carrying Jonah's coat and gloves, hugging them against her chest in a bundle. Did she still think she could find Jonah, or was she just stumbling the last quarter mile to Bert and Betty's house to collapse? She didn't even know anymore. The cold had erased everything inside her. She was blank. She was a zombie, lurching forward because she didn't know what else to do.

The flashlight found something: a dark clump, barely higher than the snow.

Zoe should have been excited at the discovery, but she felt terror wash through her instead. Whatever it was up there in the snow, it wasn't moving.

She didn't want to get any closer. She didn't want to know what it was.

She didn't want it to be her brother.

It took months to walk the next 15 feet. And even when Zoe was only a few steps away—even when the flashlight was shining right at it, bathing it in a sickly yellow light—she couldn't figure out what it was. Her mind refused to take it in, refused to record it.

She forced herself forward. She hovered over it. She peered down. It was a dark, tangled mass. It looked lifeless and still. Zoe held her breath and willed her eyes to focus.

It was the dogs.

Since they were both black Labs, you couldn't tell where Spock's fur ended and Uhura's began: they looked like a dark rug flung onto the snow. Zoe knelt down. They'd dug a shallow pit to shield themselves from the wind. She took off a glove and laid a hand on one, then the other.

They were breathing! Something that felt like birds' wings flapped around in her heart.

The dogs were groggy, halfway between sleep and something worse. It took them a minute to notice that she was rubbing their bellies. Eventually, they began shifting in their icy bed. Spock snorted and sent a puff of fog into the air. Uhura craned her head in Zoe's direction. She seemed to recognize her and to be grateful she was there. Zoe felt too wrung out to cry or she would have.

Spock and Uhura wriggled some more, trying to wake themselves up. And as their bodies untangled and parted, as they became two distinct animals again, she finally saw something she should have seen immediately, and what she saw made her hate herself for ever thinking they were idiot dogs. They were beautiful dogs! They were brave and glossy and gorgeous Montana dogs!

Because they were lying on something. On someone. They had dug a pit with their paws and pulled him into it—she could see where their teeth had torn his green hoodie—and then lain down on top of him. On top of Jonah. They had lain down on her brother to keep him warm.

TWO

Jonah was stiff as a mannequin.

Zoe wrapped him in his coat. She blew on his frozen fingers to heat them, though she could barely force any breath out of her body. And she took him up in her arms. She figured she'd have to go back for Spock and Uhura but they shook themselves off and waddled like ancient snow creatures out of the pit. Spock whined. He couldn't believe what he was being asked to do. Uhura snapped at him, as if to say, "Get over it!"

And then Zoe ran. Through the dead trees, toward Bert and Betty's. She draped Jonah over both arms and when her arms felt like they'd snap, she heaved him over one shoulder, and when it felt like that shoulder would break, she heaved him over the other. She was shaking too hard to aim the flashlight, so the beam bounced crazily in front of her. It was a miracle that she didn't smash into a tree and bust both their heads. She was like an animal running. Her heart was pounding, not just in her rib cage but in her ears—loud, like someone drumming on a bucket.

The joke was, she was probably going a tenth of a mile an hour, staggering through the snow like a drunken yeti. But she was getting there. She was covering ground. When she could finally see Bert and Betty's house through the trees, she totally lost it and cried. Even the dogs barked with something like happiness. Actually, Uhura sounded happy, and Spock sounded like he was yipping, "Are we there yet?"

Zoe laughed, and whispered to Jonah, "Oh my god, Spock is *such* a wuss." He was too out of it to reply, but she could feel his little-boy body breathing against her chest—a wheezy but unmistakable in and out, in and out—and that was answer enough.

BERT AND BETTY'S HOUSE looked like a capital A. It stood about 200 feet back from the lake, on a couple of acres of land that had been spared by the fire way back when, even though the flames swirled around it. The skies were black and the blizzard had begun to die by the time Zoe got to the front steps with Jonah wriggling in her arms. The door was unlocked. That should have seemed strange—the police had sealed the place up and Zoe's mom checked on it every few days—but her brain couldn't absorb the information. It just kept pinging with the word *shelter, shelter, shelter*.

Zoe held the door open for Spock and Uhura, but they hesitated on the steps. They'd never been allowed in the house.

"Go," was all she had the energy to say.

They looked at each other, then scrambled inside.

The flashlight had died so she felt her way to the living room in the dark, and laid Jonah on a couch. She covered him with blankets, cushions, even an antique wedding quilt she pulled off the wall. He said one feverish word ("Me?") then fell into sleep like a stone thrown in a well.

Zoe reached for a lamp but the electricity had been shut off. The heat, too. And probably the water and phone. But she didn't care. She lit some candles around the room, which was all they needed. The house was so much warmer than the woods that the couch might as well have been a hammock on a beach. And they'd made it. They'd *made* it. Now that she had set Jonah down her arms were so light they floated.

There was a spiral rag rug on the floor. She picked it up, shook some dirt out of it, and wrapped it around her like a cape. It was scratchy and stiff, but she didn't care. There was a smell in the room that shouldn't have been there—cigarettes—but she told herself she didn't care about that either. She noticed a scuzzy-looking sleeping bag bunched up in front of the fireplace like dead skin a snake had sloughed off. It shouldn't have been there. And there was a collection of empty booze bottles, all different kinds, making a miniature skyline on the floor. They shouldn't have been there. She didn't care, didn't care, didn't care.

The dogs were freaking out, though: they sniffed and growled and poked into every corner.

Zoe shushed them.

"Nobody here but us chickens," she said.

It was some weird thing she'd heard her mother say.

Her mother.

Zoe dug into her pockets for her phone, but this deep in the woods she couldn't get a signal to make a call. It was just as well.

26

She'd have to answer too many questions—and micro-questions and micro-micro-questions. She was too tired to explain anything, let alone *everything*.

Zoe knew that her mom could camp out on her friend Rufus's couch for the night, if she couldn't make it back up the mountain. Rufus was sweet, shy, and so slim that he looked like a stick that had somehow grown a beard and bought a Phish T-shirt. He was an artist. He specialized in chain-saw carvings of bears like the one he'd made for the Bissells' driveway. Depending on the season, he made them out of salvaged timber or ice. ("Carving ice is *epic*, man," he said. "It's a rad, rad journey.") In Zoe's opinion, Rufus was secretly in love with her mother. She hoped he'd blurt it out someday. Her mom acted strong for the benefit of the kids, but Zoe knew how much sadness she carried around since the kids' dad had died. It was always there, like background music.

Zoe had to tell her mom she was okay. She groaned at the thought of expending any more energy—she was, after all, about to fall asleep sitting up, draped in a rug that looked like a giant Danish. But before she closed her eyes, Zoe rallied long enough to do two final things for the day. She checked on Jonah. He lay beside her snoring lightly like a soft little machine. His cheeks were hot, but he seemed basically fine.

Then she texted her mother a single word. She knew it wouldn't go through—she knew she'd have to keep hitting Try Again—but she did it anyway.

She texted: *Safe*.

AT 7:30, ZOE FELL asleep just long enough to have a single violent dream. She was in a white room with a bare wood floor. Animals were chained all around her. She didn't know what kind of

27

animals they were—maybe they were imaginary creatures that her brain invented—but they were vicious and snarling, all teeth, claws, and saliva. And they were straining at their chains, trying furiously to rip them out of the wall. Zoe stood in the center of the room. They were inches away from her on all sides, howling and screeching. And then snow started falling into the room somehow. She lifted her face and let the flakes drift down on her. She felt relieved for a second. When she looked back down again, Jonah was suddenly beside her. He said he would fight the creatures and save her. She forbade him. She told him to stand still, to stand perfectly still. But the animals were wailing so loudly that he couldn't hear her and thought she was saying, "Yes, kill them, Jonah. Kill them all."

The last thing she could remember was Jonah saying, "Yeah, I'm definitely gonna," and stepping into all those wet, flashing teeth.

It took forever to swim up out of the dream. And the howling followed her, because Uhura was at the door making a crazy racket. She barked so loudly it was astonishing. The noise was like a physical presence in the room. Zoe couldn't think.

As for Spock, he was hiding under a rug—all you could see was a big quaking bubble.

Zoe went to the door, afraid to pet Uhura when she was so wired.

"What's going on, girlfriend?" she said softly. "Shhh. It's okay, it's okay."

She reached out to stroke the dog with her palm, but Uhura snapped at her—something she'd never done, not to anyone, ever—and began hurling herself at the door. She thumped against it three times, loud as a monster knocking.

"Do you have to pee or what?" Zoe said.

She opened the door. Uhura bolted, and Zoe followed her out, her entire nervous system grateful that the barking had ceased.

It was pretty dark, and there was no moon, but there must have been light coming from somewhere because the lake was shining. The blizzard had passed quickly. All that remained was a light snowfall. Zoe shivered and noticed again how badly her body ached. The only thing holding her bones together was pain.

She looked around for Uhura, and began worrying about how she was going to get Jonah home in the morning.

Then she saw a truck barreling down the driveway toward the house, its tires kicking up snow.

It was an ugly, banged-up old pickup. Technically, it was black but it'd been patched in so many places that it looked like it had a skin disease. Zoe couldn't see the driver. All she could make out was an arm holding a cigarette out the window. For a second, she watched, in the semidarkness, as the red dot of the cigarette floated closer and closer. It was hypnotizing.

When she snapped out of it, she saw that Uhura was flying up the driveway toward the truck—*directly* toward it, unwavering, like she could block it with her body. Zoe didn't even have a chance to scream.

EITHER THE DRIVER DIDN'T see the dog in his headlights, or didn't care. About a hundred feet from the house, there was a terrible *thud*. Uhura's body was thrown into a snowbank.

The snow kept falling as if nothing had happened.

And the driver kept coming. He pulled up to the house. Got out. Left the engine running. Slid a new cigarette into his gross, chapped little mouth and, without even glancing back to see what had happened to Uhura, turned to Zoe.

29

He looked like *hate*. He was middle-aged with a graying buzz cut and acne scars. His clothes—pleated black pants, a white shirt with blue stripes—were clearly bought to impress people once upon a time but they couldn't have gotten him far, because they were so dirty now that a washing machine would have spit them back out.

Zoe raced down the steps and knelt over Uhura in the snow. The dog was shaken, but alive.

The man didn't say a word. He certainly didn't apologize. He just stood there, his eyes sliding over Zoe's body and leaving slime trails like snails. Men had looked at her like this ever since she was 12. When she first talked to her mother about it, her mom had said, "Zoe, sit down for a second. It's time I taught you the meaning of the phrase 'horrible lowlife perv.'" Zoe had always loved her for that.

This particular lowlife was grinning, which made her veins twitch.

"You hit my dog," she said. "Are you insane?"

He laughed, then his eyes got hard.

"That ain't your dog," he said. "Just 'cause a couple old folks get themselves dead don't mean you can come along and snatch up their dogs." He flicked his cigarette on the driveway, where it fizzled out in the snow. "And whereabouts is the other one—the chickenshit one?"

He knew Spock and Uhura.

"Who are you?" Zoe said.

"Who am I? I'm somebody who hates standing in the friggin' cold. Also, I'm somebody who hates questions. Now where's the other damn dog?"

"That's a question," said Zoe.

The man barked out a laugh.

"Well, look who's got a mouth on her! Tell you what, girlie, you can call me Stan, how about that? As in, Stan the Man. I'll call you . . . Zoe. How's that grab you?"

And he knew *her*.

"Not so goddamn smart-alecky *now*, are you?" he said.

Uhura struggled to her feet. She shook the snow off her fur and started to growl again. Stan walked toward the dog with a look that Zoe didn't like. Uhura growled louder, like a rocket about to take off. Zoe stepped between them. She had no plan whatsoever.

"Well, *she* knows you," she said. "And she hates you."

"Yeah, well, this bitch here and I got some history, don't we," he said. "And I'm more of a cat person."

He stopped a couple of feet from Zoe, close enough that she could smell the cigarette smoke leaking out of his mouth, as well as the sour breath beneath it. Up close, his acne scars were so deep it looked like he'd been hit with buckshot.

"You gonna move out of my way?" he said. "I came here lookin' for money, but apparently I gotta kick a little doggy ass first."

Zoe was scared and had no idea what to do. He must have seen that, because he didn't wait for an answer.

He sprang at her.

Everything happened at once. Stan shoved Zoe down onto the driveway. Uhura lunged at him and bit his hand so hard that he let loose a shriek. It turned out that Stan was pretty chickenshit himself.

Uhura refused to let go. Stan exploded with profanity and wheeled around in pain. The dog hung on to his hand by her teeth, even when her feet were dangling off the ground.

31

"Mother of god," Stan screeched, "I am going to kill this thing *dead*."

Then, from out of nowhere, something struck him in the head. A rock. Blood trickled down around his ear. He spat out a vivid streak of curses. He and Zoe both turned to the porch, where Jonah was standing with a fierce look on his face.

"It was me, Zoe!" he said proudly. "I got him! It was me!"

Stan lurched toward Jonah, but Uhura still wouldn't let go. She was furious and wild. It was like watching someone wrestle an alligator.

Zoe ran up the steps to Jonah. He hugged her hard around the waist, then opened his fist: his pink palm was full of rocks.

"I'm gonna get him again," he said.

"*Don't*, Jonah," she said. "He doesn't fight fair, so we're not going to fight. Okay? Say okay. I want to *hear* you say okay."

"Okay, Zoe. I won't get him again—but I *could*."

Stan finally threw Uhura into his pickup and locked her in. The dog clawed at the window. Her breath fogged the glass. It was awful to watch. Jonah buried his face in Zoe's coat.

Stan was sweating now. He was shaking with rage and rubbing his buzz cut to try to calm down. Blood ran down the right side of his face. What appeared to be mascara ran down the left—he'd apparently been using it to dye an eyebrow. As sweat washed it away, Zoe could see that the otherwise black brow had a creepy tuft of pure white.

Stan went to the back of his truck, lifted a tarp heavy with snow, and pulled out what looked, in the darkness, like a poker from a fireplace. He walked toward Jonah and Zoe.

He pointed the poker at them like a weapon.

"Now *where*," he demanded, "is the *other* . . . *motherfrickin'* . . . *dog*?"

Zoe didn't answer, but Jonah flew toward the house, which gave it away. She raced after him and bolted the door the second they were inside. She could hear Stan leaping up the steps behind them.

JONAH WAS IN THE living room, pushing a coffee table in front of the doorway, like a barricade. Nobody made better forts than her brother. Well, nobody made *more* forts than her brother, anyway.

Within seconds, Stan was bashing at the front door.

Zoe tried to call the police. She couldn't get a signal. The text to her mom was still unsent, like a plane that would never be cleared for takeoff. She wished her mom had known they were safe in those few moments when they actually were.

The next thing Zoe knew, Stan had shoved the coffee table aside and stormed into the living room, his breathing heavy and ragged. Zoe and Jonah raced behind the couch just to get *something* between them and the intruder. Jonah held a floral cushion in front of his chest like it would protect him, which, even in the terror of the moment, made Zoe's heart hurt.

Stan ignored her. He loomed over Jonah.

"Hey there, little guy, I'm Stan the Man," he said. "Where's the other dog?"

He waited for an answer like he wasn't going to wait long.

Spock was still under the rug, the tiniest bit of his tail poking out. If Stan had been any less enraged, he would have spotted him immediately. Zoe willed herself, and Jonah, not to look in the dog's direction.

As Stan stood there panting, she noticed for the first time what a big, grotesque head he had—how awkwardly it bobbed on his skinny neck. He looked like a dead sunflower.

"Don't talk to my brother," she said.

It wasn't courage. It was disgust.

Jonah inched closer to her. He wasn't pretending to be brave anymore. In a moment, he was crying so hard that his shoulders started to shake.

Zoe smoothed his hair out of his eyes. She told him everything was going to be okay.

"Now don't go telling him that," Stan groaned, his white eyebrow wriggling like a caterpillar. "That is what they call a *falsehood*. Because it sure as hell *ain't* gonna be okay. In fact, it's gonna be a big ugly mess of *not* okay if you don't tell me the location of the other damn dog."

He twirled the poker like a baton. He wanted to seem menacing, but nearly dropped the thing on his foot.

Jonah struggled to speak. Finally he forced the words out, stuttering through his tears: "W-what are you going to d-do to Spock?"

Stan snorted.

"Aw, I'm just gonna give him a bath, little guy," he said.

"Don't talk to my brother."

"I d-don't believe you. And d-don't call me little guy. My daddy called me that."

This shut Stan up for a second. But what he said next was the vilest thing yet somehow: "I knew your daddy, little guy. Met him back when we was shrimpy, like you."

"Do *not* talk to my brother!"

"Your old man never mentioned me, little guy? Well, there was

34

a time when we were blood brothers. But I'm guessing he never said a word about—hell, about the first twenty years of his life, probably! You barely knew who he was. And then he died in some goddamn cave? And nobody even bothered to go get his body? What the hell kind of people are you?"

"DO NOT TALK TO MY BROTHER, YOU PSYCHOTIC DICK!"

There was a split second of silence, a stalemate where all they heard was the wind.

And then Spock sneezed.

Stan turned to the bubble under the rug and hooted with pleasure.

"Classic," he said.

He grabbed the dog, bound him up in the rug, and stuck him under one arm.

"Time for chickenshit's bath," he said, and gestured out to the frozen lake. "Hope he don't mind cold water."

He bounced the sharp point of the poker on the floor like it was a walking stick.

"Do not follow me, big sister," he told Zoe, his eyes crawling over her body once more, "or you'll get more action than you can handle."

Once he'd gone, she and Jonah sat on the couch, stunned. After a moment, she took his face in her hands so she'd know he was listening.

"I need to go out there," she said. "To get the dogs back. And I need you to stay here. Okay, Jonah? I need to hear you say okay. Can you say okay for me—and *mean* it?"

Jonah wriggled until Zoe let go of his face, then scrunched

his eyebrows down, like a teacher had told him to put on his thinking cap.

"Okay, I w-won't go outside," he said.

"Thank you," said Zoe.

"But you can't go either. That m-man doesn't f-fight fair, so we're not going to f-fight. Right? You *said*."

"How about if I just go for five minutes?"

"No, Zoe."

"Okay, how about two minutes?"

She was trying to calm him down by teasing him a bit, negotiating the way *he* always did.

"No, Zoe! *No* minutes! I want you here." He stopped and fished around for words. "Even *I* get scared sometimes."

Zoe knew if she went outside, Jonah would follow her, and she couldn't take the chance. So she did the unheroic thing, which she hated herself for. She sat on the couch with her arm around her brother and made certain he never looked out the window behind them. It wasn't as hard to distract him as she thought it would be. They found the wicker basket with Betty's knitting supplies, and Jonah starting fixing the hole at the top of Zoe's hat. For a while, the only sound in the room was the clicking of needles, though at one point, Jonah paused to scold her: "You really should take better care of your things."

ZOE TRIED NOT TO look out the window either. She didn't look when she heard Stan walk past them toward the lake, his boots crunching over the snow and Spock whimpering inside the rug. She didn't look when Jonah began rubbing his eyes and said what he always said when his body was shutting down from too much stimulation and he was seesawing on the edge of sleep: "I'm not tired. My eyes just hurt." She didn't even look when he put down the needles and fell asleep with his head in her lap.

But then she heard Stan hacking at the ice on the lake with the poker, trying to stab his way down to the water. And that's when she looked.

He was making a hole to drown the dogs in.

There were binoculars on the coffee table. Zoe grabbed them. The night was black and starless. A void. The world had just been . . . shut off.

Stan was working by the light of his truck's headlights. He struggled to hold Spock as he chipped deeper and deeper. For a second the dog managed to squirm out of Stan's arms—but he couldn't move fast enough on the ice. He slipped and slid desperately until Stan grabbed him by the scruff of his neck and threw him into the hole.

Then Stan pushed Spock's head under the water with his foot.

When he was sure the dog couldn't climb out, he loped back to his truck for Uhura.

For the next few moments, he didn't see what Zoe saw.

He didn't see the lake begin to glow, gradually at first and then—though it made no sense—brighter and brighter until it looked like the ice covered not water but fire.

And he didn't see the figure at the farthest edge of the lake moving toward them—moving across the ice, moving calmly, yes, but as fast as a galloping horse.

Zoe was at the window now, with no memory of having stood up and walked toward it. It was the window, she realized later, that made it possible for her to watch all this without thinking she'd lost her mind: not just because the pane of glass separated her from everything happening out there, but because it was like a screen and, if she was going to be honest, she'd watched a lot of crazy stuff on TV.

She walked out of the living room. Out of the house. It was like she was being pulled by a rope.

Stan slammed the door of his truck. He had Uhura locked under his arm—it was *her* turn for a "bath"—and he'd clamped her mouth shut with one hand. The dog was seething but helpless.

Zoe had the binoculars trained on Stan when he turned back toward the lake and saw it blazing in the darkness—and when he first noticed the figure shooting toward him, covering hundreds of feet in an instant.

Stan was terrified.

But, almost immediately, his face turned cocky and hateful again, as if he believed stupidity could protect him from anything.

"Now what in the hell is all *this* shit?" he said.

Stan had hardly gotten the last word out before the figure was on him. He dropped Uhura so he could defend himself. The dog ran to Zoe, who was standing off in the darkness, and leaped into her arms.

Stan tried to look tough and raised his fists. Instead, he just looked ridiculous. He hopped around the stranger like an old-timey boxer.

The stranger was X, though Zoe wouldn't call him that for days.

X was so pale that his face seemed to give off a light all its own. From a distance, she couldn't even guess at his age, though she could see he had beautiful long hair that was *actually* messy and uncared for, not just styled to look that way. He was wearing a long coat—deep blue, with an iridescent shimmer like a soap bubble. He didn't have a hat or gloves or a scarf, but the cold seemed not to touch him anyway. His face had a thin sheen of sweat, as if he were feverish.

X didn't say a word. He took Stan by the coat and hurled him onto the glowing ice. He didn't do it in anger. He didn't do it like an action hero. He just did it like it had to be done.

He never once looked at Zoe, but she could tell that he knew she was there.

Stan skidded across the frozen lake, toward the hole he had made. He came to a stop, one side of his face clawed red by the ice.

In a flash, X stood over him.

Stan looked up, trying to understand what was happening—and how he'd lost control of the situation.

"I don't know what you want, superfreak," he said, "but whatever it is, you ain't gettin' it. This is *my* party."

X still didn't speak. It was clear to Zoe that he wasn't going to bother until somebody said something worth responding to.

X walked toward the hole and pulled out Spock. The dog was wet and shivering, like he'd just been born, but he warmed instantly in X's arms. Then Spock did something he'd only ever done to Jonah and her: he licked X's cheek. X patted his head tentatively, as if he wasn't sure how. It was a tiny gesture but because of all the pain and weirdness of the last few hours, it made Zoe's eyes fill with tears.

She dropped the binoculars into the snow and went closer. Somehow, she wasn't afraid. She wanted X to see her. *Who was he? Why was he here? Why wouldn't he look at her?*

While X was comforting Spock, Stan tried to stand.

X merely shook his head no, and Stan's feet went out from under him. He fell back onto the ice.

X removed his coat. Beneath it, he wore a rough short-sleeved shirt, though (to be honest) all Zoe saw were his arms. They were ropy with muscles and covered with primitive tattoos of, among other things, animals she didn't recognize.

He wrapped Spock in his coat and set him down gently. The coat shimmered in the darkness, like a dying fire.

He turned to Stan, who was still clinging absurdly to the idea that he could talk his way out of this.

"Okay, superfreak," Stan said. "Tell me what you want and *maybe* you can have it. I'm a reasonably reasonable person."

WHAT HAPPENED NEXT WAS like a ritual from some secret society in the woods or from the Middle Ages, maybe—a trial where everybody knows ahead of time that the verdict will be "guilty."

X was shaking, but everything he did, he did calmly and methodically. He seemed to regret that he'd been sent to the lake. And that was the feeling Zoe got—that he'd been sent here, maybe even forced to come. He still hadn't looked at her, but the way these thoughts suddenly took root in her head, not as theories or guesses but as facts, as certainties, made her think that he'd somehow put them there himself. How was that possible?

Stan was on his knees now, struggling again to stand.

X put a hand on his shoulder and in an instant Stan was immobile, conscious but frozen still.

X walked a few feet, turned his back to Stan, and pulled off his shirt. His shoulders were broad, his waist slim as a swimmer's. Unlike the bruised skin of his face, X's back was smooth and untroubled. A blank canvas. It occurred to Zoe that someone or *something* had spared it—and for a reason. She honestly didn't know if she came up with this idea herself or if he gave it to her.

X spread his arms wide. His shoulder blades flashed in the darkness and his back became broader still.

Zoe couldn't help it: she took a photo to put on Instagram later.

X seemed to be summoning something up. He let out a sharp cry, like he was trying to force a sickness out of his system. Then his back came alive with images.

His skin became a screen.

What played on X's back looked almost like a home movie, jittery, dizzying, chaotic—and unearthly somehow. She and Stan watched, transfixed. Stan remained immobile. It was as if he were bound and tied by the air itself. Zoe stood in the dark not far away. They watched in shock, and then horror, each for their own reasons.

Suddenly, it occurred to Zoe that Jonah might have woken up— that he might be watching from the living room. Her eyes flew to the house.

The windows were black. Her brother might have been standing at one of them—there was no way to tell.

Zoe turned back to the movie. Bert and Betty were in it. They were cowering in the living room in the very same capital A by the lake. They were rigid with fear. Someone was circling them. Someone who'd burst into their home.

Zoe couldn't see much of the intruder's face—just a sliver of it, like a crescent moon. Still, she recognized the ugly buzz cut and the pitted skin. She saw the intruder walk to the fireplace, saw him hoist the lethal-looking poker and test its weight in his hand.

Stan tore his eyes away from X's back, unable to look at what he had done. He turned to the house, hoping for relief.

41

X expected this. He extended his palm toward the long sloping roof of the A-frame, and in an instant the images were flashing there, too. Stan was shocked. He cast his eyes down. X knelt, pressing his hand to the ice. The orange glow disappeared, and for a second the world was black. Then suddenly the movie was playing beneath them—all around them—the figures giant and distorted, the voices booming.

Zoe couldn't understand what anyone was saying. She couldn't even figure out where the sound was coming from, though it was everywhere now. But she could see that Stan, Bert, and Betty were screaming. One of them in anger. Two of them in fear.

Then, suddenly, Uhura was in the movie, trying to protect Bert and Betty. She was barking wildly, like she had when Stan's truck pulled up. Spock, amazingly, was howling, too.

In the movie, Betty took Bert's hand and pulled him toward the door, toward safety. Bert looked bewildered. Childlike. As Betty tried to rush him outside, he stopped, as if he had all the time in the world, and took a peppermint out of a dish on the coffee table.

They burst outdoors just a few seconds ahead of Stan. Seeing them escape even for a moment made Zoe's heart leap. She didn't know why—she knew there was only one possible ending.

Stan went after them, clutching the poker.

Bert and Betty stumbled to their car, and Betty started the engine, but the tires spun uselessly in the snow. By the time they'd gone a hundred yards, Stan was close behind, shouting and gesturing savagely with the weapon.

The car struck a tree.

Zoe watched as Stan yanked Bert and Betty out of the car, and went after them with the poker.

She saw Betty in the snow. She saw Bert crying like a kid. She saw the dogs snap their jaws at Stan's legs and she saw the psycho snap back at them sarcastically and then kick them in the stomach.

She saw the poker flash up and down.

Zoe saw Betty die.

She died trying to shield Bert's body with her own.

Then Zoe saw Bert die.

He died sobbing over Betty. He died hiding his face behind his hands. He died pleading over and over in a high, terrified voice, "Gimme a break, I'm just an old codger. Gimme a break, gimme a break, gimme a break."

Stan slid the Wallaces' bodies, one after the other, into the lake.

When Zoe realized what she was seeing—when the evil of it really sunk its long fingernails into her—she looked back at the house, praying again that Jonah was still asleep.

Then she fell on her knees. She held Uhura to her chest. And she threw up into the snow until her throat was on fire.

BY THE TIME ZOE could stand, X had let his arms fall to his sides and tugged his shirt back over his head. The movie had sputtered to a stop. The lake glowed fiercely once more. X, looking sickly and spent, reached down and dragged Stan closer to the hole in the ice.

Stan hadn't said a word while they watched the killings, but Zoe could see from his expression that something had been building inside him. It wasn't guilt or sorrow—or even fear, anymore.

It was rage.

"This the part where I'm supposed to say I'm sorry and so forth?" he shouted at X. "Well, don't hold your breath, superfreak. Them people were old as dirt. They was no damn use to anybody."

X still hadn't spoken. He looked down at Stan patiently, as if he knew everything he would say before he ran out of words.

Stan started up again, more quietly this time.

"Lookit," he said. "I wasn't aiming to hurt them—didn't even bring a weapon. I was just looking to *borrow* one or two valuables. I expected them to be all meek and mild, because their brains were applesauce, correct? Yeah, I knew about that. I was real *meticulous* about that robbery. Took me nearabouts a month to plan it. I mean, I really did my homework. Which is ironical because when I was in high school? *Never* did my homework."

In his terror, Stan had begun to babble.

"Anyway," he said, "the whole thing coulda been a pleasant experience for everybody involved. Relatively speaking. But that old broad was a fighter—she was trying to keep me away from her man. Scratchin' at my eyeballs and whatnot. Can't say I predicted that. So things got more, uh, *contentious* and *acrimonious*, than I planned on. Joke is, I didn't find anything worth a shit in that place. Been out here two or three times since and *still* ain't found where they hid their damn money."

Stan spat noisily on the ground.

"All right," he said, "I got nothing else to say—except that you gotta hate god if you're really fixing to drown me."

And that was the thing that made X speak.

HIS VOICE WAS DEEP, but scratchy from lack of use. Zoe couldn't tell what country he was from or even what century.

"Mark me well," X said, then stopped to clear his throat and wipe the sweat from his forehead. "No one respects god's love more than those of us damned to the Lowlands—for we know what it means to live without it." He took Stan by the collar. "Now *you* will, too."

He bent down and, though he looked too tired now to manage it, lifted Stan into the air.

Stan fought him, clung to his neck, scratched at his face.

X winced and, with what seemed like his last bit of strength, pushed Stan into the jagged hole in the ice.

Then he paused, turned—and looked straight at Zoe.

His eyes were overwhelming.

A wave rose inside Zoe's chest. X seemed to be asking her a silent question. She thought maybe he wanted her permission to end Stan's life.

Stan hadn't even been aware that Zoe was standing there. He saw her now and gave her a sickening smile.

"Call him off, girlie," he begged. "*Please.* Hell, I knew your father!"

X reddened, furious that Stan would dare to address Zoe.

"Stop your mouth," he told him, "or I will plug it with my fist."

X looked to Zoe again, and again she was shaken by the force of the connection. His eyes still held a question, but it wasn't what she'd thought it was. She could see that now. He had no intention of sparing Stan, and wasn't looking for her opinion. So what *was* he asking her then?

It came to her. Somehow X knew how much she had loved Bert and Betty. Somehow he knew that a lot of what was good and right about her was their doing—and that her hatred for Stan was like a fever under her skin. He was asking if she wanted to kill him herself.

Zoe felt a surge of something she couldn't name. She didn't even know if it was pain or relief. But it electrified her.

She walked across the ice toward X and Stan.

Stan was writhing spastically in the lake. The freezing water lapped into his horrible mouth. It was what he deserved, Zoe knew.

She walked as fast as she could without sliding sideways, planting her feet hard on the ice. She gained speed with every step. X never stopped looking at her, never stopped holding her with his eyes. Zoe still didn't know what she was feeling, not exactly. She searched around in her mind for the word, and—though it didn't seem possible—she could feel X inside her brain looking for it, too.

They found the word in the same instant.

It was not *rage* or *vengeance*.

It was *mercy*.

X's eyes flashed with surprise. He pivoted away from Zoe and hurriedly put his boot on the top of Stan's head, just as Stan had done to Spock.

He was about to push him under when Zoe hurled herself at him.

X was exhausted. Zoe was fierce.

She knocked him onto the ice before his boot came down.

46

THREE

SHE DIDN'T EXPECT X to fall, but his body collapsed under her, and they went sprawling onto the lake. For half a second, they lay entangled. His skin smelled of pine and campfire smoke.

Zoe waited for him to spring up again, but he lay on his back, twitching with pain. He was more feverish than she'd realized. She got to her feet, and turned to Stan, who was sobbing in the water, his skin turning blue-gray. The thought of touching him repulsed her, but it wasn't right that he die that way, no matter what he'd done.

She reached out with both hands and helped him out of the water. He stood in front of her shivering, his clothes soaked against his body. He looked scrawny and pathetic, like something that'd been pulled out of its shell.

"Hallelujah, girlie," he said. "Your daddy'd be proud."

It felt disgusting to be thanked by him.

Zoe said nothing. She just watched as he raced for his truck, the pale soles of his boots shining as he ran.

The engine coughed but wouldn't start. Zoe knew what an engine sounded like when it wanted to cooperate. This one just wanted to be left in peace. After thirty full seconds of profanity—in which Stan strung together curses that she was pretty sure had never been strung together before—he got out of the truck, pulled a blanket from the back, and ran into the trees like an animal.

X sat up on the ice. She expected him to be in a rage, but he just stared at her, mournful and confused.

"What have you done?" he said.

Zoe didn't answer—she didn't really *know* what she'd done, other than act on instinct.

X turned to track Stan's progress into the woods.

"Don't go after him," Zoe said. They were the first words she ever said to him and, though she often encased even the most sincere statements in sarcasm, she dropped her guard now. "Please. It's wrong."

X weighed her words.

"Yet if I do not go after him," he said, "someone will surely come after *me*."

But still he didn't move. He lingered on the ice with Zoe, listening to branches break as Stan scurried up the hills in the dark. Why wasn't X chasing him, Zoe wondered. Why was he doing what she wanted? Why would he care what she wanted?

"If you kill him, you're as bad as he is," she said. "It's not our job to punish people."

X lowered his head.

"Perhaps it is not *yours*," he said.

ZOE STUMBLED BACK TO Bert and Betty's house to retrieve Jonah, pausing just long enough to take a picture of the license plate on Stan's diseased-looking truck. Spock and Uhura followed her. X did, too. Zoe didn't look back, but she could hear him wading through the snow behind her. He didn't follow her inside. He stayed on the porch out of respect—or shyness, maybe. He hushed the dogs when they whimpered so he must have known somehow that Jonah was sleeping. Spock and Uhura lifted their heads and eventually X figured out that they wanted to be scratched under their chins. He knelt and rubbed them cautiously and whispered their names. Zoe set a candle on the windowsill and watched for a long moment.

Jonah was still lying on the couch. He appeared to have slept through the chaos. But when Zoe went to lift him his body seemed tense, not the floppy mass of bread dough it should have been.

Holding Jonah made Zoe's arms ache—she'd never get him home this way. Still, she couldn't bear the thought of rousing him and forcing him to march back through the woods. He deserved to wake up in his bed, the nightmare over and his Nerf guns and Stomp Rockets right where he left them. She wanted innocence and forgetting for Jonah—all the more because she couldn't have them for herself.

She laid him on the couch again, her palm cradling the back of his head like he was a newborn. Then she stood and waited for a solution to appear out of the ether.

Through the window, she saw X sitting with the dogs on his lap. His face was damp with sweat, and the snow on his coat was turning translucent as it melted. Spock nipped at him playfully, which seemed to startle him. Had he never played with dogs before? At last he understood what Spock wanted. He pretended his hands were birds and teased the dog by making them swoop and dive just beyond his reach.

X must have known he was being watched. He looked back at Zoe through the glass. She was struck again by how sick he'd become. But he seemed not to be asking for help but to be offering it. Did he have some plan for getting her and her brother back to their house? Because that was the only thing in the world Zoe wanted right now. She met X's eyes. She didn't move, she didn't so much as mouth a word—but he nodded.

After that, she saw flashes of sky and what seemed like a video of the trees blurring by on fast-forward.

X was dizzy and staggering and in the grip of some sickness that Zoe had never seen.

But he carried them home.

EVEN IN THE DARKNESS, Zoe could see that the snow in the driveway was untouched, and her heart sank at the sight of it: her mother hadn't made it back yet. She was desperate to see her, but it was just as well that she wasn't home. Zoe couldn't have explained the strange figure who had delivered them and who—after refusing water, shelter, gloves, a hat, a blanket, and even veggie jerky (but then who said yes to veggie jerky?)—was now retreating in the direction of the woods.

She looked out at X one last time. She saw him stagger a few feet, then fall to one knee in the snow. She made herself turn away.

Zoe opened the door of the house, a difficult maneuver now that Jonah was sleeping in *her* arms. She found the Post-it on the fridge where her mother kept all the contact information for the police, and—holding it between her teeth—struggled up the staircase with her brother.

Jonah's bed was small and shaped like a ladybug. When Zoe

50

finally lowered him onto it, he rolled onto his side without waking, and began drooling onto the pillow.

She sat on the floor by Jonah's bed with her phone, and e-mailed the picture of Stan's license plate to the police, along with a message that read: "This truck belongs to the man who killed Bert + Betty Wallace. With the poker from their fireplace. His name is Stan something. His truck is still at their house. He's maybe 45 + about 6 feet tall. Skinny. Buzz cut. Messed-up eyebrow. You're welcome."

Once she'd sent the e-mail, she scrolled through the clump of texts that had finally broken through. There were some from Dallas (who was "full-on stoked" from "rocking out" in the blizzard), Val (who had missed it entirely because she was napping), and her mother (who was just generally frantic). Part of Zoe felt abandoned by her mom, but she couldn't help but smile as she read her stream of messages: *Roads horrific. Can't even get out of grocery store. So sorry, Zo . . . Still horrific. Still sorry . . . Don't let J eat cereal before bed. Try gluten-free waffle . . . ARGH. Radio says snowplows aren't even going out tonight. No way to get up mountain . . . Still in grocery store! Will live in grocery store forever, eating chemicals and pesticides, like real American . . . Are U OK? . . . U know what? If J wants cereal, he can have it . . . OMG Rufus just rescued me in his big-ass van, like a knight. NO, he's NOT in love with me—I heard that! I'm going to crash on his couch . . . Tell me you're OK? . . . Can't sleep. Worrying about you. Did J want cereal?*

Zoe sat pondering what to text back.

We're OK, she wrote finally. *More later. I gave Jonah some Pringles dipped in cake frosting. Is that cool? Rufus is OBSESSED with you. Go 2 sleep, now! XO.*

Zoe went on Snapchat and Instagram for a while, hoping that

life might start to seem normal again. It didn't. How *could* it, after Stan and X and the hole in the ice?

She crossed the hall to her room and stood, tired and unsteady, in the doorway. On the wall at the foot of her bed there was a photo of her and her dad from one of their caving trips. They were wearing matching one-piece flight suits, which they'd bought at the Army Navy in Whitefish for 17 dollars a piece. Zoe had a battery-powered headlamp. Her father, being a dork, used an old-fashioned carbide lamp that looked like a miniature blowtorch. In the photo, he had a wide, geeky smile and some pretty crazy bed head. Her dad had *always* had bed head—he used to call it "hair salad."

Zoe heard Stan's voice spreading like dye in her brain: "You barely knew who he was. And then he died in some goddamn cave? And nobody even bothered to go get his body? What the hell kind of people are you?"

The words raced around her mind, like birds chasing one another.

Was it *her* fault that she hadn't known her father better? He was never around! Zoe'd had no choice but to rely more and more on her mom. Her mother had dropped out of medical school and worked multiple jobs to support the family while Zoe's dad came and went. She'd thrown everything she had into being a mom—and she raised the kids to be resilient and strong. When Zoe was a baby, her mother dressed her in onesies that said Hero and Protagonist. Her father's love might have been like a candle or a lantern, but her mom's was better: it never went out.

Zoe was too tired to think anymore, even if it was only 9:30. She stripped off her clothes for bed. Her whole body felt dirty and sore. Her legs were stubbly, her breath was horrendous, her shoulders were tender from where her bra straps had dug into her skin. She should have showered, brushed her teeth, *something*. But she couldn't do even one more thing today. She fell headlong into bed, like someone who'd been shot.

HER MOTHER FINALLY MADE it home in the middle of the night. Zoe heard the front door *whoosh* open in her sleep. She felt relief wash through her, and immediately had a dream in which she was a child again, laying her head on her mother's lap. She wanted to talk to her mom, but couldn't pull herself out of sleep. When she awoke again, hours later, it was because she heard voices—men's voices—rising up through the floor.

She tried to shut them out. She refused to open her eyes. She tried to grab on to the dream she'd been having but couldn't quite catch its tail.

There was music downstairs now, but it was weirdly out of place—Buddhist chanting set to keyboards, acoustic guitars, and finger cymbals. That meant her mom was trying to calm everybody down. Or she was trying to annoy them so much that they'd leave.

Zoe was wedged up against the wall—at some point in the night Jonah had crawled in with her. He always started from the foot of the bed and tunneled up under the sheets, like a gopher. She could feel the heat of his body against her back. She could feel his tiny toes against her leg.

The front door slammed. Somebody had gone outside for a cigarette. Zoe heard him coughing and crunching around in the snow. She smelled the smoke slither in through her window. The man pulled open the door again—so hard that it slammed against the side of house—and came back in without bothering to knock the snow off his boots.

53

Zoe turned onto her back. Pain shot up her neck in sparks. Soon the voices were impossible to ignore. They were squabbling like pigeons. Zoe was never going to fall back asleep. *What the hell was going on?* She drew in a long breath and released it slowly. She finally opened her eyes.

It was still night. That was a surprise—she'd assumed it would be morning. There was no moon. No wind. The snow gave off a faint blue light and the pines stood mysterious and still, as if they'd just been talking to one another. Zoe took her phone from where it was charging on the windowsill. It was 3 a.m.

She tapped the flashlight app and swept the room with it. Her mother must have been in and out because there were plates, glasses, and bowls huddled on the floor, like a ruined city. Zoe had no memory of any of it. There was red pepper, aloe leaves, sprigs of mint, a bowl of water with some yellowish tincture suspended in it like a cloud: it looked like either a frostbite remedy or a voodoo ceremony.

Nearby, there was a fat paperback lying open on a chair—a time-travel romance about a guy in a kilt. Its pages fluttered like overgrown grass in the wind. Her mother must have sat watching them for hours. She had also bandaged the cut on Zoe's forehead—she'd been in med school just long enough to learn to administer excellent first aid.

Zoe shone the flashlight over Jonah. His cheeks, which had been chapped by the wind, were glistening with aloe now, and his fingertips had been individually wrapped. For a moment, the light came too close to his eyes. He winced but kept on sleeping. One thing about her brother: he slept *fiercely*. He would sweat through his T-shirts—he was wearing one now that said I Do My Own

Stunts—and make such an indignant harrumph of an expression that it always cracked her up. What was he mad at? Who was he fighting, or protecting, in his dreams?

As Zoe shifted in bed, she felt something tug at her leg. She peeled back the comforter and sheet. Jonah must have been afraid that she'd sneak out of the room without telling him, so—as a kind of alarm system—he had tied a skateboard to her ankle with yarn. When he was scared, he hated waking up alone. It made him feel *wobbly* inside, he said.

Gazing down at her brother now, Zoe felt competing waves of guilt and relief and fear and love. He was curled against her in a crescent like a baby deer. *Look at him*, she thought. She untied the skateboard from her ankle and tied it to his own. *Tag, you're it.*

Downstairs one of the men broke a glass on the countertop.

It nearly woke Jonah. Zoe flushed with anger, and shot off a text to her mother.

It said only: *Who??*

The moment she sent it, she heard her mother push her chair back from the kitchen table and bound up the stairs. After everything that had happened in the blizzard, the sound of her mother rushing to her was so comforting that Zoe's anger dissipated in an instant and—before she even realized she was in danger of it—she started to cry.

HER MOTHER PUSHED OPEN the door of the bedroom and then closed it behind her, so that the wedge of light made the trophies along the wall gleam briefly and then go out. Zoe didn't want her mother to know how upset she was. She did what she always did in moments of uncertainty, she blurted something random: "So, you back from the store?"

Her mother laughed.

"I *am*," she said. "Anything happen around here?"

One of the things that Zoe loved most about her mother was that the woman understood her jokes even when they were totally bizarre. Very often they were the only people in the room laughing, while everyone else fidgeted uncomfortably. Not even her father—when he was alive and when he was around—had really understood Zoe's sense of humor.

"There's a stowaway in here with me," Zoe said, nodding toward Jonah. "We have to whisper."

"I can do that," her mother said.

She came to kneel by the bed.

Zoe could just barely make out the outline of her mom's face in the darkness. Neither of them spoke. The lightness of the moment drained away.

"Is Jonah gonna be okay?" said Zoe.

"Frostbite-wise, yes, he'll be fine," her mother said. "But he seems pretty traumatized by whatever you went through." She paused, and her voice softened. "Can you tell me what happened?"

Zoe searched for an answer that would sound remotely sane. Downstairs, one of the men turned off the Eastern chanting. The other men let out grunts of relief and applauded.

"Who's down there?" said Zoe.

"That's not important right now," her mother said. "But apparently they're not Buddhists."

She waited for Zoe to answer the question still hovering in the air.

"Talk to me," she said.

Zoe's instinct was always to tell her mother everything, and she wished she could pour out every crazy, hallucinogenic detail about

56

the lake glowing orange, about the movie of Stan's sins—about X. But what could she say about him? What did she even know apart from the fact that he radiated loneliness? And that she'd been drawn to him.

She fought back the image of his face. She knew if she said too much, she'd make no sense at all.

"The short version," Zoe said, "is that Jonah and the dogs went in the woods—and I let them."

Her mother let a few moments go by, like she was waiting for a train to pass.

"Okay, look, I'm sorry to be pushy," she said. "But I'm going to need a slightly longer version."

"I can't, Mom," Zoe said. "Not yet."

"Zo—"

"I mean, the longer version is that I *suck* and I almost got him killed."

"Zoe, stop. Don't do that to yourself."

"All I keep thinking is that when Jonah wakes up, he's going to look at me like I let him down. And I *did*. I let the little bug down."

She shouldn't have spoken at all. She began sobbing in that awful, hiccupy way. Her mother reached over Jonah to touch her face, but had trouble locating it in the darkness.

"I'm trying to stroke your cheek sweetly," she said. "Is this your cheek? Am I stroking it sweetly?"

"No, that's my forehead," Zoe said. "And *that* is my nose."

"Okay, well, picture me stroking your cheek," her mother said.

"I'm picturing it," Zoe said, and laughed despite herself as her mother's hand groped around blindly. "Now stop it, Helen Keller. Please. That's my ear."

57

"Zoe," her mother said, "your brother loves you like a crazy person—and that will never, ever change. The kid tied a *skateboard* around your leg."

Zoe started to say something but was interrupted by a commotion downstairs. She and her mother listened as one of the men stood, his chair screeching against the floor, and said, "Enough of this horseshit, boys." They listened to the heavy tread of the man's boots coming up the stairs. Zoe's mother didn't allow shoes in the house, so the noise sounded almost like violence.

"I wish I could give you more time," her mom said. "But I can't, baby. You're going to have to tell your story—because the police are here."

ZOE'S MOTHER SHOOED THE cop out of the bedroom immediately, and asked Zoe to come downstairs when she was ready. Zoe hadn't seen the police since her father died, and knowing they were in the house stirred some prickly memories. The police were the ones who'd left her dad's body in the cave. The cop who had just banged on Zoe's door—Chief Baldino—had decided it was too dangerous to go get it.

Zoe slipped out of bed, careful not to wake Jonah, and dressed in the dark. Minutes later, she padded down the stairs, and peeked out at the kitchen table, where her mother sat with Baldino and two of his troopers. Baldino was big, blustery, unpleasant—and actually bald. Just now, he was scratching like a dog at a scaly red rash below the collar of his shirt.

The chief sat next to a skinny young trooper whose last name was Maerz. Zoe remembered him being slightly dopey, but harmless. The chief obviously detested him.

The third cop at the table was Sergeant Vilkomerson. He was the only one who'd ever bothered to tell the Bissells his first name—it was Brian—and the only one to hug them at her dad's funeral service in town. When Zoe entered the kitchen, Vilkomerson stood and pulled out a chair for her. Unlike Baldino and Maerz, he'd taken his shoes off out of respect for the rules of the house, which were posted at every door.

Officer Maerz had been asking Zoe's mom boring background questions about Zoe—where she went to school and if she had any hobbies. Zoe's mom had been stalling so Zoe could get dressed and think through what she wanted to say. Her mother had her laptop in front of her on the table. It was open, for all to see, to a page entitled, "The Rights of Minors During Police Questioning."

Zoe loved her mother's feistiness and felt proud that she'd inherited it. Her mom worked six days a week managing a dumpy spa called Piping Hot Springs ("Relax and rejuvenate in one of our healing pools!"). She also worked as a hostess at a great café called Loula's, in Whitefish, and directed traffic on a road crew whenever they repaved Route 93. Even so, Zoe knew her family was always short on cash. She knew her mom felt like she was running down a train track, just a couple of steps ahead of the train.

Zoe's mother told Officer Maerz that Zoe's hobby was collecting trophies, which seemed to impress him. The truth was that Zoe *literally* collected trophies—she thought they were ugly and ridiculous and awesome so she bought them at yard sales and thrift stores. If you went into her room and didn't know any better, you'd be amazed that one girl could be so good at swimming, public speaking, archery, macramé, ballooning, and raising livestock.

Zoe's mom began rambling magnificently now. She described

hobbies of Zoe's that were entirely made-up. One of her supposed collections—32 of the 50 official state spoons—so piqued Maerz's interest that Zoe was afraid that he'd ask to see it.

Zoe sat down next to her mother.

"I am *all about* state spoons," she told Maerz. "I'm starting to worry that I'm *too* into them."

Zoe's mom bit her lip, and kicked Zoe gently under the table.

"Yeah, okay," Chief Baldino said gruffly. "I think we're done with the icebreakers."

He signaled to Maerz that he'd be taking over the interrogation since Maerz clearly wasn't up to it. (Zoe's mom shot her a familiar look—the look that said, *Alphas are the* worst.) Maerz shrank in his chair, looking hurt.

Baldino slid a piece of paper across the table to Zoe.

"Can you confirm that you sent this e-mail to us at nine fifteen last night?" he said.

Zoe glanced down. When she looked back up at Baldino, all she saw was the man who had abandoned her dad's body.

"Yes, I sent that e-mail," she said, "which is why it has my name on it."

Baldino put on reading glasses that seemed weirdly dainty for such a fat, overstuffed armchair of a man, and read the e-mail aloud. Zoe's mom grimaced when she heard the name Stan—if her dad had known him way back when, in Virginia, her mother must have, too—and again when Baldino got to the sarcastic final sentence, "You're welcome."

"I assume those are your words?" said Baldino. "Since they have your name on them?"

"Yes," said Zoe.

"So how about you tell us how you know all this?"

Zoe's mom made a show of scrolling down the webpage, then nodded to her. Zoe knew she couldn't tell the whole truth, but she could at least tell nothing *but* the truth.

"Jonah and I were trying to find the dogs," she said.

She glanced at Officer Maerz, who had been sullenly taking notes ever since he'd been removed from power, and then at Sergeant Vilkomerson, who gave her an encouraging you're-doing-good sort of nod. Baldino folded his arms tightly across his chest and puffed his stomach out so far that he looked seven or eight months pregnant.

"We got caught in the blizzard," Zoe said. "We went to Bert and Betty's place to warm up. We used to stay there all the time." The memory was so painful that she couldn't help but add, "After my father died—and you guys refused to go get his body."

Baldino was unfazed by the remark, but everybody else shifted unhappily in their chairs. Zoe's mom leaned over and whispered, "Don't, honey. That's not fair."

Zoe pulled away from her, surprised.

"How is that not fair?" she said.

Baldino interrupted before her mother could answer.

"So you encountered Stan Manggold at the Wallaces' former residence?"

"Yes—if that's his last name. He called himself Stan the Man."

"My god," said Zoe's mom.

She even recognized the nickname.

"And how exactly do you know that Mr. Manggold is responsible for the deaths of Bertram and Elizabeth Wallace?"

"I saw—" Zoe began, then broke off immediately. She'd been about to say, *I saw him do it*. That would have gone over well: *I saw it in a movie on the back of a superhot guy*.

"You saw what, exactly?" said Baldino.

"I saw how he bragged about it," she said. "And I saw the poker he killed them with. He thought Bert and Betty were rich. He was still trying to figure out where they hid their money. But they didn't *have* any money—and now their bodies are in the lake."

Her voice was shaking.

"Zoe," said Baldino, "did you and your brother see anyone other than Stan Manggold while you were out at the lake—anybody you knew, anybody you *didn't* know, anybody at all? I want you to think carefully about your answer. Because we're going to write it down."

At this, Officer Maerz looked up at his boss, as if to say, *Are you talking about me?* Baldino rolled his eyes and said, "Yes, Stuart, whatever she says, write it down."

Everyone looked at Zoe, waiting. X's face flashed into her head. She felt protective of him. *He had carried them home.*

Just then, there were noises from outside—it sounded like animals had gotten into the garage and toppled the garbage cans.

Zoe's mother stood.

"Raccoons," she said. "We're going to need a quick recess. No questions while I'm gone." She turned her laptop to face the policemen. "If you have a problem with that," she said, "you can take it up with legalbeagle.com."

"Would you like some help, Ms. Bissell?" asked Sergeant Vilkomerson.

"No, but thank you, Brian. The raccoons are just going to have to find a new place to play."

ZOE STOOD, HER CALVES rippling with pain, and went to one of the duct-taped windows in the living room. Outside, the clouds had shifted. The moon was a bright, white eyeball in the sky. The mountains were just wavy lines receding into the distance.

She felt weary for the thousandth time. She thought about Bert and Betty, about her father, about the big roiling mess that everything had become.

She thought about X. She knocked on the window—she didn't know why. He was out there somewhere. She shouldn't have let him go, but she couldn't exactly force him to stay.

Zoe headed back to the table. She knew what she was going to say.

"WE DIDN'T SEE ANYBODY but Stan. Why?"

The moment Zoe said it, she knew she'd made a mistake. Miscalculated, somehow. Even her mother seemed to know she was lying, but how could she? Zoe's stomach tightened again, like someone was turning a wheel.

Officer Maerz, she noticed, hadn't written her answer down—not because he'd forgotten but because he knew it would be used against her later. Zoe thought that was cool and kind. In her mind, she put a star next to Maerz's name, though she knew his little rebellion was about to get crushed.

"Stuart, write down what our young friend just said, word for word."

This was Baldino. He smiled, drummed on the tabletop, and sat up straight. Now he looked merely three or four months pregnant, like he'd just begun telling people he was having a baby.

"Brian," he said, "let's show her the photo. You got it handy?"

So there was a photo. How could there be? And of what? The wheel in Zoe's stomach turned three times in quick succession.

She was about to speak when her mother startled everyone by slamming her computer shut.

"What photo?" she said. "Why are we only hearing about it now—and why are you playing games with a seventeen-year-old girl?"

"I'm sorry, Ms. Bissell," Vilkomerson said, as he searched his phone for the picture.

"Why on *earth* are you apologizing to this woman?" Baldino said. "We gave the kid a chance to tell the truth."

"I accept your apology, Brian," said Zoe's mom. "But you"—she was pointing at Chief Baldino now—"are starting to piss me off."

IT WAS THE INSTAGRAM. Brian had an annoying daughter a couple of years behind Zoe at school, and the girl had seen the photo, thought it was hot, and left some lame comment, like *YAASS!* She'd also shown it to her dad.

The photo showed X from behind, his arms and legs spread so wide that he looked like an actual X. You could see his broad, shirtless back, lit by the glow coming off the ice. You could see the primitive tattoos running down his forearms. You could see Stan cowering miserably at his feet.

"Now, there are many odd things about this photograph," said Chief Baldino. "For instance, the lake is *orange*."

"That's just a filter," said Maerz. "Everybody uses them."

64

Zoe had stopped listening. She was staring not at X but at Stan. Her mother was staring at him, too. She seemed stunned to see him again after what must have been decades. The man was vile: The buzz cut. The shock-white eyebrow. The ugly boulder of a head. Zoe had not just let him live, she had let him *escape*. She couldn't pull her eyes away, even when she tasted bile in the back of her throat.

Baldino began hammering her with questions now: "Can you confirm that you took this photo last night? Can you confirm that you took it outside the former residence of Bertram and Elizabeth Wallace?"

Zoe felt dizzy. Only Vilkomerson noticed. He put a gentle hand on her arm, and said something she couldn't quite process. Everything was sliding. Everything was flying sideways.

And Baldino wouldn't shut up.

"We know that this man here is Stan Manggold," he said. "The truck was stolen but we ran his prints, and it turns out he's wanted by the State of Virginia for a whole bunch of nasty stuff. What we *don't* know is who the other man in the picture is—the one with the tattoos. We ran the image through our database, and came up empty. So why don't you stop wasting our time and tell us who he is?"

"I don't know," said Zoe.

"Do you know if he was involved in the murder of Bertram and Betty Wallace?"

"He wasn't involved. No way."

"How can you know that if you don't even know who he is?"

"I just *know*."

"How about you tell us everything else you *just know* about him?"

"I told you—I don't even know his name."

Baldino grunted. He was sure she was lying.

"You want to sit here all night, Miss Bissell?" he said. "I don't—but I will."

"I'm telling you the truth," Zoe said. "He came out of the woods, and then he went back *into* the woods. I didn't say two words to him. *I don't know who he is.*"

"Then why have you been lying to protect him?"

Zoe was close to tears now. She looked to her mother.

Her mother stood up.

"This is totally unacceptable," she told Baldino. "You're harassing a girl who's talking to you of her own free will. You think because I do yoga, I can't find a lawyer who will kick your ass?"

In the silence that followed, there was a racket on the stairs. It sounded like a prisoner with a ball and chain. Everybody turned.

It was Jonah, looking horribly betrayed. His fingertips were covered with Band-Aids. His right ankle was dragging a skateboard on a piece of purple yarn.

Baldino shook his head and said, quietly for once and to no one in particular, "These people are not normal."

JONAH TOLD THE POLICE everything—because, as Zoe feared, he'd *seen* everything. He had woken up on Bert and Betty's couch. He had shouted for Zoe. When she didn't answer, he'd wiped the window with a cold little hand and peered outside.

Now Jonah was sitting on Zoe's lap at the table, and pointing at the Instagram.

"That's Stan," he said. "He said his last name was The Man, but he maybe made that up so you should check."

Jonah stopped for a second.

"I threw a rock at him," he said, then looked at his mother uncertainly: "I'm sorry."

"It's okay just this once," she said. "Your dad introduced me to Stan many years ago, sweetie—way before you kids were born—and I wanted to throw a rock at him, too."

"What else can you tell us, son?" Vilkomerson asked.

"Stan was mean," Jonah said, his voice breaking for the first time. "He hurt Bert and Betty, and he *tried* to hurt my dogs. I don't know why. This other person in the picture, the kind of naked one . . . I don't know his name, but he's magic—and he saved them. He also made the ice get all orange like that."

When Jonah finished speaking, everyone let his words settle. No one spoke, except for Officer Maerz who said, "Seriously—it's a filter."

Baldino turned back to Zoe.

"Young lady, can you corroborate any of what your brother is saying?"

"I can *corroborate* all of it," she said.

Did he think she didn't know what the word meant?

"Interesting," said Baldino, the patronizing edge creeping back into his voice. "Even the part about the magic?"

"*Especially* the part about the magic."

CHIEF BALDINO ANNOUNCED THAT he was sick of being lied to—of being "trifled with by a damn teenager"—and soon he and his men were driving off into the night. The Bissells watched from the front door until darkness swallowed the squad car a quarter of a mile down the road.

Zoe's mom asked her and Jonah to follow her out to the garage.

"There's some mess we have to clean up," she said.

"Now?" said Zoe.

It was four in the morning.

"Now," said her mother.

"I hate raccoons," said Zoe.

Her mother seemed not to have heard her—she probably hadn't slept in 24 hours—but at length she responded.

"Hmm?" she said. "Yeah, I hate them, too."

The garage stood on the other side of the circular drive. Zoe had lived on this plot of ground her whole life, but it still amazed her that it could be so quiet—deep-space, science-fiction quiet—when it was nighttime and there wasn't a wind. Silence, her mother liked to say, could heal you or it could make you crazy. It all depended on how you listened to it.

Zoe couldn't tell what the silence would do to her tonight.

"Why'd you tell me to shut up when I said the thing about the cops not going to get Dad's body?" she asked her mother.

"First of all," her mother told her, "I would never tell you to shut up, because those are uncool words. But nothing good's going to come from stirring everything up now. The police didn't do their job. End of story."

Zoe let it go, and they trudged along some more.

"I know you think we were lying about what happened with Stan," she said as they crossed the drive.

"We weren't, Mom," Jonah interrupted. He had stopped to stab holes in the snow with a stick. "We weren't lying *at all*."

"Of course you weren't, sweetie," said Zoe's mom.

"Stan really did hurt Bert and Betty," he said. "And the magic man really did save Spock and Uhura."

"Of course he did, sweetie."

Zoe was annoyed by the way she was just yes-ing him. She fell behind to walk with her brother, who was still hacking at the snow like it was his enemy.

"Can you *not*?" she told him. "The snow is dead. You killed it. You win."

She loved Jonah, even during his weird outbursts. She felt it strongly now. She wished the night could have bound them even closer to their mother, and for a while it'd seemed as if it would. Now her mom was floating away from them, looking up at the stars like Zoe and Jonah weren't even there.

"We didn't lie, Mom," said Jonah, trying to reel her back in. "We *didn't*."

"Just drop it, Jonah," Zoe said. "It's not important that Mom believes us—because *we* believe us."

They were 20 feet from the garage, and only now was it taking shape in the darkness, like the bow of a ship approaching through fog. It was a shingled shed built for two cars and divided down the middle by a thin wall. Jonah was strong enough to open the doors all by himself. He rushed forward delightedly.

"Which one?" he asked his mother.

"The one on the right," she said. "But let me do it, please."

The carport on the left held her mother's silver Subaru Forester. Zoe's car—a heinous old red Taurus that she referred to as the Struggle Buggy—used to be parked on the right. But Zoe had let Jonah convert her side of the garage into a mini–skate park so he could practice year-round. Her brother had installed a quarter pipe and a rail, and covered the walls with posters that said, Shred Till Yer Dead, and, Grind on It!

Zoe's mom let out a sigh that made a cloud of vapor in the air. She asked Jonah to step back. Jonah wasn't happy about it—he stamped his feet in the snow like an impatient horse—but he did.

Zoe stood by her brother, his partner in pouting. From inside the garage, she could hear scratching and scrabbling. She pulled Jonah even farther away, prepared for the raccoons to come tearing out. They were nasty animals. She picked up a snow shovel that was leaning against the garage and gripped it like a baseball bat.

Zoe's mother reached down to open the door, then stopped and turned to them.

"I do believe you guys," she said. "I'm sorry if it seemed like I didn't."

She appeared to have more to say, but she opened the door before continuing. It swung up with a metallic groan.

"Later, I want to hear all about the magic man," her mother said. "But right now—"

Zoe saw a dark figure huddled on the floor of the garage. The figure turned to her, his face damp and beautiful and as pale as chalk.

"Right now," her mother said, "you've got to help me get him inside."

PART TWO

A Binding of Fates

FOUR

X HEARD A FLURRY of noises outside the garage: Voices. The rustling of clothes. Boots in the snow.

The door rose with a shivery *screech*, and the wind rushed in around him. He felt feverish, nauseated, depleted. Every sound was like a detonation in his head.

He looked up and saw three figures approaching in a funnel of light. It was the girl from the lake and her brother. A woman stood in front, shielding them. Their mother, surely. X winced and closed his eyes, as if it would make them disappear. He wasn't afraid that they would do him harm. He was afraid they'd try to save him.

X knew he *couldn't* be saved. Bounty hunters like him were just glorified prisoners, and they were bound by laws. He had been reckless—he had trampled on every one of them.

The most ancient commandment was None Must Know, meaning that mortals could never learn of the Lowlands' existence. It could never be more than a story they told one another, a legend about a lake of fire they called hell. They could never have *proof*. That way, the living could be judged on how they behaved when they thought there would be no consequences. Bounty hunters were never to be seen by anyone but their prey. They were to strike quickly: in shadows and in silence.

X had put himself on parade. He'd spoken to the girl. He'd carried her and her brother through the stark woods. Worst of all, he had let the soul he'd been sent to collect escape into the trees, like a virus gone airborne. Had a bounty hunter ever failed to return with the soul the lords had sent him for? Had a bounty hunter ever *refused* to do his duty? X had never heard of such an outrage, until he had committed it himself.

And why had he been so weak? Why had he let Stan vanish into the hills? *Because the girl had wanted him to.*

No, there could be no saving him now. The fever that racked his body was called the Trembling. It was his punishment, and it had only just begun.

A DAY EARLIER, X had lain entombed in his cell in the Lowlands, a wholly different pain just beginning to stir.

He didn't know if it was day or night—he never did—for the prison was plunged deep in the earth, like a tumor. He'd been trying to sleep for hours. He lay on his side, curled like a question mark on the rocky floor, when the ever-present bruises beneath his eyes began to burn. He ignored it at first, desperate for rest. But the pain grew until it was as if his face was on fire.

It was a sign—a signal. One of the lords would come for him soon and force him to capture some new soul.

X had heard stories about a Higher Power that ruled the

Lowlands, but the lords were the most ferocious creatures he'd ever encountered. There were both men and women in their number, and they'd once been prisoners themselves. Now they were a race unto themselves. They wore golden bands that lay tight around their throats, and vivid cloaks that flashed in the gloom. Like the prisoners they ruled over—X knew of only one exception—the lords did not age. The ones who had been damned when they were young remained young forever. Often they were gorgeous and stately. The oldest, however, were a walking nightmare. X sometimes saw the elders stalking around the Lowlands, hissing and howling and sharpening their curling talons on the rocks. Some had long gray hair that rippled down their backs and bony hands that pulsed with veins as fat as worms. When X looked at their faces, he could see their skulls trying to press through.

He wondered which lord would come for him now—and to which corner of the earth he would be sent.

X MUST HAVE DRIFTED off. He woke up shouting.

The prisoner in the cell to his right, who was known as Banger, had overheard the exclamation.

"Bad dream, dude?" he said. "Heard you freaking out."

The souls were forbidden from knowing each other's true names, and Banger had earned his nickname in the simplest way possible: by beating his forehead on the floor to ease his mental anguish. Banger had been a bartender in Phoenix. It wasn't long ago that, in a fit of rage, he had stabbed a patron in a bar. Then he'd fled to South America, abandoning his wife and four-year-old daughter. Banger was 27 when X hauled him to the Lowlands. Now he would be 27 for all eternity. The lords didn't allow the guards to beat the prisoners, because they knew the prisoners found pain a welcome distraction. Banger, and many souls besides him, did violence to themselves instead.

X walked to the door of his cell and peered down the corridor, hoping a guard would quiet his neighbor. The nearest one, a giant Russian with a lame foot who wore a blue tracksuit and aviator sunglasses for no reason whatsoever, was 30 yards away.

"You heard not a word," X told Banger, "for I spoke not a word."

A third voice joined their conversation without warning: "Dissembler, dissembler, dissembler!"

It was Ripper, who occupied the cell to X's left. To distract herself from her own searing thoughts, Ripper ripped her fingernails from their beds, then waited impatiently for them to grow so she could wrench them out once more. Back in the 19th century, in London, she had watched one of her servants spill soup onto the lap of a dinner guest. She'd stood up from her chair, followed the young woman to the kitchen—and killed her with a single blow of a boiling teakettle. Afterward, she instructed two footmen to deposit the servant's body on the cobblestones behind the house. She knew the police would be too intimidated by her wealth to question her. Ripper had been 36 for nearly 200 years.

Many of X's fellow prisoners were wretched men and women whose souls had been transported to the Lowlands when they died. A smaller number, like Banger and Ripper, had been snatched out of their lives by bounty hunters when earthly justice failed to punish them.

Ripper was now pacing in her cell and loudly reciting a poem from her youth: "'Deceiver, dissembler / Your trousers are alight / From what pole or gallows / Shall they dangle in the night?'"

She was a beautiful, formidable woman. She had trained X to be a bounty hunter, and dozens of others, as well. Lately, however, she seemed separated from insanity by the width of a dime.

X glanced down the corridor again. The Russian guard had heard Ripper ranting, and was on his way, dragging his left foot behind him.

Banger hissed at Ripper: "Jesus, Rip, shut it, would you?"

"But he is a deceiver! I heard his exclamation as well!"

"Okay, fine," said Banger. "But chill the hell out. And by the way, the real version of that thing is, 'Liar, liar, pants on fire / Hang them from a telephone wire.' Just sayin'."

This caused Ripper to cackle.

"Yes, of course," she said. "I shall alert Mr. William Blake to his error when next we meet."

The Russian arrived and poked his club through the bars of Ripper's cell.

"Vy sexy lady talk so much?" he said. "Must shut mouth."

"I already warned her, dude," said Banger. "I'm on it."

The guard shuffled over to Banger's cell.

"I am not needing assistance of dung beetle like you," he said. "Please to shut up, also."

"Or what?" said Banger. "You gonna hit me? Oh, that's right: you *can't*. Because your job suuucks. Do you even get health care? You obviously don't get dental."

"If anyone is to be struck, it should be *moi*," Ripper interjected. "I must insist, I really must."

The guard cursed, then shuffled back to Ripper's cell. After a furtive look around, he gave her a quick jab with his club. She was cooing with pleasure when he limped away.

"Nothing for me?" Banger called after him.

"*Nyet*," said the guard, "because you are jackass."

Silence reigned awhile. X lay back on the rocky ground, the bones of his face still glowing with pain. Just as his heart had begun to settle, he heard Banger's annoying whisper.

"Talk to me, man," he said. "Tell me your life story. I'll tell you mine."

X fought back a wave of anger. He had no desire to talk. He spoke harshly to snuff out the conversation.

"Banger, your story is well-known to me," he said. "Do you forget that it was I who conveyed you to this place? Or that it was I who trained you to be a bounty hunter just as Ripper trained me? I know your crimes only too well. Hearing them again would only disgust me."

"Jeez," said Banger. "Way to be a dick."

When it was quiet again, X closed his eyes, already regretting his outburst. He had collected 14 souls for the lords of the Lowlands, and Banger was by no means the worst of them. But X hated telling his story: it only reminded him of the injustices of his life.

X had committed no crime.

He was an innocent.

Unlike every other soul he'd ever encountered, he did not know why he had been condemned. He did not know what outrage he had supposedly committed—or even how or when he might have committed it. But rather than making him feel pure, X's confusion only convinced him that there was something vile and corrupt in his heart that he would one day discover.

The pain beneath his eyes was excruciating now.

It was time.

Even Banger knew it. He was standing at the bars of his cell, gazing out.

"You got company, stud," he said.

X looked through the bars, his heart like a drum.

A lord had leaped from the stony plain, and was hurtling at him through the air.

THE PRISONERS WERE FORBIDDEN from knowing the lords' names, as well. But the personage who swept into X's cell now had a royal, African bearing and was quietly referred to as Regent, out of respect for his proud posture, his great height, and his shining, ebony skin.

X lay down on his back, readying for the ritual that was to come.

Regent came and towered above him, the golden band around his throat and the brilliant blue of his robe shimmering in the darkness.

He lowered his hand over X's face like a mask, and began intoning a speech X had heard many times before.

"The Lowlands require another soul for its collection," he intoned. "He is an evil man—unrepentant and unpunished. I bring you his hateful name. Will you receive this name and will you bring the man to me on his knees?"

"I will," said X.

"Will you defend the secrecy of our world all the while? Will you defend the ancient, inviolable wall between the living and the dead just as bounty hunters have defended it since before time was even scratched in stone?" said Regent.

"I will," said X.

The lord gripped X's face harder with his taloned hand. X's skull seemed to ignite. The pain coursed down his neck, traversed his shoulders, and so on until it had consumed him entirely. He could not breathe. He knew from the 14 previous occasions that the terror would pass, yet he could not prevent himself from bucking and kicking. The lord's hand pressed down harder still.

But X did not think Regent cruel. Even as the lord held him fast, he stroked X's hair paternally with his other hand, taking care that his nails did not lacerate X's skin. Soon something behind X's eyes burst like a dam, and he saw nothing but an overpowering whiteness. When he retrieved his senses, he found himself in the Overworld—on a mountain, in a blizzard.

Regent had set a man's sins swimming in X's veins.

X was like a dog who'd been given the scent of his prey.

Now he could hunt.

The man's name was a boring little brick: Stan. It wasn't just Stan's story that rushed through X's blood, but also the story of everyone whose lives he had infected. There was an old couple called Bert and Betty. There was a boy lost in the woods without a coat or gloves. A pair of dogs.

And a girl.

X could have summoned her face and pictured it with perfect clarity, but he was careful not to. He merely glimpsed her out of the corner of his mind's eye, and saw enough to know that she was too lovely—too fierce and full of hope—for him to recover from.

FIVE

THE GIRL HOVERED OUTSIDE the garage now. She was just standing there, squinting at X and rubbing her nose, her hair askew from sleep. Yet he was so transfixed by her that everything in his body stopped. She had wavy, light brown hair that just barely grazed her shoulders. There was a dark beauty mark on her left cheekbone that drew attention to her eyes, which were wide and glinting and seemed to change from blue to gray even as X looked at her.

He turned away and coughed savagely. Stan's sins had been polluting his body ever since Regent set them loose in his bloodstream. Now that X had let Stan go free, the pain had intensified. The Trembling was the lords' way of ensuring that the bounty hunters would follow orders and return to the Lowlands with their prey.

X had never suffered like this before because he'd never refused his duty before. Still, he knew that his misery—the fever, the pain, the delirium—would only increase unless he renewed his search for Stan. Even if X could endure his sickness, the lords would send another bounty hunter after him—or maybe Regent himself would arrive, seething and bent on vengeance.

When his coughing subsided, X turned back to the girl and her family. The mother was holding her children at a safe distance. Still, the boy managed to break free, and rushed at him. X's body stiffened reflexively—no one ever approached him unless they meant to do him harm—but the boy only wanted to hug him and to whisper, "You saved my dogs!"

He embraced X so tightly that X gasped.

"Stop it—you're hurting him," said the girl. "*And* you're being weird."

"Step away from him, Jonah," said the mother.

The boy did as he was told. The mother peered around the garage.

"My god, it's hot in here," she said. "How is that possible?"

X had warmed the air with a simple rubbing together of his hands. Seeing the mother's concern, he made a circular motion with his palm and the garage was frigid again in an instant.

"Wow," said the mother, even more alarmed than before.

"*A-mazing!*" said the boy.

The girl said nothing. She hadn't stepped any closer. Was she afraid? Disgusted? X couldn't blame her. He was repulsive even to himself. He saw her notice the bruises beneath his eyes, then look quickly away. Shame radiated through him. He wished that she and her family would flee. He wished they would burn the garage down around him. He did not want them to bind their fate to his. Now that he had betrayed the lords, he was a body in free fall, gaining momentum as he fell.

X touched the boy's back gently to let him know that he had not hurt him. He stole another look at the girl, afraid he would see horror in her eyes. Instead, he saw a soft expression that he could not identify. Was that what pity looked like?

He managed to speak, which came as a surprise even to himself. He said four words with as much force as he could muster: "Leave me. Protect yourselves." Then, so quietly it was as if he were speaking to himself, he said two more: "Jonah. *Zoe*."

He began to lose consciousness then, and darkness poured in from every side. He heard one last exchange. The boy said in wonderment: "He knows our names, Mom! How does he know our names?!" And the mother answered—though it was not truly an answer but an exhausted kind of prayer—"I just wish I knew what I was bringing into my house."

IT TOOK ZOE AND her family ten minutes to devise a plan for ferrying X inside. As he waited, he drifted in and out of consciousness, like a boat that couldn't decide whether to sink or float. Each time he came to, he begged them to abandon him. He could not make them understand the dangers. Finally, Jonah and his mother left to fetch something from the house. X and Zoe were alone.

Even in his fever, X could feel the awkwardness of the moment. He felt Zoe's eyes flit over his face again—his hair, his lips, his eyes—and again he was ashamed to think how he must look to her. He'd seen others like her from a distance before, and they'd never stirred anything in him. But Zoe . . . He could feel her gaze on him even when he turned away—even when his eyes were closed. Her face gave off such warmth that it was a kind of light. No amount of horror or hatred could make an impression on X anymore—but loveliness and kindness laid him flat.

"Who are you? *What* are you?" said Zoe, after an agonizing silence. She paused, and laughed to herself. "Do you skateboard?"

"Do I—?"

"Sorry," she said. "I have a blurting problem."

Again the awkwardness was everywhere. X wanted so badly to speak to her, to make her comfortable, to let her see something in him that was not wretched.

"I do not . . . skateboard," he said.

She laughed for some reason, shook her head, and put her face in her hands. She stared out into the darkness to see if her mother and Jonah were on their way back. They were not.

"Zoe," said X, wondering if he had the energy to speak the words swarming in his head. "You *must* abandon me. I am not like you. You have seen what I am capable of—and creatures even more dangerous will come after me soon. They will demand that I recapture Stan, and they will destroy anyone whose shadow falls across their path. Zoe, truly, I can offer you nothing but peril."

She knelt by his side.

The closer she came, the more his fever cooled. He had never experienced the phenomenon before.

"You saved my brother and me," Zoe said. "And I can handle a little peril." She smiled faintly. "What's your name? I don't even know your name."

"I do not have one," he said.

"That's messed up," she said. "Okay, listen, whoever you are, we are *not* going to let you freeze to death out here. You helped Jonah and me when you didn't have to, and you didn't kill Stan when you could have—and *that's* when I saw what you are capable of."

"Zoe, I beseech you—"

"*No.* There will be no beseeching."

Her voice was stern now. He feared he had angered her, but saw that she was struggling with many emotions.

"My family's had a shit year," she said, then stopped to gather herself.

"You need not speak if it brings you pain," he said.

"No, I want to," she said. She started again, speaking slowly, carefully: "We've had a shit year. There was nothing we could do about it, but there *is* something we can do about you. So we're going to help you, no matter what you say—or how weirdly you say it."

X searched her mind to see if her will was as strong as it seemed. He moved slowly, feeling his way into her thoughts, like he was parting branches. Almost immediately, she shivered and shot him a warning look.

"Stop it," she said. "There will be no mind-melding—or whatever that is. You have to promise. Not with me *or* my family."

"I give you my word," he said. He added—he was not sure if he should—"And I have never been able to do it with anyone but you."

This seemed to surprise her, and she smiled.

The awkwardness was lifting, dissipating like smoke.

"What will you call me?" he said.

"I'll think of something," she said.

The front door slammed in the distance—a dead sound with no echo. X turned to watch Jonah and his mother cross the drive. Jonah ran excitedly. He was carrying a round, red sled. He was holding it in front of him, like a shield.

TOGETHER, THEY PULLED X to the house. With every bump and jolt, he arched his back in agony. Once inside, they

85

maneuvered the sled through the kitchen, then the living room. Zoe and her mom tugged at the rope, while Jonah cleared the path and shouted frantic, sometimes contradictory, instructions.

At the bottom of the staircase, they managed to get X to his feet, like a team of workers lifting a statue. Zoe and her mother held his arms to steady him, and Jonah shoved as hard as he could from behind to prevent him from toppling backward. After five nerve-wracking minutes, they reached the landing. Jonah wanted X to sleep in his room with him, and when his mother hesitated, he began chanting, "Sleepover! Sleepover! Sleepover!" In the end, it was decided that X would sleep in Jonah's bed, even though it was small and shaped like a ladybug. The Bissells would all share the floor. The mother didn't want her children alone with him.

Zoe helped X onto the bed, putting a palm against his chest to steady him. X closed his eyes to hide his surprise. His shirt had a rough V at the throat, and Zoe's right forefinger had landed on the patch of bare skin. For the next few moments all he could feel—all he was aware of in the world—were the tiny movements of her hand as she inched her finger back onto cloth.

X was still dizzy and weak. The moment Zoe took her hand away he fell back onto the mattress with such a *thud* that the lady-bug's antennae twitched. Zoe unlaced his boots and put them under the bed. When she went to hang his overcoat in a closet, he shook his head no.

Zoe smiled.

"Security blanket?" she said.

X did not recognize the phrase, but he could tell there was kindness in it.

Zoe placed her palm on X's chest again—avoiding his exposed

skin so carefully that he felt her touch even more keenly than before—and said, with a strange kind of sweetness, "Good night, moon."

As she turned away, he reached out to touch her arm. Had he not been in a fog and half out of his senses, he'd never have had the nerve.

"Why endanger yourselves?" he said. "Why do all this for me?"

Zoe looked down at where his hand lightly gripped her. She gave him a smile, a trace of light in the darkness.

"There's nothing good on TV," she said.

Jonah fell asleep first and began battling someone or something in his dreams. Zoe's mom tossed on the floor awhile—she gave a little yelp every time she rolled onto a toy that Jonah had left on the carpet—then slipped off as well, one arm draped lovingly over her son.

X lay quietly, unable to rest despite his exhaustion. He turned to face the window next to the bed. A frantic beetle was flitting back and forth between the panes of glass, trapped forever with the wide world in full view. X knew what it felt like to be that bug. For a moment, he allowed himself to imagine escaping the Lowlands and living. *Truly* living. He pictured himself with Zoe in the summertime when the world wasn't hardened by ice and swallowed in snow. When there was no Trembling. No fear.

He shook his head. The vision was ridiculous—and dangerous, besides. The longer he resisted returning to the Lowlands, the more he imperiled them all.

Yet even the sound of Zoe's breathing in the darkness captivated him. It was nearly five in the morning now. They were the only ones left awake. Some protective instinct made it impossible for him to sleep before she did. So X and Zoe just lay there in the dark. He listened to her breathing—waiting for it to deepen and slow—and had the sensation, though he had a hard time trusting it, that she was listening to his.

THE BLIZZARD HAD MAULED Zoe's and Jonah's schools, and they had to be shut down for days. The flagpole at the high school had snapped in half and flown through the front doors like a missile. Half the windows on the northern side of the building had been shattered: all that remained of the glass was a rim of tiny, pointed shards that looked like vicious little teeth. Over at the elementary school, the classrooms were flooded with muddy water. Handwritten essays about climate change and drawings of horses floated through the hallways like lily pads.

X had fallen into a sleep so long and unbroken it was nearly a coma, his chest rising and falling, his legs dangling off the end of the ladybug. He slept through most of Monday. He was only vaguely aware of the comings and goings downstairs. He heard voices. He heard cupboards squeaking open and clapping shut. He heard branches being dragged across the snow and tossed onto a pile.

In the afternoon, a friend of Zoe's arrived in a truck thumping with music. X heard Zoe call him Dallas, but wasn't sure that was actually a name. Dallas had brought Zoe a coffee, which seemed to delight her ("Oh my god, does this have actual *milk* in it? Do *not* tell my mother."). Still, she sent him away without letting him into the house. X knew that he himself was the reason, and he was just conscious enough to feel shame trickle through his chest.

Hours later, he woke again: another car engine, another friend. The sky was black, except for the fuzzy yellow lights of another town on the horizon. X's shirt was soaked with perspiration.

This friend must have known Zoe well. She didn't bother to knock on the front door—she just strode into the front hall, calling her name. The instant Zoe tried to send her away, the friend said, "Why are you being weird? Gloria and I take *one* four-hour nap—okay, it was five hours, shut up—and now you're dissing me? And, by the way, what the hell was up with that insane Instagram? People are asking *me* about it."

Even feverish and half-asleep, X could feel Zoe grow tense.

He heard a wooden step creak as she sat down: She didn't want her friend anywhere near X. She was blocking the stairs.

"I'll tell you everything, Val," she said, finally. "But first tell me what you've heard."

Val sighed.

"I hate this game," she said. "Okay, I heard you solved the Wallaces' murder, met a hot alien, and made the chief of police cry like a bitch." She paused. "Let's start with the alien."

"He's not an alien," said Zoe.

"I'm disappointed," said Val, "but go on."

"I met him during the storm," said Zoe. "He helped me and Jonah."

"And?" said Val.

X didn't understand the question, but Zoe clearly did. She lowered her voice to a whisper, not knowing how keen X's hearing was.

"And he's so hot I can't even," she said.

"You can't even?" said Val.

They were giggling now.

"I can't even *begin* to even," said Zoe. "Ask me about his shoulders. Ask me about his arms. I mean it—pick a body part."

"Okay, okay, I get it," said Val. "Just because I think heterosexual sex is gross and immoral doesn't mean I don't understand what a hot guy is."

Zoe laughed.

"It's immoral now, too?" she said.

"Hello, overpopulation! Hello, world poverty!" Val said. "But I'm trying to be open-minded. Say more about the alien."

"Still not an alien," said Zoe.

"Still disappointed," said Val.

X sank back into sleep like someone pushed down into a river. He only half-understood what he'd heard.

HE AWOKE ONLY TWICE on Tuesday.

The first time, Zoe propped his head up against a pillow and spooned broth into his mouth, saying gently, "Three more sips . . . Two more . . . One more . . . Come on, don't fight me."

The second time, she leaned over him with a glass of water and attempted to push something into his mouth. X was confused. He began to choke. Jonah, who'd been playing with dinosaurs and wizards on the floor, looked up and said in a shocked voice, "He doesn't know how to use a *straw*?"

"Shut up, Jonah," Zoe said. "Don't embarrass him."

Now that he was under Zoe's care, X began to surface from dreams more regularly. The Trembling had loosened its grip. Stan's sins flowed more quietly through his veins, though they never disappeared entirely.

Sometimes, he heard the Bissells wonder aloud about him when they thought he was sleeping. Was he from hell—was that what he meant by the Lowlands? Why was he sent there? *What had he done?* Was he alive? Was he undead? What were his superpowers and what were his weaknesses? These last two questions came from Jonah, who, as X's eyes fluttered open momentarily, had also crept close and asked if he was one of the Avengers.

Zoe's mother suggested they all write their questions down on slips of paper and put them in a metal mixing bowl she had placed on the nightstand. When he had recovered, she said, she'd see to it that he answered them all.

Now, even as he slept, X could sense the bowl beside him filling with paper. He dreaded answering the questions, and the dread crept into his dreams like a rising flood. He saw terrible images: a parade of every soul he had ever dragged to the Lowlands. He saw the fear he inspired in his victims and, sometimes, even his own hands in a ring around their throats. X was certain that the more Zoe knew about him, the more repulsed she would be. He had only done what the lords had commanded him to do—but he had done it.

X FINALLY HAD THE strength to sit up on Wednesday morning. Zoe and the others were curled on the floor, still murmuring low in their sleep. The Trembling should have forced X back to the Lowlands by now but, thanks to Zoe's presence, the pain was muted. He gazed out the window, hungry for air. The frozen river glinted at the bottom of the hill like a long glowing ribbon.

He went outdoors, and the frigid wind blasted away the last remnants of sleep. The sun was not yet visible but it had sent a flood of orange and red across the sky to announce its arrival. X was grateful that the day was not yet bright. He had lived so long in a cell that his eyes were accustomed to darkness and to close quarters. He was most comfortable at this hour, when the world revealed itself slowly.

X had been trained to ignore the beauty of the Overworld. He had been taught to cast his eyes downward, or to stare straight ahead like a horse pulling a carriage. Any memories he formed here—not just of mountains and sky, but of the dogs nuzzling his face or of Zoe placing her hand against his chest—would make him suffer all the more when he returned to the Lowlands.

And he *would* be forced to return—he couldn't let himself forget it. The lords would eventually haul him back home. What terrified him was that he didn't know when or how—or what plague they would visit on Zoe's family for giving him shelter.

X was weaving his way down the hill when he heard the door open behind him. He turned to see Zoe coming toward him. She had thrown on a coat and snowshoes, and her face wore a dark expression.

"Are you bailing on us?" she said.

"Bailing?" said X.

"*Leaving*. Are you *leaving*?"

"No, I assure you I am not."

Zoe seemed not to believe him.

"Because enough people have left us already," she said. "And Jonah *likes* you. You know who else was allowed to sleep in the ladybug? Nobody ever."

"Zoe," he said. "I am merely testing my lungs." He paused. "Will you walk with me? I would be glad of your company."

He could see, in her eyes, that she was struggling to trust him— and he could see the instant she decided to try.

"Yes, kind sir," she said. "I, too, should like to test my lungs."

"Do you mock me?" he said.

"Verily, I do," she said.

92

They walked in silence, down toward the snow-burdened trees. Zoe did not assault him with questions about who or what he was, and he was grateful for it. He could not remember a time when he'd simply walked beside someone with no horrible destination in mind. He could not remember anyone being so calm in his company. Zoe seemed not to fear him at all. Once, as they were crossing the frozen river, she even bumped against him playfully. He felt the whole length of his body flush with heat.

They found themselves, almost without realizing it, on the path to the lake. The dead part of the forest loomed ahead of them—the trees stood stripped and charred, as if they'd been decimated in an atomic blast. X watched as Zoe took in the grim sight. He offered to turn back. She shook her head no, like it was something she knew she had to overcome. To distract herself, she began singing: "'Row, row, row your boat / Gently down the stream /Verily, verily, verily, verily / Life is but a dream.'"

"Even I know that tune," said X. "Yet I think you have misrepresented the words."

Zoe laughed: "Have I? I don't think so."

Again she gave him a little bump with her hip, and again he felt heat ripple through him.

When they reached the lake, Zoe walked directly to the hole that Stan had made, as if to convince herself that she hadn't dreamed it all. X trailed after her.

The hole had mostly frozen over. It looked like a scab that was healing.

X wanted to pull Zoe away, wanted to protect her from the memories he knew would be sinking like pins into her brain.

She spoke before he could conceive of a plan.

"So Stan really did know my father," she said. "That disgusting reptile knew my *father*. I thought he was lying when he said they were friends."

X searched for something suitable to say. He was so unused to talking that forming even the simplest sentence felt like building a wall. Every word was a stone he had to weigh in his hands.

"Stan is poison," X said carefully. "You must not let a single syllable he uttered into your blood."

Zoe nodded, but he could see that she was distracted and had not truly heard him.

"You'd think that once my dad died," she said, "he couldn't disappoint me anymore." She stopped and kicked at the ice with the tip of a snowshoe. "There goes that theory."

X saw both hurt and anger in her—they were like competing storms.

"Yet you loved your father?" he said. "Or the disappointments would not pain you?"

Zoe hesitated just long enough that X felt his cheeks redden and wished he hadn't spoken.

"I loved him," she said. "Sometimes I think I loved him just enough to screw me up for the rest of my life."

X was silent a moment.

"You do not seem . . . You do not seem *screwed up* to me," he said.

Zoe laughed.

"Get to know me," she said.

This time X spoke without thinking.

"Would that I could," he said.

Zoe frowned and turned away. X wondered if it was because

he'd reminded her that he would eventually have to leave. He decided it was better that she not forget it. It was better that neither of them forget.

She was staring down at the ice now. The edge of the hole was speckled—decorated almost—with Stan's blood.

Zoe shivered, and straightened up again.

"There's other stuff that Stan said," she said. "I can't stop hearing it in my head. He said he heard my dad died in 'some goddamn cave' and that we just left him there."

"More poison," X said.

"No," said Zoe. "It's true."

There was another silence and, because the wind had quieted, it felt deeper somehow. X waited. Zoe began to tell him about her father—about the morning she woke up to find him gone, about the search for his body. She seemed surprised that the story flowed out of her so freely.

"I was pissed when I realized he'd gone caving without me," she said. "I mean, it wasn't just our thing—it was our *only* thing. If he thought I wasn't ready to go caving in the snow or whatever, he should have waited for me. He should have trained me. We had one thing! How hard is it to keep *one thing* sacred?"

Zoe stopped for a second. X didn't know if she would continue.

"I figured he'd gone up to Polebridge," she said, at last. "There are two really tough caves up there—Black Teardrop and Silver Teardrop—so about 20 of us helped the cops look for him. It was insanely cold. My friends Val and Dallas came. They don't even like each other, but they pretended to because I was so freaked out. Dallas brought a big jug of this disgusting, like, weight-lifter shake that he said would give us 'the strength of a thousand badasses.' I refused to drink it." Zoe paused. "Jonah came, too. I mean, it was nuts that he was there. Some therapist told my mother it was a good idea. The kid was still *seven*—and he was up in the mountains looking for his dead dad."

Zoe fell silent again.

"I'm sorry," she said. "You don't want to hear all this."

"I do," said X.

Zoe searched his eyes to see if he was telling the truth.

"It's a horrible story," she said.

"Perhaps telling it will take away some of its power," he said.

She nodded, and continued. X didn't recognize all the words— some swam past him in schools, like exotic fish. Still, he felt Zoe's pain seep into his chest and become his own.

"We searched around Silver Teardrop first," she said. "We didn't find anything. The caves up there both have supersteep caverns— just straight, like, hundred-foot drops—so nobody actually went inside. But at Black Teardrop, we found the rope my dad had used to lower himself down. One end was tied around a tree. The other just kind of disappeared into the cave." She looked at X, and paused. "Jonah was the one who found the rope. He had this happy, little-kid look on his face, you know? He was like, 'I found him! I found him!'"

Zoe turned away from X now.

"Then Jonah saw the blood on the end of the rope and all of a sudden he dropped the thing like it was a snake and started crying." Zoe stared up at the sky. "I took the weight-lifter shake from Dallas and chugged the thing," she said. "I ended up puking all over the place. Attractive, right?"

X could find no words to offer.

"Your father," he said, when the silence had become uncomfortable. "He had fallen into the cave?"

"He must have stopped to take a picture while he was rappelling down," said Zoe. "He probably wanted me to see some ice formation, or something. That's actually the part that . . ." She couldn't finish the sentence. "You know? Because he was doing it for *me*. And it would have been okay except that he used to wear this nerdy old helmet that had an actual flame for a light. That's the way my dad was: he would do things *because* they were dorky. The flame must have burned through the rope. I used to love what a dork he was. But this time it got him killed."

Zoe's words hung in the air.

X put a hand on her shoulder. He couldn't remember the last time he'd touched anyone that way. He wasn't sure he ever had.

"The cops promised they'd go get my dad's body, but they never did," said Zoe. "They just fenced off the cave and left his body down there, all mangled or whatever. We had a memorial service in town, which was totally awful. Even the food sucked. Then my mom and Jonah and me had a little ceremony in our backyard. Jonah wanted to bury one of our dad's T-shirts. He decorated a cardboard box with purple stars—that was, like, the coffin, I guess?—and put an old T-shirt in it that said Ninja Dad. We buried it under a tree that Jonah'd be able to see from his window. We couldn't bury it very deep because the ground was too hard. Anyway, it was this whole big thing. Jonah wrote a poem, but he was crying too hard to read it, so we just passed it around. I could only read, like, two lines before I started losing it. The first two lines—seriously—they were like, 'Now that Daddy Man and I are apart / I don't know what to do with my heart.'"

When Zoe had finished her story, X felt desperate to tell her

97

something about himself, but every thought, every memory, every feeling was stuck in his throat.

He told her this in his stumbling way.

She shook her head.

"I didn't tell you all that because I wanted you to tell *me* something," she said. "I told you because I trust you."

"And I *you*," said X. "Yet still I stand here, dumb as a stump. Everything I know about myself shames me."

Zoe looked at him so sadly now that X feared he had only compounded her pain.

"Just tell me *one* thing about your mom and dad," she said. "One tiny thing. It doesn't have to be some huge deal."

X considered this.

"I do not know who they were," he said.

Zoe breathed in sharply. X felt a stab of embarrassment.

He told her about the Lowlands a little. He wondered if she would believe him. When he saw that she did, his shame at who—and what—he was kept spreading. Zoe seemed to know it. She stepped forward and hugged him. He was too stunned by the gesture to hug her back.

"It's time we gave you a name," she said when they pulled apart. "I'm thinking Aragorn—or Fred."

Later, they climbed the hill back toward the Bissells' house, the white drifts sighing beneath their feet. Zoe pointed out the willow where they had buried her father's T-shirt. It was a slender tree, heavy with snow and bending so low to the ground it looked as if it were trying to pick something up. It struck X as a lonely sight. He stepped forward and took the branches one by one in his hand. He shook the snow off gently until the tree could stand upright.

He felt Zoe's eyes on him all the while.

BACK IN THE HOUSE, Zoe informed everyone of X's new name.

Her mother laughed and said, "That's not technically a name, but okay." Jonah shouted, "I'm gonna call you *Professor* X!" And then immediately forgot to.

Zoe's mother steered everyone into the living room, where an awkward silence fell. The silver bowl full of questions had migrated downstairs, and sat on the coffee table now. X cringed at the sight of it. He dreaded telling the Bissells even more of his story. They should have cast him out days ago, and once they knew who he truly was, they would.

Zoe was next to him on the couch.

"You don't have to tell us anything you don't want to," she said softly. "And *no one* will judge you."

Zoe's mother picked up the bowl and handed it to X.

"Time to find out who we're dealing with," she said.

She did not say it unkindly, but it stung.

X took the bowl and set it on his lap. Immediately, he felt anxious and unsettled, like there was an animal loose in his chest. Even if Zoe had told them everything she knew about him, they knew only the bare beginnings. But that was not the only reason he feared what was about to happen.

He stared down at the nest of papers.

He could not convince his hand to reach into the bowl. He sat paralyzed.

"Pick one!" said Jonah.

X pulled out a strip of paper. The bowl made a pinging sound as his knuckle brushed against it. He unfolded the strip and stared down at the words in his hand. The letters swam in every direction, as they always did.

He looked to Zoe, helplessly.

She did not understand—but then, all at once, she did. She leaned toward him to whisper a question.

But Jonah beat her to it: "You don't know how to read?"

X shook his head the slightest bit.

"Nor write," he said. "Nor draw, now that I think of it."

X knew that Zoe's mother was gazing at him now. Was she disgusted? Scared? Was she strategizing about how to separate him from her children? He was afraid to turn to her, so he didn't know.

"I can show you how to do that stuff," said Jonah. "It's actually *not* that hard."

"Thank you," said X.

Zoe took the paper gently from his hands so she could read it aloud. Her voiced quavered just enough to tell X that she was nervous, too.

"'Why'd you get sent to the Lowlands?'" she read. "'Did you kill somebody? Did you kill *a whole ton* of people—like, with a catapult?'"

"That one's mine," said Jonah.

"We know," said Zoe.

X took a breath.

"I know this beggars belief," said X, "but I committed no crime. I was never even accused of one. I will swear it upon anything you like."

Across the room, Zoe's mother coughed what sounded like an unnecessary cough.

"I'm sorry," she said, "but that actually does—how did you say it?—*beggar belief.*"

"Stop it, Mom," said Zoe.

"Do not censure your mother on my account," said X. "This is her home. She has shown me nothing but kindness."

"Thank you, X," said Zoe's mother.

It was the first time anyone had used his name. Even in the unhappy circumstances, he liked the sound of it. It made him feel centered—*present* somehow, like a picture coming into focus.

"I read about a lot of religions when the kids' dad died," Zoe's mother said, "and there was something in all of them that helped me. I'm kind of a walking, talking Coexist bumper sticker now." She paused. "And, I'm sorry, but . . . I've never heard of people getting sent to hell for no reason."

Zoe took the bowl from X's lap and set it angrily on the coffee table, where it vibrated noisily.

"This was a bad idea," she said. "We're done."

"No," said X. "Your mother is correct: No one gets sent to the Lowlands without cause."

He turned to Zoe's mother now, and found her eyes.

"But, you see, I was not *sent* to the Lowlands," he said. "I was born there."

No one spoke as X's words settled. The only sound was Spock and Uhura barking in the distance. X hated speaking the sentence, yet now that he *had* he felt freer somehow.

Zoe reached into the bowl.

"'Is it weird to be three hundred years old, or whatever?'" she read.

X surprised them all by laughing.

"And whose query is this?" he said, glancing around the room.

"Mine," said Zoe. "I mean, no offense, but you talk like Beowulf."

Jonah giggled.

"Wolves can't *talk*, Zoe," he said. He turned to X uncertainly: "Can they?"

"I do not believe so," said X. "As to my age, I was but a whelp when a woman we call Ripper began training me to be a bounty hunter. For years, hers was virtually the only voice I heard. I suppose I learned to speak as she does—and she was wrenched from your world nearly two hundred years ago."

"So how old *are* you?" said Zoe.

X heard an urgency in her voice, as if this question mattered more than the others.

"Ripper tells me that I am twenty," he said.

"Twenty?" said Zoe. "For real?"

"Yes," said X. "The only reason I have to doubt her is that she is quite nearly insane."

"Wow, twenty," said Zoe. "If you want, I could help you apply to college."

X recognized this as a "blurt" and let it pass.

Zoe unfolded another question.

"'*Where* are the Lowlands? *What* are the Lowlands?'" she read.

"Those are mine," said her mother.

"Good job, Mom," said Jonah.

X sat motionless, trying to compose an answer in his head. Finally, he turned to Jonah and asked him to gather up all the little figures from his room—the soldiers, the animals, the wizards, the dinosaurs, the dwarves—and bring them outside in a basket.

"I am not certain I can *explain* the Lowlands," he said. "But perhaps I can build them for you."

SIX

THEY STOOD IN THE BACKYARD, looking at X as if he'd gone mad. He was rolling a mammoth snowball, circling them faster and faster as he did so, the tail of his shimmering blue over-coat taking flight behind him. Uhura chased him ecstatically, as if a game was afoot. Spock lay nearby, eating snow.

"I believe the first query was, '*Where* are the Lowlands?'" X said.

The snowball was about four feet tall now, and he had at last come to a stop.

"Yes," said Zoe's mother.

X gestured to his creation.

"This is the earth," he said. "Or as good a likeness as I can produce."

He was warming to his task. The dread he'd felt had been beaten back—replaced by the desire to give a true and clear accounting of himself. They deserved that much, and more, for taking him in when they had every reason to fear him.

"The Lowlands," he continued, "are *here.*"

He thrust his left fist deep into the heart of the globe, breaking it open with such force that Jonah stepped backward and exclaimed, "Holy shit."

X had never heard the phrase—the words didn't seem to belong together—but Zoe's mother found it unacceptable, and told Jonah so.

X had begun to perspire. He removed his coat—the left arm was encrusted with snow all the way up to the shoulder—and draped it over the low branch of a tree. Jonah and his mother, who'd crossed their arms and were shuffling their feet to stay warm, once again looked at him as if he were a lunatic. Zoe merely smiled. It pleased X to think that his ways were becoming familiar to her.

"The query that followed was, '*What* are the Lowlands?'" he said.

Zoe's mother nodded.

X knelt beside the ruins of what had, until recently, been the earth, and gestured for Jonah to join him. Together, they used the snow to sculpt a tall, curving wall that ran along the edge of a plain.

Zoe's mother stopped X as he was piling the plain with rocks, and drew him aside to say something only he could hear.

"I'm not sure I want Jonah to see this," she said.

"I shall make it a game," said X. "And I shall endeavor to hide from him what I say to you now: the Lowlands are an abomination."

X TOLD JONAH TO imagine that the snow was black rock, porous and damp. He instructed him to carve a grid of holes into the wall—he called them "the rooms where we sleep" rather than "cells"—and to tuck a figurine into each of them.

"Guys or girls?" Jonah said.

"Either," said X. "Both."

"Civil War guys or World War II guys—or knights, maybe?" said Jonah.

"You may use any of them," said X. "There are souls of every kind in the Lowlands, all of them in the clothes they died in. I myself reside *here*, among the bounty hunters"—he pointed to a cell in a row midway up the wall—"and have two neighbors. To my left lives a man I call Banger. I brought him to the Lowlands in 2012. To my right lives Ripper, whom I spoke of earlier. She drew her last mortal breath in 1832."

"Are they your best friends?" said Jonah.

X considered this.

"Yes," he said. "If I can claim any friends at all."

He hadn't meant it to sound self-pitying, but he noticed that Zoe frowned at the words, then came to sit next to him in the snow.

Zoe and her mother watched as the Lowlands came to life. When the cells were filled with "residents," X told Jonah they required five or ten more figurines.

"To play the role of the guards," he explained, before correcting himself and referring to them as "the helpers."

Jonah asked him to describe the helpers. "So I can get a mental picture," he said. X said that they were fat and simple-minded, more often than not—and that they had waxy skin and bulbous noses, and were highly pungent.

Jonah asked what "pungent" meant. Zoe spoke up and said, "They like puns," which seemed to satisfy him.

X asked what sort of figures Jonah would suggest for the helpers, and Jonah scrunched his eyebrows down and made his thinking-cap face.

"What about orcs and dwarves?" he said.

X asked to see representatives of each species. Jonah pulled a few from the basket, and held them out to X, their ugly bodies lying on their backs on the chubby starfish of his palm.

"Well chosen," said X. They placed the motley guards in a row atop the wall. "Now," he continued, "we shall need a river and a tree."

"I have a tree!" said Jonah. "It's Pooh's honey tree. I don't play with it anymore. *Obviously*."

He plucked it from the basket and handed it to X, who regarded it with a smile.

"This is a far lovelier tree than the one in the Lowlands," he said. "Yet for our purposes it is perfect."

He set it carefully on the plain, covering its base with snow so it wouldn't topple, and then he and Jonah began discussing what might pass for a river. They were stumped, and were about to dig a long, snaking ditch through the plain when Zoe unwound the blue scarf from her neck and offered it up. X bowed his head in thanks—she thought he did it in jest, but he did not—and arranged the scarf so that it curved along the ground.

When X announced that their model was nearly complete, Jonah made a confused face and raised his hand, as if he were in school.

"Where does the devil live?" he asked.

X faltered.

"It's said that some Higher Power rules the Lowlands," he said. "Yet I have never seen evidence of such a presence, nor have I heard the same tale told about Him twice."

So X told Jonah about the lords. He'd delayed describing them because he didn't know how to disguise how terrifying they were. In the end, he simply said that they were angry beasts, and that he and Jonah must use the fiercest of figurines to represent them.

Jonah's hand shot up once more, his fingers wiggling excitedly.

"T. rexes?" he said.

Soon a half dozen dinosaurs were stationed in the miniature Lowlands. A few were raging on the plain, jaws agape, teeth flashing. Others were scaling the great wall and reaching into the cells.

"The lords are the ones who sent you here?" said Zoe.

"They are, indeed," said X. "They put Stan's name into my blood like a poison, along with the powers I needed to capture him. My powers are only a fraction of their own, however, and they will strip me of them when I return to the Lowlands."

"What if you never return?" said Zoe. "What if you *stay* in our world?"

Hadn't he told her already? Didn't she understand how he endangered them every moment he lingered in the Overworld? Why was she so reluctant to believe him?

"I suspect," he said, "that they would obliterate everything—and everyone—you ever loved."

BUILDING THE LOWLANDS, EVEN out of snow and toys, put X into such a grave mood that once it was finished he could hardly stand to look at it. Jonah continued to play. X was touched to see that he freed the prisoners from their cells and locked the lords and guards in instead.

Zoe's mother seemed as troubled as X. She took her daughter's arm and steered her around to the front of the house, not knowing how keen X's hearing was.

"He's cute—I get it—but I want him *out*," he heard the mother say.

The words, though wrapped in wind, were so clear that she might have been standing in front of him.

"I'll give him another day to make sure he's recovered," she added. "That's it."

"You want to send him *back* there?" said Zoe. She sounded as if she'd been struck. "Now that you know he's innocent? Now that you've seen what the Lowlands are like?"

"Yes, it has T. rexes, I know," her mother said.

"You think he's lying?" said Zoe. "You didn't see what Jonah and I saw on the lake."

"Honestly, I don't know *what* I believe," her mother said. "But last night—when I woke up at two in the morning in a sweat—it occurred to me that the best-case scenario is that he's a delusional psychopath. I mean, that's what I'm *rooting* for."

In the distance, X could hear a car—a truck, from the sound of it—shifting gears as it plodded up the mountain. He'd been so comfortably ensconced in the Bissells' home that he had forgotten there was anyone else in the world. The reminder was unsettling.

"I won't let you send him back," said Zoe. Her voice was rising now. "I won't."

"I'm not sending him anywhere—except *away*," her mother said. "He warned us not to take him in. It was the first thing he said. Look, I know he helped you and Jonah—"

"He saved our lives," said Zoe. "From Stan—somebody *you* should have warned us about."

"Don't do that," said her mother. "I made your dad stop speaking to that man back in Virginia twenty years ago."

"Why didn't you ever tell me about him?" Zoe asked.

"Because it's not a pretty story," her mother said.

"Yeah, well, I want to hear it anyway," said Zoe. "Right now."

Her mother sighed.

The truck had grown louder. X watched it rattle into view. It turned out to be a van and—unlike Stan's pickup, which had been as corroded and sinister as the man who drove it—the sides were painted to resemble the top of a snowy, majestic mountain. Strapped to the roof was a wooden carving of a bear. It appeared to be a permanent fixture for it was positioned to look as if it were the king of the aforementioned mountain. It was a happy bear, smiling and waving as it rode through the countryside.

X knew nothing about transportation, but to him the van seemed . . . silly. For a moment, it stalled. The tailpipe coughed up smoke, like someone experimenting with his first cigarette. But the driver got it started again and resumed the climb. X chastised himself for having let the van distract him. He turned his attention back to Zoe and her mother.

"Stan was disgusting even as a teenager," Zoe's mother was saying. "But he could convince your father to do anything. They broke into a teacher's house. They stole a garbage truck. Seriously: a garbage truck! You know what they did with it? They actually went around collecting people's garbage. Have you heard enough now? Can I please stop—*please*?"

"No," said Zoe. "I want to hear everything."

"You *don't*," said her mother.

There was a brief stalemate.

The van labored closer.

"When they hit eighteen or nineteen, the crimes started getting less and less cute," her mother said. "It was like Stan was trying to figure out how weak your dad was and how far he could push him. There was stuff so ugly that your father cried over it. Eventually, he and Stan got arrested for something—I don't even remember what, I've blocked it out—and I gave him an ultimatum: *him or me.* We got married a year later. I don't think he changed his last name to mine because he was some big romantic—I think he did it because he had a criminal record. Now, should I have told you all that when you were a kid, Zoe? About your *father*? Who was a big enough disappointment *anyway*? Should I tell Jonah? How do you think that would go?"

Zoe said nothing. X suspected she was crying. When her mother spoke again, her voice was hushed and kind.

"I'm grateful to X," she said, "and that's why I didn't turn him in to the police. But, sweetie, I think Jonah's getting too close to him." She paused, as the van drew nearer. "And I *know* that you are."

X was still waiting for Zoe to deny it when the van turned up the Bissells' driveway, about a hundred yards away. The engine sounded absurdly, almost catastrophically, loud.

"Crap, it's Rufus," said Zoe's mother. "What's he doing here?"

"What do you *think* he's doing?" Zoe said, still rattled by their conversation. "He's obsessed with you, and it's time for a new episode of *World's Slowest Courtship*. 'This week, Rufus starts growing a rose!'"

"Don't do that," her mother said. "If he heard you say something like that, it would really embarrass him."

Rufus pulled up near the garage and killed the engine.

"Get X into the woods," Zoe's mother told her, "unless you think you can explain who he is to Rufus. Because *I* certainly can't."

The words jolted X. Why had he just been standing there, eavesdropping? He could not afford to be seen by yet another citizen of the Overworld. Every person who saw him was another person he endangered. He might as well have dangled them over a furnace.

He scanned the woods. He could reach them in an instant, but he feared he would alarm Jonah if he ran. He looked down at the boy. Jonah's back was turned, and he was kneeling in the snow, fussing with Zoe's scarf.

X headed for the trees. He forced himself to move slowly. It was agonizing. He was barely a hundred feet away when Jonah—apparently not as entranced by his game as X had imagined—stood up, brushed the snow off his knees, and began shouting: "Rufus! We're in back! Come meet our new friend!"

Zoe came around the house and ran toward X.

"Is there any chance you can talk like a normal human being for even two minutes?" she said.

"I shall endeavor to do what the circumstances require," he said.

Zoe rolled her eyes.

"We are *so* screwed," she said.

Rufus came around the back of the house now, too, and saw them. He approached Jonah first, playfully baring his teeth and hissing like an animal.

"I am One Tooth, ancient ruler of the cat tribes of the tundra!" he exclaimed.

"And I am Many Teeth, the usurper!" Jonah shouted back.

The exchange cracked both of them up, and they ran to hug each other.

Watching, X was hit by a wave of jealousy—he hadn't realized how attached he'd become to the little boy.

Zoe's mother, meanwhile, looked alarmed.

"Perhaps all is not lost," X told Zoe quietly. "I have spent years listening to Banger in his cell, and he died not so long ago. I believe I can do a tolerable imitation of him."

"Then start *now*," said Zoe.

Rufus came toward them. He was flushed with happiness. He extended his hand to X in greeting. Rufus was maybe five years younger than Zoe's mom. He had a friendly, open face, an unruly, reddish-brown beard, and dark hair that clumped together in a strange way. He caught X staring at it, and smiled such a wide, unself-conscious smile that X's jealousy turned a deeper shade.

"Yeah, I'm thinking about dreads," Rufus said. "But I'm only *thinking* about them, so don't judge me. Your hair's pretty epic, too, bro. What's your name? I'm Rufus."

X took his hand.

Zoe and her mother stared at him, waiting. He had never even spoken his name aloud.

"'Sup, dude?" he said. "I'm X."

SEVEN

THAT NIGHT, AFTER ZOE was safely launched into her dreams, X padded around the quiet house. He had lived such a barren life that the rush of faces and voices and attachments had unnerved him. He could not sleep. The lords would be strategizing even now about how best to punish him. He knew he should return to the Lowlands before they struck. And yet Zoe had all but silenced the Trembling. She had all but silenced everything. She had *filled* everything. When she had hugged him for just that instant on the lake . . .

If he could just have one more day with her.

He remembered Zoe's mother saying that Zoe had gotten too close to him. Zoe hadn't denied it. Could it be true that she thought of him as more than an object of pity? He couldn't stop wondering. The thought was like a train on a circular track.

X gazed out the living room window. The moon was high and nearly full. The ice on the river was shining with its borrowed light, and looked lovely in the darkness. X was reminded of his own filthiness.

He went outside and descended the hill under a vast and humbling sky full of stars. His own world had no equivalent. In truth, it had *nothing* that one would willingly gaze at.

When he reached the river, he knelt at its edge. The surface was decorated with cloudy whorls, and pocked here and there with stones and reeds that had been trapped in the ice.

He removed his shirt and pants and laid them on the ground beside him. His body was a map of bruises from grappling with Stan. He wondered how far his prey had gotten by now. Had he fled as far as he could without looking back? Had he crept into some innocent family's home? Was he still nearby, shivering among the trees? Thanks to Zoe, very little of Stan remained in X's veins. The man could be anywhere.

X leaned forward and pushed against the ice, testing it. He clenched his left hand and raised it. He was about to bring it down on the ice when he felt himself being watched. It was as if someone's fingertips were grazing his neck.

He reached for his shirt, now dusted with snow, and wrapped it around his waist. He turned to the house, and ran his eyes along the windows. There was no one there.

He turned back to the river, knelt once more, and punched at the ice. It shattered instantly, cracks racing in every direction. He cast his shirt aside.

The water glimmered darkly, like oil.

He stepped into it.

The river closed over him as he sank to the bottom, his hair floating above him in tendrils. It was like traveling through the earth to the Lowlands—a slow, blurry drift that existed outside of time. When he reached the bottom, he drew his knees to his chest and wrapped them with his arms. He hung suspended for two or three minutes—a new sort of sea creature—then burst up to the surface.

Zoe was there.

"Are you insane?" she said.

X looked nervously for his clothes.

"Relax," she said. "I can't see anything."

Even so, X pulled his shoulders under the water.

She laughed at his shyness.

"Oh my god, *here*," she said.

She thrust his pants at him. He pulled them under the water and put them on, feeling ridiculous.

"Why do you inquire after my sanity?" he asked her.

"Because it is *freezing cold* out, dork," she said.

"No harm will come to me," said X. "I have warmed the water."

Zoe took off a glove and dipped her hand in the river. Surprised, X floated backward until he could feel the edge of the ice behind him. When Zoe's hand touched the water, her eyes registered surprise.

"I told you true, did I not?" said X.

"You told me true," said Zoe.

She sat down in the snow, and stared off at the dark ridge. The air was still. The only sound was the lapping of the water as X floated, his tattooed arms working effortlessly in the water.

"Your query about my age," he said. "Was it the only question you asked the bowl, or are there others still awaiting me?"

"I only asked two," said Zoe. "The other one was stupid."

"You will not share it?"

"It was about the first time I saw you—when you were going after Stan. I wanted to know why you turned the ice orange."

X sank below the surface and hung suspended a second time. When he finally shot up again, he pressed his palms to the ice and pushed himself out of the river. The weight of the water dragged his pants down low on his hips. He felt Zoe watching, and pulled them up as quickly as he could, then sat on the ice facing her.

"You did not ask the bowl about the bruises beneath my eyes," he said. "Were you ashamed on my account—is that why you shrank from the question?"

Zoe was a long time in answering.

"I didn't ask because I already knew the answer," she said. "Someone's been hurting you."

X said nothing.

"Who?" said Zoe. "And for how long?"

"The lords," said X. "It is part of the bounty hunter's ritual. The pain is fleeting, I promise. Do not think on it."

"I can't help it," said Zoe. "It pisses me off. They have no right—"

He interrupted her.

"No, Zoe," he said gently. "I am the one without rights. I was born into their midst. I am no one's son, no one's brother. I belong to the Lowlands itself. My parents . . . I cannot imagine how they stole even a moment in each other's company to produce me, but they broke every law of the Lowlands to do it. I am just the living embodiment of a crime—if I can even claim to be 'living.'"

X stopped, and looked at Zoe. She had put her hands in her coat pockets to warm them. She seemed not to know what to say.

"No one ever told you who your parents were?" she said finally.

"They never even told Ripper," said X. "I suppose they feared I

116

would look for them. And, in that, they are correct. When I was young, I used to console myself by inventing a love story about my mother and father. I told myself that my mother wept and my father tore his hair when the lords wrenched me away." He paused. "You did not expect such a dreary monologue," he said. "Shall I end it there?"

"Please don't," said Zoe, then quoted something he'd told her himself: "Perhaps telling the story will take away some of its power."

"I suspect my father was unaware of my existence and my mother was glad to be quit of me," X said. "After all, they were almost certainly prisoners—and of rough character. I have scant memories of my first decade. It was an oddity for a child to be growing up among the damned. I have never met another. Only *I* needed to eat because only *I* needed to grow. Only I was aging at all."

"It's why you can't read," said Zoe softly. "Because no one bothered to teach you."

"Many of the prisoners hated me when I was a child," X continued. "Many still do. Perhaps I remind them of their own lost innocence. Perhaps they're jealous because they think that, unlike them, I will grow old and one day die and escape the Lowlands."

"Will you die?" said Zoe. "*Can* you?"

"I do not even know," said X. "There is not another like me to ask. Maybe I will rot little by little but never actually perish. I see that my words pain you, Zoe, but you should know what sort of creature you have befriended." He stopped, before returning to his story. "As a child in the Lowlands, I was kicked and punched by other prisoners. I was beaten even by some of the guards, who resented having to bring me water and meat. I was given nicknames, but they were forgotten, one after the other, because no one cared enough about me to remember them. Then, when I was ten, one of the lords simply shoved me at Ripper and told her to train me to hunt souls. 'Let's see if he's worth keeping alive,' he said."

"Ripper," said Zoe. "You like her."

"I owe her everything," said X. "I learned to hunt quickly. Banger was my first soul. I took him when I was just sixteen. I found him in a tavern. He looked at me like I was a child, a nuisance—so I struck him in the throat. Ripper seemed astonished when I brought him back to the Lowlands and threw him at the lords' feet. She told me I was special. I swear to you, her praise kept me alive. She couldn't teach me to read, for she had no books, no paper, no pens. She didn't even have fingernails to scratch letters into the rock, because she had ripped them all out. But she taught me to be quick and strong and hard—just as your mother has taught you."

"I wish I could meet Ripper," said Zoe.

X laughed quietly.

"Arranging such an interview might be complicated," he said.

"Right?" said Zoe.

She was laughing now, too.

"Yet Ripper would adore you," said X.

Zoe blushed at this. X did not know why.

"You haven't explained the ice on the lake," she said. "Why did you turn it orange?"

X looked pained.

"Am I to have no secrets at all?" he said.

"I showed you mine," she said playfully.

X stood, and drew closer to her. He saw her smile and roll her eyes at the sight of his bare feet on the ice. Something about this girl loosened the ever-present knot in his chest. Just the sight of her unclenched every part of him.

Zoe handed him his shirt. She turned away, but just slightly, as he tugged it on. The closer they came to each other, the more the air itself seemed to want to pull them together.

"I set the lake afire because I knew you were there," he said. "It was not a necessity."

Zoe arched an eyebrow.

"You were showing off for me?" she said, grinning.

"I shall leave you to your conjecture," he said. "I have no more to say on the subject."

Zoe leaned toward him.

She pushed the wet hair from his eyes, her face just inches from his.

X jerked away in surprise. Zoe cast her eyes down, mortified.

Immediately, self-loathing flooded through X. She'd meant to kiss him, and he had flinched! He had ruined the moment.

But, no, he would not let the moment go.

Now *he* moved toward *her*.

He could feel himself shaking. He hardly knew what he was doing. So little in either world frightened him—and yet *this* did.

Zoe saw that he was nervous, and leaned in to meet him. At the last possible moment, she turned her lips from his and kissed the bruises beneath his eyes, one after the other.

The knot in his chest fell to pieces.

He knew then that he loved her.

Zoe took a pen from her pocket, and drew a wide black symbol on the back of his hand.

"That's an *X*," she said.

She drew two smaller letters above it, but only smiled when he asked what they meant.

He took her arm, and they turned toward the house. She leaned her head against his shoulder and closed her eyes.

She never saw, as he did, that her mother was watching from a window.

EIGHT

X WOKE IN THE MORNING to an empty house. He smoothed the sheets of the ladybug as he had seen Jonah do. Then, for an hour, he rambled around, trying to think of something other than Zoe and the feeling of her lips on his cheek. He took some food from the buzzing metal box in the kitchen, the cool air brushing pleasantly against his face. He stood at the front door waving to the dogs as they charged around the yard. He tossed a stick to Spock, as Jonah had taught him to. Spock ran after it, but seemed not to know he was supposed to pick it up and return it—the dog seemed to think the point of the game was simply to prove that the stick still existed.

Later, X sat in the living room studying family portraits, and was struck by how Zoe's essential Zoe-ness—the bright, wide eyes that promised something but demanded something, too—had remained constant even as the years passed and her hair lengthened and shortened and curled and flattened and was briefly blue

for some reason, and even when her teeth were temporarily decorated with miniature railroad tracks.

X was so taken by her face. Everything he knew about loveliness
began and ended with her.

He could still feel Zoe's lips on his skin. He replayed the moment
so often in his head that he began to think he'd never have another
thought. In truth, he didn't *want* another.

Perhaps Zoe's mother would recognize that he and Zoe had
forged a true connection. Perhaps he could stay. Perhaps the lords
of the Lowlands had forgotten him. *Perhaps he could stay.* He was
but one soul in an infinite sea of bodies, and—though he'd never
had the audacity to remind them—he'd done nothing to deserve
damnation.

X heard the Bissells' car in the drive. He went to the porch and
stood waiting, eager as a dog. A cold rain had begun to fall. It did
not concern him. He was too happy for that. He looked at the sculp-
ture that Rufus had made for the Bissells: a bear standing, waving,
smiling ridiculously. He felt a kinship with it.

But Zoe and her family got out of the car in a dark mood, slamming their doors.

"You'd better tell him," Zoe's mother told Zoe as they climbed
the stairs toward X.

Zoe lingered on the porch, but did not speak.

X could not bear the silence.

"She requires that I leave this instant?" he said. He cast his eyes
downward. "I cannot fault her, though I have made myself drunk on
delusions that I might stay."

"It's not just that," said Zoe. "We were in town, and we saw a cop
we know named Brian." She hesitated a moment. "The police can't

find Stan—and he's killed somebody else. He could be in Canada now, he could be in Mexico, they don't know. They may have lost him for good."

THE NEWS STRUCK X like a blow. Every bit of hopefulness and joy fled his body. He'd been a fool to think he deserved anything at all in this world. His rage—at Stan's evil, at his own weakness—produced a sharp pain in his head. It was as if someone had released a bee into his skull. He stood outside until long after Zoe had gone in, only half-aware that he was being drenched by the rain. He felt the Trembling reawaken in his blood.

Eventually, Zoe returned and insisted he come inside. She put a blanket around him, and placed a hand consolingly on his shoulder.

"Stan's gone," she said. "You couldn't go after him if you wanted to."

X couldn't bear to be touched. The bee in his skull had been joined by a dozen others. He pushed Zoe away—more roughly than he intended.

"It is my duty to hunt him down, even if he flees to the end of the earth," he said. "It is all I am made for."

Zoe backed away.

"You can't go," she said.

"And yet I can't stay here—pretending I am something other than I am," he said.

He saw how his words wounded her. He tried to explain, but she waved him off and sank onto the couch, refusing to look at him. Outside, the rain fell harder. It froze the instant it landed, encasing the driveway, the trees, the world in ice.

Soon the power failed with a spooky sighing sound they all felt in their stomachs. The house went black. Candles were lit and distributed. They flickered and glowed, but were in no way comforting. The Bissells huddled on the couch, growing colder and listening to the rain as it entombed them bit by bit. X slumped against a wall, his head in his hands. The storm had grown so intense that it worried even him.

Late in the afternoon, Zoe used her phone somehow to see when it was expected to stop, only to discover that there were no reports of rain (or sleet or power outages) anywhere within 500 miles.

"Idiots," she said. "How can they not see this storm?"

X began to fear that the storm was meant for them alone.

Spock and Uhura pawed at the front door, begging to be let in. They'd finally been admitted into Bert and Betty's house, and were now trying their luck here. Jonah looked at his mother with such pleading eyes that she finally groaned and said simply, "Okay, fine."

Jonah clapped ecstatically, ran to the door—and discovered that it had been frozen shut. X listened as Zoe and her mother tried and failed to wrench it open. He could hear Spock and Uhura on the steps, whimpering. He pictured them shivering, their fur rattling with ice.

Above them, the roof groaned, threatening to cave in.

Then, suddenly, the rain stopped.

But the relief was short-lived, for soon the silence was torn by the sound of trees surrendering to the ice and splitting apart.

At first it was just a branch or two that snapped and fell onto the snow. Soon, though, the noise was terrifying and constant, like a thousand bones breaking. Trees that had stood more than a century were shattered in an instant. X could see Zoe and the others registering every loss. Jonah rushed to a window that looked out on the backyard. "Daddy Man's tree!" he said. The willow had not cracked, but it was bent low again and threatening to snap. X was powerless to help. His head was boiling. He slumped farther down the wall, draped in the blanket Zoe had given him.

The blizzard had damaged the forest, but this decimation seemed nearly vengeful, and it could not be ignored, for there was no wind or snow to cover the sound. Even to X, who had heard every sort of agonizing sound the universe could produce, the destruction of the trees sounded raw and pitiless—a kind of mass murder.

Zoe's mother, electric with anger and worry, said that there hadn't been an ice storm in years.

"This doesn't make any sense," she said.

At that moment, X felt the bruises beneath his eyes begin to burn.

One of the lords had come for him.

X felt him calling out. He could envision the lord's gnarled hands summoning up the storm—conducting it like an orchestra. X had no choice but to go to him. To end this.

HE BECKONED ZOE TO his side.

"I have hurt you," he whispered.

His voice was hoarse.

"A little," she said.

"I am sorry, and ashamed, besides," he said. "This storm, this rain—it is not from your world, but mine. A lord awaits me in the woods. I feel his rage in every part of me. He has come to put me back on the path."

"Let him wait," said Zoe.

She said it blithely, but he heard the fear in her voice.

"I must finish what I began," he said. "I must drag Stan to the Lowlands where his kind belong. You must let me go."

"No," said Zoe.

"Yes," said X.

"No," said Zoe.

"Yes," said X, laughing softly at her willfulness. "How long shall we continue in this vein?"

"I can go all night," said Zoe.

She sat down next to him on the floor.

"Don't you realize what the lords have done to you?" she said. "You were a little kid—totally innocent—and it *killed* them. So they made you hunt souls. And you were grateful, right? Because you got powers for a little while. Because you got to leave your cell every so often on some, like, supernatural hall pass. And the whole time— *the whole time*—they've been trying to turn you into *them*. And now you think you belong there! Which you don't. I am *so sick* of losing people, X. Don't make me lose you."

She was crying now. X wanted to touch her—she was the only proof he'd ever had that there was light and life and warmth in the world—but he knew if he so much as brushed her skin with his fingertips, he wouldn't have the strength to leave. He would sink into her, and all would be lost.

"I have brought evil to within a hundred yards of your door," he said, "and I will face it before it crawls even one inch closer."

Zoe looked away, defeated.

"Stay within these walls, no matter how fiercely they groan," X continued. "The lord will not risk being seen by any who walk this world. It is an unbreakable code. I, myself, am about to discover the penalty for breaking it."

He staggered to the door. He drew in a breath, gathering his strength so that he might break the seal of ice. He looked up at the ceiling as if his visitor from the Lowlands were hovering just above his head.

"If you want me," he cried, "*let me out!*"

He pulled so fiercely that the wood burst along the hinges.

The door flew open.

Spock and Uhura rushed into the house, delirious with relief. Their fur was beaded with ice, just as X had imagined. Their legs made a crinkling sound as they ran.

Jonah and his mother rushed to the dogs. The last thing X saw was them covering the animals with the blanket that had fallen from his own shoulders.

HE STALKED TOWARD THE woods, his head lowered, his broad back curved against the cold. He had gone a hundred feet when he heard Zoe call out to him.

"Will you come back?" she shouted. "When you've found Stan—when you've brought him to the Lowlands—will you come back?"

It was an impossible question. Surely she knew that. Though he was scared, he wanted to make her laugh, if he could.

"Unless I get into college!" he shouted. When Zoe smiled, he added, "That was a blurt."

"Yes, I know!" she said. "But, seriously, will you come back?"

Would it be a lie to say yes, if he truly didn't know?

Nothing could induce him to lie to her.

He began striding toward her through the snow. The lord would have to wait one more moment.

Zoe cried even harder when she saw X coming. He could see her shoulders rise and fall.

"If I do not return," he said, "it is only because not one but *two* worlds conspired to stop me."

Zoe came down the steps in just her hoodie and jeans. X all but flew the remaining feet. He removed his coat, and wrapped it around her. It brightened briefly, like coals being stoked.

He took her face in his hands, and pulled her mouth to his. Her lips were cool and smooth.

He lifted her off the snow when he saw she was standing in her socks.

THE TREES LOOKED BRITTLE and translucent: a forest of glass.

X moved slowly, pulled toward the lord by an unseen force. He feared that if he brushed against a branch, he might shatter it. He dodged and ducked the tree limbs. Where the tree trunks were thickest, he crawled. Up ahead, he heard the ice cracking and trees splitting apart. He knew the lord was close.

He came into a clearing littered with fallen trees. The lord, who was in a fury unlike any X had ever witnessed, stalked maniacally before him, pushing down firs with a single shove.

"I beg you to stop," said X. "I have come."

It was not the ebony-skinned Regent, but a crazed and vicious lord they called Dervish. He stared at X, eyes alight with anger.

"You will beg for MANY things before the horizon swallows the sun," he said.

Dervish resumed the destruction of the trees, stripping branches and snapping trunks so that their interiors lay exposed.

X stepped forward hesitantly.

"Yes, yes, draw near!" Dervish screamed. "Mark well what I do to these trees for it pales next to the violence I shall visit upon you—and those creatures who have sheltered you."

The lord had pointy, ratlike features. His face was as gray and papery as a wasps' nest.

"You were hoping the one you call Regent would come for you, no doubt!" said the lord. "But he is too soft a kitten, you see. He coddled you. And in return? You shamed him by letting your prey escape, and by mingling with mortals! When you return to the Lowlands, do not be surprised if you see Regent's bones floating in your soup." He paused, then added with relish: "*I* am your master now."

"I shall do whatever you ask," said X. "But I beg you to spare the family that took me in. They know nothing of who I am."

At this, the lord squawked with laughter.

"And now you would LIE to me?" he said. "I have borne witness to your every moment in that house. I have heard your pathetic mewling. You were like a love-struck schoolboy plucking petals from a flower."

X repeated his plea, even more softly: "Spare the family, I beg you. I will do whatever you require."

"Indeed you shall," said the lord. "And I shall require things that will reduce your heart to ash!"

He stomped toward X.

"On your knees, bounty hunter," he demanded. "It is time you took Stan's sins into your blood once more."

Dervish grasped X's face with both hands, and began reciting the familiar speech: "The Lowlands require another soul for its collection. He is an evil man—unrepentant and unpunished."

As he continued, the lord's fingernails—long, curling, and yellowed—punctured X's skin and sent blood down his cheeks.

X felt the lord's power flow through his body. Once again, Stan's story entered him. It was even more hateful this time, because new sins had been added to the old. When Dervish had finished, he shoved X to the ground, where he shook as if in a seizure.

The lord left him writhing, and stalked toward the Bissells' house, leaving a wake of splintered trees.

X was terrified for Zoe and her family.

He found the strength to stand. He stumbled through the darkening woods, crashing against the very branches he had labored to preserve. He imagined the lord's sickening hand closing around Zoe's pale throat. The thought of it nearly caused him to empty his stomach into the snow.

X found Dervish at the edge of the forest. The lord was lurking behind the last row of trees, making certain he could not be seen from the house. He wheeled around toward X. He smiled so widely that his crooked teeth glinted in the dusk.

"So this is where you have played house with your pretty little mortals," Dervish purred horribly. "Do you know how easy it would be for me to murder them all? How easy—and how pleasing?"

"I do," said X, fearing that if he added even one more syllable it would enrage the lord.

"Bring me the soul whose name swims in your blood," Dervish said coldly, then pointed toward Zoe's house. "Do not fail a second time. Else I shall return here tomorrow night—and I shall swim in *theirs*."

NINE

X DOVE INTO THE GROUND as if it were water. He blazed through snow, dirt, rock. The earth itself parted before him and closed again once he had passed.

Stan Manggold's sins were flowing through him in a rush once more, this time coupled with X's own fury. He had released the man— he had shown him mercy—only so Stan could murder again. Now X had been torn from Zoe. Now his heart was in ruins, all the worse because he'd only just discovered what his heart was actually for.

X burst out of the earth in a hot, sludgy marsh. He was in a part of the country he had never seen. He tried to orient himself, but there was no time: noises were already assaulting his ears. A hundred yards off, a pack of hunting dogs barked riotously, a squadron of geese swarmed the sky, and a half dozen shotguns crackled, decorating the air with smoke.

For all the villainous men and women he had encountered, X had never heard gunfire. The noise jolted him. He felt it under his skin.

Three birds plummeted from the sky. The hunters lowered their guns, and broke into chatter about the wind and the light. They drank from silver flasks that winked in the day's last light. Some of them already had dead geese strung around their necks on giant necklaces. They reminded X of stories Ripper had told him about cannibals who wore skulls across their chests. He was no better than the hunters—or even the cannibals. He might as well have worn 14 skulls on a necklace of his own for all the souls he'd taken.

Stan's skull would be next.

The hunters collected their trophies and pressed on. As he waited for them to disappear, X's mind crept back to Zoe. He pictured her wearing his coat in the rain. He was glad he'd left something of himself behind. She would wear it, even if it was too long for her, even if it hung down around her ankles. He knew she would. And someday soon he would knock on her front door and say . . .

What would he say?

He would say, *I forgot my coat.*

She would like that. She would smile. And then he would kiss her for the second time. She'd expect him to be shy, but he was finished with shyness forever. There was no time for it.

When he could no longer hear the dogs, X climbed out of the marsh and wrung the water from his pants. The ground was flat for miles. It looked nothing like Montana. There were clumps of trees here and there, but mostly it was just wetlands marked by wide rivers and tiny, tufted green islands. It looked as if the world had been flooded and the water had only just begun to recede.

There was no road in sight, but X didn't need one. He moved at a superhuman pace. The anger in him fed the longing, and the longing fed the anger. The marshy ground exploded with water as he passed. Had anyone been watching, they would have seen what looked like a comet cutting through the landscape.

After a mile, X felt the pain coursing through him deepen. The Trembling was guiding him. He was on Stan's trail.

HE FOUND HIM JUST a few minutes later. Stan was walking the main street of a dusty town, eating an ice cream cone and peering into a shop window, looking as innocent as a child. X was repulsed by the sight of him. But there were too many people dotting the street for him to charge at Stan and snap his neck. He stepped out of sight, and waited for his prey to turn down some quiet passageway.

X didn't know the name of the town. Half a mile back, atop a pole wrapped in vines, there had been a sign, shaped like a coat of arms. He had stared at it, sensing that it welcomed him to the town of Somewhere in the State of Something. The name of the state had an *X* in it. He recognized it from what Zoe had written on the back of his hand. He looked down at his hand, wishing she'd told him what the other letters meant.

The message was already beginning to fade: My X.

He shook off the thought of her. He had to deliver Stan to the Lowlands. If he did, there was a chance he could see Zoe again one day. If he failed, she and her family might not even survive until morning.

When he looked up, Stan had disappeared.

X headed down the sidewalk, catching his reflection in a store window. He looked like a wild creature. His pants were filthy. His shirt was torn. And his hair ... His hair looked as if it had been in an ice storm and a marsh. Every strand was straining in a different direction.

He'd draw too much attention like this.

He found a shop with a horse etched into the door, and a rack of colorful shirts on the sidewalk. X peeked inside. No one was watching. He slipped one of the shirts off its hanger. It was purple with decorative white stitching that looped across the chest. X put it on over his own shirt. It was too small for him, and he could not even begin to manage the pearl buttons, so he left it hanging open. He stared at himself again in the window. Now he looked like a wild creature wearing a purple shirt.

He shook his head and went after Stan.

The pain told him which way to go as surely as a compass.

When he found Stan, he saw that he'd bitten the bottom off his ice cream cone and was sucking out the last dregs. Ice cream dripped off his chin and onto his stomach.

Stan finished the cone, and strolled to the edge of the street, which was lined with trucks and SUVs. He examined a dark green pickup to see if it was worth stealing. He made up his mind against it, rubbed his nose, and kept walking.

Halfway down the next block, Stan swung open the door of a store and stepped out of sight. X followed. He couldn't read the name on the store window, but, on the door, there was a pair of scissors and a woman caressing her silky hair.

X peeked over the lacy curtains that lined the windows. In the front of the store, behind a glossy desk, there was a bored young woman taking a photograph of her toenails. In back, there were half a dozen women in smocks milling about. Stan was already behaving ridiculously—dancing around a handsome, brown-skinned woman in a way that seemed vile. The woman kept gesturing nervously to the chair.

X was so close to Stan now that his body began to shiver. But revealing who he was—*what* he was—to another half dozen people seemed like madness. He leaned his head against the window, hoping the pain would pass.

It did not. It grew and grew, until X felt as if he were a puppet whose master was violently shaking his strings. He had broken so many laws of the Lowlands. What was one more indiscretion?

He swung the door open.

He was in such discomfort now that the woman behind the desk was just a floral, lipsticked blur.

"Welcome to the House of Uncommon Beauty," she said in a drawl.

Before X could respond, the woman had taken in his preposterous hair.

"Oh, sugar," she said, "I don't think we can help you with *that*."

X tried to center himself, to clear his mind. He could hear Stan in the back, yammering. He was telling the woman cutting his hair to call him Stan the Man or—"depending on how cozy we get"—Stanley the Manly.

The woman behind the desk rolled her eyes.

"That one's trouble," she said. "Minute he walked in, I said, 'Mister, you been drinkin'?' And he hoots and says, 'Since I was fourteen!' I'll tell you what, I'm calling the sheriff if he gives Marianna any trouble."

X growled, half in anger, half in agony, and stumbled toward the back. He ignored the woman when she called after him.

MARIANNA HAD LAID A hot towel over Stan's face. Steam rose off it now, as he reclined in his chair, moaning with pleasure.

"You ain't beautiful, but you sure as shit ain't ugly," he told Marianna. "Why don't you come sit on Santa's lap?"

He reached out blindly to grope her, but she sidestepped him like a bullfighter.

X gestured for Marianna to stay silent. He drew close to Stan, disgusted and furious and raked with pain.

He grasped Stan's throat.

Marianna gasped. The other women fled, half of them in smocks, their wet hair flying. But Marianna seemed too shocked to move.

Stan tore the towel from his face. He saw X in the mirror. He began kicking and punching wildly at the air.

X laughed darkly.

"It was my dearest wish that you would fight," he said.

"Yeah, well, I sure as hell will, superfreak," said Stan. "And, by the way, *nice shirt*, cowboy. Tight enough?"

Stan cast his eyes around as X closed his grip around his throat. There was a pair of scissors glinting on the counter.

He jabbed them into X's thigh and twisted them viciously.

X cried out, more in annoyance than pain. He pulled the scissors from his leg, and sent them clattering across the floor. He did not let go of Stan's skinny neck even when blood began to soak through his pants.

He turned to Marianna.

"You would be safer elsewhere," he said, as gently as he could. He gazed around the salon, and saw his reflection multiplied endlessly in the mirrors, like he was the front line of an army.

"What are you gonna do to him?" said Marianna.

"I am going to propel him through the wall," said X.

Marianna rushed out of the salon now, too.

Stan continued to struggle. He didn't seem to realize that the more he lashed out, the harder X squeezed his windpipe.

"You ain't taking me with you, superfreak," he rasped. "You'll have to kill me first."

"Yes," said X. "I will."

Stan grabbed things from the counter and hurled them at X: spray cans, bottles, a brush, a hair dryer. X pushed him hard against the chair. He regarded Stan pityingly, as one would look at a child having a tantrum. When Stan had run out of projectiles, X pulled him out of the chair and dashed him to the floor.

Stan tried to scramble to his feet, but X raised his boot and brought it crashing down on his back. They remained motionless for a time. Then, breaking the silence, came a terrible new sound.

Stan was crying.

X had no pity.

"Has your courage fled so soon?" he said.

He took a step backward. Stan rolled onto his back, and cradled his enormous head in his hands, sobbing dismally. X loathed the man so much that the noise had no effect on him. It might have been the screeching of a scavenger bird.

Soon, Stan was listing the many reasons he did not deserve to die. X had heard such speeches from many men. (Banger was the only exception: he'd simply asked X if he'd be able to get cell service where they were going.) Stan moaned, lied, and made excuses for himself so vehemently that spittle flew from his lips. X only half-listened.

Finally, Stan quieted. X stood and removed both the purple shirt and the threadbare one beneath it.

"Oh, come on," said Stan. "*Again* with the damn strip show?"

X stretched out his arms, and felt Stan's sins gathering force within him. Images began to bloom on his back:

A car was stalled by the side of an unlit highway. An old man with a friendly, open face had pulled over to help, and was shuffling toward the car. He was wearing flip-flops, a pink Izod shirt, and khaki shorts. His legs were knobby and white as an uncooked chicken.

He rapped his knuckles on the driver's window.

The driver was Stan.

He'd been lying in wait for a Good Samaritan. He thrust open his door, knocking the old man onto the road. The man looked up in confusion. He reached up a hand for help. Stan kicked him in the ribs.

The old man crawled into the highway to get away. Stan followed, laughing and kicking, until the man lay in the middle of the road, the double yellow lines under his back.

Cowering in the salon, Stan turned away from the images. He could not bear to watch.

X extended a palm toward a mirror, and the mirror jumped to life. The movie now played there, too. In an instant, it jumped to the next mirror and then the next and so on around the room, as if the mirrors were catching fire one by one.

X pulled Stan's head up high and forced him to watch.

"I gave you your freedom on the lake," he shouted. "I gave you your life! And *this* is what you squandered it on!"

In the movie, Stan was hooting with happiness as he slid into the old man's car and peeled away.

His victim lay stranded in the middle of the highway. He tried crawling and rolling. He tried pulling himself across the blacktop with his fingernails. His flip-flops had fallen off and lay behind him in the road.

Now a truck could be heard coming around the curve. Its head-lights were high. Its brakes were screaming.

Not even X could watch the rest.

He clenched his fist, and the movie vanished. Outside the salon, he heard police sirens, howling like cats. They were half a mile away and growing louder.

X looked at Stan with a glimmer of compassion. It was then that Stan knew he was truly about to die. He was so scared he could barely bleat out a word.

"Now?" he said.

"Now," said X.

"Don't you gotta take me back to that lake?" said Stan.

"No," said X. "We can reach our destination from anywhere. We can reach it from here."

X dressed slowly. When he had finished, he closed his eyes for a moment and the room instantly went dark.

"Why'd you turn out the lights?" said Stan.

He was stalling.

"Respect for the dead," said X. When Stan gave him a puzzled look, he added simply, "*You*."

He picked up Stan. He threw him over his shoulder.

He turned to the great round mirror at Marianna's station.

"Will it—will it *hurt*?" said Stan.

"Only forever," said X.

He leaped at the mirror. The glass exploded as he and Stan passed through it. The shards, rather than raining onto the floor, were pulled in after them. X left the shell of Stan's body behind—a worn and ugly casing for the police to find—as he pulled his soul down into the dark.

TEN

THEY FELL INTO A HALF-LIT VOID. The air rushed past them so fiercely that it obliterated all sound. X was accustomed to it, but he knew Stan would feel a crushing pressure on his eyeballs, a hammering in his ears. He saw Stan panic and resist the fall. He watched as Stan clawed at the air with his hands, as if he could climb back to the surface. As if there *was* a surface. The wind thrashed them in every direction.

X fell faster than Stan. He had tucked himself into a ball, like a diver. When he saw Stan struggling, he unfurled his body, reached up, and grabbed ahold of Stan's ankle to steady him. Stan kicked ferociously, but gave up after one last pathetic spasm. X suspected his senses were so overwhelmed that they had stopped functioning. Stan let his arms drift over his head. He let X drag him down.

After they had fallen for a time, Stan recovered some of his equilibrium. X knew what would happen next. He could predict it almost to the second: Stan would be hit with a sadness so severe it was nearly blinding. Regret, remorse, and rage would overtake him, as they overtook all new souls. It was always at this moment that they realized they were not traveling down a holy tunnel toward a shimmering light but rather falling down a shaft to oblivion.

Stan began crying again, right on schedule. X was grateful that he couldn't hear it this time. Just the distorted, wailing look on Stan's face was enough to turn his stomach. All freshly plucked souls wept—never for their victims, only for themselves—and X found the self-pity galling. They all believed they were innocent, no matter what they had done. As the wind howled around them, Stan cried voluminously. His tears flew upward, like bubbles.

The air grew cold. It was the breath of the river rising up to greet them. The journey, X knew, was nearly over.

He looked down and saw the river that cut through his hive in the Lowlands. It was just a pale thread at first, but it came at them fast. There were only 1,000 feet left to fall. Then 500. Stan must have seen the roiling current, too. He shut his eyes, filled his cheeks with air, and clutched his nose like a child jumping into a pool. X closed his own eyes and pictured Zoe's face, soft and welcoming. He promised himself again that he would return to her, that he would take that face carefully in his hands—that he would say, *I forgot my coat.*

The water hit them like a wall.

THE RIVER IN THE LOWLANDS raged as always, but X reached the banks with ease, even without the powers he enjoyed in the Overworld. He had delivered Stan so the Trembling had vanished. Along with his powers went his pain. For a brief time, his body would feel relieved and renewed.

Behind him, Stan screamed at the arctic cold of the current. He scrambled for the banks, but the river kept sucking him under. A handful of guards crowded the water's edge, laughing at him. When Stan finally made it to the riverside, his lungs were heaving. He bent over and vomited water (and ice cream) into the dirt. A guard approached him with a kindly expression, picked him up—and threw him back in.

The others roared with delight. Stan began to make for the other side of the river, but there were guards waiting there, too.

X sat in the dirt and waited for someone to bring him a blanket and a wedge of bread, as they always did when he returned with a soul. He noticed, with a shiver of dread, that Dervish stood preening nearby. X wished again that it was Regent instead.

He drew in a deep breath and steeled himself for a confrontation. He would be humble, hang his head, beg forgiveness a hundred times. He would endure whatever humiliation Dervish could devise. Sooner or later, his crime would be forgotten—carried away as if by the river. He would be sent back to the Overworld to collect the next soul, and he would steal away to see Zoe. An hour with her would sustain him for a year.

But Dervish did not so much as glance in X's direction. He clapped when Stan stumbled. He whistled and hooted when the current dragged his big, fuzzy head under the water. Dervish was draped in gaudy necklaces and bracelets, all of them stolen from the souls of the Lowlands. The jewelry shimmered and clattered as he hopped around.

"Well done, guardsmen!" he shouted. "Well done!"

X stared openly at Dervish now, anxious for his punishment to begin. He knew the lord would still be boiling with rage. Yet the creature continued to ignore him. X had not expected this reception and it worried him.

The light had left his body now. The reality of the Lowlands—the way it sucked all the hope and happiness out of you, the way it stank like the mouth of some enormous beast—flooded into him instead. His anxiety deepened. Still no blanket. Still no bread.

X stood and waded into the river.

Stan continued to battle the current. He was red-faced and panting, wailing about the cramps in his legs. X grabbed him around the waist and hoisted him over his shoulder yet again. Even without supernatural powers, he had no trouble lifting a knot of wire like Stan.

He carried him to the side of the river.

"Thank you, superfreak," said Stan, shouting to be heard over the rushing water. "I don't like *anyone* here so far."

The guards jeered when they saw that there was no more fun to be had. But even this was a comfort to X because it meant that life, such as it was in the Lowlands, would lurch back into motion.

He laid Stan on the ground, and waited for the guards to descend on the terrified new prisoner.

At last, Dervish sliced the air with his long, taloned forefinger and screamed, "SEIZE HIM!"

But something was different.

Something was wrong.

The lord was pointing at *him*.

THE GUARDS RACED AT X from all sides, like lions on a fallen deer. Their merriment at the river had been a ruse. They had been waiting for the lord's signal all along.

They stripped X of his purple shirt. He saw it pass through many hands. He saw it fought over, bartered for, and, finally, carried off triumphantly like a newly captured flag.

Dervish instructed the guards to carry X to the tree on the plain. There was some grumbling at this—the men were as small and round as hobbits and unaccustomed to true labor—but they did as they were told.

X did not resist. At least now his punishment had begun, which meant that someday it would end.

It was a long march through foul, humid air. The guards groaned angrily under their burden—why had this traitor's punishment become their own?—while Dervish strutted in front of them. The guards pinched and poked X as they bore him along. When they saw that the lord not only did not object to X's mistreatment but rather whooped with pleasure at it, they *accidentally* dropped him to the ground and dragged him a dozen feet at a time.

The souls in the lowest ring of cells sensed something was afoot. They could see from the tattoos decorating X's arms and from the bruises on his face that he was a bounty hunter. It was unusual to see one punished—and thrilling. Word was passed up to the top ring of cells and out to the farthest edges. Soon, the great black wall seemed to shake as prisoners hollered in the tongues of a hundred countries and thousands of years. All X heard as he passed was a storm of hate and anger. Occasionally, one voice could be heard above the others: "What the hell have you done, boy?"

Ripper and Banger recognized X as he was carried across the plain. Ripper was so upset she twirled manically in her cell. She wept and spat, and cursed her fingernails for not yet being long enough to tear out. Banger suggested that she take a "chill pill," which only confused her, and tried to shout down the souls who surrounded them, calling them haters and tools.

The procession finally reached the tree. It was 30 feet tall, ugly and bare and elephant gray. Its trunk consisted of a dozen tortured, intertwining strands. Its mottled branches bent and swerved in every direction, as if in search of something they would never find. Its roots sank into the dirt like veins.

The guards thrust X against the tree and bound him to it, which brought a wave of applause from the cells. The rope sawed at X's skin, but he knew better than to complain. When the guards had finished, they stepped away and Dervish approached.

"Lovely to have you back among us, X!" he said brightly. "I may call you X, I hope? As all your pretty new friends do?"

The lord circled the tree, testing his men's work.

"I fear this rope may not serve," he said. "Be a dear, X, and ask the guards if they might be so kind as to tighten it. I do *very much* want you to feel its embrace."

There were four guards, but they looked like a single, multi-headed beast. They were foul and pocked. Their clothes were a bizarre patchwork for, like the lords, they dressed in whatever they could steal from the prisoners. They wore frayed vests, ruffled shirts blackened with dirt, pinstriped pants and jeans, as well as a scarf or two, despite the heat. One of the guards—he was the shortest and stoutest of them, and his nose had been broken so many times it was nearly flat against his face—appeared to be the chief. He wore a white turtleneck and a red tie.

"Guards," said X, "might you be so kind as to tighten my rope?"

The men laughed, as if he had told a bawdy joke.

"Of course, luv," the stout one said. "'Twill be an honor!"

The guard fussed with the rope, which, in truth, could hardly be made any tighter. Dervish tested it once more—X's blood was beginning to leak out from under it—and nodded his approval.

The lord faced the vast wall of souls, who were still shouting oaths at X. He motioned for silence.

"BEHOLD A MAN WHO THINKS HIMSELF BETTER THAN YOU!" he bellowed. "BEHOLD THE BOUNTY HUNTER WHO CALLS HIMSELF X!"

The cells began to rumble once more.

"Perhaps he is THE VERY ONE who ripped you out of your life and ferried you here!" the lord went on, animated by the screams. "Even if he is not, I daresay he would have done it gladly. Now, it seems, our noble bounty hunter has grown BORED of our company. He has attempted to flee—for he has FALLEN IN LOVE! What say you, souls of the Lowlands, shall I let him go?"

Not even Dervish could have predicted the violent gust of profanity that emanated from the cells now.

He turned to X, his eyes wild with delight.

"My heavens!" he said. "It's as if they don't like you!"

The lord looked back to the wall.

"I believe I shall let you punish this man yourselves," he shouted. "WOULD YOU ENJOY THAT?"

The cells erupted yet again.

Fear slipped its cold hands around X's heart.

Dervish called to the guards patrolling the wall. He ordered them to release some prisoners from their cells.

"A hundred or so, shall we say?" he said. "Let them come down here and mete out whatever justice they see fit!"

X could not just hear the prisoners' bloodlust now—he could

146

smell its sour odor drifting down from the cells. Out of nowhere, he remembered Zoe telling Jonah that "pungent" meant "someone who likes puns." He was warmed by the memory.

Dervish noticed.

"Look how he smiles!" he shouted. "THE BOUNTY HUNTER DOES NOT FEAR YOU!"

Cell doors clanged open. Prisoners thundered toward the steps. The wall was in a frenzy, chanting for X's blood.

"I must take my leave," the lord told him. "I do so *abhor* violence."

THE FIRST WAVE OF souls pounded toward him across the plain. The whole hive seemed to shudder under their feet.

The guards hastily fled.

"I don't get paid enough for this shite, do I?" said the stout one with the red tie, as he ran.

"You get *paid*?" said another.

"It's a figger o' speech, innit?"

The first souls to reach X merely spit at him or dealt him a single blow. He looked each of them in the eyes. He refused to so much as bow his head.

The beatings soon grew fiercer. X forced his mind to drift. He remembered building the Lowlands out of snow and toys. He pictured Zoe, Jonah, and their mother crowded around him in a yard fringed by waving pines.

He was jolted out of his reverie by a voice he recognized.

"Dude, wake up! This shit is *nuts*."

It was Banger, peering worriedly into his face. Ripper stood next to him. She was swaying in her filthy golden dress as if she were at a high-society ball in London.

"Why should I wake?" said X. "I wake only to a nightmare. Nothing can stop these men from doing what they will."

"Shut up," said Banger. "That's just negative thinking."

"Shut up, *indeed*," said Ripper. She stopped midtwirl and fixed X with her eyes. "You are dousing what promises to be a quite thrilling rescue!"

X had always suspected that Ripper's mania was largely a pretense. It was as if she still expected to be put on trial for murdering her servant with that boiling teakettle, and planned to use madness as a defense. Despite the flights of lunacy, X could see in Ripper the steely woman who had trained him. A dozen bounty hunters stood close by her now, their faces all wounded like X's from the lords' fingers. Ripper had mentored them all—and they had come when she called.

"I am grateful for your friendship," said X. "But if you free me, you merely postpone my punishment till another day—and endanger yourselves. I will endure this now, and be done with it."

"Don't be so bloody noble," Ripper said. "You'll bore the arse off me." She paused, her brain spinning in search of a plan. "If you won't let us free you," she said, at length, "then we can at least place our bodies between you and the threat. You are one of *us*, and we will not stand by while they make pulp of you."

Ripper called to the bounty hunters.

"Form a ring, my daisies!" she shouted. "And *do* try to look at least a little fierce?"

The hunters made a human chain around the tree. Banger and Ripper paced in front of them, the first line of defense. X was surprised—and moved—that so many of his fellow bounty hunters had come to his aid.

Prisoners spilled forward in greater numbers. The chance to

scrap with a bounty hunter or two was too tempting to pass up, and they all wanted to try their luck at getting through to X. The human chain may have been intended as a protective measure, but it took on the air of a challenge.

Banger alone trounced half a dozen men, but soon the prisoners attacked him two at a time. Ripper came to his aid repeatedly, jumping on their backs, gouging at their eyes, and trying to tear their fingers off with her teeth. (She actually succeeded once, tossing the finger at her dazed victim's chest and exclaiming, "Oh, don't weep, you infant! Your nanny can sew it back on!") Soon, the prisoners grew bored of losing. They attacked the tree in one vicious mass, surging past Banger and Ripper and assaulting the chain of bounty hunters with rocks and branches.

X strained at the rope, but it only cut deeper into his skin. A handful of men were raining down blows on him now: A bearded giant crashed a rock against the side of his skull. A tiny pink worm of a man jabbed him with a stick over and over in the very place that Stan had stabbed him with the scissors. X was losing consciousness when he heard a voice so furious and commanding that it could only belong to a lord.

"Enough! The next man to deliver a blow will receive a hundred back from me!"

It was Regent, the princely lord. A hush fell over the plain. Exhausted, Banger put his hands on his knees and tried to steady his breathing. Ripper wiped blood from her mouth, looking irked that she could not detach any more fingers.

As Regent approached X, the bounty hunters disbanded and sank back into the crowd. The lord wore his royal blue robe, but no jewels or bangles. He had stolen nothing from his charges. He alone of all the lords seemed to remember that he had once been a prisoner himself.

Regent shouted for the guards to drive the mob back up to the cells. The prisoners complained loudly, but knew better than to resist. Only Banger and Ripper remained. They would not abandon their friend, and the guards let them be.

Regent tore away the rope that bound X and, when his bruised body fell forward, caught him and eased him to the ground.

"I am sorry for the evil done to you," he said. "Dervish is a villain for engineering this torture, and he will shortly have a conversation with my fists."

"You have my thanks," said X. "Yet I broke the laws of this place, and was deserving of punishment."

The lord shook his head.

"You were not deserving of this," he said. "Never of this."

From behind them there came a wordless holler.

It could only be Dervish.

Banger saw him and groaned: "This guy *sucks*."

Ripper turned to Regent.

"Say the word," she said, "and I will relieve this crazed lord of his fingers."

"Do nothing," he told her. "I shall settle the matter myself."

Immediately upon his arrival, Dervish began berating Regent.

"How DARE you set my prisoner free?" he said. "How dare you even call yourself a lord? Do you really imagine yourself my equal, you filthy creature?"

Without a word, Regent struck Dervish across the mouth, sending him flying onto the rocky plain.

The prisoners, still rumbling up the staircases, stopped to watch the confrontation. Soon, a dozen other lords streamed in from the tunnels, moving so quickly they seemed to fly.

"I told your little friend that your bones would soon swim in his soup," said Dervish. "And now I shall drink it down myself."

Ripper laughed at the threat.

"Please," she said to Regent. "His fingers? May I?"

"Your proposal has its merits," he said. "But no."

The other lords poured in around X now, men and women in a riot of wildly colored garments and gems. Up on the steps, the prisoners were stunned to see so many lords roosting in one place, like brightly feathered birds. Even the guards were mesmerized.

The cavern grew silent as the lords took in the strange scene before them. Regent stood in front of X, protectively. When Dervish tried to stand, he nudged him back to the ground with the heel of his boot, causing the prisoners and guards—and even some of the lords—to titter. X was relieved to find that his champion had such standing, yet feared that humiliation would only strengthen Dervish's resolve. He wanted no enemies here, no celebrity—no scrutiny of any kind that might endanger his return to the Overworld and to Zoe.

The lords broke into debate about what was to be done. They murmured in low voices so the prisoners could not hear.

Dervish was outraged at the delay. He pointed at Regent and shouted, "Strike down this rough beast!"

The lords ignored him.

"Why do you tarry, fools?" he screamed. "I will have satisfaction!"

Regent cleared his throat, and addressed the lords, not caring if the prisoners on the steps listened.

"This man has been most horribly abused," he said, motioning toward X. "Did he violate our laws? He did. Did his actions cry out for punishment? They did. But he did not deserve the horrors that *this* hateful forgery of a man"—now he was pointing at Dervish—"devised for him. I would defend any soul against such abuses, and this man is not just any soul."

X had no idea what Regent meant by that last statement, and was shocked to hear other lords murmur their assent.

Dervish finally stood. He screwed up his face, as if he had a bitter taste in his mouth.

"What could you possibly mean by such nonsense?" he said. "If X here—you *do* realize, by the way, that he has given himself a name, which is an outrage all its own—if this troglodyte before me is better than the basest of souls, I should like to hear why."

"You know very well why," said Regent. "Do not pretend to be even more slow-witted than you are. Your stupidity is already a towering achievement."

"Well, if *I* know why he's so special and *you* know why he's so special," Dervish goaded him, "then why not simply speak it aloud?"

"Because, as you are certainly aware, the law of the Lowlands forbids it," Regent said coolly. "Yet *you* seem quite blustery today. Perhaps you would like to educate everyone yourself."

"You think I am too frightened?" said Dervish. He gestured at the lords, who were drawing closer and flashing him looks of warning. "You think I am scared of *them*? They are weak. They cannot so much as scratch their asses unless it is voted upon and approved on high!"

X could not hold his silence.

"What can be so shocking about me that no one dares speak of it?" he said.

Dervish looked ready to answer. The lords threatened him with their eyes.

"This disgrace you call Regent believes you are special," Dervish said, "because he believes your mother was special."

At this, the lords swarmed forward and began dragging Dervish away. He struggled and kicked, outraged that they dared to touch him.

"Who was my mother?" cried X, to anyone who would answer.

He looked at Regent.

"Who was my mother?" he said. "Please."

Regent looked at him regretfully, but did not speak.

Dervish made himself heard a final time.

"She was *nothing* and *no one*, just as your father was," he screamed. "Your father was less than dirt. Your mother was a traitor—and a whore."

Then his voice was muffled and lost.

X needed to know more. His chest was heaving. He found himself near tears.

Regent must have pitied him, for he took his arm and began walking him slowly toward the great stone steps.

"Does he speak the truth about my parents?" X asked him.

"That desiccated mouse has no idea who your father was," Regent said quietly. "I can assure you, however, that your mother was no whore. She is now a prisoner in a secret corner of this place—but, once, she was a true friend to me. Dervish is correct when he says that she is the reason I believe there is hope for you yet."

He paused, and all the world seemed to pause with him.

"Your mother was a lord."

ELEVEN

X WOKE WITH HIS HEAD on Ripper's lap, as she tended to his wounds. He was shocked to find her in his cell, with no guards in attendance. He'd never known two prisoners to be left together for even an instant. Regent must have made it possible.

Ripper sat with her legs folded under her, the ruined golden gown spilling everywhere. Beside her, there was a stone bowl filled with healing water. She dabbed at X's face with a cloth, humming a dreamy tune as she worked. A crude metal lantern threw her silhouette against the wall.

Something about the shadow and the song awakened a memory in X.

"You have ministered to me before," he said. "When I was a child. You sang that very song."

Ripper submerged the cloth, then twisted it over the bowl.

X winced at the sight of her hands: They were all bone and knuckle. What fingernails she had were ingrown and crusted with blood. Still, there was a gentleness to her, a glow, that he hadn't witnessed since he was small.

"It is one of the few tunes I remember," she said. "And do not inquire after the words, for they have gone *poof* out of my brain. Something insufferable about a sparrow, no doubt."

She pressed the cloth to X's brow.

"They never told you my mother was a lord?" he asked her. "Truly?"

"Never, I swear it," said Ripper. "I knew there was *something* special about you, and I told you as much. You were a finer and fiercer bounty hunter than I by the time you were seventeen—and, as you know, I am a veritable legend."

Once she'd cleaned X's wounds, Ripper began to bandage the more severe ones, beginning with the gash on his leg. X did not have the strength to lift his head and survey the damage. Still, he knew it must be profound, because his friend frowned at the sight of it.

"This nastiness on your leg concerns me," she said. "It is a jagged valley of tissue and blood. Does it burn?"

"Yes," said X. "As if with white flames. And please do not describe it again."

"My apologies," said Ripper. "I fear it may be infected, though I am not a doctor, merely a murderess."

X ground his teeth to distract himself from the discomfort, and looked up at Ripper. Her skin had hardly suffered from centuries in the Lowlands, and she was still beautiful by any measure. She had strong, clean features, a sturdy, dimpled chin, and ageless blue eyes. Because it had been decades since she had hunted a soul, even the bruises beneath her eyes had faded. Today, her dark hair was swept up in a knot atop her head, a single silver lock weaving through it like tinsel.

"Do you miss being a mother?" X asked her, after a time.

Conversation was a welcome relief, and he saw that he would have to feed it, as one feeds a fire.

Ripper nodded.

"I was a good one," she said. "Alfie and Belinda were always rosy and plump. Unfortunately, one's children grow distant after they've seen one bash a servant's skull with a teakettle."

X asked if she'd ever looked in on them—peeked in their windows, or stood across the road in disguise—when she had been out collecting souls.

Ripper shook her head wearily.

"I could not see my children without embracing them," she said. "I could not have survived it." For a moment, she was lost in thought. "A hundred years after I was brought here, another bounty hunter discovered for me what had become of my family. My husband took a new bride—an American, of all things—and they sailed for New England, like those ghastly pilgrims. When Alfie was eleven—"

Ripper stopped for a moment, deciding whether to continue.

"When Alfie was eleven," she said, "he perished in a fire in a stable. He was trapped under a post or a beam or the like. Belinda tried to push it off his chest, but she was only nine and had not the strength for it. She never recovered from the grief, I was told. She was deposited in some asylum, because my husband's new wife could not countenance her wailing."

"Your husband," said X. "Did you love him?"

The question seemed to break Ripper's cloudy mood.

"Good god, no," she said. "When he refrained from talking—

and from putting his sweaty hands on me—he was an amiable enough companion. Yet I suppose a tall plant could have served the same purpose."

X closed his eyes. He listened as she tore a length of bandage.

"I believe—" he began, but stopped when he felt his cheeks flush with embarrassment.

"Yes?" said Ripper. "What is it that you believe?"

"I believe that I . . . I believe that *I* may be in love," he said.

If Ripper had laughed, or smirked, or even paused to let his words ring, he would have clamped his mouth shut.

She did neither.

"Yes, I thought it must be something like that," she said. "Else you wouldn't have broken so many of the laws I taught you. I half-expected the lords to punish *me* for your transgressions, you know. If they did not think me irretrievably mad, they might well have."

"Even I have thought you mad," said X.

"Yes, well, I nearly *was* for a time," Ripper said. "After I learned of that fire in the stable, I mean. And in that interval I learned that the appearance of madness has its uses."

She stood and, with a dramatic flourish, tossed the contents of the bowl into the corridor. The water splashed the prisoners down below, and there was a chorus of profanity, which caused Ripper to titter.

She sat beside X once more.

"Tell me about this girl you love," she said. "Quickly now—before the guard comes to eject me."

"Had you told me such a person existed," he said, "I would have called you a liar."

"Is that so?" said Ripper, arching an eyebrow. "Without pausing to think, tell me three things you especially love about this astounding creature."

X thought for a moment.

"*Without* pausing to think," said Ripper. "I should have thought the rules of this game were plain enough."

"Her strength," X began. "But three is too few—I cannot do her justice."

"Oh, *do* stop your whinging," said Ripper.

"Very well," said X. "Her strength. Her blurting. Her face."

"Her blurting?"

"I cannot describe it."

"Please don't," said Ripper. "Yes, well, all that does indeed sound like love—at least as it was described to me once upon a time. As I have said, love was not a sea I myself ever swam in."

A guard loped down the corridor now, rattling his club against the bars. Ripper readied her things to leave, and X rose up on his elbows to gaze around the cell.

The purple shirt with the wild white stitching had been returned to him. It lay folded on the ground by the door. He was shocked to see it again.

"A guard returned it while you slept," said Ripper. "The fact that your mother was a lord is now a well-traveled secret."

X lowered himself to the ground again. The footsteps outside grew louder. He knew, from the scrape of a dragging foot, that it was the Russian.

"What do you think the lords will do with me?" said X.

"There will be a trial of some sort, I would think," said Ripper. "Dervish will insist that you be shredded by lions, or something equally theatrical. Still, you are an innocent soul—and the son of a

158

lord. That makes you a special case. In truth, I wonder if the lords even have the authority to punish the likes of you. As you know, there is a Higher Power that rules this place, and the lords quake before Him—or Her, as I like to imagine it."

The guard drew close. Ripper spoke quickly.

"At the trial, you will be allowed to speak but once," she said. "Apologize for your actions in words as honeyed as you can manage. Perhaps they will let you remain a bounty hunter—and, eventually, turn their back on you long enough for you to visit your blurting girl. You are aging, unlike the rest of us. I should hate to see you rot in this cell until there is no skin left to make a bag for your bones."

Her speech finished, she placed a motherly hand on X's cheek. Her palm was raw, yet he felt its warmth.

"I have enjoyed our conversation," Ripper said. "It's been years since I spoke so many coherent words in a row."

"Thank you for your counsel," said X.

He smiled gratefully, and found he was not ready to let her go.

"Ripper," he said.

"Yes?"

"I wanted to say," he began awkwardly, "I wanted to say that I very much like your dress."

"Well, thank you, kind sir," she said, looking pleased and brushing some dirt off the decaying embroidery. "In truth, it was never particularly dear to me. But I did not know, when I laced it up on that last morning, that I was dressing for eternity."

The Russian twisted the key in the door and entered the cell. The lantern threw a faint light on his powder-blue tracksuit.

"Is time," he said. "Party over. Now ve cry, boo-hoo."

Ripper gave X a final nod, then contorted her face into the mask of insanity she had invented for the Lowlands. It was as if someone entirely new inhabited her body now.

X watched in admiration as she spun around, hissed at the guard like a feral cat, and swept back to her cell.

THE DAYS PASSED, BUT X's bruises were slow to fade—his skin remained a landscape of purple, yellow, and blue. Soon, though, he was strong enough to pace in his cell and do simple exercises. He still daydreamed about Zoe constantly. But he managed to divert his thoughts, as a town might divert a river, from losing her to finding her again.

One day—as usual, he could not have said if it was morning or night—X awoke to the sound of a rusty key scraping in the lock. A squad of guards stood huddled outside. They were the same ones who had abandoned him on the plain. The squat chief in the turtle-neck and red tie stepped forward, and helped X off the ground.

"Been meanin' to apologize, I 'ave," he said. "Me and the men behaved poorly with respect to you. Cowardly, like. You deserve betta."

The guard was only groveling because he'd learned that X's mother had been a lord. Still, X had no appetite for cruelty.

"Thank you," he said. "I could not ask for a more sincere apology."

"Been practicin'," said the guard.

The guard gestured for X to follow, and steered him toward the wide rock staircase. The prisoners rattled their bars and hollered as they passed.

"Where do you take me?" X asked.

A cloud passed over the guard's face.

"Promised I wouldn't tell," he said.

"I understand," said X.

"But seein' as how you been so gracious 'bout the other matter, I'll tell you anyway," said the guard. "The waterfall what feeds the rivva—you know it?"

"Yes," said X.

"Well, behin' it," said the guard, "there's a tunnel, an' at the end of the tunnel there's a kind of meeting hall, like. Very grand, it is. The lords do their business there—their shoutin' and lawmakin' and whatnot." He paused as X negotiated the first step down. "I'm told they're all waitin' for you. They been handlin' assorted matters all day, but you're to be their main course."

THE WATERFALL RAINED DOWN so fiercely that X could hardly penetrate it. Finally, with the help of two guards, he emerged into a long stone passageway he had never seen before.

No one spoke. The only noises were the crackling of torches, the echoing of boots, and the dripping of garments as they walked. X knew they must be drawing close to the meeting hall. So many lords congregating together sent out an unmistakable energy—a pulse, like a hive of bees.

As if to confirm X's suspicion, the passageway began to transform. The walls had started out as ugly, rough-hewn rock. But the farther the company walked, the more polished the tunnel became until it shone like silver. There were enormous gems embedded in the wall now, too. They flickered and winked as the guards passed by with their torches.

At the end of the tunnel, there was an ornately carved blue door. Two sentinels with terrifying black rifles stood in front of it.

The sentinels were a higher species than the fleshy, bumbling

161

guards and barely acknowledged them. They turned to the door with choreographed precision and pulled it open without a word.

X passed through the door, and was hit with a burst of light. He and the guards had entered a stunning white amphitheater made entirely of marble. The lords—hundreds of them—sat in a circle around a small stage, their clothes so colorful and fine they looked almost like plumage. They stopped talking when they saw X. They watched as he was led down the steps to the stage.

The stage was empty except for a single stone seat and a podium. The guards, trying to impress the lords, pushed X roughly into the chair, and streamed single file back up the steps.

X's eyes slowly adjusted to the light. The walls were like the inside of a pyramid—carved with thousands, maybe millions, of words and drawings, as well as an immense map that seemed to represent every inch of the prison. The ceiling was a huge, transparent dome, above which the Lowlands' wide river rushed without a sound.

X hadn't been seated long when the stone chair began to revolve so that no matter where the lords were seated they had a chance to inspect him. The crowd quickly bored of this, however, and broke into a hundred conversations. The chair continued to turn. It moved slowly, then quickly, then slowly again. X listened to the belligerent shouting, the jagged laughter, the angry stomping of feet. He watched queasily as the faces streamed by in a never-ending loop. He was waiting for the trial to begin, and then it struck him . . .

This *was* the trial.

He fought the urge to panic. He searched the crowd for Regent, but couldn't find him. Surely Regent was there? Surely he wouldn't abandon him now? X kept searching. There were so many lords. Their robes were flapping. The golden bands at their necks were glinting. Dervish sat in the middle of a row, laughing wickedly with his fellow lords. Were they laughing at X?

At last, amid the confusion, a lord no taller than a child mounted the stage. X watched as he stepped behind the podium and hushed the crowd. In a high, nervous voice, the lord announced that they would now hear final arguments before voting on whether the prisoner was to remain a bounty hunter or be locked away forever.

Final arguments!

X's mind reeled. He was dizzy from the motion of the chair. His purple shirt was damp with sweat. The gash in his leg seemed to glow beneath the bandage.

He closed his eyes, and when he opened them—he saw Regent. At last! The lord rose from his seat and approached the stage.

Before Regent addressed the audience, he leaned down to X and confirmed what Ripper had said: X would be allowed to speak, but only once. X saw the sympathy in the lord's eyes, and was moved by it. Without thinking, he whispered, "You have been so kind to me. Might I know your true name?"

The lord was shocked by the question. He turned away without answering.

Regent told his fellow lords he was disgusted that they were even contemplating further punishments to the soul who sat before them. He reminded his audience that, though X had committed no crime, he had spent his life in the Lowlands—that he had learned to crawl and walk and speak in a cell barely bigger than his body. *Of course* he had been tempted to run! *Of course* he had fallen in love!

It was a stirring speech. The lords seemed rapt by it.

Regent talked about X's mother, about the rare blood that ran in his veins, about the appalling torture he had suffered on the plain.

X longed to speak on his own behalf—and was afraid he'd miss his chance. He remembered Ripper telling him to grovel. He practiced silently in his head: *My lords, my actions have been disgraceful. I beg to remain a hunter, so that I might continue to serve you. I recant everything—and everyone—else. My only love is the Lowlands.*

He loathed every word and meant none of them.

When Regent finished, there was a light rain of applause. Dervish, who seemed to live in a perpetual state of outrage, was so scandalized that he didn't even bother taking the stage to give his rebuttal. He pushed past the lords seated next to him, and began shouting from the aisle.

"This knave MUST NOT and CANNOT remain a bounty hunter," he declared. "He has ALREADY revealed what weak, lovesick stuff he is made of. He has ALREADY betrayed us. And yet some among us would let him remain a hunter and stroll the Overworld at his leisure? Nay, I say! NAY, NAY, NAY!"

Dervish expected his own round of applause. But after that bizarre string of "nays," Regent said loudly, "Forgive me, but has a horse entered the room?"

Laughter rippled through the chamber.

Dervish stood hunched in the middle of the aisle, recalculating his plan of attack. A thought came to him. X could see it register in his eyes.

"The TRUTH," bellowed the vile lord, "is that this knave does not even DESIRE to remain a bounty hunter. All he truly desires is to nuzzle his SLUT! I should have MURDERED her when I had the chance—and I may murder her yet!"

X rose from his seat. He was so furious and dizzy he could barely see.

Regent tried to calm him: "He bluffs in the hopes of enraging you. Do not be provoked!"

But X could hear nothing but the blood pounding in his ears. He stumbled off the stage, and lurched down the aisle toward Dervish.

"If you lay a hand on Zoe," he cried, "I will make your face even uglier—with a rock!"

"You are hardly in a position to hinder me," taunted Dervish. "I shall lick her neck, if it pleases me."

Regent flew down the steps to hold X back. But, dizzy as a child spun around during a birthday game, X lashed out at Dervish with his fist.

He struck Regent instead.

A gasp flew up from the lords. The sentinels raced forward with their rifles. X looked to Regent, whose face was a mask of fury and surprise.

"I never intended—" said X.

Regent raised a palm to silence him.

"You have spoken," he said, his tone suddenly clipped and officious. "And you may not speak again."

X COLLAPSED BACK INTO the stone chair. All was lost. He would never be a bounty hunter again. He would never see Zoe. His insolence might even cost her family their lives.

He gazed at the bandage on his leg. Blood rose through it like a little lake. To distract himself, he pressed his fingertips into it and felt the pain rush through him. Maybe, with Ripper's help, he could prevent the wound from ever healing, so that he could jab at it forever—a permanent reminder of his loss.

When it came time for the lords to vote, Regent helped him out of his chair.

"Be silent, no matter what occurs," the lord told him. "I have done all that I can."

X forced himself to look out at his judges. Few of them returned his gaze, which told him everything he needed to know about his fate.

The diminutive lord who'd opened the proceedings called out the official referendum in his reedy voice: "Shall this soul remain a bounty hunter—yea or nay?"

A nay was shouted, and then another, and then two more.

X felt as if he were watching his future with Zoe vanish and die. He had promised to return to her unless two worlds conspired against him—what a reckless promise! All it had taken was his own anger and pride, his own voice leaping out of him unbidden.

He tried to shut his ears to the proceedings. Yet listening to his own thoughts was no less a misery. How long would it take Zoe to admit to herself that X had failed her—that he was never coming back?

The ninth—or was it the tenth?—nay was bellowed out.

X hoped Zoe knew that he loved her. He couldn't swear he had actually said those words. When he had kissed her, every part of him was flooded with feeling. Had she known it? Would she remember? Or would she decide that he had never cared for her? Might it be better if she did?

His mind ached. Every question was like dry wood exploding in a fire.

He could ask Banger to take Zoe a message when Banger was sent to retrieve another soul. Banger was a loyal friend, that was clear. He would do it. But what would the message say? The words "I'm sorry" were so small.

Regent voted in X's favor, and X felt an absurd flutter of hope.

Three more nays followed. X was surprised how much they stung him even now.

He needed this to end. It was torture.

The lords had grown tired of the vote. They began standing and pushing toward the aisle. The man-child behind the podium shouted for order. They ignored him, and jostled each other. X wondered how such a pack of adolescents could rule the Lowlands.

And then it struck him: They *didn't* rule the Lowlands. Not really. Ripper's words came back to him: the lords answered to the Higher Power.

Suddenly, X heard a voice cry out: "I question your authority!"

He was shocked to discover that it was his own.

Regent shook his head violently, reminding X that he was forbidden from speaking again.

But X would not be silent. Zoe wouldn't have been.

"I question your authority!"

Every head turned.

"On what grounds?" said the little lord.

X stole a look at Regent, hoping for encouragement. The lord gave him the slightest of nods.

"On the grounds," he began slowly, "on the grounds that you do not have the right to judge me—for I am the son of a lord."

Silence swept the cavern. Ripper had counseled X well.

"There is one who rules over even you," X continued. "Only *He* has the power to punish me. Only *He* can decide my fate. Ask Him to judge me—if you dare."

BANGER HUNG ON EVERY word of X's story. The guards had ushered him back to his cell, and they could not get their fill of his tale either. They stood clustered in front of the bars, openly admiring X's courage ("The bollocks on 'im! Imagine!") and soaking up every detail in amazement. Ripper danced noisily in her cell, feigning madness, but X knew that she listened and was proud.

As for X himself, he careened between ecstasy and shock. He tried to calm his blood, reminding himself that his fate was still uncertain.

"You said, 'I question your authority'?" Banger asked, not for the first time. "You *seriously* said that?"

"Desperation drove me to it," said X.

"And then what 'appened?" said one of the guards, who had a wizened old face like a shrunken apple. "Mayhem, I figger?"

"The lords exploded into debate," said X. "The noise was terrible. The lords circled me, outraged by my insolence. They threatened me with medieval punishments. Dervish stuck his nose within inches of my face, and asked if I was aware of how many different ways there were to skin a human body. But I was so inflamed with righteousness that he did not scare me, and I let him know it by replying, calmly as I could, 'Seven?'"

This brought a round of laughter.

"Despite the lords' fury," X continued, "no one suggested that they *did* have the authority to judge me. I grew bolder and bolder, and began exclaiming, 'Ask *Him* to judge me! Only *He* can judge me!' Once, I believe I even shouted, 'Can He hear us now? Is He listening?! Tell Him that He must answer!' I was demented. Then, suddenly, amid the chaos, something so peculiar happened that I do not know how to credit it."

X was silent for so long his audience squealed in frustration.

"The chamber itself seem to *awaken* in some way," he said at last. "The river that rushed over our heads darkened. The walls became slick with moisture, as if they were made of skin. Then they took to vibrating. It was a mere tremor at first. But it grew steadily, and was soon accompanied by . . . Again, I hardly know how to describe it. It was accompanied by a *hum*. It began as a sort of growl, like something issuing from the belly of a beast. But the hum grew higher and higher, and soon it was transformed into a piercing sort of whistle. I cannot *begin* to relate how unkind a noise it was. It was like a spike driven into our ears."

"I 'ave 'eard that very sound!" said the shriveled apple.

"Oh, you never did!" said the stout chief.

"I saw fear transform the lords' faces—even Regent's," said X. "He ordered the sentinels to remove me from the chamber. I resisted, for the lords had not yet informed me of my fate. But the place was in such a tumult that I could do nothing to further my cause. As I was hurried away, I turned back toward the lords for a moment. I do not suppose you will believe this, but I saw that the gold bands the lords wear about their necks had commenced to glow. All at once the lords dropped their hands from their ears and clutched at the collars as if they were being choked. The sentinels and I had to push past one of the lords to exit the chamber, and the last thing I saw was a curtain of blood sliding down his neck."

X's last words landed in silence. Then, yet again, the shriveled apple felt compelled to speak.

"I seen that meself!" he said. "I seen that very fing!"

The stout guard turned.

"Liar," he said wearily.

"All right, fair enough," said the apple. "Howevva, I 'ave many a time seen their lordships strain and tug at them gol' bands, as if they was a nuisance."

In the cell next door, Ripper stopped carrying on and surprised the party by interjecting.

"Mr. Ugly has struck upon a truth," she said. "Those gold bands are not signs of power—or, rather, not *just* signs of power. They are chains."

"Well stated," said the apple. "Bein' called Mr. Ugly hurts a person's feelin's, but I will let it pass, as you are a well-known loony."

Before Ripper could respond, Banger warned them of movement on the plain below. Regent was pacing on the rocky ledge. X could not make out his features, but his agitation was clear.

"Right," said the chief of the guards. "We betta be off, then. Come along, Mr. Ugly."

X stared down at the plain as the squad lumbered off. Regent was brooding and pacing in such a tight loop that it looked as if he might wear a groove into the rock. X knew he would come to him— and soon. Yet he could not imagine what news he would bring.

The dark feeling in his heart told him it would not be good.

At last, Regent stopped pacing. He turned to the vast black rock of cells and leaped toward X, landing in front of his cell with a tremendous *thump* and a blast of air. He motioned X toward the bars.

"I have been commissioned to tell you that you must bring the Lowlands one more soul," he said. "If you fail to locate this final bounty, if you grow sentimental and release him, as you released

Stan—or if you waste a single instant chasing your newfound love—you will never leave the Lowlands again. You will never even leave this cell."

"And if I do precisely as I am instructed?" said X. "If I bring the soul back on his knees? Then I can remain a bounty hunter?"

"No," said Regent. He took a pause that seemed endless, before continuing. "Then you can be free."

It took X a long moment to find his voice.

"Free?" said X. "Forever? I have never heard of such a thing."

"Nor have I," said Regent. "But you are innocent, and the son of a lord. You were never meant for a cage. Perhaps this is the Lowlands' attempt at justice."

"I do not mean to appear ungrateful, for you have been a great ally to me," said X. "But I fear this is a trap."

"Then pray it is not," said Regent. "And I will pray with you."

The lord made sure no one was watching, then slipped his hand through the bars and shook X's firmly.

"What I am about to reveal to you, you must never breathe to another soul," he said. "Do I have your word?"

"You do," said X. "Of course you do. I owe you the world."

"Very well," said Regent. "My true name is Tariq."

PART THREE

Promises to Keep

TWELVE

ZOE TRIED SLEEPING in a dozen positions, as if she were inventing an alphabet with her body. Outside, the trees rustled peacefully, and a breeze brushed the window. The world was returning to normal, as if the word "normal" still meant something.

Whole days had slipped by since X had left. There would be school tomorrow. School! How absurd was that? Whenever Zoe felt a wave of sadness about to hit, she remembered how she'd stood in her socks in the driveway—how X had put his coat around her shoulders, how he'd pulled her body toward him. His mouth had been so warm it had made her lips glow like the ring on a stove.

At midnight, her door creaked open, and Jonah crept in, along with a cone of yellow light from the hall.

Zoe pretended to be asleep. Dealing with her brother was not on her list of priorities.

She let out a loud snore.

"I know you're awake," said Jonah. "Duh."

Zoe snored louder.

"Faker," said Jonah. After a moment, he added, "Where's X? Why isn't he back? I liked it when he was here."

Zoe groaned, and sat up in bed.

"He had to leave," she said. "You know that, bug."

"But, like, *leave* leave?" said Jonah. "*Forever* leave?"

His voice faltered.

The reality of the situation flooded through Zoe, too. Maybe she'd never see X again. Maybe their kiss had been so engulfing, so singular, because it would be the only one.

"I don't know about forever," she said. "All I know is that he *wants* to come back and that he's stubborn, like us."

Jonah seemed to accept this. He approached the foot of Zoe's bed and prepared to burrow under the blankets.

"No, bug," she said. "You can't sleep here. Not tonight."

He didn't think she was serious. He lifted the covers.

"*No*, bug," she said, snatching away the sheet and blanket.

Jonah left the room without a word, trailing a cloud of hurt. Zoe fell back onto the bed. Through the wall, she could hear Jonah push open their mother's door and say, "Zoe is the worst. Can I snuggle with you?"

Zoe changed positions yet again. She missed X—there was a lake of pain where her heart should have been—and now she felt guilty, too. Up on the roof, a clump of snow broke apart. It slid down the shingles, dropped past the windows like a body falling, and landed in the snow with a *thunk*.

She was never going to sleep.

Exasperated, Zoe sat up and hurled her pillow across the room. It struck the shelves above her desk, and sent some trophies clattering to the floor. She tried to assess the damage, but, in the darkness, could only identify an award for Best Sheep Shearer among the casualties. The trophy was of a golden half-naked sheep. It was one of Zoe's favorites because it reminded her of Val, who shaved the left side of her head. (Val was so gorgeous she could get away with it.) Zoe had bought the trophy at a thrift store in Columbia Falls. The man behind the counter—he'd been dozing and she had to wake him up with the shiny hotel bell— was so surprised that someone wanted the thing that he said, "For real?"

Zoe banged the back of her head against the wall in frustration. Once, twice, three times. Her mother must have thought she was knocking because she knocked back. It was a comforting sound.

Zoe realized she didn't really want to be alone.

The door to her mom's room stood open. Zoe entered tentatively, wondering if she'd be turned away. Her mother and Jonah lay huddled under the blankets, whispering like conspirators. Jonah heard Zoe's footsteps and lifted his head.

"This room is for sad people only," he said.

He'd been crying.

"I'm sad, too," said Zoe. "I promise."

Jonah put on his frowny thinking face. Finally, he nodded.

Zoe went to the foot of the bed and tunneled under the blankets like a gopher, for Jonah's benefit. When she popped her head out, she saw him snuff out a smile he didn't want her to see.

Zoe settled against the wall so that she and her mother lay shielding Jonah like parentheses.

"Your body's so warm," she told him.

"I get warm when I'm sad," he said. "Because of science."

Zoe and her mother took turns patting Jonah's hair. A clunky metal fan that their mom used to lull herself to sleep spun noisily in a corner, like the propeller of an old plane.

Jonah fell asleep within minutes, and Zoe's mother drifted off soon after. Zoe lay on her side, her thoughts swirling. Was this what love was like—one part pleasure, two parts pain? Zoe thought of Val's obsession with Gloria. She understood it now. She'd never felt anything like that with Dallas—it had never even *occurred* to her to make a Tumblr about his feet. For one thing, she was pretty sure he waxed them.

Zoe laughed softly, and her body relaxed, muscle by muscle. She could feel sleep coming for her at last.

But then Jonah, who'd apparently *not* been sleeping, announced into the darkness, "I'm not going to school tomorrow."

Zoe clenched.

"Shhh," said her mother, her voice soggy with sleep. "We'll talk about it in the morning."

"Okay, but I'm not going," Jonah said, as defiantly as he could. "And you can't make me."

"We will talk about it in the *morning*."

"I know you'll try to make me. But I won't. I hate it."

Zoe knew she should keep her mouth shut. But the idea that Jonah hated school was ridiculous. His homeroom teacher, Miss Noelle—he *worshipped* her. Once, he'd drawn a picture of her on his arm, like a tattoo.

"You don't hate it, bug," she said. "Don't say that."

"I hate it if I say I hate it," he said.

He sat bolt upright, and kicked the covers to the bottom of the bed.

Crap, thought Zoe. *Here comes a meltdown.*

"Jonah, control yourself," her mother said. "Please."

"Only *I* know if I hate school," he said. "So Zoe shouldn't say I *don't* hate it. I hate it if I *say* I hate it."

Zoe got out of bed, and stalked across the room, allowing herself a childish outburst of her own. She was carrying around enough pain already. She couldn't add her brother's misery to the pile. Not this time. It wasn't fair. Didn't Jonah know that she missed X, too? Didn't he know that she was thinking about him with every breath?

On her way to the door, she kicked over the idiotic fan with her bare foot. Behind her, Jonah said, "See how she just left? *Nobody* says good-bye."

THE MORNING WAS A nightmare. Zoe avoided Jonah as she printed an essay for English, but she could hear his shouts of "I hate it if I say I hate it" ringing through the house. He wouldn't eat, wouldn't brush his teeth, wouldn't get dressed. Zoe felt her mother's impatience rise. As she passed Jonah's bedroom, she saw her mom trying to dress him herself. Jonah refused to cooperate. He stiffened his body like a war protester.

Zoe motioned for her mother to come into the hall.

"I can't believe he's being so heinous," she said.

"He's in pain, Zo," said her mom. "We all process pain differently."

"Yeah—and he processes it heinously," Zoe said.

"Anyway, look, there's no way I can go to work today," said her mom.

"Can you afford to take a day off?" said Zoe.

"No, but I can't afford a sitter either," said her mother. "And who

179

could I call? All the sitters are going to be in school, which is where children are *supposed* to be."

Jonah must have overheard them because he called out from his room.

"Could Rufus be my babysitter, maybe?" he said. "I would never be heinous at Rufus."

Zoe's mom didn't like the idea. She didn't want to take advantage of Rufus's crush on her, probably. But Zoe thought it was genius, and she wanted this morning, this crisis, this escalating Jonah nonsense over with.

She called Rufus herself. He sounded surprised by the request—chain-saw artists are rarely asked to babysit—but before she could say never mind he had declared the idea to be rad.

"Thank god," said Zoe. "I was afraid you'd think it was gnarly."

"You're making fun of me, I know," said Rufus, laughing, "but tell my man Jonah to prepare himself for an *epic* hang."

Twenty minutes later, Rufus's van could be heard negotiating the mountainside. Zoe saw the wooden bear affixed to the roof as it rose above the treetops, waving like the queen.

AT LAST SHE WAS free. She drove the decrepit Struggle Buggy to school as if it were a race car. Every nerve in her body seemed to be humming. Every song on the radio seemed to be about X.

Zoe's and Jonah's schools were nestled next to each other in Flathead Valley near a dense settlement of chain stores (Target, Walmart, Costco) and beef-slinging restaurants that Zoe's mom referred to as the Cannibal Food Court (Sizzler, Five Guys, House of Huns). Students were allowed to eat lunch at the mall once they became juniors. For everyone else, it merely shimmered across the highway like an unreachable promised land. Zoe was a junior, but the thrill of eating in the Cannibal Food Court had lost its shine. It was partly because her mother's ethics had sunk in over the years—Zoe wasn't a vegetarian, but she felt a cloud of guilt whenever she ate meat—and partly because House of Huns was where she'd told Dallas she didn't want to go out anymore.

Val had begged Zoe not to see Dallas in the first place. She thought he was cocky and kind of a douche. But Val's relationship with Gloria was so intense that she had a skewed idea of what was generally possible in 11th grade. Zoe loved that Dallas was a caver like her and her dad, that he was fun and uncomplicated, and that—so sue her—you could see his triceps through almost any shirt. When she told Val that she was going to give him a chance, Val said simply, "I weep for you."

They began dating in September, and Zoe soon discovered that there were many sweet things about Dallas: His favorite color was orange. He still slept in pajamas. He used a photo of his mom for the wallpaper on his laptop. Val didn't want to hear any of it. Once, when Zoe and Dallas passed her in the hallway, Zoe sang out, "Still dating!" Val nodded, and sang back, "Still weeping!"

In November, when her dad died and she was crying constantly and everything was so raw and dizzying that she felt like she'd been thrown out of a moving car, Zoe decided to strip away everyone who wasn't essential to her life. And Dallas just *wasn't*. She broke the news to him at House of Huns, which was a Benihana-type place where shirtless men grunted like barbarians in front of a massive circular grill. At first, Dallas flatly refused to be dumped. He told Zoe she was in too messed-up a state to be making "mega-life-altering decisions." Zoe had face-palmed—she couldn't help it—and said, "Dude, this is *in no way* a mega-life-altering decision. I *know* what a life-altering event is, okay? My father just died."

"I'm sorry," said Dallas. "I didn't mean to compare this to—to *that*. To your dad. I just think you're a badass. And you're hot. And those are, like, the two best things."

Dallas asked if they could still hang sometimes—as friends, or whatever. He said it very simply and genuinely. Zoe said of course. Dallas grinned and told her that there was another girl at school he was kind of into anyway—and that he was pretty sure if he asked her out she'd say yes. He said Zoe was probably "too complicated" for him anyway. The air cleared, Dallas then turned his attention to the comments card and the miniature-golf pencil that had been left on their table: *How was your meal? Let us know!* Dallas reflected for a moment, and wrote, *Solid salad bar!* When Zoe left, he stayed behind to apply for a job.

Today, Zoe swung the Struggle Buggy into the parking lot that connected the schools. She was an hour late, thanks to Jonah's meltdown. She gathered up her books and bags, and slammed the car shut—a complicated process that involved pulling the handle up and to the right because the door had been sideswiped by a snowplow and now sagged several inches too low.

No one at Jonah's school even looked at Zoe sideways when she told them that he'd be out sick. Everyone knew that Zoe's family had slipped into a dark tunnel. She'd always been an A student, but lately her grades had been sliding. Given the awful stuff that had happened, she found it harder and harder to believe that there was really an earth-shattering difference between an A and a B, or even between a B and a C. Today, Jonah's vice principal, Ms. Didier, asked if Zoe was doing okay with so much compassion—with so much eye contact—that Zoe knew rumors must be circulating about what had gone on at the lake with Stan. God only knew how the story had been twisted in the retellings.

"I'm okay, yeah," Zoe told her. "Jonah's kind of . . . *not*."

"Well, look," said the vice principal, "this is incredibly scary, upsetting stuff. There's no handbook. But we will do whatever your family needs. Let Jonah know we're thinking about him. Who's with him now?"

"Our friend Rufus," said Zoe.

"The chain-saw guy?" said Ms. Didier.

"Yes," said Zoe. "But he's—"

"Oh, no, no, I love Rufus," said Ms. Didier. "I didn't mean to sound critical. He made a moose for me."

By the time Zoe got to the high school, the only period left before lunch was Spanish. Zoe sat between Val and a girl named Mingyu, who penciled little wings at the corners of her eyes, dressed in layer upon layer of black, and drew pentagrams and 666's on the undersides of her wrists during class. Mingyu played bass in an all-girl punk band called the Slim Reaper and claimed to be a Satanist. Zoe didn't believe the devil-worshipping part. But sitting down next to Mingyu now, she wished the girl actually *was* a Satanist, so she could freak her out.

Hey, Mingyu, guess where my boyfriend's from!

The Spanish instructor, a slender woman named Ms. Shaw who had what Zoe and Val agreed was by far the best teacher hair, rapped her wedding ring on the Smart Board to get the class's attention. Zoe raised her hand four times in the first eight minutes, so she could spend the rest of the period staring out at the mountains and thinking about X without being called on.

She tried to imagine where he was now. Had he found Stan or was he still hunting him down? All she could picture was the model of the Lowlands that he'd built with Jonah, so she imagined him talking to a Revolutionary War soldier while an orc from Lord of the Rings waved a club nearby. Zoe was terrified for X, but she told herself that she would see him again. She *would*. Meeting X had convinced her that things were possible. She didn't even know what things, but it didn't matter. Things!

She'd take him swimming in Tally Lake—not just at the dinky, roped-off pebble beach, but in the big blue bowl of the water. She'd go huckleberry picking with him. She'd take him hiking on the Highline in Glacier National Park. She'd tell him all the names of the wildflowers. She'd ask what his tattoos meant. She'd ask if he had ever kissed anyone but her. She was pretty sure he hadn't—his lips had trembled just the slightest bit.

His lips were *so warm*. Had hers been too cold? Had he noticed? Was he disappointed?

Okay, she was seriously losing it. When she surfaced from her daydream, Val and Dallas were making bug eyes at her and motioning toward her desk. Zoe looked down, and saw a quiz she was supposed to be taking.

As soon as the bell rang, Val rushed up to her, but Zoe floated past her and spent the rest of the day in a daze.

IN THE STRUGGLE BUGGY after school, Val started up again.

"Okay, *what* were you high on in Spanish? You know that quiz counts, right?"

"Counts how?" said Zoe. "Counts toward *what*? My total life score? *Esta quiz no es me importa para mi!*"

184

"Yeah, see, even that was terrible Spanish," said Val.

Zoe laughed.

"Sí, usted eres razón," she said.

"Ugh, just stop," said Val. "You're mauling a beautiful language."

They were crossing farmland on a long roller coaster of a road. The car shook and rattled. The windshield had a spiderweb crack—there was still a rock, about the size of a blueberry, wedged into the center—and the floorboard on the passenger side had rusted through so that, if you moved the rubber mat, you could actually see the ground fly by underneath.

By the time the Buggy sputtered up the driveway, Zoe had told Val as much as she could about X, though she substituted "aspiring musician" for "supernatural bounty hunter." It was what she'd told Rufus when he'd shown up unannounced that day. And it seemed plausible, if nobody pressed too hard about why an aspiring musician was on a frozen lake in the middle of a blizzard—and how he'd fought off a murderer.

Zoe had never withheld anything from Val before. She told herself she wasn't lying about anything significant. Where X was from and what he was didn't matter as much as *who* he was—how he'd woken her whole life up and helped her set aside some of her pain. All this from a guy who had never been given anything ever.

She pulled up to the house, and turned off the ignition. The Buggy bucked and chortled even after she and Val slammed the doors and walked away.

Before they could make it up the steps, Rufus stepped outside. He looked weirdly serious. Was something wrong with Jonah? Zoe had to fight an impulse to push past Rufus and run into the house.

"Just wanted to give you a heads-up," Rufus said. "Oh, hey, Val, what's shakin'?"

"Hey," said Val.

"*Talk*, Rufus," said Zoe. "You're scaring me."

"No, no, no, it's all good, it's all good," he said. "I mean, it's mostly good. I mean, honestly, it's not great. The little guy's just super-super-bummed. Like in shock, almost. I couldn't get him out of the house at all. Not even a step. He just froze up. He's in real bad shape."

Zoe groaned.

"He wouldn't go outside after our dad died," she said. "I'm not going through that again. I'll give him some tough love."

"Actually," said Rufus, "I think that might just make things worse."

Zoe ignored him. She liked Rufus, but didn't need him telling her what was best for her own brother.

"It's okay, I can fix this," she said. "Jonah just got really tight with that guy X I introduced you to."

Val couldn't help but interrupt: "Rufus got to meet X, but *I* didn't? What kind of hot garbage is that?"

"The musician dude?" said Rufus. "Supercool guy. *Epic* hair. And I don't blame him for not wanting to talk about his musical inspirations, or whatever. I'm an artist, too. I get it. You gotta blaze your own trail."

Rufus scratched at his bushy reddish beard, which he allowed to go wild in the winter. It was currently edging perilously close to his eyes.

"But, see, this isn't about X anymore, I don't think," he said.

"It is," said Zoe impatiently. "I know my brother."

Rufus shook his head, and his fledgling dreads swung back and forth. His stubbornness surprised her. In her experience, he disliked confrontation and would go with the flow no matter where the flow happened to be headed.

"Look, we talked about X," he said. "And honestly? I think him taking off was a bigger deal for you than for Jonah. Jonah liked him, heck yeah. He's bummed he split, heck yeah. But this stuff—the crying and the shell shock and the not leaving the house—this stuff is deeper than that. This thing's got roots like a big-ass tree. This is about something else now."

The front door opened. Jonah hovered near the threshold. He had his shoes on, which could have meant something—or nothing.

"I want to talk to you," he told Zoe. "I have a question."

He was a single step away from the outside world. A wind came up and rattled the storm door in its frame.

"I can't hear you," said Zoe. "Come closer."

Rufus shook his head and leaned toward her. "Don't get your hopes up," he whispered. "I tried this."

Zoe ignored him. Why hadn't he left already? She waited for her brother to answer.

"No," said Jonah. "I know what you're trying to do."

"I'm not trying to do anything, bug. I just can't hear you."

Rufus turned away, as if he didn't want to see what was about to happen.

"He's just not ready," he said. "You're playing with matches."

"Stop it, Rufus," Zoe said under her breath. "You're not his sister."

Jonah eyed them all suspiciously.

"I have to talk to you, Zoe," he said again. "Because of my question."

"Just come out on the steps," she said. "You can go *right back* inside."

Val put her hand on Zoe's shoulder.

"Maybe Rufus is right?" she said.

Zoe gave Val a look: *You, too?* She focused on Jonah again. He was leaning against the door, his hair flattened into a fan.

He pushed the door infinitesimally forward.

Come on, that's right, thought Zoe. *Come on, just do it, you little shit.*

He pulled it shut again.

"You're trying to trick me," he said.

"I'm not, bug."

"Don't call me bug when you're trying to trick me."

"Look, if you can't come out on the steps for *two seconds*, then let's talk later. Your question can't be very important."

"I want to know—"

"*Later*, Jonah."

She hated being cruel, but someone had to get tough with the kid or he was going to turn into a shut-in. When somebody was scared of the water, weren't you supposed to just throw them in the pool? Wasn't that a thing? If it wasn't, it should be.

"You stopped calling me bug," said Jonah. "That means you *were* trying to trick me. You didn't use to try to trick me."

Zoe walked toward the door—slowly, like someone trying not to frighten a cat.

From behind her, she heard Val say worriedly, "What are you doing?"

Zoe ignored her and climbed the steps. She heard Rufus say, "I can't watch this." She ignored him, too. She was going to put an end to this before it got any worse.

She opened the door. Jonah withdrew farther into the house. There was fear in his eyes, distrust.

Zoe smiled. She held the door open with one foot.

"Hug me?" she said.

Jonah made a confused face. He shivered as the wind slipped inside. After a moment, he inched forward and held out his arms. Zoe reached for him.

She clamped her arms around him and bolted outside.

Jonah panicked. He fought and screamed and pulled Zoe's hair. She kept going. She was convinced that what she was doing was right. Later, he would understand.

Rufus and Val stared at her like she was insane. She veered away from them. The ground was snowy and rough. She nearly fell. Jonah was heavier than she remembered. She tried to soothe him. She whispered in his ear, "I know you miss X. So do I! But he'll come back. I promise, I promise, I promise."

"So *what!*" Jonah wailed. He was beating on her back with his fists. "I don't *care* about X! I don't even miss him!"

"You *do*," said Zoe. "And it's okay!"

"I don't, I swear to god I don't!" shouted Jonah. "I miss Daddy!"

He landed a kick to her right knee. Zoe's legs buckled and she collapsed into the snow.

Jonah fled into the house.

Rufus managed to slip in after him before he locked the door.

ZOE LEANED AGAINST THE Buggy and cried a long time, mortified by what she'd done. Val put an arm around her. She tried to console Zoe by describing every idiotic and embarrassing thing *she* had ever done, which took almost 15 minutes. None of it was as bad as traumatizing your little brother just as he reached out to you for help. None of it was as bad as allowing an obsession with a guy make you forget that your father was dead, that he'd been abandoned in a hole, and that you and just about everyone you loved were still wrestling with grief.

Finally, Zoe went inside and called Jonah's name like a question. She didn't expect an answer and didn't get one. She peered up the steps to the bedrooms. Jonah had kicked a stack of laundry that their mother had folded before leaving for work. T-shirts, bras, and plaid little-boy boxers were strewn over the staircase. Zoe hung her head and climbed.

Rufus sat outside Jonah's door, trying everything he could think of to get the kid to open it. When he saw Zoe, he stood, hugged her, and—without saying *I told you so*, god bless him—lumbered down the stairs.

Zoe sat, and scratched at the door playfully. Jonah didn't answer. She could hear him jumping on the ladybug.

"I'm sorry, Jonah," she said. "I'm a really bad example of a person right now. I know that."

The bouncing stopped. The bed squeaked as Jonah hopped off it. Zoe heard him come to the door. Rather than open it, he sat on the other side and said nothing. It was a gesture, at least.

"I shouldn't have tried to trick you," she told him.

She spoke gently. She could hear him breathing.

"And I should never have said your question wasn't important," she added. "And I should never, *ever* have bought such an ugly car."

Silence.

There was a gap between the bottom of the door and the carpet.

She slipped her fingers through it and wiggled them. A gesture of her own. She was about to pull her fingers back when she felt Jonah's hand grasp hers.

Zoe didn't want to scare him off, so she kept quiet. Soon Jonah let go of her fingers, stood, and retreated farther into his room. A minute later, he slid a piece of paper, which he'd folded a ridiculous number of times, under the door.

"You're an excellent folder," said Zoe. "Everyone says so."

She opened the paper and smoothed it against the carpet. Even before she read the message, she smiled fondly at Jonah's handwriting, which was ... *eccentric*. His lowercase *y*'s, for instance, were always uppercase—they stood up proudly wherever they happened to fall in the sentence, like gold medalists raising their fists. Zoe never teased Jonah about it. She knew that his ADHD made it hard for him to write—the pen couldn't keep up with his brain, for one thing—and that he was ashamed that his classmates had pulled so far ahead of him.

She read his message:

> *WhY didn't DaddY Man take You with him to that cave? He alwaYs took You.*

Zoe didn't know what to say.

She bought herself some time by telling him, "I don't have anything to write with, bug."

Jonah padded off and then back again. He rolled something under the door—a sleek black pen attached to a beaded silver chain. He must have yanked it off the desk at the bank. Zoe would let her mom have *that* conversation.

She pressed the paper against the door.

I don't KNOW why he didn't take me. I have wondered
about that MANY times—even more times than I've
wondered why I bought SUCH AN UGLY CAR. Maybe
Dad was sad? Or maybe he thought I couldn't handle
the cave?

They continued passing the paper under the door. Jonah stopped folding it, which seemed like a sign that he was opening up to her.

WhY was DaddY Man sad?

Money stuff maybe. NOT because of you or me or
Mom. He LOVED us. LOVED LOVED.

There was no answer. Zoe couldn't tell if the conversation was over. There was a jittery, unresolved feeling, like a field of static, in her chest.

The paper finally came back. Jonah had folded it a zillion times again. The sight of it made Zoe's heart fold in on itself, too.

WhY did we leave him DOWN THERE? I hate it &
worrY he is cold.

Zoe turned the paper over. The other side was blank, though creased a dozen times and starting to tear. She wrote another message. It was a promise to Jonah and a promise to herself. She didn't pause to think about it. It just spilled out of her.

Bug, she wrote,

> *I will MAKE the police go find Dad's body—or I will go*
> *in that cave and find it myself. I swear to god. I always*
> *wanted to prove I could. And if I can't get Dad out of*
> *there myself, I will at least make sure he isn't cold. I*
> *WILL BRING HIM A BLANKET.*

She'd written the message in huge letters and even signed it, dated it, and drawn a small picture of herself as a superhero wearing a cape and flexing her biceps.

Jonah opened his door, looking happy and shy. Behind him, Zoe could see that he'd jumped so hard on the ladybug that the bed had drifted away from the wall.

DOWNSTAIRS, ZOE ASKED RUFUS if he could babysit a couple more hours—she was so ashamed of how she'd behaved that she could barely make eye contact—and then went outside, where Val was doing a handstand in the snow. (Val did not believe in being bored for even one second.)

After Val had tumbled back onto her feet and wiped her hands on her jeans, Zoe handed her the paper that she and Jonah had scribbled on. Val pored over it, turning it this way and that as necessary.

"Jonah is so awesome," said Val. "I mean it. I just want to squeeze him till he pops."

Zoe nodded, and walked past her to the car.

"I'm going to the police station," she said. "I'm going to tell them they *have* to get my dad's body. You wanna come?"

"Is there gonna be a big confrontation?" said Val.

"Probably," said Zoe.

"Then I *absolutely* want to come," said Val.

They didn't talk in the car. They just took turns fiddling with the radio. Zoe was deep in a country music phase, and Val liked a station that played the same four pop hits over and over and over, like a psychology experiment. The landscape that had seemed so bright and hopeful on the drive home from school now drifted by the windows looking hopeless and dead.

Zoe parked outside the police station, and took one of those "deep, cleansing breaths" her mother was always talking about.

"What do you want me to do in there?" said Val. "Can I play a character? Can I improv?"

"Just be my friend—and don't let me get arrested," said Zoe.

Val made a pouty face.

"What if *I* want to get arrested?" she said.

"We'll come back another time for that," said Zoe. "With costumes and stuff. Cool?"

"Very."

She and Val high-fived. They pretended to do it ironically, but the truth was that they just liked high-fiving. The only time they had ever tried fist-bumping neither of them wanted to make the stupid explosion sound.

The station was bustling, but the one cop Zoe liked, Brian Vilkomerson, stood up behind his desk when he saw the girls enter. He must have seen the tension pouring off them, like a vapor trail.

"Is this about Stan Manggold?" he said, before Zoe and Val even reached his desk. "Because—"

Stan Manggold! Zoe hadn't thought about that psycho in days, and hearing his name threw her off balance.

"No," said Zoe. "Stan's been taken care of."

Fortunately, Brian didn't ask what she meant. What could she have said? *You guys had your chance. Now my boyfriend's taking him to hell.*

"This is more important," Zoe said quickly. "This is about my father."

She told Brian she didn't want to talk to Chief Baldino. She referred to him as "the mean one—the one who looks pregnant."

Brian pursed his lips to kill a smile.

"Why don't you and your friend sit with me for a minute?" he said.

He gestured to two green chairs by his desk. Zoe could hear Baldino back in his office, noisily unwrapping a sandwich and laughing on the phone about something that probably had nothing to do with police work.

Brian reached out to shake Val's hand. Not everybody was that respectful to teenagers. Also, Brian didn't do the patronizing triple take that virtually all adults did when they met Val. First, they'd see the half-shaved hair with orange streaks, and grimace as if they were passing a wreck on the highway. Next they'd notice how hot Val was. Finally, their brow would furrow, and they'd wonder why on earth a girl that pretty would *blah yadda blah*. It never bothered Val. She had the same opinion of people that Zoe had of trophies: that they were both ridiculous and awesome and all you could do was collect the coolest ones.

Zoe was grateful that Brian just stuck out his hand and said hello and didn't treat her friend as if she were some Object of Interest. There was already a star next to his name in her head, so she added a second one, along with an exclamation point.

"Hey, there, I'm Sergeant Vilkomerson," he said.

"And I'm Val," she said. "I'm Zoe's attorney."

Brian tilted his head at this, but let it go.

Now that Zoe was sitting there, with a sympathetic audience leaning forward, she found she no longer wanted to scream or make threats. She just wanted to be *heard* and to be taken seriously. She tried not to be too rattled by the noisy everyday life of the station—the radio squawking, the baby crying, the officers jabbing at their keyboards. The hardest thing to block out was the sound of Baldino on the phone, doing impressions he thought were funny. The sound of his voice repulsed her.

"It's been months since my dad died," she said.

She stopped for a second, surprised by how much emotion that one sentence kicked up in her.

Val put an arm around her shoulder, which made her even sadder somehow. She shrugged it off.

She told Brian that the thought of her dad's body lying in a cave was eating away at her family. She told him about Jonah locking himself in the house, about the notes he'd passed under the door. Brian looked pained. Zoe could tell he was trying not to look at the pictures of his daughter that stood like monuments all over his desk.

"Look," he said. "This is so, so complicated—and not just because that particular cave is so dangerous."

Zoe waited to hear *why* it was so, so complicated, but as Brian was searching for words, Chief Baldino ambled heavily out of his office, like a bear. Zoe's stomach did its tightening thing. She prayed that he wouldn't notice her. If he said one rude thing to her, she'd lose it.

She watched Baldino out of the corner of her eye. He crumpled up his lunch bag, compacting it into a tight ball as if it were a feat of strength. Then—though Zoe could count at least four garbage cans in plain sight—he handed it to Officer Maerz and said, "Throw that away for me, would you, Stuart? Can of Coke Zero on my desk, too."

The chief yawned, stretched, and surveyed his kingdom.

He noticed Zoe.

He grimaced and moved toward her. It was clear he hadn't forgotten that nasty night at the house. It was clear that he loathed her as much as she loathed him. She just prayed he wouldn't say anything to set her off.

Baldino came so close that all she could see was his gut. Crumbs from his shirt fell onto her lap.

"I *thought* I smelled teenager," he said.

Zoe sprang out of her chair. She began talking too loud, her hands shaking all the while, as if they wanted to disconnect from her body. The whole station got quiet. Everyone stared.

Just as Zoe finished shouting—and just before Baldino, whose face had swelled with anger like a balloon filling with water, began yelling, "You're a disrespectful brat, and your old man can *stay* in that hole for all I care"—she heard a microwave *ding* preposterously in the silence. Somebody's burrito was ready.

Val and Brian were standing now, too. When had they stood up? Everything was blurring. They each had a hand on one of Zoe's arms, and they were steering her toward the door. She didn't want to cooperate. She stiffened her body, like Jonah when he refused to get dressed. Finally, Val whispered, "I love you, but *stop it* or you really are gonna get arrested. I'm saying this as your lawyer."

Baldino seemed to notice Val for the first time now. He did the least subtle triple take Zoe had ever seen.

Val gave him a wide smile—god, she loved Val, she was a born blurter, too—and said, "I could show you how to get this look, if you want."

Baldino snorted.

"Get your little friend out of here," he told her.

Zoe let her body go slack.

There were tourists at the door, openly gawking at her. Brian cut a path through them.

"It's all good," he told Zoe gently.

The door swung open. She felt cold air on her face. She heard car tires hissing on the wet street. Already, she'd forgotten everything she had said to Chief Baldino. She knew she'd been loud, but had she been clear? Had she been *heard*? Had she told him what she'd promised Jonah?

She turned back to the chief. Brian's head sagged. He just wanted this to be over. And it was. Almost.

"If you guys don't go get my dad, I'm gonna go get him myself," she told Baldino. "And then you may have *two* bodies to fish out of that cave, not just one."

VAL TOOK ZOE'S CAR keys and escorted her to the passenger side. Zoe was still in such a cloud that Val had to help her with her seat belt.

Brian leaned in through the window.

"Let's all just breathe for a second," he said.

He rested against the Struggle Buggy, hands stuffed in his pockets, head tilted up at the sky.

Zoe waited for the tension of the last ten minutes to dissipate, for the wind to sweep in and break it up and turn it into rain, or something. She regained her equilibrium slowly. Everything started to come back into focus.

Brian patted the roof of the car twice in an okay-let's-do-this sort of way. He crouched down beside Zoe's window again.

"First, the good news," he said.

He waved a small bag of candy—sour gummy worms, it looked like—and offered it to the girls.

"I confiscated these from my daughter this morning," he said. When they smiled, he added, "It was a routine stop-and-frisk."

Zoe and Val each took a handful of worms—Brian winced when he saw how many they were about to ingest—and dropped them one after the other into their mouths. The girls squirmed as the bitterness corroded their tongues.

"Thith ith horrible," said Val.

"*Weally* horrible," said Zoe.

When they'd calmed down, Brian did another one-two pat on the roof of the car.

"Can we talk for a second?" he said.

"Yeth," said Zoe.

"Abtholutely," said Val.

Brian cast his eyes back at the station to make sure no one on the force was milling around.

"I know the chief doesn't seem like the world's awesomest guy," he said. "And I'm not going lie to you, Zoe—he is *not* the world's awesomest guy. Between us, his wife is leaving him and he's pretty torn up about it. Anyway, the point is . . ."

He paused, frowning.

"The point is, he's not saying no about your dad because he's some colossal jerk," he continued. "He *wanted* to recover the body, believe me. There's some good cave-rescue units out there. He was in touch with them."

Brian paused again, looking tortured.

"But he was told to let it go," he said. "Well, not *told*, really. I shouldn't put it that way. He was *asked* to let it go."

Zoe and Val replied simultaneously:

"By who?"

"It's not my place to say," said Brian. He dropped his head, like a dog that knew it had done something wrong. "I'm sorry."

Zoe needed an answer. She made Brian look at her. Her eyes, she knew, were teary and bloodshot. Good. Let him see the kind of pain she was in.

"By *who*?" she said again.

Brian groaned. He swept a hand through his hair, which settled back down into an even messier formation.

"I just *know* I'm going to regret telling you this," he said.

He thumped the car a final time, by way of good-bye.

"Your mother."

ZOE SLIPPED DOWN IN the passenger seat, her mood darkening by the second. There was a bank of black clouds approaching. It looked like the underside of a massive spaceship.

"You should call your mom," Val said quietly.

"Yeah," said Zoe. "But can we just sit here a second?"

"Whatever you need," said Val. "I'll sit here forever if you want. I'll sit here until they tow the car to the junkyard. I'll go in the trash compactor with you, if I have to."

"Thank you," said Zoe.

"I mean, I'd prefer *not* to go in the trash compactor," said Val.

Zoe laughed despite herself.

"You want to hear something weird?" she said.

"Of course," said Val. "Have we met?"

"When the cops came to ask us about Stan," said Zoe, "I made some comment about how they were idiots and how they'd never gotten my dad's body out of the cave. And my mom gave me this look, like, *Nothing good will come from stirring all that up!* Now I know why—because she told them to leave him there. Because she was glad he was gone."

"Maybe there was another reason," said Val.

"Like?" said Zoe.

Val twisted her mouth into a frown.

"I got nothing," she said.

When Zoe was ready to call her mom, Val slipped out of the car to give her some privacy. She gave Zoe an encouraging shove as she left.

Zoe watched Val disappear into a thrift store across the street, then finally called. Even the phone sounded jittery as it rang. It took her mother forever to answer.

"Zoe, what's up? Are you okay? I'm working."

The first fat drops of rain had begun to detonate on the windshield.

"Zoe? Are you there? What's wrong?"

Zoe hardened her voice so she wouldn't cry.

"What's wrong is that you told the cops not to go get Dad's body," she said. "Which is *so* messed up! And you *lied* to me about it."

There was a long pause. Zoe waited. She could hear the everyday sounds of the Hot Springs in the background—the *ping* of the door opening, the *beep* of the cash register, the scuffling of bath slippers on the concrete floor.

"Look, this is a long conversation," her mother said. "And I can't have it right now. I've got people asking for their money back because they don't want to sit outside in the rain—like I'm responsible for the *rain*."

Zoe slid over to the driver's seat and switched on the windshield wipers so she could see out. The rain was already coming down hard, hitting the roof like nails.

"I don't care how long a conversation it is," she told her mother. "I want to have it *now*."

Across the street, Val was waving at her through the thrift store window. She was modeling a red suede blazer, and asking Zoe's opinion. Zoe shrugged in a *meh* sort of way. The red clashed with the orange streaks in Val's hair.

"I told the police to leave him because I didn't want someone else to get themselves killed," said Zoe's mom. "And *that* is the truth."

Zoe considered this.

"You're full of crap," she said.

"Zoe!" said her mother.

"I'm sorry, but you *are*," said Zoe. "That may be part of the truth, but it's definitely not all of it."

"So tell me," her mother said. "Why'd I do it?"

"Because of all that stuff you told me about him and Stan," said Zoe. "Because Dad was never around. Because he was a 'disappointment' or whatever you called him. Because you *hated* him."

"You're wrong," her mother said. "I never, ever hated your father. I wouldn't have spent twenty years with someone I didn't love. If nothing else, I wouldn't want to set an example like that for you and Jonah. You're going to have to guess again."

"I'm sick of guessing," said Zoe. "I told you before X left that I want to know everything."

"And I told you that you *don't*," her mother said.

There was another silence, a stalemate.

"Listen," said her mother. "There's stuff I'm still sorting through. There's stuff I'm still forgiving your father for. I'm not ready to talk about all of it yet—and I don't think you're ready to hear it. I'm sorry."

Val appeared in the shop window again. She was holding an absolutely enormous plastic skunk. *How about this?!*

Zoe laughed silently, so her mom wouldn't hear her.

A car cruised past, kicking slush up against the windows. Her mother was still waiting for her to say something.

Zoe wasn't ready to forgive her. She just wasn't.

"You know what?" she said. "I don't really care what *you* thought of Dad. Jonah and I loved him, even if he was lame sometimes." She paused. "I warned the police, and now I'm gonna warn you. Dad taught me how to cave—and you know what that means? That means I know how to go get him."

VAL TROTTED BACK TO the car in the rain. She crossed in the middle of the street and, when a pissed-off trucker honked at her, responded with a quick curtsy. She slipped into the car, and handed Zoe a bag. She'd bought her a trophy at the thrift store. It had a weird golden *O* at the top.

"You won Best Donut," said Val.

Zoe broke out of her mood long enough to smile and accept the award graciously.

"There are *so* many people I want to thank," she said.

Zoe set the trophy on the backseat, and started up the Struggle Buggy. The engine coughed before catching, annoyed at being woken up. But soon they were out on the wide, rain-slicked highway to Kalispell. Zoe told Val they had to make one more stop. They had to see Dallas. When she began to explain, Val interrupted her.

"You want to see him because he's a caver," she said. "You want him to train you in case you have to go into Black Teardrop." She paused. "Hello? This is *me*, Zoe. I'm the one you don't have to explain things to."

The rain was gentler now. The clouds were pulling apart, and there was a small blue hatch in the sky. Zoe felt herself beginning to breathe again. She had a plan—*and* she'd won Best Donut. On the road in front of them, there was a massive pickup with dual back tires and a bumper sticker that read, Montana Is Full! I Hear North Dakota Is Nice.

TEN MINUTES LATER, ZOE pulled into the giant lot outside House of Huns, where Dallas had gotten his dream job on the grill. Val still wasn't a huge fan of Dallas. He'd never asked out The Girl Who Was Gonna Say Yes, and Val was convinced he still had a thing for Zoe.

She told Zoe she was going to hit FroYoLo.

"I can't stand to watch Dallas drool over you," she said.

"Dallas and I are just friends," she said. "He gets that."

"Yeah, okay, whatever," said Val. "I don't actually care if you hurt him because—bottom line—that dude is *basic*. I mean, he was named after a TV show."

"He says he was named after the Dallas Cowboys," said Zoe.

"Of course he does," said Val. "I'd say that, too, if I was named after a TV show."

Zoe felt the greasy air settle onto her skin as she entered House of Huns. Dallas and three other cooks were grunting around the giant grill, which they referred to as the Ring of Doom. They were all comically hunky. They carried rubber-tipped spears and wore cone-shaped leather hats, which were ringed with fake fur. They had wide leather straps crisscrossing their chests and backs, but were otherwise shirtless. Because of the heat, they perspired constantly. Every so often drops of their sweat hit the grill and sizzled.

The grill itself was an imposing black circle with a hole in the middle for scraps. Customers handed over the frozen meats, veggies, and sauces they had selected from the salad bar—placards suggested at least five ladles of sauce, and recommended various combinations—and then pushed their tray along the cafeteria rails that surrounded the grill as the cooks fried the stuff up and chanted nonsense that sounded Hunnish. There was a miniature gong positioned nearby that patrons could strike with a mallet if they put something in the tip jar. Whenever the gong was struck, the cooks stopped whatever they were doing and flexed.

To say that Dallas loved his job would be a tremendous understatement.

He beamed when he saw Zoe—then remembered he was supposed to be a Hun.

"What want?" he barked theatrically.

"Can I talk to you?" said Zoe.

"No talk," said Dallas. *"Eat."*

Zoe gazed down at the grill. It was heaped with grayish chips of what purported to be pork and beef. A handful of frozen peas rolled around like marbles.

"I'm not eating this stuff," she said.

She saw, with a pang, that she had insulted him.

"No eat, no talk," he said. "Mrgh!"

"Seriously?" she said.

At this, Dallas transformed back into Dallas for a second and said, almost pleadingly, "Come on, Zoe. Work with me!"

Another cook—was he Head Hun?—stomped over to where they were standing and pounded a fist against his pecs, which were glistening with sweat and body lotion.

"Girl no eat?" he said to Dallas.

Zoe rolled her eyes.

"Okay, okay," she said. "Girl eat, girl eat. Mrgh!"

LATER, WHEN DALLAS WAS on break, he sat across from Zoe as she twirled noodles around a fork.

He'd taken off his Hun hat, and pulled on a white V-neck T-shirt torn slightly at the base of the V. He was fanning himself with a laminated menu.

"What's up?" he said cheerily. "I haven't seen you in here since you dumped my ass."

Zoe smiled.

"Yeah, sorry about that," she said.

"You kinda broke my feelings, dawg," he said.

"I know," said Zoe. "I didn't realize—"

"You didn't realize what?" said Dallas. "That I had feelings?"

"Kind of?" said Zoe.

Dallas surprised her by laughing, and she saw a flash of the cute, unpretentious guy she used to make out with in the handicapped bathroom at Target.

"Totally honestly?" he said. "I didn't really know I had feelings, either. But it's all cool. No worries. I mean, I'm about to ask somebody out, anyway."

"The Girl Who's Gonna Say Yes?" said Zoe.

"She *is* gonna say yes," said Dallas.

"I know she is," said Zoe. "I'm seeing somebody else, too."

Dallas's face fell.

"Ugh," he said. "Why'd you have to tell me that?"

"You just said *you* were asking someone out," said Zoe.

"But still!" said Dallas.

Zoe ate a sickly looking chip of pork as a goodwill gesture. Dallas pretended not to care, but she could see a flicker of pride in his eyes.

"It's better than you thought, right?" he said.

Zoe nodded.

"It's really not," she said.

Behind her, another cook began beating the gong in a low steady rhythm to signal that Dallas's break was over. When Dallas didn't immediately stand, the cooks added an unintelligible chant on top of the beat. Dallas looked over Zoe's shoulder at the half-naked savages who were his co-workers.

"I should go soon," he said. "Before my bros get rowdy."

"I can do this quick," said Zoe. "I want to go caving again, and I want you to go with me. I don't know how to do it in the snow, and you're the only caver I know who's as good as my dad was."

Dallas shook his head.

"No way," he said.

Zoe's heart fell—until he continued.

"Your dad was way better than me," he said.

"Here's the messed-up part," said Zoe. "I told Jonah I'd go into Black Teardrop if the cops wouldn't. Actually—this is crazy, but whatever—I told him I'd bring my dad a blanket."

Dallas took this in. The cooks were chanting louder now. Dallas looked up and shouted something that sounded like, "Furg!"

"Why would your dad need a blanket?" he asked Zoe. "He's . . . dead."

"Jonah thinks he's cold," she said.

"Wow," said Dallas.

Zoe waited.

"Will you help me?" she said.

"This is pretty bat-shit crazy, Zoe," said Dallas. "And really gruesome."

"You know what would be more gruesome?" she said. "If I didn't give a shit what happened to my father's body."

Dallas's face took on a meditative expression.

"True dat," he said.

"And, look, maybe the cops will deal with it," Zoe said, "and I won't have to."

"But you're not just bluffing, are you?" said Dallas.

"No," she said.

"That cave's a beast," said Dallas. "Obviously."

"Yeah," said Zoe.

"Black Teardrop's only a couple hundred yards from Silver Teardrop, which is less of a ballbuster," he said. "We could do a training run there, and see how you do." He paused. "This new boyfriend you like more than me—is he a caver?" he said.

The question surprised Zoe.

"Sort of?" she said. "But I'm asking *you*. Will you help me?"

"Well, I'm not gonna let you go alone," said Dallas. "But we're going to have to do it fast because when the snow starts to melt, those caves are going to be like waterslides. Also, if we spend too long training, you're gonna get all attracted to me, and then *that's* gonna be a whole big thing."

She laughed.

"True dat," she said.

Dallas stood and slipped back into character, like a Method actor about to hit the stage. He put on his Hun hat. Then, with a loud cry, he ripped off his V-neck T-shirt with both hands. (The tear at the base of the V made it easy to shred and, Zoe suspected, had been put there for that very purpose.) An older woman sitting nearby hooted happily at the sight of Dallas's biceps. He tossed the shirt to her, then leaned down to Zoe and whispered proudly, "They give us the T-shirts for free."

Zoe sat alone awhile, pushing around noodles. She was nervous about the plan—she'd be an idiot not to be—but she was doing it for Jonah, and she wasn't going to let him down.

There was a commotion on the other side of the restaurant. Zoe looked up and saw that Val, having finished her frozen yogurt, was outside the window. She was bored and doing jumping jacks to get her attention.

A strange thought struck Zoe as she headed for the door: she was going into the earth for her dad, while X was trying to get *out* of it for her.

THIRTEEN

ZOE AND DALLAS PLANNED the Silver Teardrop trip like it was a military operation. In the gleaming, high-ceilinged halls at school, they passed each other notes about rebelays, cowstails, and carabiners, and about whether they should use 11-millimeter rope, which was the safest, or 9 millimeter, which was lighter to carry. Dallas was the treasurer of a caving club with the unfortunate name of the Grotto of Guys. His enthusiasm reminded Zoe so much of her father that sometimes when Dallas was waving his hands around and babbling excitedly about the trip, she felt her eyes prick with tears.

It was a Friday night now, close to midnight. They were going caving in the morning. Zoe lay on the couch in the living room, a list of supplies and a map of Silver Teardrop in her hands. Her body felt jangly. She couldn't get her mind to sit still. The moon, bright and big, was blaring through the window next to her. A larch scratched at the window with its skeletal hands.

Silver Teardrop was just a practice run. It was less daunting than Black Teardrop, where her father had died—but still, she had never gone caving in winter. She'd never dealt with snow and ice. She'd never gone without her dad at all.

Her father had treated caves like they were holy ground. Zoe thought some of the graffiti on the walls of the caves was cool, especially the ancient-looking stuff. But it used to make her dad mental. He'd shine his headlamp at a wall where somebody had carved *Phineas* in the rock, and he'd shake his head: "Even in the 1800s, some people were assholes." Her dad had shown her caves with amazing domed ceilings, caves with lakes so blue they seemed phosphorescent, caves with enormous, glassy stalagmites that looked like a pipe organ.

"Here's the deal, Zoe," he'd tell her. "There are still a million unexplored places on earth—places where no human being has ever set foot. How cool is that? *How freakin' cool is that?!* It's just that they're all underground."

Zoe's father had always been a few feet in front of her, testing the tunnels and drops and underground rivers. He'd always been *right there*, smiling goofily and shouting over his shoulder, "You're freakin' awesome! You can do this! You're my girl!"

But not anymore. Not ever again.

She took her phone from the coffee table and texted Dallas to psych herself up.

Tomorrow Tomorrow TOMORROW!!!! she wrote.

Dallas texted back instantaneously, as if he'd just been waiting to hit Send.

Pumped! he wrote. *Just gotta get out of work. Huns are being HUGE a-holes. Stand by.*

WTFF? Zoe texted back. *Don't you dare blow me off!*

Never! I'm PUMPED!!! G2G—I'm shaving. (Not my face.)

EWWWW. Tell the Huns if they don't let you go, I will kick them in the MRGH and shove a spear up their FURG.

Ha!

Too much?

Hells no! LMNO!

N?

Nuts, Zoe. NUTS!

She set her phone on the coffee table and stared at the map of the cave. In the top right corner, there was an inscription:

Silver Teardrop. Bottomed March 2, 2005. Team leaders: Bodenhamer & Balensky. Water temp: 32°–33°.

The map, which had been drawn by hand, looked like an illustration of a digestive tract, like they used to give out in ninth-grade Bio. The entrance to the cave (the mouth) was a narrow crawlway. It was going to be claustrophobic, and they'd have to be roped and harnessed as they crawled, because after 50 feet the passage arrived at a steep, 175-foot drop (the esophagus). Water ran down one of the walls year-round. How much water there would be—a trickle or a waterfall—was the only question mark that nagged at Zoe and Dallas. They hoped the snow outside the cave hadn't started to melt and flood underground.

Zoe's eyes drifted down the map. At the bottom of the drop, there was a big, bell-shaped chamber (the stomach), where the waterfall splashed against a giant rock and spilled onto the floor. She and Dallas would be touching down in a freezing lake. They'd have to wear wet suits under their clothes.

The chamber was what the cavers came for. It must have some spectacular ice formations hanging from the ceiling: it was called the Chandelier Room.

Zoe let the map drop to the floor and rubbed her eyes.

She could hear her mother upstairs, pacing around. They hadn't spoken in days. Zoe still felt angry and hurt, but she missed her mom. She felt disconnected from the world, like she was floating in space without a tether. The fact that X was gone made it worse. Zoe listened as the ceiling creaked under her mother's step. Every sound made her feel lonelier.

Zoe was going caving because Jonah needed her to—why couldn't her mom understand that? Did she think she was only doing it to cause trouble? Or because she needed a distraction while she waited for X? Jonah was still in too much pain to step outside the house. He was waiting for Zoe or the police to make it to the bottom of Black Teardrop. He'd become pale and weepy. He gnawed endlessly at his fingers. Every weekday morning, Rufus rumbled up in the truck with the waving bear, but even he—with his vast repertoire of silliness—couldn't cheer the kid up. When Rufus and Jonah played hide-and-seek, Jonah hid in the old freezer in the basement like he used to with their dad, but even that seemed to upset him. Rufus refused to take any money for caring for him. At first, Zoe assumed this was all part of his one-mile-per-hour courtship of her mother. Then, one afternoon, she saw Rufus holding her brother's hand and delicately clipping his tiny fingernails—and she realized that he actually just *cared about Jonah*. That was the day Zoe decided the guy was a saint.

Tonight, before Jonah went to bed, Zoe had dictated some extra supplies she'd need, and—in a rare burst of energy—he'd written it as best he could in a spiral notebook.

Zoe went over the list one more time:

H2O

Proteen bars, 3?

Hair ties for tYing hair

Raisens

Flashlights, 2

Swis ArmY Knife

Battories

Wool socks reallY thick ones

Dish-washing gloves (WIERD!)

Knee pads for knees

Garbig bag for poncho, <u>just in case</u>!

Everything was stuffed into packs now. Zoe let the paper float to the floor. There was nothing left to do but somehow make it to morning.

SHE WAS STILL AWAKE at 2 a.m. She forced herself off the couch. She went to the front hall closet—why hadn't she thought of it before?—and took out X's blue overcoat. It shimmered even in the muted light of the hallway. The metal hangers made a tingling sound when they touched.

Zoe pressed her face to the coat. It smelled of wood smoke, pine, and the faint tang of sweat. The memory of colliding with X on the lake, of feeling his body collapse beneath her, of breathing him in for the first time, flooded over her. She squeezed the coat hard, as if he were in it. Dallas was cute. He had a sweet, lopsided grin, but X . . . X was kind of astounding. Zoe rubbed one of the buttons on the coat. It was made of stone. It warmed in her hand.

She carried the coat to the couch and huddled under it. X was five or six inches taller than Zoe, so the coat engulfed her, cascaded over her, made her feel *certain* and *safe*. She imagined X finally returning. She imagined him walking up the steps. He would be too nervous to look at her at first. She would say . . . What would she say?

She would say, *You forgot your coat.*

At 3 a.m., she decided to write X a letter, even though she had no way to deliver it *and* he didn't know how to read. The pen with the beaded chain that Jonah had taken from the bank lay on the coffee table. She picked it up. She took the supply list off the floor, turned it over, and pressed it against her knee. She didn't care that X would never see the letter. She just wanted, just *needed*, to capture some of the thoughts flying in circles in her head.

She wrote without pausing until she'd filled the page. At 3:15, she folded the letter and slipped it into a pocket of X's coat as if it were some kind of supernatural mail slot. She fell asleep within seconds. The stolen pen was still in her hand. The coat flowed over her like warm water.

AT 8:58, ZOE WOKE to the sound of Dallas blasting his horn. He was two minutes early and, since she had last been in his car, he'd apparently customized the horn to play the first five notes of *The Simpsons* theme song. Zoe stumbled to the kitchen window. She made a slashing motion across her throat (*Stop honking!*), spread the fingers on her right hand (*I need five minutes!*), and then repeated the slashing gesture (*Seriously, honk again and you die!*). She was exhausted. Her neck ached from sleeping on the couch. She was in no condition to go caving. Adrenaline was going to have to get her through the day.

Upstairs, she pulled on her wet suit and, over that, as many layers as she could handle without walking like a mummy. She did a quick check of her backpack and the duffel bag that held her gear. All good. On the way down the hall, she peeked into Jonah's room, hoping he'd be awake so she could hug his toasty little body before she left. He was deeply asleep, though—flushed pink and 20,000 leagues under the sea.

Downstairs, her mother hovered like a ghost in the kitchen. She was at the counter, stirring tea.

"I'm going," said Zoe.

Her mother didn't answer. Didn't even turn.

Zoe didn't want to leave like this.

She could hear Dallas outside, blasting a Kendrick Lamar rap in his 4Runner.

"I'll be careful," she said.

She meant it as a kind of peace offering, but her mother wheeled around angrily.

"If you wanted to be careful—if you wanted to respect my wishes—you wouldn't go at all," she said.

"Mom, listen—"

"No, Zoe, I'm not listening. Just go, if you're going."

Her mother refused to say another word. She picked up the orange box of tea and began reading the back, as if it were interesting.

Zoe was a wreck when she got in the 4Runner. Dallas stumbled around for something to say. Zoe felt bad about it. Dallas was so PUMPED! PUMPED! PUMPED! for the expedition, and here she was like some pathetic chick getting all messy with her *feels*. She was not this person.

In a surprising flurry of thoughtfulness, Dallas had brought Zoe a cappuccino from Coffee Traders and switched the radio to a country station she liked. Fiddles and acoustic guitars filled the car. Zoe could tell Dallas hated it, but he didn't say a word. She put a star next to his name in her head.

"The Huns let you come after all," she said finally. "That's cool."

"The Huns suck," said Dallas, relieved to be talking. "Don't get me going on how hard they suck."

He pulled up to a red light.

"Check this out," he said. "My boss, right? We're supposed to call him King Rugila, which is stupid and hard to pronounce—his name's actually Sandy. Anyway, King R gives me a *massive*, nut-busting guilt trip about the sacred code of the Huns and how they didn't just abandon their brothers for some chick." He paused. "*You* are the chick, by the way."

"I got that," said Zoe.

"So I go on Wikipedia, right? I never actually read about the Huns before because I kinda wanted to create my own character. But check this out: the Huns *had* no code! That was the point—they just attacked stuff!"

The light bloomed green. Dallas let a string of cars turn in front of him before pulling forward. He was a weirdly polite driver.

"Sorry to get all riled," he said. "King R just makes me insane."

"I don't want you to get in trouble because of me," said Zoe. "You're not going to get fired, are you?"

"No, I'm definitely not going to get fired," said Dallas. "Because I quit."

"Dallas!" said Zoe. "Because of me?!"

"*Yeah* because of you," he said shyly. "Shut up."

She'd embarrassed him. Who knew Dallas could even *get* embarrassed?

"They'll be begging me to come back by Monday," he added. "All those hot moms don't come in for the food—which I bet isn't even all that authentically Hunnic. I'm not saying I'm the biggest stud they've got. That would be conceited. But I'm definitely in the top three. King R's got, like, *back hair*."

Zoe laughed, grateful that Dallas was so deeply, defiantly . . . *Dallas*.

THEY STREAMED PAST COLUMBIA Falls and turned north toward Polebridge. Civilization quickly petered out. All cell and Internet service evaporated, and the last of the stores and restaurants gave way to empty, rutted roads that curved through the woods. Signs saying Private Property and Be Bear Aware were nailed to firs along the roadside. Every so often a log cabin sent up a fat plume of smoke. Otherwise, the world was empty. Zoe felt it in her stomach. The closer they got to Silver Teardrop, the more anxious she felt about going caving again. Dallas must have sensed it.

"You nervous?" he said.

"Yeah," she said.

"Seriously?" said Dallas. "Because we're going to *crush* this cave. We're both total ballers. Repeat after me: *crush, crush, crush!*"

"Crush, crush, crush?" said Zoe.

"That was feeble," said Dallas. "Nothing was *ever* crushed by anybody who said 'crush' like that."

"It's not just the cave," said Zoe.

Dallas frowned.

"Do you want to—do you want to talk about your *feelings*, or whatever?"

Zoe just stared at him. She couldn't help it. It was the last thing that the Dallas she'd gone out with would ever have asked.

"Have you been practicing how to talk to girls, dawg?" she said.

"Maybe," said Dallas. "Maybe with my mom—who's a therapist. I'm saying *maybe*."

"Well, it's sweet of you to ask," said Zoe. "But I *know* you don't actually want to hear about my feelings."

They came to a narrow curve in the road. Another car was approaching. Dallas slowed down and drove onto the shoulder so it could pass.

"Here's the thing that girls don't understand," he said.

"Oh my god," said Zoe. "Please tell me what girls don't understand—because I've always wondered."

Either Dallas didn't hear the sarcasm, or decided to ignore it.

"What girls don't understand," he began earnestly, "is that guys actually do want to hear about their feelings—they just don't want to hear about *all* of their feelings. They want to hear about *some* of them."

"How much are we talking?" said Zoe. "Do you want to hear, like, thirty percent of our feelings?"

Dallas mulled this over.

"Maybe fifty percent?" he said. "Depending? We just want there to be time left at the end to talk about something else. But with you guys—with you *girls*—everything is always connected to everything else, so you start talking about *one* feeling and that leads to *another* feeling, which leads to *another* feeling." He looked at her with his dimpled, wide-open face. He was absolutely sincere. "You know? There's never any time left."

219

They were just outside Polebridge now. Dallas turned onto the road to town. Polebridge was a tiny, pony express sort of place in the middle of nowhere. There were maybe a dozen buildings—a café, a general store, a cluster of cabins, a red outhouse with a crescent moon on the door. Except for the satellite dishes, it might have been 1912. There was a rail for tying up your horse.

Dallas parked in front of the store, shut off the engine, and turned to Zoe, apparently still waiting for the lowdown on her feelings.

What the heck, she thought.

"Okay, here are the highlights," she said. "My mom's pissed at me for going caving. Jonah won't leave the house. He's like a crazy person in a play. I haven't seen X—my boyfriend—I haven't seen him in *days*. I'm sorry. I know you don't want to hear about him. What else? I miss my dad. I've never gone caving without him. I don't even know *how* to go caving without him." She made herself stop talking. "So those are my feelings. Which fifty percent do you want to hear more about?"

To Dallas's credit, he said exactly the right thing: "You need some sugar."

He disappeared into the general store and returned five minutes later with a bag of pastries, which he dumped onto the seat between them, like a pirate's treasure. There were chocolate chip cookies, cherry turnovers, and huckleberry bear claws. It was far more food than the two of them could eat. Zoe unwrapped a bear claw and began to devour it, licking the frosting off her fingers. She hadn't realized how hungry she was.

"When we're finished with Silver Teardrop, I want to go see Black Teardrop, okay?" she said. "I haven't seen it since . . ."

She trailed off, and Dallas finished the sentence for her: "Since we looked for your dad?"

"Yeah," she said.

"You really ready to see that place again?" said Dallas.

Zoe laughed. She wasn't sure why. Maybe it was the sugar.

"Who knows," she said.

THEY LEFT POLEBRIDGE AND drove the last ten miles to Silver Teardrop, the car bucking and rattling over the road. The forest in this part of the mountains had recently burned. The trees were stripped and charcoal black, and rose out of the snow naked as needles. They reminded Zoe of the woods near Bert and Betty's house, of course—and that reminded her of chasing Jonah and the dogs through the blizzard, of meeting X, of meeting Stan. It was just like Dallas said: everything was connected.

Silver Teardrop lay under a frozen creek bed that ran alongside the road. There was nowhere to park. Dallas drove an extra half mile, and finally the road widened enough for him to pull over. For the next five minutes, he blared Kanye West's song "Monster" at top volume, which seemed to be a pre-caving ritual of his. Zoe stood outside the truck, watching in amusement as Dallas duplicated every move from the video. Finally, the tune ended. Dallas emerged from the truck, red-faced and beaming.

"*Woot!*" he shouted, not so much to Zoe as to the universe.

He gestured for Zoe to follow him. He walked to the back of the 4Runner and opened it with a flourish.

"Behold!" he said.

Zoe couldn't speak for a moment: It was a gearhead's paradise. There were beautiful coils of rope hanging from hooks. There were drills, bolt kits, harnesses, ascenders and descenders, caving packs with holes in the bottom so water could drain out. There were folding shovels and gleaming ice axes. There were whole unopened boxes of Clif Bars and CamelBaks full of water. Everything was meticulously curated and cared for. Everything was *shiny*. Zoe's dad always used as little gear as he could get away with: he liked to improvise, and he was kind of a slob. Dallas had four identical orange helmets. He even had a stack of jumpsuits, which were a lighter shade of orange. They appeared to have been ironed.

"Turns out I have a little OCD," said Dallas.

Zoe didn't want him to feel self-conscious.

"No more than, like, a serial killer," she said.

Dallas took a jumpsuit from the pile, popped it open, and stepped into it. The suit used to have a breast pocket, but Dallas had removed it so it wouldn't fill with mud when he crawled. The front of the suit had tiny holes in the shape of a U where the pocket used to be.

Next, Dallas inspected the row of helmets. Zoe wondered how he could even tell them apart. Finally, he picked one, rigged it with an LED headlamp, and strapped it on. He was square-jawed and handsome in his orange helmet-and-suit ensemble.

"How do I look?" he said.

"Like a Lego," said Zoe.

She put on her own jumpsuit, which had been crushed in a ball at the bottom of her duffle. It was off-white, and so stained with mud that it looked like an abstract painting. Her helmet came next. Her dad had given it to her when she turned 15. It was dark blue, and scarred from low ceilings and falling rock. It was slightly too big and poorly padded. Whenever she nodded, it did a dance on her head.

For ten minutes, Dallas and Zoe geared up. Everything Dallas owned seemed to have been scientifically engineered—even his gloves looked like something you'd use to repair a space station. Zoe's stuff was all shabby crap from the land of misfit clothes. But Dallas didn't judge her, and she didn't embarrass easily, anyway. She pulled on her yellow dish-washing gloves like they were made of silk.

Zoe and Dallas double-checked their headlamps, their batteries, their backup batteries, their drill. Dallas got pissed when he realized that he'd forgotten to bring walkie-talkies. Fortunately, Zoe had thought to pack a pair. She dug them out of her duffel, and handed him one.

"Please come prepared next time," she said.

Dallas locked up the 4Runner—*cheep! cheep!*—and they hiked back down the road, trudging along stiffly under all the layers of clothes. After a few minutes, they came around a bend and saw some deer in the snow up ahead. The deer's eyes were wet and nervous. Their coats, thin and red in summer, had turned coarse and gray to survive the cold—and hunting season. They stared at Dallas and Zoe, then darted away, jumping high like horses on a carousel.

IN THE SILENCE, ZOE'S anxiety began to seep back in. She tried to clear her mind, but couldn't. A story her dad had told her when she was 10 or 11 came back to her and the minute she remembered it, she couldn't shake it. The story was about British cavers in the '60s who got caught underground when a freak thunderstorm flooded their cave.

She'd never forgotten the details: Rescuers came running from their pubs. They built a dam, but it kept collapsing so they had to hold it together with their bodies. They worked through the night to pump out the water. Finally, they wriggled into a small tunnel to search for survivors. Deep in the cave, the lead rescuer found the bodies of two dead cavers blocking the way. He had to crawl over them to find the others. They were just corpses now, too. The last of them had squeezed into a tight fissure in a desperate hunt for air. The lead rescuer began his retreat, knowing all was lost. The volunteers behind him were crying and throwing up in the passageway. He said to the first one he saw, "Go back, Jim. They're dead."

Dallas noticed that Zoe wasn't talking.

"What are you thinking about?" he said.

"The British cavers," she said.

"The dead guys in the tunnel—*those* British cavers?" he said. There wasn't a caving legend that Dallas didn't know. "That's a horrible thing to think about, dawg. Hit Delete right now. Seriously."

Zoe shoved the story into the Do Not Open box. It didn't want to go in—it wrestled with her—but eventually it did. She imagined herself sitting on the box to keep the thing trapped.

But still she felt unsettled as they trudged through the wilderness. Between the silence and the snow and the burned-out forests sliding past, Zoe felt like she and Dallas were characters in some postapocalyptic movie—survivors of a deadly virus that only they were immune to.

Dallas didn't seem remotely nervous. He never did. He seemed stoked, giddy almost, oblivious. They were within arm's reach of each other, but still miles apart.

"It's this way," said Dallas, who'd been staring down at his GPS. He thrust a fist in the air: *"Woot!"*

He led her to the side of the road, and down the steep embankment. If there had ever been a trail, it was buried now. The slope was piled with fallen trees, which plows had shoved off the road. Their trunks were charred and blistered.

Zoe struggled to climb over the logs. The weight of her pack kept pulling her off balance.

Getting to the cave was supposed to be the easy part.

Dallas was just ahead of her. She tried to step exactly where he stepped. She started to sweat under her clothes. She was near the bottom of the embankment when her snowshoe landed on a rotten log.

She had a sick feeling, like the ground was disappearing.

It *was*.

She pitched forward, her arms churning helplessly.

Dallas was still babbling. He had no idea. Zoe fell toward his back, arms outstretched and grabbing at the air. A branch shot past her face. It missed her eye by an inch.

She crashed against Dallas.

He gave a grunt of surprise, then fell forward, too. The whole thing took only an instant. Less than an instant.

The sky spun above Zoe's head. She landed on her side in the snow. She heard a sharp, dry *crack*—the sound of a bone splintering—and waited for the pain, but it never came.

Dallas lay in a heap a few feet away. He'd tried to break his fall with his hands. He was clutching his wrist. His mouth was an O, and he was about to scream.

DALLAS INSISTED THAT ZOE could crush Silver Teardrop without him. He was *not* going to wreck the day for her. It was too

225

huge. He popped some Advil from his pack, and sat on his butt at the bottom of the embankment, his wrist plunged in the snow to stop the swelling. He swore he was fine—that it was probably just a sprain and that he'd only screamed because of the shock. Zoe argued with him, and lost.

They followed the creek bed awhile, and soon the GPS informed them that they'd arrived at their destination. Zoe saw nothing resembling a cave. The entrance had to be deep under snow.

She and Dallas removed their snowshoes and climbed down to the frozen creek. A couple hundred feet up, it ran into a rocky hill and slipped underground. Zoe helped Dallas off with his pack, took out a folding shovel, and began to clear the mouth of the cave. Dallas insisted on helping. He'd filled a pocket with snow, and he kept his right hand buried in it as he hacked away at the entrance with an ice ax. They worked slowly to conserve their energy. They didn't talk much, although at one point, Dallas looked at Zoe's yellow rubber gloves, shook his head, and said, "Can I please give you a better pair? I promise to give yours back if we have to wash any dishes."

Zoe's fingers were already so cold they seemed to be burning. She nodded so forcefully that Dallas cracked up.

When they'd cleared the snow, they found a dense wall of ice blocking the mouth of the cave, as if defending it from intruders. They chipped at it for half an hour. Zoe's arm began to ache. Shards of ice flew up at her face. But as the entrance of the cave emerged from the ice, she found she was grinning like an idiot. She locked eyes with Dallas. Even injured, he had the same loopy, blissed-out expression.

"Right?!" he said happily.

The map hadn't done justice to how narrow the entrance was. It

226

was shaped roughly like a keyhole, and not much more than two feet wide.

"Man, that's tight," said Dallas. "I couldn't have gotten in there without scraping my junk off."

"Thank you for that image," said Zoe.

She and Dallas crouched down, and their headlamps flooded the tunnel. The ceiling was slick with condensation, the floor littered with broken rock and bubbles of calcite that cavers called popcorn. But none of this was as troubling as the fact that the tunnel never seemed to widen. Zoe would have to crawl down a meandering, 50-foot corridor *on her side*. Neither of them spoke, and while they were not speaking, a giant wood rat wandered into the light and stared up at them indifferently.

"You got this," said Dallas.

"I know," said Zoe. She thought of the tattoo on his shoulder. "'Never don't stop,' right?"

"Exactly!" said Dallas. "'Never, *ever* don't stop!'"

He hesitated.

"Unless," he said.

Zoe had never seen Dallas hesitate.

"Do *not* mess with my head two seconds before I go in there," she said. "Or I will scrape your junk off myself."

"No, no, no, you got this," said Dallas. "*But.* If you get in there and there's a shit-ton of running water, you gotta get out. Promise me you won't get all intrepid."

Zoe promised, but they both knew she was lying.

She put on her seat harness and descender. Dallas double-checked them so carefully it actually made her *more* nervous. He was acting like she was about to jump out of a plane.

Zoe tested her walkie-talkie. All she had to do now was stop stalling.

She took a last breath of fresh air.

THE FIRST TEN FEET of the cave were furry with ice. Her father's voice popped into her head, like a cartoon bubble: "That's *hoarfrost*, Zoe! Also known as *white frost*. Come on—know your frosts!"

She ducked into the tunnel, and lay down on her side. She shimmied forward like a snake, pushing a fat coil of rope and a small pack in front of her.

The passage was insanely claustrophobic. The walls were like a clamp.

She made it about five feet before the back of her neck was slick with sweat. She could already hear the waterfall pounding up ahead. She thought of the British cavers who drowned—she couldn't help it—and of the men who rushed from their pubs and tried to save them.

"Go back, Jim. They're dead."

She had to focus. That's the first thing you learned as a caver— you focus or you get hurt. Actually, the *first* thing you learned was that it was nuts to go caving without at least two other people. That way, if someone got injured, one person could stay with her and the other could run for help.

She twisted her legs so she could push with both feet. She dragged her body over the rubble and calcite. Even through a wet suit and four layers of clothes, she could feel them bite.

When the tunnel grew even narrower, she filled her lungs with air, then released it so her chest would shrink and she could keep crawling. She made it another five or six feet. She had to crane her neck to see where she was going. Her helmet bobbled and scraped along the ground. Every so often it scooped up a stone and she had to shake her head until it tumbled back out. In the distance, the waterfall grew louder. She'd forgotten how ferocious water sounded in an enclosed space—how it got your heart drumming even if you weren't afraid.

And then it struck her: she didn't *have* to be afraid. She was cold, her body was tense as a wire, she felt like she was crawling into an animal's throat—but she didn't have to be scared. She knew how to do this. She *loved* doing this.

And she wasn't even alone, not really. She had a whole support team in her brain: Dallas, Jonah, X. Even her dad, in a way.

Especially her dad.

"You're freakin' awesome! You can do this! You're my girl!"

She arrived at a bend in the tunnel and wriggled around it. She imagined she was a superhero who could transform into water or molten steel—who could flow through the rock and then reconstitute at will.

Her stupid grin was back.

Suddenly, the walkie-talkie trilled. By the time Zoe finished the laborious task of taking off her glove and fishing the thing out of her pack, it had stopped. Annoyed, she called Dallas back.

"I'm being molten steel!" she said. "What could you possibly want?"

There was a pause during which Dallas presumably tried to figure out what the hell she was talking about. When he answered, his voice was so distorted that she had to work to fill in the missing words.

"Where (you) at?" he said. "You killin' it? Can you (hear the) water?"

"Of *course* I'm killin' it," she told him. "Go away!"

She slid the walkie-talkie back into her pack, wiped her nose, and put her glove back on. Even in that brief interval, her hand had become stiff with the cold, and she had to flex her fingers to get some life back in them.

Just ahead, a thousand daddy longlegs hung from the ceiling in a clump, their legs packed in such a dense mass that they looked like dirty hair. Zoe was used to spiders, but she was surprised to see them so late in February. She slid under them and squinted up. She heard her father's voice again: "Daddy longlegs aren't *spiders*, Zoe! They're Opiliones! Come on—this is Insects 101!"

When she was small—five, maybe? six?—her dad gave her an ecstatic lecture about this stuff. There were two things she'd always remembered. The first was how her father's face glowed with excitement. The second was a gruesome tidbit about how daddy longlegs could play dead by detaching one of their legs to trick predators. They'd leave it behind—still twitching!—while they crawled in the opposite direction. Only her father could have thought that was a cool thing to tell a little kid. And yet it kind of *was*.

Zoe shook her head and smiled. Her helmet did its dance.

She'd already lost track of how long she'd been in the cave. Time had a way of shattering underground. The waterfall roared even louder now. She kept crawling in the dark, telling herself to focus.

The tunnel finally widened, then stopped at the edge of the giant drop that led down to the Chandelier Room. Zoe rolled onto her stomach. She lowered her head to the ground, and exhaled gratefully, like a swimmer who had just barely made it back to the beach.

Her neck ached. The left side of her body felt ravaged. She dreaded looking at the bruises. Were superheroes supposed to get this tired?

She rotated her head slowly, her headlamp sweeping the walls. There were bolts on either side of her that another caver had left in the rock—a primary and a backup. She unspooled her rope and rigged up with loops like bunny ears. She struck the bolts with a buckle and leaned close to hear the solid, reassuring *ping*.

There were still five feet between Zoe and the giant shaft that plunged down to the Chandelier Room. She pushed herself up into a sort of Gollum-like crouch, and inched toward it, hoping the waterfall wouldn't be as ferocious as it sounded.

The shaft was roughly circular. Its walls were jagged and embedded with pockets of ice that glinted in the light of Zoe's headlamp. Off to her right, an underground river burst through an icy hole in the wall, then tumbled down, like Rapunzel's hair. It wasn't the trickle that she and Dallas had hoped for. She was glad he wasn't there to say, *Forget it, dawg, this is waaaay too intrepid.* She was sure that if she rappelled straight down, she could avoid most of the spray.

She tested the bolts in the wall again, though it didn't tell her anything definitive: if they were going to pop out, they were going to pop out when she was hanging in midair. She hooked herself onto the rope. She took a deep breath and turned around.

She stepped backward off the edge.

She could have cried with joy when the soles of her boots found the wall. She began to descend. Slowly. Cautiously. Just a couple of feet at a time. Her right hand never left the brake. A cold cloud of mist from the waterfall enveloped her. The noise was immense. Her heart thumped even louder. It was like she was being chased.

She tried to ignore the waterfall, but it was shooting out of the wall with the force of a fire hydrant. Water splashed her boots as she descended. The spray crept up her body, drenching her legs, her arms, her chest. She was grateful for the wet suit beneath her clothes. She fought the impulse to drop faster, to drop farther, to free-fall to the bottom.

The water found her neck now. Her face. It was so frigid it felt like a claw against her skin. She twisted away. She needed a new plan. She needed to get farther away from the falls.

Zoe began inching sideways, away from the torrent. She was descending at an angle now, like a pendulum. The muscles in her legs were objecting, tensing up, sending out warning shots of pain. The rope was scraping against the rocks. Zoe crept five or six feet sideways, but still the spray lashed at her. If she could just make it a couple more feet. She reached out with the toe of her right boot.

It landed on ice.

She slipped. Her heart flew into her mouth.

She felt herself being yanked back toward the falls, her body twirling like a top. She couldn't stop—couldn't find anything to grab. Up above her, the rope sawed against the edge of the cliff.

Zoe was swinging so hard she was pulled under the falls. The water pounded her back, furious and cold. It banged on her rickety helmet. It soaked every part of her. She tried to move, to push off the wall, to do something, anything, but her body was rigid with shock, and suddenly there was a terrible flower blooming in her head.

This is how my father died—terrified and swinging on a rope.

At last, the rope pulled her back out of the water, as if it had all been gravity's way of telling her that the only way down was straight. Zoe hung suspended for a moment, tears clouding her eyes. She felt shaken, stupid, humiliated. The walkie-talkie trilled in her pack. Did Dallas somehow know what had happened? Had she shouted and not known it? Had he heard her? He couldn't have.

She didn't answer. Dallas would hear the shakiness in her voice and tell her to come out. She was fine now. She was *fine*. But for a sliver of a moment it'd felt like the bottom had dropped out of the world and she was hurtling downward.

She took the glove off her right hand, tearing at the Velcro with her teeth. She dropped it into the darkness.

She inspected her harness and her brake. The metal was so cold it seemed electrically charged. She brushed the ice off everything as best she could. Her heart was galloping.

She couldn't get the thought of her father out of her head.

This is how he died.

She found herself staring at her bare right hand, weirdly fascinated by it, as if it didn't belong to her.

There'd been blood and skin on her dad's rope. Was it from his hands? From his *neck*? Had the rope wound around his throat? Had it choked him—suffocated him—like he was a baby trying to be born?

She was sobbing now. She would have made an awful noise if there hadn't been a torrent of water spilling along with her tears.

THE WALKIE-TALKIE RANG again, and she answered it angrily: "Can you *please* leave me alone, please!"

"Can I (what)?" said Dallas.

The explosions of static were worse than ever.

"Can you please leave me alone for a second!" she said.

"Can I *what* for a *what*?" said Dallas.

Screw it, she thought.

Zoe dropped the walkie-talkie now, too. She didn't hear it land, but pictured it smashing on the rock down below, the battery springing out and skittering across the floor of the cave. She turned off her headlamp. She just wanted to hang in the dark a moment. She didn't care about the spray from the waterfall. She couldn't get any wetter.

The darkness was absolute. It was as if the water, with its astonishing noise, had decimated all her other senses.

She thought of her dad. She thought of X. She thought of how they'd both be *extremely* concerned about the borderline-crazy adventure she was embarked on. It was so strange that they would never meet. One had exited her life just as the other entered it. They'd brushed past each other, missing each other by moments.

Zoe twisted slowly on the rope in the dark. She concentrated on the water now. She tried to pick it apart, tried to hear every tiny sound in the middle of the roar. She let the relentlessness of the noise drive all thoughts out of her head—to douse them like fires, one after the other. Her heartbeat began to slow. Her breathing got deeper.

Later—she couldn't have said how long it had been—she switched her headlamp back on, and continued her descent. The ice in the rock sparkled all the way down.

THE CHANDELIER ROOM WAS breathtaking—Zoe's eyes didn't know what to devour first. In the middle of the chamber, there was a giant boulder encased in translucent ice. The waterfall struck it dead center, then splashed in every direction like a demented fountain. The walls were coated in ice as well. Here, though, the ice was as thick and wavy as cake frosting, and it glowed with the sleepy, blue-green light of an aquarium. Every 20 feet or so, there were massive, almost melted-looking columns of rock. (Her father wouldn't shut up today: "They're not *columns of rock*, Zoe! They're *limestone pillars*! Come on—respect your rocks!")

Zoe stepped carefully on the frozen floor, running her bare hands along every surface, then shoving them inside her jacket to warm. She was transfixed. Everything in the chamber seemed as ancient as the earth, yet somehow still evolving, still breathing, still being formed. And just when Zoe thought the Chandelier Room couldn't get any more mesmerizing . . .

She looked up.

The ceiling was hung with icicles of every conceivable size. It looked like an upside-down forest, like some massive musical instrument that had yet to be invented. It was gorgeous. She swept her eyes along the ice, greedily. Her headlamp made the whole thing glow.

It was only when Zoe felt something *crunch* under her feet—a shard of plastic from the walkie-talkie—that she remembered Dallas. He'd be up there, pacing around with his injured hand in his pocket, possibly freaking out. The walkie-talkie was busted beyond repair but she collected all the bits she could find and stuffed them in her pack.

She returned to where the rope hung down the shaft. It was covered with ice, so she thwacked it against the wall like she was beating a rug. Looking up, she could see fragments of the water—little jets and beads—catch the light of her headlamp as they fell.

She hooked herself onto the rope once more, and began to rise.

ZOE CRAWLED OUT OF the cave 20 minutes later, dizzy and drenched. The crystals of frost at the entrance floated down on her shoulders like a good-bye present.

She struggled to her feet, dropped her pack in the snow, and gulped in as much air as her lungs could hold. Her legs felt rickety. She wobbled like a newborn colt for the first few steps. Otherwise, she felt lighter in every way. She felt lifted.

Dallas stepped toward her, beaming and offering an orange towel from his pack. He seemed not to know if he should hug her, so Zoe threw her arms around him and squeezed gratefully.

"Thank you for bringing me here," said Zoe.

She worried it wasn't sufficient so she added, in his own language, "You're a full-on baller and a boss—thank you!"

She felt exhilarated. The air was lighting up her blood.

"Okay, okay," said Dallas, breaking off the hug. "You're starting to feel attracted to me. I *warned* you."

"How long was I down there?" she said. "Half an hour?"

"Two and a half hours," he said.

"Two and a half *hours?*" said Zoe. "I'm so sorry."

"Don't be, dawg," said Dallas. "Shit like this is special."

Zoe took a picture of them in front of the entrance to the cave so she could Snapchat it to Val when she had a signal again. She scrawled a caption across the top in yellow:

Cave: Silver Teardrop! Crushed by: Zoe!

Dallas's wrist was still buried in his pocket. He wouldn't show it to Zoe, so she assumed it was swollen and purple. He promised he was fine. He insisted they still go check out Black Teardrop. Maybe she was being selfish, but Zoe needed to see the place her father died, no matter how wet she was—she needed to see it *right now*, while the adrenaline was still racing around in her blood.

"We're just going to look today, right?" said Dallas. "We're just gonna say hello, or whatever? You're not gonna trick me, and rig up?"

"No tricks," said Zoe. "But you have to promise that we'll come back if the police won't do their job."

"With a blanket," said Dallas. "For Jonah. I remember."

"Was that a promise?" said Zoe.

"That was a promise," said Dallas.

"Because now you know I'm not scared of any cave," said Zoe.

Dallas's snowshoes thumped softly behind her.

"I knew that already," he said.

THE HIKE TO BLACK Teardrop was short, but exhausting. The snow rose in front of them in huge, untouched swells. Zoe could feel her back and legs complaining to each other, ready to mutiny.

Her body recognized the cave before she did. She felt the storm gathering again in her stomach as they clomped over a final snowy rise, and looked down to see the rocky gash in the earth. Black Teardrop was ringed with a chain-link fence now, and hung with warning signs. The fence was about eight feet tall—but more or less useless. The wind had blown it back and forth, so that whole sections tilted crazily, like loose teeth.

Zoe was surprised by how ordinary the cave appeared. It was just a hole in the ground. Still, the longer she stared at it, the more it seemed to be surrounded, not just by a fence, but by some kind of force field. She stared at it longer than she should have.

Dallas had caught up, and stood silently beside her. The cave lay a couple hundred feet in front of them. Zoe found it hard to move forward.

"I'd go with you," said Dallas, "but I can't get over that fence with one hand."

"No worries," she said. "I got this."

Zoe clomped down the hill. The snow was powdery and deep. She paused at the fence. She didn't know what she was supposed to feel, but what she *did* feel was a confused rush of emotions, each of them struggling to get to the front of the line: sadness, fury, fear.

Zoe tried to give each of the emotions a moment in her heart. Wisps of warm air, which had been trapped inside the cave for months, slipped out the entrance. It looked like a mouth exhaling smoke. It was as if there were a dragon in there, rather than her father's body.

She dropped her pack, unstrapped her snowshoes, and climbed the fence. Once again, she could tell that the muscles in her legs hated the idea. Still, they obeyed, and soon she was dropping over the other side. Now the only problem was that she didn't know why she had come, or what she intended to do.

She forced herself forward. On the ground, close to the entrance, there were two objects just barely peeking out of the snow. She knelt and brushed them off.

A stone crucifix. A stone Buddha. They were lying on their backs, staring up at the sky.

Someone had been there since the search for her dad's body. Someone had visited. Someone had left the statues as a gift.

Her mother.

Only her mother would have brought a Buddha *and* a cross. When she said she'd never stopped loving Zoe's father, she'd been telling the truth. Then why wouldn't she let the police bring his body home?

The statues seemed to have fallen from an outcropping of rock above the entrance to the cave. Zoe picked up the crucifix, shocked by the weight of it. She wiped it clean, then climbed up the rocks, and set it back on its shelf. She did the same with the Buddha.

The statues radiated calm, and seemed to be urging Zoe to find some peace of her own. She wanted to say something. But what? She was still angry that her father had been so reckless. When he fell into the cave, it was like he'd pulled all of them down with him. But she did love him. Maybe there was a way to say all that?

She closed her eyes, and tried to find the words.

"I love you for everything you were, Dad," she said finally. "I forgive you for everything you weren't."

"PS," she added. "Jonah is going nuts without you, and I'm in love with somebody from out of town."

She opened her eyes, wishing she could do more.

An idea lit up her brain. She searched the ground and found a piece of bark in the snow. She asked Dallas to toss her the multi-tool knife from her pack.

Zoe scratched and gouged at the bark for five minutes. By the time she was finished, she was sweating, her arm was aching, and she'd started to lose the feeling in her hands. But she was proud of her handiwork. She set it on the ledge with the statues, and took a selfie to text to Jonah later. She'd even put it on Instagram so the police would see it and know how serious she was about going into the cave, if she had to.

She'd carved a message to her father into wood:

I WILL COME BACK.

FOURTEEN

DALLAS SWORE UP AND DOWN he could drive the stick shift with just his left hand, but Zoe said she'd defied death enough for one day. She steered the 4Runner down the rutted roads and out of the wilderness.

The instant they hit Columbia Falls—and civilization—their cell phones finally picked up a signal, as if they'd just splashed down from space. Zoe pulled over to text her mother. Seeing the Buddha and cross her mom had left at the cave had softened her a little. She wasn't ready to forgive her mother entirely, but she figured she deserved to know that she was okay. So she texted her the same one-word message she'd sent on the night of the blizzard: *Safe.* As she pressed Send, she felt not just déjà vu, but amazement at everything that had happened since she saw X hurtling toward her and Stan across the ice.

Her mother answered before Zoe even had a chance to put the phone back on Dallas's dashboard.

Thank god! she wrote. *Thank EVERY god! OX!*

"OX" was her mom's version of "XO." Zoe had begged her to stop using it because every time it popped up on her phone she thought, for a split second, that her mother was calling her an ox.

I'm still pretty pissed at you, Zoe texted back.

Her mother began typing. The "..." bubbled up. As always, it seemed to promise something profound.

I know you are, Zo. I get it & don't blame you. I've been a wreck—so worried about you getting hurt that I haven't been able to eat/breathe/operate heavy machinery. I'm at the hot springs. Come and let me hug you?

Maybe. Not sure. Let me see if I can get un-pissed.

Please-please-please?

OK, OK, I will—just so you don't start sending me emojis. OX (as you wd say).

Thank you. And do NOT make fun of the ox! :)

PIPING HOT SPRINGS WAS a run-down old place nestled in a hillside above Flathead Valley. It boasted two pools. (Literally: there was a sagging banner out front that read, We Have Two Pools!) Both were outdoors and fed by rejuvenating, mineral-enriched waters that shot up through the earth. One was an ordinary-looking swimming pool kept at 84 degrees. The other, a giant, kidney-shaped concrete-bottomed lake, was always precisely 104 degrees. Zoe's mom was a conscientious manager, but the owners lived out of state and were always on the verge of selling the business and didn't want to sink any more money into it. So every season Piping Hot Springs looked a little grubbier, a little more desperate. The green fiberglass slides were rickety and rusted. The colored pennants decorating the walls were faded. The enormous '70s-style digital clocks were all malfunctioning so that, rather than telling the time, they seemed to be making announcements in Chinese.

These days, the rich tourists all went to spas where they got microfiber bathrobes and shiny wire baskets with lotions and loofahs. The more adventurous tourists drove up to Canada, where hot, swirling pockets of water appeared, as if by magic, in the middle of freezing rivers. Piping Hot Springs mostly attracted elderly couples who sat against the wall of the big pool with their arms draped sweetly over each other's shoulders. There were also some European tourists and some drunk twentysomethings who thought the place was hysterical. Zoe would have been embarrassed about Piping Hot Springs except that she'd never seen anyone leave without looking blissed-out and dreamy and pink. The waters worked.

It was early evening by the time Dallas had his wrist wrapped at an urgent-care place on the highway and then dropped Zoe off at the hot springs. Zoe caught her reflection in the door on the way in: she looked like hell. Beneath X's overcoat, her clothes were wrinkled and torn. Thanks to the caving helmet, her hair looked like roadkill.

Her mom sat perched behind the front desk, folding towels and watching for her. She stood up the minute Zoe stepped inside. They inched toward each other shyly, like a couple that's forgotten how to dance.

Zoe let herself be hugged but made a point of not hugging back. Her mother ignored the awkwardness.

"Oh my god, that *coat*," she said. "Is that X's?"

"Yeah," said Zoe. "It *heals* you. The minute you put it on, it starts, like, erasing your bruises and mending your bones."

"Seriously?" said her mother, her eyes wide.

"No, it's just a coat," said Zoe. "It's superwarm, though."

Her mom laughed and swatted her on the shoulder.

"Look, I need to apologize to you," she said. "Come fold some towels with me, and let me try?"

They sat with a basket from the dryer between them. Zoe remembered folding towels with Bert after he'd become senile. He'd been obsessed with how warm and fluffy they were, how clean they smelled. She had to stop him from shoving his face into them.

"So," her mother said now, "do you want the short, medium, or long apology?"

"Start with the short one," said Zoe.

"I love you, and I'm sorry," said her mother.

"Not feeling it," said Zoe. She smoothed a towel with her hand. It crackled with electricity. "Try the medium one."

"I love you, and I'm sorry—and I was wrong to tell the police to leave your dad's body in the cave," her mother said.

"Why *did* you?" said Zoe. "I don't get it."

Her mother sighed.

"I'm just going to blurt it out, like you would, okay?" she said. "I think maybe your dad killed himself, Zo."

Zoe said nothing.

"He was really unhappy toward the end," her mother continued. "He felt like a failure. He hated who he was. And he thought I'd stopped loving him, which . . . It kills me that he thought that." She paused. "I'm only telling you all this because you've asked me so many times, and I think you can handle it."

"I can," said Zoe. "Don't stop."

"Look, I don't know anything about caving, but it seems like he was too smart to die in some freak accident," her mother said. "So I thought maybe he killed himself, and I didn't . . ." She paused again, and pressed her hands against her eyes. "I didn't want the cops to go in there and prove I was right."

Zoe leaned forward. She hugged her mother for real this time.

"I *know* Dad wouldn't have done that," she said. "He just messed up. He stopped to take a picture—and he fell. When I was in the cave today, I could picture exactly what happened. I could *feel* it."

Her mother nodded.

"I'm sure you're right," she said. "I want you to be right."

"I *am* right," said Zoe. "So you'll tell the police to go get him now? I kicked ass today, but it was scary as shit—and Silver Teardrop is nothing compared to Dad's cave. I don't actually want to die doing this."

Before her mother could respond, an elderly, German-sounding couple came through the door. Zoe's mom took their money, and handed them flip-flops, towels, and locker-room keys. She and Zoe watched them shuffle down the stairs, arm in arm, and didn't speak until they'd descended out of sight.

"I'll talk to the police," she told Zoe. "I promise I will. And I'm sorry I didn't tell you all this sooner." She paused. "Being a grown-up is the worst," she said. "You'll be better at it than me. I can already tell."

HER MOTHER'S SHIFT WAS supposed to end at six o'clock, but at 5:58 an employee she referred to as the Flaker called to say that he had weird spots on his tongue and *was it cool if he bailed?* Her mom was exhausted—she didn't even have the energy to brush her hair back when it fell in her eyes—and her shoulders sagged at the news. Zoe was still on a high from crushing Silver Teardrop. She offered to cover the shift herself. Her mother did the whole I-couldn't-ask-you-to-do-that thing, but Zoe said, "Shut up, I'm doing it. Shut up, I'm doing it"—and so on until her mother gave in.

Zoe's mom told her the pools were basically empty: there was the German couple, who were now making out in the big pool, and a single dad throwing a birthday party for his beastly six-year-old daughter in the smaller one. She reminded her that there was a lifeguard on duty at each pool, and that if she couldn't find Lance, the security guard, he was probably in the locker room doing Pilates. Her mom told her that she could close up early if the place emptied out—and, on a sort of creepy note, that she should watch the security monitors because they'd been having some sneak-ins.

"There's one other thing," she said. She opened her laptop, which lay on the desk in front of Zoe. "I was going to let this wait until morning because I wasn't sure you could handle it after the cave and everything. But you're going to want to see it."

Zoe's mother called up a news story. She swiveled the computer toward Zoe, and took a step back.

"It looks like X found Stan," she said.

Zoe's eyes raced over the article:

> A man murdered in a hair salon in Wheelwright, Texas, earlier this week has been identified as Stan Manggold ... Mr. Manggold, 47, was a native of Virginia . . . He was wanted by police . . . The coroner's report indicates that Mr. Manggold died of blunt-

force trauma to the neck when his body was thrown headfirst into a mirror above one of the stylist's stations . . . Hairdressers described the assailant as an agitated, black-haired Caucasian between the ages of 18 and 21. He was said to be wearing dark boots, black pants, and a purple cowboy shirt. Police have released an artist's sketch, but have no leads at this time.

Purple cowboy shirt? thought Zoe.

She clicked on the link to the sketch.

The mouth was all wrong. The eyes didn't have enough depth. Still, there was something about the drawing—the long, wavy hair, the bruises on the cheekbones—that evoked X so powerfully that Zoe felt the blood rise in her cheeks.

She shut the computer and pushed it away.

"It's over now," her mother whispered. "The craziness is over. X, the cave—everything. We're going to be okay."

But Zoe didn't want the craziness to be over. She wanted X back. She couldn't help but hope that now that the lords had Stan in their clutches, they might let X out to hunt more souls.

ZOE'S MOM TOLD ZOE she'd pick her up later, and left her sitting behind the desk idly eating yogurt pretzels and watching the bank of snowy, out-of-date security monitors. The single dad ushered the flock of six-year-olds into the night. The old German couple eventually wandered out, too, the wife's hand on the husband's butt. Nothing else happened for hours.

Zoe sent Val ten texts to pass the time. Three of them were about caving, five were about X, and two were about yogurt pretzels. Val must have been with Gloria—on the weekends, they often got in bed with a ton of food, hacked into Val's brother's Tinder account, and swiped right on all the girls they thought were hot— because she wrote *Can't talk* and (when Zoe wouldn't leave her alone), *New phone who dis.*

After that, it seemed as if even time itself had gotten itchy and bored, and decided to nap. Zoe padded down the damp hallway toward the pools, and told one of the lifeguards he could go home. That killed about ten minutes. She returned upstairs and stretched her legs, which ached from the cave. That killed about eight.

As Zoe dragged herself back to the front desk, she cast her eyes over the monitors. Everything was empty. The halls and stairways were newly mopped. The vending machines glowed silently. A ghostly cloud of vapor hung over the pools.

She was about to sit when her eye caught on something.

The upper left-hand monitor. The big pool.

Somebody had snuck in.

The man's back was to her. He was in the water, but wearing a knit hat pulled down low over his ears. The tiniest bit of scruffy hair spilled out from under it.

Zoe called Lance on the locker-room phone—he sounded out of breath from Pilates, as her mother had predicted—and told him to kick the guy out. She checked the monitor again. She saw Lance come into the frame and call out to the guy in the water. The guy didn't move. He ignored Lance entirely—which was not a thing Lance sat still for.

Lance was a preposterously big, broad dude. He lived for

confrontations. His only complaint about being a security guard was that no one had the guts to stand up to him. More than once, Zoe had seen him swat at a fly and say, "Yeah, you *better* run."

She watched as Lance went to the edge of the water and knelt on one knee, like the former football player that he was. Zoe closed her eyes. She just wanted to go home. She didn't want to watch Lance administer a beatdown.

When she opened them again, she got a jolt—Lance was staring right at her in the security camera. His face filled the screen. He gestured for her to come down to the pool.

Zoe's stomach clenched. She slipped on X's coat, locked the front door, and walked to the stairs as slowly as she could.

By the time she made it outside, the stranger had swum to the far side of the pool. He was obscured by the darkness and the rising steam. He was just an outline, really—a head, shoulders, and hat glinting above the water.

Lance stood by the door, looking annoyed.

"What's going on?" said Zoe.

"The dude says he knows you," said Lance.

Zoe peered at the man in the water. The mist looked eerie tonight. It curled around him like a wreath—as if he'd summoned it. She didn't know the guy. No way. She was about to tell Lance to get rid of him when the stranger spoke.

He said just one sentence, but it stopped her cold: "Your name's Zoe—and you love X."

Zoe walked slowly around the pool.

She drew near to the man. He had dropped some clothes by the water. She couldn't quite make them out in the dark. They lay tangled like a nest of snakes.

248

She tried to think of something to say but the stranger spoke up again—and stunned her a second time.

"That's X's coat, right?" he said. "Kinda big for you."

She crouched for a better look at his face. He was in his late 20s. Handsome in a battered sort of way—but shaky somehow. Unhealthy. The whites of his eyes were streaked with red.

He smiled up at her. His friendliness made him seem all the more menacing.

She inspected him closely, without speaking.

He had dark, crescent-shaped bruises near his eyes.

They looked like X's bruises.

"Who are you?" she said.

"I'm Eric," he said. "'Sup?"

The sunniness of his voice was freaky.

"X never mentioned anybody named Eric," she said.

"X doesn't use my real name," he said.

He drew an arm out of the water—he had a wild sleeve of tattoos almost identical to X's—and lifted his hat the tiniest bit. Zoe winced. His forehead was horrifically bruised.

"He calls me Banger."

HE'D COME WITH A message from X, he said.

Zoe couldn't tell from his face if it was good news or bad. The anticipation was awful.

She told Lance and the remaining lifeguard that they could leave. They looked shocked. Still, they reluctantly headed up the stairs.

Zoe waited for Banger to speak, but he seemed to enjoy her impatience. He was an odd sight in the water. He'd taken off his shirt but he was still wearing his hat and his jeans, which were so drenched they clung to his legs. He floated on his back to the center of the pool, and gazed up at the bright needlework of the stars.

"What's the message?" said Zoe. "Tell me."

Banger smiled, and floated even farther away in the dark, his white belly shining. He never took his eyes off the sky.

She followed him around the pool, picking up dirty towels and stray flip-flops as she went.

"Don't mess with me, Banger," she said. "I don't care if you're dead—I will seriously injure you."

"Can I just swim *one* more minute?" he said. "You know how long it's been since I've felt warm water?"

Zoe felt a twinge of sympathy. She straightened a row of white deck chairs that should have been trashed years ago and went inside.

After ten minutes, Banger climbed out of the pool, put on his shirt and shoes, and joined her. He'd pulled his hat back down over his nightmarish forehead. But he still looked feverish and sickly to Zoe, and then it struck her: he had the Trembling.

"You're supposed to be hunting somebody?" she said.

He turned to her, surprised. He wiped the perspiration from his face with the back of his hand.

"Yeah," he said quietly. "Guy who drove a school bus while he was high on crack. I'll spare you the details."

He drifted around the lobby, inspecting every poster, every piece of furniture, and every knickknack to see what they could tell him about the years that had passed since he was yanked down to the Lowlands. Zoe wished everything in the place wasn't so shabby and old. She asked if he wanted to see her cell phone. His eyes sprang to life. He spent ten minutes playing with the thing, then handed it back with an air of regret, saying, "I had a BlackBerry. Thing *sucked*."

Zoe asked Banger if he was hungry.

"No," he said. "Because I'm dead, if you want to get technical about it. But what are you offering?"

"I've got some seitan and quinoa my mom made," said Zoe.

Banger lifted an eyebrow.

"Those aren't real words," he said.

"There's also junk food in the vending machine," said Zoe.

Now his eyes were shining.

"Are Skittles still a thing?" he said.

Zoe opened the register for cash, then she and Banger trooped downstairs. The vending machines hummed expectantly in the vacant hall. The drink machine was the only new thing in the entire building: it was the science-fiction-y kind that sends a miniature elevator up and over to retrieve your selection. Banger gazed at it in fascination. He agonized about what to buy for five minutes. Zoe found it touching. They returned to the lobby with 14 dollars' worth of energy drinks, candy, chips, and gum.

They sat on the stone floor, the loot piled between them. The night sky had turned from blue to black. Zoe wasn't particularly hungry. Still, she got a kick out of the way Banger devoured the candy. She leaned back on her hands and watched. Eventually, she figured, he'd get around to delivering X's message.

"Sorry I've been jerking you around," he said at last. His face was still pink from the hot pool, his mouth smeared with chocolate. "I know you want to hear about X. It's just that I know once I tell you everything, you're going to get bored of me and kick me out."

"I won't," said Zoe softly. "I don't have anywhere to go. I mean, my boyfriend's in *hell*."

Banger smiled mysteriously.

"Not for long, maybe," he said.

Her heart jumped.

WHEN BANGER FINALLY BEGAN to spill, Zoe could barely take in all the details because her brain was spinning so fast. All she wanted to hear, all she cared about in the world, was finding out whether she'd see X again.

The lords had put him on trial, Banger said. X had shouted them down—he'd questioned their authority!

Banger was shocked that X had it in him.

"I mean, the dude never even talks," he said. "Am I right?"

"Stop it," said Zoe defensively. "He's shy—but he talks!"

"Oooh," said Banger. "Somebody's got a crush."

Zoe blushed, but recovered quickly.

"Do not *even* make fun of my star-crossed supernatural love," she said.

Banger grinned. His teeth, Zoe couldn't help but notice, were chipped and gray.

"Anyway, X does talk *now*," he said. "You must have taught him how to stand up for himself. I can already tell you're a lot cooler than him."

Banger poured half a bag of Skittles into his mouth—a strange decision given that he was already chewing gum. Zoe watched, weirdly mesmerized. How could he swallow the candy without swallowing the gum? She'd never seen anyone even try.

"Were you always this disgusting?" she asked him.

"Oh, *much*, much more so," he said.

His mouth was grinding away like a cement mixer as he continued his story.

The trial had ended in chaos, he said. Finally, one of the lords brought X the verdict.

Here, Banger appeared to get hit with a sugar high and, at the pivotal moment in his story, went on a tangent that Zoe found excruciating.

"The lord that showed up?" he said. "Only cool lord in the whole place. We call him Regent. He treats X like a son, almost. Anyway . . . Sorry. Lost my train of thought." He giggled. "Choo-choo! Choo-choo!" he said. "*Train* of thought—get it?"

Zoe gave him a stern look.

"Tell me what happened," she said. "Or I will take away your candy."

Banger opened his mouth wide to air out his tongue.

"You gotta take a chill pill," he said.

"No one says that anymore," said Zoe.

"Yeah, they didn't even say it when I was alive," said Banger. "But it's a solid expression. Hey, is Taylor Swift still a thing? Is Chipotle still a thing?" He thought for a moment. "Is saying 'is that a thing' still a thing?"

Annoyed, Zoe reached forward and began pulling the candy away from him piece by piece. A Reese's. A PowerBar. A Twix.

"Not the Twix!" said Banger. "It's a candy bar *and* a cookie."

He delivered the rest of the story in a rush:

"They told X he has to collect *one* more soul. If he doesn't screw it up, if he doesn't run crying to you or whatever—he'll be set free. He can leave the Lowlands forever."

Zoe listened as Banger spoke, her heart charging ahead of her.

"Forever?" she said. "I didn't know that was even possible."

"Me neither," said Banger. "I still don't understand half the rules. Friggin' place should have a website."

Zoe stood, so full of energy and emotion that she all but ran across the lobby. She didn't want Banger to see her face.

"I can't believe it," she said. "It's so—it's so *fair*. Because he shouldn't have been there in the first place. He was an innocent little kid and they treated him as if he was some kind of monster like—"

She broke off.

"Like me?" said Banger.

"I'm sorry," said Zoe. "I'm not judging you. All I know is you were a bartender and you stabbed somebody in a bar—I don't even know why. I'm just glad that X doesn't have to suffer anymore."

NEITHER OF THEM SPOKE, as Zoe absorbed the astounding news about X. The only thing that stopped her from tap-dancing around the room was that she felt sorry for Banger. He would *never* be free. He shoved the remaining junk food into his pockets now— she could hear the potato chips splintering into dust as he forced them in—and threw the empty wrappers into the trash.

"You don't have to leave," said Zoe. "Do you? Can you stay a bit?"

Banger seemed touched by the invitation. He smiled, and sat back down on the stone floor. Zoe pointed to a tattoo on his right arm: a weird, spotted animal with a spiked tail and a long curving neck that nearly touched the ground.

"X has that one, too," she said. "I never asked him about it. You have different animals in the Lowlands, huh?"

Banger snorted.

"We actually don't," he said. "The guy who inks all the bounty hunters? He's this senile old dude who's been dead since, like, Pompeii—and he *doesn't remember* what a lot of animals actually look like. This one is supposed to be a giraffe."

"No way," said Zoe.

"Way!" said Banger.

"People don't say that anymore either," said Zoe.

"I figured," said Banger. "Anyway, I wigged out when I saw the tat. This thing with the horns is supposed to be a monkey."

Zoe laughed. She thought of "Never Don't Stop." Would she *ever* date a guy with normal tattoos?

"Does X know they aren't real animals?" she said.

"I never told him," said Banger. "It'd break his heart, and I'm kind of protective of him—because, like you said, he's an innocent. Don't you tell him, either, okay?"

"I won't," said Zoe. She smiled. "I'm kind of protective of him, too."

Zoe glanced at her watch. It was nearly ten. Soon, her mom would be outside honking for her. She didn't want Banger to go. He was her only connection to X, and she liked him. But he had an evil bus driver to find. His eyes had lost their glint. His sugar high had ended. He seemed to be crashing, and was sweating faintly again.

Banger had endangered himself by taking even an hour to deliver X's message—he'd put himself at the mercy of not just the Trembling but the lords. Zoe had been so obsessed with her own feelings that it hadn't occurred to her.

"Are you going to get in trouble for coming here?" she asked.

Banger shrugged.

"Yeah, maybe," he said. "But after the mess I made of my life, they can't do anything to me I don't deserve."

255

He stared down at his hands just for something to look at. They were calloused and bruised and held nothing.

"You know how you said you didn't judge me?" he said.

"Yeah," said Zoe.

"You *should*," he said. "I'm not anything like X. I wish I was."

Zoe didn't know what to say. She waited.

"You know why I stabbed that guy?" said Banger. "Because he was acting like a dipshit, and I was in a bad mood." He paused. "My whole life was a bad mood."

Zoe didn't want to hear any more.

"You don't have to talk about this," she said.

"I want to," Banger said. "After I killed him, I emptied the cash register and bolted. Never spoke to my wife or daughter again—because what would I say?" Again, he paused. "My daughter was autistic. She had this thing where you couldn't hug her. It just, like, overloaded her system. She'd totally freak out. She'd be eight now. Probably has no idea if I'm alive or dead." Banger looked away. "So, anyway, yeah—you can judge me."

It was Zoe's turn to look at her hands.

"Are you sorry?" she managed.

"God, yes," said Banger. He pulled off his hat, revealing again the catastrophic bruises that he'd inflicted on himself. "Have you met my forehead?"

Zoe frowned—seeing his forehead the second time was no easier than the first.

"Being sorry's got to count for something," she said.

"Does it?" said Banger, as he pulled his hat back on. "I'm not so sure. It's pretty easy to say you're sorry—especially once you get caught."

Zoe asked him if he ever thought of trying to visit his wife and daughter while he was out of the Lowlands.

"I'm too ashamed," he said. "I've had a lot of time to think deep thoughts, and here's the thing: you can't do what I did to my family and expect them to forgive you. Hearts are fragile—the good ones, at least. Best thing would be if they decided I was just a bad dream."

Banger stood, wincing as he unfolded his long limbs. Zoe followed him to the door. The candy in his pockets creaked and crunched with every step.

Outside, the wind was blowing the snow around. After the warm, humid air inside Piping Hot Springs, it came as a shock to the skin. There was a lamp above the door. Banger stood in the small cone of light, as if it would warm him. He rubbed his bare arms, and squinted into the distance.

"You can't go running around Montana without a coat," said Zoe.

"What's it gonna do—kill me?" said Banger.

Zoe groaned at the joke. She went inside and retrieved X's overcoat. She held it open for Banger.

"You serious?" he said, slipping his arms into the sleeves before she could change her mind. "You are the bomb diggity."

Zoe rolled her eyes—but fondly. There was no way this guy had *ever* kept up with slang.

"Will you tell X I love him?" she said. "And will you give him some of the candy?"

"I'll tell him you love him," said Banger, "but no way can he have my candy."

He stepped out of the light, and onto the snow.

"No matter what happens with you and X," he said, "I'm glad he ran into you. He's a good dude—and you've given him a little bit of a life."

"Do you think the lords will really set him free?" said Zoe. "Be honest, I can handle it. No, wait—don't be honest. I *can't* handle it." She released a long, tired breath. "The odds aren't very good, huh?" she said.

Banger was just a voice in the darkness now.

"Who cares about odds?" he said. "What were the odds that he'd ever meet somebody like you?"

PART FOUR

A Divided Heart

FIFTEEN

ONE MORE SOUL.

The words shouted in X's brain.

He turned on his side in his cell. Despite Ripper's nursing, his wounds weren't entirely healed, and they cried out as they scraped the ground. He didn't care. He lived in his mind now. His body existed only to prop it up.

One. More. Soul.

He could only see Zoe again if he brought the lords a final bounty. He thought of the Overworld—of the hunters with their necklaces of geese, of the cannibals who wore skulls on a rope. How many could you wear before the weight of the dead pulled you to the ground?

He would snatch their soul for them. Of course he would. All that troubled him was how simple it sounded. He turned the phrase "one more soul" over and over in his head. He searched for the trapdoor hidden between the words. What if they required an innocent man? What if they demanded a *child*? He was consumed with seeing Zoe. Thinking of her, thinking of Jonah—even thinking of their mother who had grown cold toward him—sent a bolt of anguish through him. Still, there were things he would not do, even if the lords commanded him. It was not that he was too noble. He wasn't. It was that he didn't want to disappoint Zoe. She would not want horrors committed in her name.

X decided that he himself was the only true danger. When Regent—it was too perilous to even *think* of him as Tariq—sent him to the Overworld to hunt the last soul, would he run to Zoe instead? Would he enrage the lords and obliterate his single hope for happiness? Could he stop himself? Even now, he could feel Zoe's fingers on three very particular places: his lips, his hips, his shoulders. He shivered, as if she were in the cell with him, wrapped around him like a vine and breathing onto his neck. How could it be that the thing that made him strong also brought him to his knees?

A sudden noise interrupted X's thoughts. The Russian guard was escorting someone down the corridor. X heard a voice say, "Chillax. It's not like I forgot where my friggin' cell is, dude."

It was Banger.

X leaped to his feet. He had to know if his friend had seen Zoe, as he had asked him to—had *begged* him to, really. It was all he could do not to scream the question in front of the Russian. He held his tongue. He waited for the men to come into view. The guard strode in front. Rather than his usual powder-blue tracksuit, he wore a shining cherry-red one. He was so towering and wide—and strutted so proudly in his new finery—that X could barely see Banger behind him. But there he was. And he too was dressed in some new garment. It was so deeply blue it was nearly black.

X did not recognize it for a moment.

Then it struck him.

It was his own overcoat—Banger had seen Zoe.

The guard thrust his key into the cell next door. He waited for Banger to catch up, idly snorting up phlegm and then swallowing it.

Banger shuffled into his cell. X craned his neck, desperate to catch his eye, but the Russian blocked his view. X cursed silently. He was about to withdraw into his own cell when Banger leaned back out and looked directly at X. He flipped up the collar of the coat—and winked.

The Russian loitered for ages. Mostly, he paraded manfully back and forth in front of Ripper, who took a perverse pleasure in flirting with him.

"You have noticed new suit, yes?" said the guard.

"Oh, I have indeed," said Ripper. "You cut a dashing figure. You will be the talk of the Lowlands!"

"You may touch suit," said the guard. "Do not tell others. They may *not* touch suit."

The guard reached his arm into Ripper's cell. X shook his head as he watched. He was not in the least surprised when Ripper bit the man.

"You are monster!" cried the Russian, pulling his arm back and inspecting his cherry-red sleeve for rips. "You have teeth of animal!"

Still, he lingered at her cell another half hour. X had nearly exploded with frustration when he heard Banger whisper.

"Come to the bars," he said. "Fast."

X did as he was instructed.

"One, two—*three*," said Banger.

He thrust the coat through the bars. X grabbed for it and pulled it into his cell.

"Zoe rocks," said Banger. "She said she loves you, and I said you love *her*, et cetera, et cetera. It's all good in the 'hood." He paused. "There's a candy bar for you in the pocket."

"How can I thank you?" said X.

"It's just a candy bar, dude," said Banger.

"You mistake my meaning," said X. "How can I thank you for being a true friend to me—when I was never much of a friend to you?"

The words must have meant something to Banger, for he was silent awhile.

"Ain't no thang," he said.

"You are wrong," said X. "It is very *much* a thang."

A thought occurred to him.

He took off the purple shirt with the curly white stitching. He folded it carefully, smoothing out the creases as best he could. It was a garish object, yet he had seen Banger covet it.

X crouched down by the bars.

"One, two—*three*," he said.

He passed the shirt to Banger. He could hear him giggling as he slipped it on.

"Dude," said Banger. "I look friggin' *hot* in this."

BY THE TIME THE Russian lumbered away, Banger had fallen into a deep, animal sleep, exhausted by his adventures in the Overworld. X sat against the wall, the overcoat spread over his lap.

It was wet from Banger's fall into the river. Still, when X pressed his face against it, he could detect the faintest scent of Zoe's skin. It went through him like a flame.

Thanks to Jonah, X actually knew what a candy bar was, and, looking for relief from his thoughts, he slipped a hand into one of the coat pockets.

Instead of candy, he found a piece of paper.

Both sides were covered with markings he could not identify. The mystery of what it said was unbearable. Maybe it was a message from Zoe?

He asked Ripper if she was awake. He spoke just loudly enough to ensure that he would wake her if she wasn't.

"I am always awake," said Ripper. "Surely you know that by now? My brain is like a fireworks factory."

"Might you read something to me?" said X. "Something I have discovered in my coat?"

"Pass it to me," said Ripper. "Quickly. That ridiculous Russian will soon be back for another bite."

X maneuvered the paper through the bars. He listened as Ripper unfolded it, his heart racing.

"It is a list of some kind," she announced at last. "Is this the hand of your blurting girl? Heavens, she scrawls like an unschooled child. She is incapable of spelling 'raisins'—and her fondness for the capital Y borders on the terrifying."

She studied the paper further.

"Wait," she said. "The writing on the other side is not nearly so maddening."

"Read it out to me?" said X.

Ripper cleared her throat, and began:

*Dear X: Here is a letter for you. You're probably
thinking that (a) I have no way of sending it and (b)
you don't know how to read anyway. So, yeah, this isn't
a totally practical letter. I get it. Can we move on now,
please? I have to get these words out of my brain—
they're killing me. I don't care if they never go farther
than this piece of paper. Maybe that will help. Anyway,
here's the main thing I want to say (I'm taking a
superdeep breath—picture me taking a superdeep
breath, okay?) . . . The minute you left, I realized I
loved you. Crap, I'm already running out of paper. I
should have written smaller.*

Ripper broke off suddenly.

"I must say, she is a *very* unconventional correspondent," she said.

"Is there no more?" said X desperately.

"Yes, yes, there's more, my lovesick boy," said Ripper. "Restrain yourself."

She continued:

*The minute I wake up now, my thoughts go straight to
you, like gravity pulled them there. You tried so hard
not to take Stan. You trusted me when I said it was
wrong. Watching you suffer for what was right was the
first thing that made me love you, I think. Then there
were a ton of other things that I don't have enough
paper for. I hate your sadness, X—even more than I
hate my own. When you come back (please come back),*

let's get rid of our sadness, okay? When you come back
(please, please come back), let's bury our sadness under
15 feet of snow. Love, Zoe.

X said nothing. Zoe's words faded into the air, and he leaned forward, listening hard, as if he could pull them back into being.

"Would you read it again?" he said.

"Of course," said Ripper, "for even I think it is lovely in its way. But might I ask how many times you shall require me to read it?"

"Until it is fixed in my memory—and I can speak every word back to you," he said.

After a dozen readings, X finally let Ripper rest. She returned the paper to him, and withdrew to the back of her cell, complaining about the state of her throat. X ran his fingers over the letter, trying to connect the markings on the paper with the words he had memorized. He taught himself "love" and "Zoe," as well as "superdeep" and "crap."

Then he sat for hours holding the paper and the coat. He wondered when Regent would send him for the final soul. He wondered if he could survive the terrible wait.

He whispered to Ripper that Regent had told him his true name.

Ripper did not answer immediately.

"Do not even tell *me* what it is," she said. "He is a lunatic for having revealed it."

"I will never tell a soul," said X.

The churning of his brain finally tired him. Sleep hit him so

267

unexpectedly that he dropped off while sitting against the wall and balancing Zoe's letter on his palm as if it were made of glass.

HE DREAMED HE WAS back in the lords' giant chamber. It was empty. He had snuck in. The marble steps gleamed, the river rushed overhead. He had only seconds to do what he needed to do. He strode to the wall where the map of the Lowlands was embedded in the marble like some massive fossil. He searched for clues about where his parents were held. He ran his fingers along the symbols. There were too many—and he could not decipher them. The rock began to burn under his touch. He was not supposed to be there. The map *knew* that, somehow. His face was hit with a wave of heat.

When X wrenched himself from the dream, he found that the dark bruises on his cheeks were burning, and that Regent had come with the name of the 16th soul.

X was startled to see the lord in his cell. How long had he been there? Why hadn't he woken him? What reason could there be for delaying, even by a moment, his final hunt?

X rubbed the sleep from his eyes, but that only made the pain worse. He took a breath to steady himself. He looked up again at Regent, and saw that his face was heavy with sorrow. Something was wrong. The certainty of it hit X's heart like a hammer.

Regent didn't speak, didn't move. He just regarded X miserably, his dark, muscular arms hanging at his side, as if the blood were draining out of him. Nothing about the moment was ordinary. Nothing was right. X wanted to ask Regent what he meant by his silence, but his brain was so frantic now that it could not build a simple sentence.

X began to stand, desperate to break the stillness of the cell.

Regent, moving for the first time, like a statue suddenly coming to life, shook his head and gestured for X to lie on his back. X should have been relieved that the ritual was about to begin—that the moment he could touch Zoe again was finally drawing nearer, that something like life would finally unfold. Instead, he lay down as if into a grave.

Regent knelt beside him. He opened his right hand. X could see the lines that ran like rivers through his palm. He closed his eyes and waited for the hand to descend. It did not. After a moment, X opened his eyes again. He stared up at the lord questioningly. He did not think he could bear another moment.

At last, Regent spoke.

"The Lowlands require another soul for its collection," he began, as he always did. "He is an evil man—unrepentant and unpunished."

Instead of going on, Regent paused and another maddening silence filled the cell. When he spoke again, he departed from the ritual's ancient text.

X had never heard a lord sound so wounded and raw.

"This name," said Regent, "is not of my choosing."

X opened his mouth to speak, but before he could get a word out the lord had plunged down his hand. The name entered X's blood.

The name was Leo Wrigley.

It meant nothing to X.

But then Leo's story hit X's veins, and X howled like an animal at the shock of it.

He tried to push Regent away, flailing for his arms, his neck, anything. Regent stared down, his eyes full of pity. He tightened his grip on X's face until the bones threatened to snap—and pinned him to the ground.

Suddenly, X was on a rocky beach somewhere, his brain black with pain and rage. He began stumbling along the water's edge. The winds blew cold at his back. The tide, foaming and gray, swarmed over his boots.

He'd planned to collect this last soul as quickly as he could, so he could rush back to Zoe. But that was impossible now that he knew the man's story. He plodded forward almost against his will, his heart full of lead. Beneath him, the ground was strewn with enormous logs that had been bleached by the sun. They looked like bones.

The Trembling grew stronger as he walked, pulling him forward like a chain. Still, the pain was nothing compared to X's anger.

Who had chosen Leo Wrigley? Had the name been passed down from the Higher Power, or was it a ploy of Dervish's? The Lowlands had no need for the puny man that X had been sent for—X was certain of that. The man had sinned, yes, but was he really unrepentant? X didn't believe it. And if the Lowlands wanted this soul why hadn't they sent a hunter decades ago? No, the one the lords truly wanted to punish was X. He had defied them. He had stood up. He had told them he was better than they were, that he was pure and noble—that he was worthy of love! And now they would strike him down. They would strip him of everything.

X stomped over the rocks. Above him, the clouds were dense and dark. It was as if his own fury had put them there.

When he had walked a half mile down the beach, a hard rain began to fall and made the ocean boil. There were only a few people within sight—old men who waved strange metal instruments over the sand, then stooped every so often to dig up a can or a coin. They rushed for the boardwalks between the cliffs now. X kept walking, indifferent to the storm. The rain was cold, and slipped down his face.

He could not take this soul. He knew that. The lords knew it, too. They knew that he'd give up every hope of freedom first.

Still, he wanted to lay eyes on the man he was about to sacrifice himself for. He continued down the beach. It would not be long before he was back in the Lowlands. His cell was a stony mouth waiting to swallow him forever.

NEAR THE END OF the beach, X felt the pain in his body flare, and looked up to see his prey coming toward him in the rain. The man was tall and wiry. He wore glasses and a red wool hat, which bobbed up and down as he walked. It was the only fleck of color in sight.

The rain crashed down in sheets now. The shore was deserted except for the bounty hunter and the soul he had come for.

Between them, there was a cliff that had been hollowed out by the tide. It rose up and over the beach like a giant, curling wave. The man ducked beneath it to get out of the rain, and took a seat on a fallen tree trunk. X stopped a hundred feet away, his boots sinking into the spongy sand. Should he turn back or continue? Every possibility, every thought, every emotion rushed at him at once.

The man saw X standing in the downpour. He cocked his head: *What are you doing out there?* He waved for him to come under the cliff. He gestured to the tree trunk he sat on: *Plenty of room right here.* Even in his torment, X found the innocence of the

271

invitation touching. The man had no idea that X had been commissioned to kill him.

X stepped into the shelter, and sat without speaking. Above them, rainwater struck the top of the stony wave, then dripped off its outermost edge, like a beaded curtain. X looked at the ocean, at the bed of stones at his feet, at the smooth, curling wall of rock behind him—at everything but the man sitting beside him.

"Gonna be a while," said the man.

X wanted to turn, wanted to speak, but found he could do neither. The man barreled ahead, unfazed.

"How freakin' awesome is this rock?" he said, pointing up at the cliff behind them. "Sandstone. Coolest thing I've ever seen."

X finally turned to him.

The man looked as harmless as a leaf.

X searched for something to say, but there was so much violence in his brain that it crowded out all thought.

The man smiled expectantly.

"Is this your first time in Canada?" he said.

X furrowed his brow.

"Is this Canada?" he said.

The man laughed, and X realized, with relief, that he thought he was kidding. The man was in his forties. He had a mop of brown hair and surprising green eyes that X recognized somehow. Beneath his jacket, he wore dingy clothes. His boots, coat, and glasses had all been repaired with the same shiny black tape. His clothes smelled like fish. He saw X notice the odor.

"I've been doing some ice fishing," the man said. "It's awful hard to make any kind of living up here."

X felt an intense wave of loneliness pouring off his bounty.

Ordinarily, he didn't pretend to know what went on in people's hearts, but loneliness was one of the few emotions he felt qualified to judge.

The man removed a glove and offered his hand to X.

"I'm Leo Wrigley," he said. "What's your name?"

X looked down at the man's hand, which was pink and splotchy from the cold. He couldn't make himself take it. Was it because of what the man had done? Was it because X was ashamed that he was meant to murder him? He wasn't sure, but it was as if his arms were bound to his sides.

The man's smile faltered. He withdrew his hand and gave X a long, hurt look.

Only now did X realize why he had recognized the man's eyes: they looked like Jonah's eyes.

X stood. He had to get away. The pain was too much.

"Your name is not Leo Wrigley any more than mine is," he told the man. "It may be what you call yourself now, but it is not your true name."

X ducked through the curtain of rainwater that fell from the cliff, and walked toward the noisy sea. He thought of Zoe. He would go to her now and see her one last time before he descended back to the only home he had ever deserved. He didn't know how he would tell her—or *if* he would tell her—that her father was still alive.

SIXTEEN

Zoe woke up giddy, as if someone had injected her with light. It was Sunday morning. Her body ached from caving. Still, it was the right kind of ache—an athlete's ache. At nine o'clock, her mother peeked her head in and asked if she wanted to go into town with her. Zoe could hardly turn her head toward the door.

"Only if you have a stretcher," she said.

"Terrific," said her mother, leaning down to stroke her hair. "Now I have two kids who can't leave the house."

"Stop, stop, stop," said Zoe. "That hurts."

"Your *hair* hurts?" said her mother. "Is that even possible?"

"Apparently," said Zoe.

When her mom left, Zoe inched her way to the edge of the bed, her muscles resisting even this tiny journey. Once upright, she staggered out of her bedroom and lurched across the hall to Jonah's room, where she shouted, "Move, bug, move!" and collapsed onto his bed a fraction of a second after he had scrambled out of it.

Jonah listened to her groan for five minutes, then clambered back onto the ladybug, kissed her on the cheek, and said, "You are in *no* condition to be in charge." He went down to the kitchen and made a tremendous amount of noise while constructing some sort of breakfast for her. Zoe heard so many machines *ping* and grind and whirl (the microwave, the blender, the Vitamix, the dehydrator, the *cake mixer*?) that she shuddered to think what lay in store for her. Still, it was the first time in days that Jonah had seemed . . . like Jonah. It was because she'd gone caving. She would have done a dance if her body had been up to it. Jonah's laptop was open on the floor. He'd made her I WILL COME BACK photo his desktop background.

At 9:30, Jonah pushed the door open with his bare foot and entered bearing a breakfast tray, which he laid beside Zoe with great ceremony. Zoe forced herself upright. Gazing down at the tray, she was surprised to find that Jonah had spent 30 minutes on a bowl of cereal, a glass of chocolate soy milk, and a bottle of Advil.

"What was with all that noise, bug?" she said.

Jonah looked confused.

"I was just playing," he said brightly. "Did you think I was making you Eggs Benedict? I'm eight!"

ZOE EVENTUALLY LIMPED DOWNSTAIRS to the couch. She'd spent so many hours there lately that the cushions were molded in the shape of her body. She tried to do some calculus homework, but even the textbook seemed to know her mind was elsewhere: "Solve for X," it told her. Zoe napped. She reread the article about Stan obsessively (where had X found a purple cowboy shirt?). And she ate lunch, thanks to Jonah who made her a peanut butter and banana sandwich on gluten-free bread in just under 35 minutes. By afternoon, she was bored, so she guilted Val into visiting by playing up her aches and pains and Snapchatting her five selfies, in which she made increasingly miserable faces.

Val came over in her pajamas: red flannel bottoms and a pink T-shirt that said, I Wanna Be a Housewife. As always, she brought a great jolt of energy into the house. She scratched Spock's and Uhura's bellies. She painted Jonah's toenails green. She raved to Zoe about her girlfriend, Gloria, in such minute detail that it seemed insane, then touching, and then insane again. Spending time with Val was so effortless that Zoe found herself almost teary with gratitude. It was like being lifted by a tide.

Just as it got dark, they heard a truck in the drive. Zoe's legs were so stiff that they buckled as she went to the window.

"It's Dallas," she said.

"Ooh," said Val. "This should be interesting."

"You will be nice," said Zoe.

"I doubt it," said Val.

Jonah scampered to the door. Dallas's wrist was still bandaged from his fall, and he was carrying a shopping bag, but Jonah wanted a piggyback ride into the living room—and got one. Zoe always felt a pang when she saw how much her brother loved having guys in the house. It was like the sonar *ping* on a submarine. Zoe knew that not even the sum total of X, Rufus, and Dallas could fill the empty place where their dad used to be.

Dallas's goofy smile faltered when he saw Val. He knew she only tolerated him for Zoe's benefit.

He set his bag on the floor shyly. There was a present peeking out of it, wrapped in fancy blue-and-gold paper. The corners were so crisp and perfect that Zoe figured one of Dallas's parents had done it for him. He remained standing because Jonah was still hanging off his back, like a cape.

Zoe watched as Dallas's neck got pink, then red.

"Jonah, get off him, okay?" she said. "He needs to do stuff like breathe."

Her brother did as he was told, but the moment Dallas took a seat Jonah plopped down on his lap.

There was silence for a while. Val was not just reveling in the awkwardness now, but actually *bathing* in it. She pointed to the package at Dallas's feet.

"I can't stand the suspense," she said. "What'd you get me?"

Dallas sagged, embarrassed. He looked at Zoe.

"It's just something to commemorate you killing it at Silver Teardrop," he said. "You can open it later. It's probably stupid."

"Thank you, Dallas," said Zoe. "I was pretty hard-core, right?"

"You were *full-on*, dawg," he said.

"Open it now," said Val. "I'd like to see what it is."

"Me, too," said Jonah, who was rocking back and forth on Dallas's lap.

"I'm gonna wait, bug," said Zoe. She turned to Val and whispered, "Stop being a dick."

It was too late, anyway. Jonah was off and running.

"Open it! Open it!" he said. "Please and thank you! Please and thank you!"

Dallas drew the present reluctantly from the bag.

"Actually, Jonah sort of inspired it, so it's kinda for him, too," he said.

He handed the box to Jonah, who tore into the wrapping paper.

The noise brought Zoe's mom to the room. She'd just returned from town and stood leaning against the doorway. The whole situation was out-of-control awkward now. Zoe's heart went out to Dallas, who was reddening again.

Jonah pulled the lid off the box. Inside, there was what looked like an antique quilt. It was covered with hexagons in a dozen colors. Even from across the room, Zoe could see how beautiful it was, though she couldn't figure out what it had to do with caving. Jonah frowned into the box. He was trying to decipher it, too.

"Wow, that's a gorgeous quilt," said Zoe's mom, just to break the silence.

"It is," said Val. "I'm not even kidding."

"Thank you so much, Dallas," said Zoe. "I love it. But—"

She was about to say that she didn't exactly *understand* it, but she feared it would hurt Dallas's feelings. Fortunately, Jonah turned out to be smarter than she was.

"It's a blanket for Dad," he said. "So he won't be cold."

Thirty seconds later, Zoe's phone buzzed, and she looked down and saw that Val had texted her from the other end of the couch: *The dude is IN LOVE with you. YOU'RE the one being a dick, you dick! Tell him NO HOPE! Tell him X!*

TOLD him already, Zoe texted back.

Tell him again! HURT him if you have to—better now than later!

Zoe put her phone down before it became obvious to everybody that she and Val were texting each other. Within a few minutes, she had kicked everyone out of the room as politely as she could. She asked Dallas to hang out a second so they could talk.

278

Once everyone had drifted away—Val had hugged Dallas good-bye, and not even ironically—Zoe sat up on the couch and fished around for words. The sun was dropping behind the mountains. The room was more shadow than light. Dallas stared at her glumly, knowing that he'd done something wrong, but not knowing what it was.

"I need to know the name of The Girl Who's Gonna Say Yes," said Zoe. "And I need to know when you're gonna ask her out."

"Why?" said Dallas nervously.

"Because I need to know it's not me," said Zoe.

"It's not you," said Dallas. "Stop it."

"I hope not, dawg, because I swear to god I will *not* say yes," said Zoe. "I am The Girl Who's Never Gonna Say Yes. I mean, I think you're awesome. You've totally grown on me—as a *friend*. However . . ."

Dallas was in misery. He would not look at her.

"Stop, stop, stop," he said. "I don't want the Friend Speech. It's Mingyu, okay? I'm going to ask out Mingyu."

Zoe was shocked.

"Mingyu from Spanish?" she said. "Mingyu the Satanist?"

"She's not an actual Satanist," said Dallas. "She's just . . . complicated. And complicated's good, right?" He looked up at Zoe. "I finally figured that out."

Zoe beamed.

"Happy to help," she said.

That night, after her friends had all gone, Zoe finally departed the couch, her muscles still aching. She was trudging around the kitchen like a wounded Civil War solider when her mom offered to drop her off at the hot springs for a soak. They tried to coax Jonah

279

into coming along for the ride. He refused and threatened to lock himself in his room if they asked again.

Jonah watched from the window as Zoe and her mom left. He'd never been alone in the house before.

THE HOT SPRINGS WERE so still and dark that the mountains seemed to have gobbled them up. After her mom dropped her off, Zoe let herself in, singing loudly and switching on every light she could find, including the strings of white Christmas lights that had yet to be taken down from the windows. The empty locker room spooked her slightly, thanks to a hundred high school horror movies. She changed quickly—her bathing suit was a black retro one-piece with a halter top that she'd spent too much money on and literally never worn—and then grabbed a towel and darted back into the hall. She had forgotten flip-flops. She tiptoed down the cold concrete corridor, avoiding the puddles that covered the floor like a chain of lakes.

Outdoors, the air was frigid. Zoe had forgotten how the cold took your breath away—how it electrified your skin even as you walked to the pool. Within seconds, her shoulders were shaking and her hands were in fists.

The water was shiny and dark. She stepped into it and crouched down low so it could spill over her shoulders. Her muscles relaxed, but her brain just wouldn't. She didn't like the way the mountains loomed over her in the dark. She felt stupid for having come alone.

Zoe turned onto her back, and paddled to the center of the pool. Her dad had taught her the names of all the constellations, but she'd forgotten most of them. So she gazed up, and—trying to distract herself—invented new ones. She named one cluster of stars the Candy of Banger and another, X's Arms. After that, she closed her eyes and floated around peacefully, her legs and arms flung wide like the spokes of a wheel.

Then she began to feel that maybe she wasn't alone.

She heard a hum that did not sound like the wind. She became weirdly conscious of the rustling of the trees. She thought about how she was miles from anywhere, how she was surrounded by black mountains, how she'd left her phone in the locker, how she didn't even have a car. She kept her eyes closed, but couldn't shake off the nervousness. It felt like someone dragging their fingernails up the side of her body.

When she finally opened her eyes, she was so surprised by what she saw that her heart began hammering. The water that she floated on—the water that held her up and splashed in tiny waves over her legs and arms—had turned orange and red.

It had begun to glow.

SHE PIVOTED TOWARD THE stream that fed the pool. It looked like a river of fire—and someone was rising out of it.

A man was coming toward Zoe. The water was streaming off him. She waited, barely breathing. She told herself that it had to be Banger.

It was X.

"You are *such* a show-off!" she shouted. "You scared the crap out of me!"

X didn't answer until he reached her. It seemed to take forever. Finally, he knelt by the pool, his beautiful face emitting its usual pale light.

"I was so desperate for you I could not think clearly," he said. "Might that serve as an apology?"

281

Zoe smiled.

"Yeah, that'll work," she said. She reached up for his hand. "Can you help me get out?"

X leaned toward her.

"A little closer?" she said.

X bent over the water, obediently—and Zoe pulled him in.

When he had righted himself, he stood waist-deep in the water, looking confused. His hair and overcoat dripped into the pool.

"That's what you get for scaring the hell out of me," said Zoe. "By the way, if you were a regular person you would *never* have fallen for that."

He looked down at her body and seemed to see it for the first time.

"Your limbs are bare," he said.

Zoe waited for him to look away shyly.

Instead, he said, "They are beautiful."

"Thank you," she said. "No one's ever said that about . . . my limbs."

X pushed his hair back behind his ears. His face and neck were covered with droplets of water that picked up the light. He took off his coat. He laid it at the side of the pool. He drew Zoe close and put his hand at the small of her back. She could feel it pulsing there. All his shyness had vanished. He seemed hungrier for her than he'd ever been.

"Are you free?" Zoe asked him. "Have the lords let you go?"

"Do not make me answer," he said. "Let me have this moment."

He took Zoe's hands and placed them on his hips.

She knew what he wanted her to do.

She pushed up his shirt, her hands sliding slowly up his body.

His skin was hot to the touch. The heat jumped to her own palms and traveled up her arms. She felt as if she and X were part of one continuous body now. She tried to hold his eyes, but he looked away as her fingers grazed the welts and bruises that covered his ribs.

"Don't be ashamed," said Zoe, her voice a whisper. "I don't want you to *ever* be ashamed, okay? You haven't done anything wrong."

X nodded, but she wasn't sure he believed her.

Zoe tossed the shirt to the side of the pool. She missed. The shirt landed on the water and hung suspended like a jellyfish. Zoe didn't notice. She stared at the tattoos along X's forearms. She smiled.

"What is it?" he said. "Tell me."

"Nothing," she said.

She'd been looking at the "giraffe" with the spiked tail.

X pulled her even closer now and took her face in his hands. He tilted it up toward him.

"I loved your letter," he said.

Zoe had forgotten about the thing. She let out a squeal of embarrassment.

"Oh my god," she said. "It was in the coat!"

"I insisted that Ripper read it to me until I had committed every syllable to memory," said X.

"Shut up," said Zoe. "You did not!"

X cleared his throat.

"'The minute you left, I realized I loved you,'" he said. "'Crap, I'm already running out of paper.'"

"Stop, stop, stop," she said.

They stood smiling and swaying in the water. It was becoming impossible to keep their bodies apart. There was no such thing as close enough.

X ran a thumb over her lips. She parted them at his touch.

She waited for his mouth to come to her—and it did.

WHEN SHE EMERGED FROM the locker room in her street clothes, Zoe saw that X was trembling. Now she knew for certain what she'd already suspected: he hadn't collected his final soul. He had defied the lords. He had come to her instead. She couldn't imagine what the consequences would be. Under the stark fluorescent lights of the lobby, X began to look afraid. Was he afraid for himself—or for her?

Now she understood why he hadn't wanted to talk.

She didn't want to talk either.

Instead, she wanted to show him something. But it was far. She didn't know how they'd get there.

X understood before she said a word.

"Wherever you want to go, I will carry you," he said.

Zoe remembered how X had carried her and Jonah home through the woods. At the time, she'd been so out of it that all she remembered was a feeling of immense safety and the sight of the trees pulsing by.

X made a basket of his arms now, and she reached around his neck. She felt warmed. Protected. *Enclosed.*

Her cell phone buzzed. She fished it out of her coat, and found a text from her mom.

You ready? it said. *Should I come get you?*

Zoe sank gratefully into X's chest.

No, she texted back. *I've got a ride.*

And then X launched them into the snowy night. This time, the journey in his arms was bumpy and nauseating, and Zoe realized

284

that holding on to a comet seemed really cool until you were actually holding on to a comet. She clung to X's neck, shouting directions. They moved faster than she thought possible. The landscape blurred by, trailing streaks of light. Zoe saw everything in flashes: the snowy ski runs; the dark, twisting river; the thick puffs of smoke that rose out of the trees as if giants were lying on their backs in the mountains and smoking cigars.

A hundred miles rushed by. Soon, X descended and skidded to a halt, snow swirling everywhere. When they'd finally come to a stop, he set Zoe down with infinite care.

She lurched forward and threw up.

And then she spent the next five minutes trying to get her ears to pop. X was mortified, but Zoe reassured him.

"It's fine, it's fine," she said. "I thought it'd be romantic."

Zoe had guided him to a deserted spot in the mountains. Only now did she realize that, with the moon locked behind clouds, they wouldn't be able to see a thing.

X seemed unconcerned.

"Which way are we bound?" he said.

"That way," she said, pointing vaguely into the darkness. "I think?"

X knelt and placed his palms against the snow. A tunnel of light burst in front of them, 10 feet high and 20 feet wide. It illuminated the hills and evergreens as far as Zoe could see.

She shook her head in disbelief.

"I'm keeping you," she said.

SEVENTEEN

X FOLLOWED ZOE OVER A SNOWY RISE. The drifts were deep, and their progress was slow. He could hear her just ahead of him, panting and swearing. Occasionally, she would turn back and say, "We're almost there" or "Okay, I was lying, *now* we're almost there."

He himself did not speak. He couldn't shake the image of Zoe's father from his brain. He kept picturing the man's hand extended toward him, reddened and chapped from the cold and waiting to be shaken. He kept picturing his eyes—*Jonah's* eyes.

There was nothing but snow in every direction. He'd had enough of the snow.

Finally, they staggered down the other side of the rise. At the bottom, there was a fence and a hill of rocks, on which stood a small cross and a stone Buddha. X had seen souls arrive in the Lowlands with the same images around their necks—just as he'd seen necklaces with golden stars and crescent moons. New souls never fought so hard as when the guards tried to steal them away.

Without a word, Zoe began scaling the fence. It rattled as she climbed, and X felt a wave of concern. He wondered if he should stop her. But then he remembered that one of the things he loved most about her was that no one could *ever* stop her.

Zoe dropped down on the other side of the fence and landed with a deep, muffled thud. She turned to X.

"This is Black Teardrop," she said. "This is my father's cave. This is where he died."

X's heart lurched.

This was the moment to tell her that her father was still alive. *This was the moment.*

He couldn't do it. The words wouldn't come.

He wanted to give Zoe one more minute of happiness, of innocence—of *not knowing.*

Did he have to tell her the truth? What if he didn't? He could take her father's soul to the Lowlands and be free—and Zoe could keep believing that her dad had died in a cave. She didn't have to know about her father's sins. She didn't have to know that he had run from his past as long as he could, or that when it finally caught up with him he'd chosen the most cowardly course: faking his own death and leaving her and Jonah and their mother to cry their hearts out by a tree in the backyard. Zoe could have a *whole lifetime* of not knowing.

She was staring at him. Her eyes were teary. He had to say something.

"Show me the cave," he said.

He leaped over the fence and joined Zoe. There were already tracks, half buried in snow. They followed them up to the cave, then climbed to where the statue and the cross sat on the ledge.

"I feel bad for these guys standing out here in the cold," said Zoe.

X did not reply. His mind and heart were aching.

"But I guess Jesus and Buddha can handle a little snow," she said.

She sat down on the rocks, surrounded by the light that X had summoned up. She began talking, shyly at first.

She told him about the cave and about her father. X found it hard to concentrate on the exact words—they blew by him like a wind. She said that she'd gone caving the day before. She said that there was a moment during the descent where she suddenly knew what her dad had gone through when he died—not just the mechanics of it, but the terror, too. She said she'd felt the rope wind around his throat, as if it were her own throat. She'd seen the flame on his headlamp singe the rope, then burn through it as he struggled. She'd imagined the fall—the sudden, heart-in-your-mouth naked panic of it—as if the cave were devouring *her* instead.

She paused.

She apologized for talking so much.

She looked at him, desperate for him to speak. But still X said nothing. And every second that he said nothing felt like a lie. Could he lie to her for the rest of their lives? And would the two of them be able to build anything on top of the lie and still call it love?

Zoe pointed at the statues. She said her mom had left them there. She'd been shocked when she found them. She'd thought that her mother hated her father, but clearly she hadn't been able to cut him out of her heart. None of them had. Jonah, she said, was a *legit basket case*.

She picked up the piece of bark from the ledge above the Buddha and the cross.

"See this?" she said. "'I will come back.' I carved that for my dad. I wanted him to know we're not gonna just leave him here."

X was startled by the words.

"What do you mean?" he said. "What do you mean you're 'not gonna just leave him here'?"

"We're gonna come back and get him," said Zoe.

He saw the seriousness in her eyes. *No one could ever stop Zoe.* This time, he thought it not with a pang of fondness, but of dread.

"I'm sorry I'm babbling, but I'm babbling because you aren't talking," she said. "Why aren't you talking? You must have a million things to say."

"I do," said X miserably. "And yet no way to say them."

Zoe climbed down from the rocks. She took off a glove. She laid her palm against the side of his face.

"Try," she said. "Try just telling me *one* thing."

X took her hand from his cheek. The softness of her hand—the kindness of the gesture—only hurt him.

"You cannot go into this cave," he said.

"I'm not going to," she said. "The police are."

"They cannot go either," he said, growing heated. "You must trust me. You must stop them. *No one* must enter this cave. Let them seal it forever."

Zoe pulled away from him.

"Why?" she said.

His mind spun in search of an answer.

"Why should I stop them?" she said.

"Because I am asking you to, Zoe," he said. "Because I am *begging* you to. Because everything depends upon it." He was going too far.

He was saying too much. "Because I will destroy the cave with my own hands before I let anyone venture into it."

Zoe recoiled from him.

"What is *wrong* with you?" she said. "*Why should I stop them?* I'm going to keep asking until you answer me. And you know me—I can go all night."

This time, he interrupted her before she could get the question out.

"Nothing but the most desperate pain can be found in that cave," he said. "You might recover from it, but I am not so strong as you, Zoe. I could not bear to watch rags made of your heart."

His tenderness had no effect.

"You're not answering me," Zoe said angrily. "Why should I leave my father's body in a hole? He would never have left me. Why shouldn't we go into the cave? Tell. Me. *Why.*"

X felt the answer fly up his throat, like a sickness.

"Because your father is not there," he said. "And because you are wrong—he *did* leave you. He left all of you."

Zoe staggered back a step, her face suddenly unrecognizable.

"What are you talking about?" she said.

He stepped toward her. She drew back, as if in fear.

"What are you talking about?"

"The lords gave me one last commission—one last soul I must take if I am to be free," he said.

"I know," she said. "Banger told me."

"The soul they sent me for, Zoe—it was your father," said X. "He is alive. I have seen him."

The color was gone from Zoe's face now. He reached for her again. She wouldn't let him touch her.

"You've—you've seen *my father*?"

"In Canada," he said. "On a barren coast. Not so many hours ago."

Zoe shook her head.

"It couldn't have been my father," she said. "Tell me how you knew. Tell me exactly what he said."

"We spoke but little," said X. "He gave off a strong scent of fish. He begged my pardon for it—he said he had been fishing through the ice."

Zoe's eyes suddenly flared with hope.

"My father didn't fish," she said. "He didn't know how. If *he* knew how, *I* would know how. He would have taught me."

"It may be that he has learned," X said gently. "This is a man who fled his life—who shed even his name. I suspect he lives on the margins and in the shadows now. He calls himself Leo Wrigley."

This last detail seemed to wound Zoe more than anything that had come before.

"We used to have a cat named Wrigley," she said, her voice breaking. "And Leo is—it's Jonah's middle name." She was quiet a moment. "What else did he say? This is *insane*."

X searched his mind. He had spent so few moments with the man—and he had been in such a tortured state.

"He praised the rock we were sheltered under," he said. "He said it was sandstone, and remarked on how 'freakin' awesome' it was. I grieve to tell you, Zoe. But it *was* your father."

Zoe burst into sobs.

He reached out to her again, and yet again she shrank away. Not being able to touch her was excruciating. X clenched his hands so tightly that his nails drew blood.

"Did you—did you *take* him?" said Zoe. "Did you take my father to the Lowlands?"

"No, Zoe," said X. "How could I? He sits on that beach still, for all I know."

"What did my father *do*?" she said. "What were his crimes?"

"Do not ask me," said X. "Spare yourself *something*."

Zoe rubbed frenziedly at her eyes, but the tears kept coming.

"I need to know at least a little," she said. "I mean, it was bad, what he did? Bad, like . . . bad, like you're used to?"

X shivered. Every word she spoke pierced him, but the words he was forced to speak in return were worse somehow—because they pierced *her*.

"Much of it occurred in his youth," he said. "Yet—"

Zoe could not wait for him to complete the thought.

"Yet what?" she said.

"Yet I have taken souls for less," he said. "There was blood on his hands when he was still a young man. And there is fresh blood on them today."

He watched as the last remnants of hope drained out of Zoe.

"What happens now?" she said.

He reached out to her a final time, and this time she let him hold her.

"I regret this answer above all the others," he said. "What happens now is for you to decide. Either your father goes free—or *I* do."

X WAITED FOR WHAT felt like years for Zoe to speak.

"Take me to him," she said finally. "Take me to my father."

Her voice sounded so hard now. X turned from her. He stared down at the feeble metal fence, which shook and rattled in the wind.

"Please," she added. "Or I'll go myself. I'll find a way. You know I will."

"Yet what will you say to him, Zoe?" X said. He did not look back at her. He couldn't. "And what will you have me do? Will you ask me to stop your own father's breath? Will you watch as I circle his neck with my fingers? And, once I am done, will you ever be able to look at me again?"

Zoe was silent a long time.

"I don't know," she said. "But I want to see him with my own eyes. I want him to know . . . I want him to know that *I* know what he's done. I don't want him thinking he got away with this—not for one more second." She put a hand on X's shoulder. "Will you take me?" she said. "Even if I don't have all the answers yet?"

He turned back to her. Her eyes, even in distress, were so familiar. They never failed to unravel him.

"You know that I will," he said.

Zoe texted her mother: *I'm not going to be home tonight. I'm OK, I promise. Please trust me ONE more time.*

She turned off her phone so she wouldn't hear it explode. She nodded to X. She was ready.

He picked her up and pulled her to his chest. He did not bother leaping over the fence—he just let out a howl and kicked it down with his boot.

HE CARRIED HER UP and over the powdery banks and then down the icy road that wandered through the mountains. The moon had broken through the clouds. The snow gave off a faint blue light. Zoe was silent now—overwhelmed by the shock of it all, he imagined. Her eyes were open, but she appeared to see nothing.

He tried to think of a story to tell Zoe as he carried her. He thought that hearing his voice might console her somehow. Talking would never come naturally to him (how many words had he even spoken in his lifetime?), and he realized now that he didn't know very many stories—and certainly no pleasant ones.

So he told her *their* story.

He began with her knocking him down on the ice.

He told her that she'd smelled like the dogs, adding nervously that he meant it as a compliment, that he'd *liked* it. He told her that he was changed the minute she smashed into him, that by stopping him from taking Stan, she'd woken him up—challenged him not to hate himself and to think of himself as something more than a killer. Because that's all he was when they met, wasn't it? It didn't matter if you killed only bad men. You were still a killer. Even if Zoe and X had never spoken (never touched, never kissed) he wouldn't have forgotten her. *Couldn't* have. He'd have guarded the memory of her with two cupped hands, like it was a flame in a draft.

Was Zoe listening? He wasn't sure. But he liked telling the story. It soothed him.

He told her about how they'd argued when her family found him in agony in the garage—how he'd begged her to abandon him, even though he was praying that she wouldn't. He described riding to the house in Jonah's sled and sleeping in a bed shaped like a fat insect. Why was it shaped like an insect? He'd worried it was a stupid question, so he had never asked.

X told her how he used to lie waiting for her to fall asleep. He told her that she snored just the tiniest bit—but maybe he shouldn't have said that? He changed the subject. He talked about Jonah. He said he could feel his hard little hugs even now. He confessed that when he was tiptoeing out of the room one night he'd stepped on one of Jonah's toy animals and broken its horns. How ashamed he'd been! He'd meant to apologize, but never did. He didn't know what kind of animal it was. It had horns, so maybe it was a monkey?

Zoe's lips twitched at this last detail—she nearly smiled.

She was listening. And she looked warm in his arms.

X talked for another hour. They were out of the mountains now. They were on a road lined with evergreens. X saw poles strung with wires. He felt civilization rising up to greet them. Still, it would take them ages to reach her father.

As if she'd read his thoughts, Zoe stirred in his arms and spoke.

"Why are you walking?" she said.

Her voice was flat and tuneless, but he was grateful to hear it.

"Why aren't we *zooming*—or whatever you call it?" she added.

"I have seen the effect that zooming produces in you," said X, "so zooming must be our last resort. In truth, I am happy to walk—for the more slowly we go, the longer I can hold you."

Zoe was quiet a moment.

"Thank you," she said softly. "But it's okay to zoom." After another silence, she added, "Do you really call it zooming? I was just guessing."

"No, we don't call it that," said X. Fearing that he'd been unkind, he quickly added, "But we certainly can."

Satisfied, Zoe withdrew into her thoughts again. The moon, appearing to follow her cue, ducked behind the clouds once more. Even to X, the darkness was alarming.

EIGHTEEN

THE INSTANT ZOE AWOKE, she knew her father was near.

She lay in a bare wooden hut on a beach in what she guessed was British Columbia, the ocean crashing and sighing on every side of her. She could feel her own version of the Trembling spreading beneath her skin. Her heart, her nerves, her lungs—everything in her body told her how close her father was.

X was not beside her. Zoe remembered only flashes from the night before: the hut had been locked, and X had smashed his fist through the door so they could get in. He'd warmed the place by simply rubbing his hands together, but still they'd slept huddled against each other, as if they were in danger of freezing. X had made a pillow for her out of his coat.

An hour ago—could it have been more? she wasn't sure—X had opened the door, and a wedge of sunlight had fallen across her face. She'd woken, briefly. He told her he'd be back. He told her to keep sleeping. It was such a lovely thing to be told: "Keep sleeping."

Zoe's mind must have churned as she slept because she woke up knowing exactly what she and X had to do about her father. The answer had been sitting in her brain for hours, waiting for her to awake. She knew X wouldn't like it. She'd have to find the right time—and the right way—to tell him.

She sat up and leaned back against the wall. The place was one of those changing-room huts that families rented on the beach during the summer. It was tiny. There were hooks for clothes and rough wooden drawers. Otherwise the inside of the hut was stark, white, and empty. Zoe could hear the wind whistling outside. When she peered through the slats in the wall, she saw a line of snow-covered trees leaning almost horizontally over the edge of the cliffs.

She pulled her phone from her pocket. It was 8 a.m. There was a string of texts from her mother, beginning with one that read, *What do you MEAN you won't be home?* There was also one from Dallas (*Do you really like the quilt I got you? I got a gift receipt just in case*), and one from Val (*Why isn't your butt at school?! Is your butt malfunctioning?!*)

To Dallas, she texted: *I love the quilt, shut up, go away.*

To Val, she wrote, *Loooong story. Who told you about my butt??*

To her mother . . . Well, what could she say?

Zoe stared down at the phone, and began typing:

I'm in Canada, I think.

CANADA? YOU THINK?!

Road trip. Hard to explain. I will be home soon. Pls don't freak.

Waaaay past freaked. Who are you with?

. . .

WHO are you WITH?

. . .

297

Zoe? Are you there?

I'm with X.

Zoe couldn't explain the situation. Not in the state she was in. For all she knew, X was on his way back with her father right this minute.

She stuffed the phone in her pocket, put on X's coat, and pushed open the door.

The hut turned out to be on stilts, and—because the tide was high—standing in three feet of frigid water. The outside walls were bright red. On either side of it, there were identical huts, painted yellow and powder blue. Zoe had planned to walk on the beach, but the ladder at her feet was so swamped with water it had begun to float. She might as well have been on a houseboat.

Zoe sat in the doorway, the cold sun on her face, the wind playing games with her hair.

She tried not to think about her mother. Her mom would understand—eventually.

She tried not to think about her father. When she *did* think of him, all that came to her was a rage so dark it was like a storm front. Maybe that was for the best. She was going to need her anger.

Zoe caught sight of X coming down the beach. He waded toward her through the water, his pants soaked, his shirt flapping against his chest like a sail in the wind. He was carrying two plastic bags. When he noticed her perched in the doorway of the hut, he lifted the bags high and shouted the most surprising thing she'd ever heard him say: "Breakfast!"

X climbed the ladder, and handed Zoe the bags. For a moment, he stood in the doorway, wringing the cold salt water out of his

298

pants. His face was flushed from the wind. He looked weirdly happy. Giddy, almost. Zoe had seen him twirl Stan like a baton. She had seen him stagger into the ice storm to confront a lord. But she had never seen him as proud of anything as he was of having successfully ordered takeout.

She watched as X converted his coat into a picnic blanket—she made a mental note to get the thing dry-cleaned—and unpacked the bags.

They held three Styrofoam containers, which were still so warm that they perspired slightly. There was also a bizarre number of cans: a Canada Dry Ginger Ale, a Big 8 Cola, a Jolt Cola, an RC Cola, a tomato juice, and a Diet Dr Pepper.

"I *demand* that you explain this amazing triumph," said Zoe.

X looked at her sheepishly.

"Surely there are more important matters before us?" he said.

"I can't think of any," she said. X seemed unconvinced so she added, "I need to hear something happy. Everything else is too awful. Let's just talk about food for a little while? Please?"

He said he'd taken the money from Zoe's pockets as she slept— he still felt bad about it—then wandered along the road until he discovered a restaurant. It was a bright, loud place, full of laughter and clinking glass. Everyone swiveled toward him when he walked in—partly, he supposed, because he wasn't wearing a coat and his hair was not quite presentable.

Zoe snuck a look at X's hair, and smiled. It pointed in every direction like a sign at an intersection.

X said that he'd panicked as the diners inspected him. He thought of fleeing, but a woman with bright yellow hair and a pencil welcomed him and set him at ease. X pretended he couldn't speak

English. The yellow-haired woman found this endearing. She toured the establishment with him, miming that he should look at everyone's plates and point to what he wanted.

"Oh my god, she was *flirting* with you," Zoe interrupted. "I may have to go back and have a talk with her."

X had been telling his story excitedly—breathlessly, almost. He stumbled to a stop now, confused by Zoe's comment.

"Never mind," she said. "Keep going. This is my favorite story of all time."

All the diners, X said, wanted him to choose *their* food. It became a game. They lifted their plates to him as he passed, hoping for his approval. Whenever he selected something, a cheer would go up, and the waitress would scribble on her little rectangle of paper. His only difficulty had been choosing the drinks because he couldn't see what was inside the cans. He hoped she found something here acceptable?

She assured him that she did. She took the ginger ale for herself and, when he reached for the Jolt Cola, guided him toward the tomato juice instead, saying, "I think you're jacked up enough already."

Next came the ceremonial opening of the Styrofoam boxes. X watched as Zoe gazed inside them. He looked so nervous that it would have moved her to tears if she hadn't been starving. In the first box, there were two thick, buttered slices of French toast, each with a whorl of cinnamon in the center, and a side of wavy, gleaming bacon. In the second, there was a golden mound of onion rings and a small container of blue cheese dressing. In the third, there was a slice of molten chocolate cake so enormous that an elastic band had been stretched around the box to keep it safely inside.

X stared at Zoe, desperate for a verdict.

"I do not pretend to know what constitutes a meal," he said.

She leaned over the boxes, put a hand behind his neck, and pulled him close for a kiss.

"These are the best foods on earth," she said. "How did you know?"

X beamed.

"Should we begin with this?" he said, pointing to the chocolate cake.

"Obviously," said Zoe.

The waitress had forgotten to give them silverware—or paper plates or napkins—so they ate with their hands.

They ate until there was nothing left but crumbs. They ate until their hands, their shirts, their faces—somehow, even their necks— were sticky with grease and frosting. They ate until the tide had receded, until the sun sat overhead, until X was so high on syrup and cake that he was hopping jubilantly around the tiny hut and doing impressions of Ripper, Dervish, and the Russian guard. Zoe laughed, remembering Banger and all his candy bars. *Come to me, ye Men of the Lowlands*, she thought, *and I shall give you sugar! And maybe even caffeine!*

Seeing X so happy calmed everything inside her. She wouldn't have thought it was possible. She had gotten so used to pain and to loss and to impossible questions—and yet right here in front of her was love, was hope, was an *answer*.

After the inevitable sugar crash, X slept for hours, his long legs sticking out of the hut. Zoe watched him every moment, just as he had watched over her all night. Her father had abandoned her, but X never would. Not willingly. She smoothed his hair as best she could with her hands. She traced the tattoos on his arms with her fingers: the giraffe, the monkey, a knife, a tree, a band of stars. She worried that it was wrong to touch him while he slept, but she couldn't help herself. And, anyway, she could have sworn that his breathing deepened whenever her skin touched his. She pressed her lips to the insides of his wrists and the soft hollow at the base of his throat. She kissed his fingers one by one, and took them into her mouth. She did it all softly so he wouldn't wake. Her face flushed with heat. Everything tasted of maple syrup.

THEY WERE SO CLOSE to Zoe's father that the Trembling returned as X slept. Being with Zoe always quieted his body, but never cured it altogether. X's skin became damp and feverish. Zoe opened his shirt wide to let the air cool him, allowing herself the brief pleasure of placing her palm against his chest and feeling his heart pump beneath her hand. As the hours passed, the sickness grew stronger. X shook and thrashed his head in his sleep.

Zoe's phone trilled in her coat.

The screen said *ME!!!* was calling. Jonah had programmed himself in.

She stepped down the rickety ladder so X wouldn't wake, and balanced on one of the narrow rungs. Birds that had drifted in from the water were tracing circles around her. The waves roiled just below her feet.

Jonah began talking before she'd even said hello.

"Why aren't you here?" he said. "Where are you? What are you *doing*?"

Zoe answered the least complicated of the questions.

"I'm looking at the ocean," she said.

"Where is there an ocean?" said Jonah suspiciously. "We don't *have* an ocean."

"I'll tell you everything when I see you, bug," she said. "I can't talk right now."

"Don't hang up!" he said. "If you hang up, I will call back sixteen times! You have to come home, Zoe. Right now! Mom said you'll come home when you're ready, but I'm ready right now!"

"I can't come yet," she said. "Soon."

"I'm all by myself!" he said.

"Wait," she said. "Why?"

Jonah gave an exasperated grunt, then poured out the following without pausing to breathe: "Rufus is late 'cause he got in an accident—the bear fell off his van, I guess?—and Mom couldn't wait 'cause she had to go to work, and now I'm alone and I *hate* it and it's scary, and why do you have to look at the ocean when we have stuff *right here* you can look at?"

It took five minutes to get him off the phone.

Zoe pocketed her cell and climbed the ladder. The birds sensed food now. Zoe eyed them anxiously. Their bodies, their bills, their moist little eyes—everything was jet-black, except for their wings (which had streaks of white) and their legs and feet (which were bright red and reminded her, strangely, of the bottoms of expensive shoes). She ducked into the hut and began bundling up the bags.

She wasn't fast enough: one of the birds dove through the door.

The instant it was in the hut, it freaked out. It banged against the ceiling and walls, trying to escape. Zoe saw X register the noise in his sleep. She was desperate for him to rest and wanted to protect him like he had protected her, but she just couldn't drive the bird out. She felt sure it'd been sent to remind them that there could be no sleeping—no touching, no forgetting, no *relief*—while the Lowlands were watching.

Zoe finally trapped the bird in X's coat. She carried it to the door. She released it, watched it disappear over the waves, then sank down in the doorway. The agitation had pushed her over the edge. X, who'd slept through all the commotion, woke up the instant she began crying. She found that moving somehow: that he could ignore anything but her.

He touched her shoulder.

"I dreamed you were kissing me," he said. "I dreamed you were kissing my fingers, my hands, my throat."

Zoe turned and smiled guiltily.

"Weird," she said.

She dried her eyes on her sleeves, embarrassed that something as random as a bird had upset her.

"Can you stand?" she said.

He nodded and stood.

"Can you walk?" she said.

He nodded again.

"It's time to find my father," she said. "I've made a decision."

X nodded a third time, and took his coat from her. Even the simple act of pulling it over his shoulders seemed to exhaust him.

"What is your decision?" he said. "I must know."

Zoe stood now, too. The birds were still circling the hut.

"The lords gave you his name to punish us, right?" she said.

"To punish *me*," said X. "You have done nothing to chastise yourself for. I beg you not to imagine otherwise."

"Why do they want to punish you?" said Zoe. "Because you're

innocent—and they're not? Is that what it is? They're just . . . *assholes*?"

"You may think me innocent," said X. "But they do not. They think me arrogant and vain, for I have put myself above them. I have put *you* above them. Now they mean to show me how weak I truly am."

"Because they don't think you can do it?" said Zoe. "They don't think you can take my father, no matter what evil crap he's done? They think you'd rather go back to the Lowlands forever than do something that would hurt me?"

"And I fear they are correct," said X.

Zoe opened the door and began descending the ladder again.

"They are *not* correct," she said. "You are *going* to take my father and you are *going* to come back to me. Not just because he deserves to be punished, but because—even if you're a dork and don't believe it—you deserve to be free."

THEY HEADED UP THE beach to the road, the rocks sliding and clacking under their feet. It was afternoon now. Zoe knew it wouldn't stay light for long. They walked half a mile without speaking, and she was grateful for the silence. If they talked, they'd have to talk about the fact that X was growing sicker by the minute—that he was tripping over his feet and hanging on to Zoe for support. She had never seen him so weak. Being close to her was not helping him now.

Once again, Zoe's body told her that her father was near, just as X's body told him. She saw omens and metaphors everywhere. It wasn't just the dark birds back at the beach. It was the frigid wind, which pushed at their backs as if goading them on. It was the black road, which was riven down the middle with cracks, as if something was trying to break out of the earth.

After ten minutes, X and Zoe passed a junky-looking truck parked on the shoulder of the road. There was a path just ahead. X led Zoe to it, and they entered the dense, snowy forest. It was like the woods near her house. Every awful detail from the day she had chased Jonah and the dogs came back to her unbidden—everything about Bert and Betty, the fireplace poker, and the hole in the ice. And here she was preparing to collide with another soul marked for the Lowlands.

Zoe looped her arm through X's. She didn't know if she could survive another day like that.

The forest was hushed except for the creaking of the trees. Some of the firs were so deeply encased in snow that Zoe couldn't see the slightest hint of green. They leaned over in every direction—giant, hooded figures bowing to each other. Snow ghosts, she'd heard them called.

Zoe thought of how much she'd once loved the woods. She remembered running through them in summer, patches of sunlight bright on her skin. She remembered snowshoeing through them on days so crazily cold that it hurt to breathe. She remembered Jonah's laughter lighting them up, no matter the season. But too much had happened. She feared forests would always feel hostile now—claustrophobic somehow, as if the trees were waiting for her to look away so they could rush at her from all sides.

X's fever was spiking. When they came to a larch that had fallen across the path, Zoe cleared some snow from the trunk and snapped off a half dozen spindly branches. She helped him sit.

"How much farther?" she said.

She was desperate to get there. And desperate *not* to.

"Perhaps a half mile," said X, each word draining him even more. He pointed at the path ahead of them, which was tamped down and streaked with mud. "These tracks," he said, "are your father's."

Zoe's stomach did its tightening thing, where it felt like someone was turning a wheel. This time, it felt as if her skin was caught in the gears.

"My throat is in flames," he said. "I feel as if glowing coals were being shoveled down it. Still, there is counsel I would give you, if you will hear it?"

"Of course," she said.

She sat down next to him on the trunk.

"It is not that your father is an evil man," said X, his voice a husk. "It is that he is a weak one. You will know it the moment your eyes encounter him." He paused, collecting his energy. "You will also know that he loves you," he said. "We are not slaying a dragon today, Zoe—just putting a wounded animal to rest. You will find it harder than you imagine. I have never known my parents—and it seems that I never will—so perhaps I have no right to advise you. However, if you find that you pity your father, you need only look at me and I will know—and I will not take him."

"Stop it," said Zoe. "Just stop it. He doesn't love anybody but himself. I understand that now. You are going to be free. Do I *seem* like somebody who changes her mind?"

THEY WALKED FOR WHAT felt like much more than half a mile. Maybe it was because the woods were strange. Maybe it was because Zoe was going to see her father. She was so tense now, so alert, that time seemed to crack open and expand just to maximize her anguish.

She was going to see her father—it seemed like such an innocent statement. Except that he was supposed to be dead. Hadn't she prayed for his soul at the cave? Yet, somehow, her father was *still alive*. He was up ahead through the trees. Doing god only knew what. Pretending to have no wife, no children, no Zoe, no Jonah, no past. Did they mean so little to him?

Rage seeped through her. She knew one thing she'd tell her father for sure: it was a good thing he'd gotten rid of his name because where he was going they wouldn't let him keep it anyway.

A squirrel jumped into a tree as they passed, sending snow down the back of Zoe's neck. She shivered as it melted on her skin. They couldn't be more than a quarter mile away now—but a quarter mile from *what*? Knowing her father, he could be living in a house, a cave, an igloo, anything. She peered through the trees. There was no plume of smoke, no sign of life at all.

Suddenly, her phone trilled again.

ME!!!! it said.

"Bug, I can't talk," she said, hoping to preempt another tirade.

"Why are you looking at an ocean?" said Jonah, his voice more desperate than before. "You don't even *like* oceans! You have to come home, Zoe! Right now, right now, *right now!* I am still alone and now it's—it's either raining or snowing, I can't tell which. But it's creepy and loud, and even Spock and Uhura are mad at you because I told them where you were."

Zoe only half-listened.

The forest thinned out up ahead. The light grew stronger.

X leaned close and whispered, "We will soon be within sight of your father."

Zoe nodded, and squeezed his hand.

"I gotta go, bug," she said into the phone. "I'm sorry. I love you."

"No, Zoe, *no*!" he said. "If you hang up, I will call back! I will call back thirty-two times!"

"Bug, stop!" she said. "I promise to call you back and make you giggle, okay? I will do whatever it takes. I will tickle you over the phone, if I have to."

"That's not even possible, *obviously*," he said. "Unless I, like, put the phone in my armpit, and probably not even then."

She felt guilty for hanging up. Jonah had suffered even more than she had. If she'd cried over her father a hundred times, he had cried a thousand. His eyes had gotten so puffy with tears that he could hardly see, and he'd let out wails that she would never forget.

There were only a hundred yards of forest left.

They could see something through the trees—a field of snow, maybe. A gray sky hung above it.

Zoe took X's arm, and they followed the path as it snaked through the firs. Anger and fear fought for her attention. The woods were so quiet it was as if the silence, rather than being passive and still, were a living thing that devoured all sounds. It was like the snow. It buried everything.

Just ahead, two snow ghosts leaned toward each other, weary under their heavy white coats. They formed a narrow archway—an exit out of the woods, an entrance to whatever it was that awaited them. Zoe peered between the trees. In the distance, she could see a dark smudge on the snow—a cabin, maybe. A hundred feet and they'd be out of the forest.

She needed this to be over, but she kept slowing down, she couldn't help it. She kept thinking of that day with Stan. She thought of Spock and Uhura huddled on top of Jonah in the snow, saving his life. She thought of Stan throwing Spock into the freezing water and holding him down with his foot. She thought of X doing the same to Stan. The boot on Stan's head, the frigid water lapping into his mouth—the images were carved into her. They were her tattoos.

They ducked under the snowy archway. The branches groaned above them. Zoe didn't trust them to hold. She held her breath, waiting for snow to bury them. She thought of the bird that had flown in for their breakfast—but now, instead of being trapped inside the hut, it was trapped inside *her*. She felt its wings banging and thumping in her rib cage.

"I want to talk to my father alone first," said Zoe.

X began to object. She shook her head to silence him.

"Just give me a few minutes," she said. "Then you can come and take him. I want him to know what he's done to us."

X agreed reluctantly.

"I will watch from the trees," he said. "If you want me, I will be at your side before you can even finish the thought."

They plunged out of the archway. The forest fell away and the world rushed out in every direction.

The smudge they had seen was not a cabin and it did not stand on a plain. It was a dingy shed, smaller even than the hut on the beach.

It stood on a frozen lake.

Zoe felt the bird squeeze up into her throat, scratching and choking her and desperate to get out.

In front of them, a small hill ran down toward the lake. They were out in the open now. If Zoe's father was in the shed, he might see her at any moment. She thought of hiding, but there were no snowbanks or bushes or rocks and, anyway, she was paralyzed. She couldn't convince her body to move.

The door of the shed swung open. The sound reached her an instant later, like an echo.

It was her father.

It was her father.

He was skinnier than she remembered, and she didn't recognize his tattered clothes. But she knew the goofy way he walked—the way his head bobbed, the way his lanky arms swung at his sides.

He carried a fishing pole.

She watched as he loped around, his eyes cast downward to inspect the frozen lake. It took her a moment to understand—to see what he saw—and then the bird in her throat let out a screech so sudden and alien that it shocked even her. X clasped her hand.

Her father turned and saw them.

There were a dozen holes in the ice.

NINETEEN

X watched as Zoe hiked down the hill. Her arms were crossed tightly around her chest. She was staring straight at her father, refusing to let him look away.

X heard noises behind him in the woods. Something was crunching through the snow. He assumed it was an animal and did not turn. He would not take his eyes off Zoe.

The Trembling made it almost unbearable for X to be so close to his prey. His fever burned beneath his skin. His hands had a will of their own, and began to shake at his sides. They were desperate to act—to kill—even if X was repulsed by the thought.

He reminded himself that killing this one last soul would set him free. But freedom was too strange and vast an idea to hold for more than an instant, and it was followed by a crushing guilt. Why must being with Zoe come at another soul's expense—and why must that soul be her father? The lords had made even freedom seem a sin. He told himself not to think of his bounty as

312

Zoe's father, but rather as a faceless, nameless creature to be disposed of: a 16th skull to hang around his neck, no different from the 15 others.

A branch snapped behind him. It was a tiny sound but X was so agitated it assaulted his ears. Still, he refused to turn.

Zoe was halfway down the hill now, halfway to her father.

Before X met her, he'd wrenched souls from the Overworld without so much complaining from his conscience. He used to tell himself that he hated it, but, when the time came, he always managed to summon up enough fury to strike his target down. He wondered if he'd been such a fierce bounty hunter because he had the blood of a lord in his veins—or because he'd never lived a true life and never known the value of a soul.

The noises returned. It was not an animal behind him. He knew that now. It was a human being.

A hiker, perhaps, or a hunter.

X could hear the man's breath.

He could not have someone stumbling on the scene about to unfold. He forced himself to look away from Zoe. He spun back to the trees. He saw a flash of gold through the parted branches of a fir.

Aggravated by the interruption, X stalked back down the path, the trees exploding with snow as he pushed past them. He would terrify whoever it was and send him running. It wouldn't be difficult. He knew how grim and malevolent he must look with his wild eyes and his hair trailing him, ragged as fire.

The glint of gold was maybe 200 feet back, still hidden by trees. X bore down on the intruder. Whoever it was would surely turn and flee before he'd even reached him.

But something strange happened. Rather than retreating, the figure moved toward him, scudding through the snow.

X himself was being hunted.

Ripper appeared suddenly, breathless and fierce and firing words.

"The lords are coming," she said. "I am here to warn you."

X was so shocked to see her that he could not speak. Ripper waited a moment, then continued, her voice rising.

"Struck dumb, are you?" she said. "You must do what you were sent to do. You have dallied too long with your lover. The thing that needs stiffening is your spine! Do you not *know* how the lords watch you? Do you not *know* how your insolence makes them seethe? I am ignorant of their plan, but they will surely unleash hell if you betray them again."

She fell silent, finally. She wore only black boots and her golden dress, which looked like a Christmas ornament against the snow. Her old bounty hunter tattoos peeked out from beneath her lacy sleeves.

"How did you come to be here?" said X.

"*That* is what you would ask me?" said Ripper angrily. "You have a friend in Regent, and I have a friend in that repulsive Russian. If you must know, I had to promise him a kiss, which I may never forgive you for. I have not kissed anyone for a hundred and eighty-four years, and I had hoped for a grander prize."

She took X's arm.

She turned him back toward Zoe's father.

"Come," she said. "Let us find that soul that needs taking. I will crush the man's throat myself if you cannot."

"I will do what is required," he said. "But you must return to the Lowlands before your absence is discovered."

314

"I will not," she said. "Not until this thing is done."

"I insist, Ripper," he said. "You have endangered yourself enough on my behalf."

"And I have done it gladly, foolish boy," she said. "I am to rot for eternity, in any case. I should be glad to think back on the one or two occasions I tried to be kind."

X accepted this, gratefully. Though the Trembling still pulsed through him, he felt stronger with Ripper by his side.

They walked through the dwindling trees, Ripper's eyes darting around with fascination. She took in the enormous pines, the streaks of sky, the snowflakes that drifted down like motes of dust. She had collected her last soul many years ago. She hadn't been in the Overworld for decades.

They stopped at the top of the hill and peered down at the tense figures below. Zoe was just now reaching the lake.

"Is that your blurting girl?" said Ripper.

"And her father," said X.

Once more the thought of taking the man's soul filled him with dread.

"This calling of ours," he said. "Did it never bring you shame? What we call 'bounties' are human beings, after all."

Ripper seemed surprised by the question.

"Surely you do not still think of them as *human*," she said. "Was I human when I cracked the skull of that serving girl—or when I left her corpse to grow cold in the street? Was I human when I rendered my babies motherless? No, these souls we take have given up all claims on humanity. They are garbage—and we are dustmen."

TWENTY

Zoe's father stared at her as if she couldn't be real. His fishing pole fell from his hand and clattered against the ice.

Zoe stomped the last few feet to the lake. Her body was shaking uncontrollably. Vibrating, almost. She hated it—it made her seem weak. She wanted her father to feel nothing from her but disgust. She wanted him to know, even before she spoke, that she loathed him, that she saw him for what he was, that he had gotten away with *nothing*.

But the sight of him stirred up tenderness, too. She hadn't expected that. Part of her wanted to run to him. He was *her father*. He used to cut her sandwiches into ridiculous shapes—once he used a cookie cutter to cut a star out of the middle. He used to tell her bedtime stories and insert her into famous moments in history—she'd cured smallpox, begged Decca Records not to reject the Beatles, and refused to board the *Titanic* when she heard there were only 20 lifeboats. You couldn't count on him, but when he hugged you, you really felt hugged.

No. He was vile. He was poison. She didn't have to know what he'd done with Stan when he was young, she didn't have to know exactly why X was taking him—because she knew what he'd done to her family. He had deserted them. He was the domino that pushed all the others down.

The lake was fringed with dead reeds poking up through the snow. Zoe picked her way through them, still holding her father's eyes. The thoughts in her head were dizzying: love, hate, forgiveness, revenge.

Her boot struck a rock in the reeds. She stumbled forward.

She landed on her knees on the ice, furious with herself for being so clumsy. When she looked up again, her father had broken out of his daze and was scrambling to help her.

"Zoe!" he called.

The sight of his teary face rushing toward her was too much. It softened her and repulsed her all in the same moment.

"Don't *touch* me," she screamed. "Are you *kidding*?"

She had never spoken to him like that before—not once in her life.

Her father backed away, palms in the air, indicating that he meant no harm. He seemed startled by the rage radiating from her.

He hung his head.

He can't even look at me, thought Zoe. *The coward.*

She got to her feet. She brushed the ice from her clothes.

"How did you find me—and who are *they*?" her father said, gesturing to the hill behind her.

Zoe was stunned to see X standing with a woman she'd never seen before. She knew from her golden dress—and her coolly ferocious air—that it was Ripper.

"You don't want to know," she answered coldly.

Her father picked up his fishing pole.

"Come into the shed. It's warmer," he said. "Let's not do this out here."

He turned away.

Zoe thought about just walking away right then and there.

Her father must have known what she was thinking.

"Don't go," he said over his shoulder. "You came this far to tell me how much you hate me—so come tell me. I deserve it."

THE SHED CREAKED IN the wind. It'd been built out of salvaged plywood and two-by-fours—one of the walls still had Post No Bills stenciled onto it in black spray paint—and sat on runners so her father could slide it around the lake. Inside, there was a thermos, a wooden stool, a copy of some ridiculous self-help book, and an electric heater powered by a small, puttering generator. Where the floor should have been, there was a five-by-five-foot patch of cloudy ice with a dark hole in the center, like a bull's-eye.

Zoe's cell rang as she entered the shed.

ME!!! it said.

Jonah was trying to FaceTime her now.

She silenced the phone, but a text popped up a minute later: *It's raining so bad! I need someone to talk to! Me and Spock are UNDER THE BED. Wait—now Uhura is, too!*

Zoe frowned, and put the phone in her pocket. She just needed a few minutes with her father, then she'd call Jonah back. In a few minutes, everything would be different. X would be here.

"Was that—was that Jonah?" her father asked.

His voice broke the slightest bit.

"Don't you *dare* say his name," Zoe told him.

Her father nodded. He stood in a corner of the shed, hugging his spindly chest with his arms as if to comfort himself. He looked as if he were going to cry. He was so much weaker than she was!

"How did you find me?" he said.

"You don't get to talk," she said.

It was unbearable to be so close to him. The air felt toxic. Even the silence was awful, the way it fed on itself and grew bigger and bigger. And yet some part of her—a part she hated, a part she'd crush if she could—wanted to hug him.

"Zoe," her father said, "I never meant to hurt you."

"You don't get to talk!" she said. "And you *definitely* don't get to say dumb bullshit crap!"

But he couldn't stop himself.

"It would have been worse if I'd stayed," he said.

"Really?" said Zoe.

She loathed the sound of his voice.

"It would have been *worse*?" she shouted.

She threw open the door of the shed.

"I can't be in here with you," she said.

She stormed away on the ice. Her father followed her. The lake had been shoveled clean. It was glassy and slick. The holes were everywhere.

When she'd put 20 feet between them, she stopped and turned to him. He knew not to come any closer.

"Jonah used to punch himself in the chest to stop his heart from hurting," she said. "Would it have been worse than that?"

"No," her father said quietly.

"I almost killed myself in a cave just so the cops would go get your body," she said. "Would it have been worse than that?"

"No," he said again.

"Mom didn't have a life when you were 'alive,'" she said, "and she has even less of a life now. Would it have been worse than that?"

"*No*, Zoe," he said. "No."

"You don't get to talk!" she screamed, then took it up like a chant. "You don't get to talk. You *don't* get to *talk*!"

Her father made a tent out of his hands and hid his face behind it. He was sobbing. It was pathetic. Zoe walked toward him so purposefully that fear flashed in his eyes, and he stepped backward toward the hut.

"Your BFF Stan?" she said. "He murdered two people we loved—with a fireplace poker. Would it have been worse than *that*?"

Her father looked stricken.

"Who did Stan kill?" he said.

Zoe let the question hang in the air, unsure if she wanted to answer it. He didn't get to talk!

"Bert and Betty," she said finally.

Her father shocked her by letting out a pained cry.

He spun away from her.

Suddenly, he seemed consumed with an energy he couldn't control.

He knelt down on the ice and checked a fishing line that ran into a nearby hole. When he'd finished, he crawled to another, and then another. He couldn't, or wouldn't, look at her again. He never left his knees. He scrabbled around like an animal. It scared her. She shouted, *"Stop!"* He wouldn't. When he'd run out of holes, he finally stood. Still, he didn't turn. It was like he'd forgotten she was there—or was trying to drive her away.

There was a giant sort of corkscrew, an auger, leaning against the shed. Her father took it and, hands trembling, began to screw yet another hole into the ice. Above them, the sky darkened. Zoe looked up at the hills. The trees were a solid black mass now, an army waiting for orders. X and Ripper stood there, watching. Soon it would all be over.

She didn't know if she was ready. Had she said everything she'd wanted to say? Had she gotten what she wanted? What *had* she wanted?

Her father was twisting the auger furiously. The hole was growing. Zoe tried to squash every bit of sympathy, but she couldn't. He looked like a man digging his own grave.

"I ran from Stan, not from you," he said suddenly.

He threw down the auger, and walked toward her.

"I grew up with him, did you know that?" he said.

His eyes were wild. It was Zoe who stepped backward this time.

"Yes," she said. "Mom told me."

"Did she tell you he was like a virus?" he said. "That he—that he—that he was hateful and merciless and—and—*lonely* even when he was a kid? Did she tell you how he polluted *everything*? When we were kids, he did things—*we* did things—that I'll never forgive myself for. I left Virginia because of him. Married your mother. Changed my name. Changed my *heart*. Truly. I mean, look, to be honest, *you* changed my heart—you and Jonah and your mom. You can laugh, if you want."

Zoe knew she was supposed to say something comforting. She said nothing. She made her face blank.

Her phone buzzed in her pocket.

More texts from Jonah. It had to be.

"I spent almost—what—twenty years looking over my shoulder," her father said. "I was terrified Stan would find me. You don't just walk away from someone like that. They won't accept it. They're—they're—*feeding* on you. But I got away from Stan. I tried to be a dad. Tried to forgive myself. Tried to make some goddamn money so we could—so we could at least freakin' *live*. You all used to laugh at my schemes, but every time I was away—every time I was on the road, every time I 'disappeared'—I was trying to get something going. I'm not smart like you, Zoe. No—don't make that face, it's okay—I'm just not. I mean, look at me. But I tried every legitimate, law-abiding thing I could think of. You think I *wanted* your mom to work as hard as she did? Be careful who you fall in love with, Zoe. You've got a big, big heart. Don't waste it like your mother wasted hers on me."

Her father stopped talking as abruptly as he'd started. He picked the auger off the ice once more and began drilling, desperate to do something with his hands.

"Why did you freak out about Bert and Betty?" said Zoe. "You never loved them like the rest of us did. You barely knew them—because you were *never around*. So why do you care what happened to them?"

Her father seemed not to have heard her.

"Twenty *years* I looked over my shoulder," he said.

"You said that already," said Zoe. "Answer my question."

But it was as if her father were talking to himself now.

"I was *so* careful," he said. "Because I knew Stan would never stop looking for me."

Zoe's phone buzzed again, jittery as a bomb. She was about to read Jonah's texts when something caught her attention out on the edge of the lake: the ice had begun to change.

Color was seeping in. It was darker than the time with Stan—more red than orange—and it spread slowly, like a sickness.

Her father was too obsessed with his hole to notice.

"But you can't hide forever, can you?" he said. "I mean, you found me here. And this place—this place isn't just off the grid, it's never even *heard* of the freakin' grid." He wiped the sweat from his forehead. "So Stan found me. Tracked me down in Montana. And he saw, in two seconds, how desperate I was. How *broke* I was. How ashamed I was of just years and years and *years* of failure. I mean, I was good in a cave, but—let's face it—I was always pretty useless aboveground."

Zoe looked back to the hill.

X and Ripper were sweeping down it now. Ripper's dark hair was swept up in a bun. Her bare neck was glinting.

Zoe's father still hadn't seen them.

"Why did you freak out about the Wallaces?" she said again. "Answer my question."

X and Ripper came to the bottom of the hill, and, as if they'd planned it, leaped simultaneously over the reeds. They were close now. The red tide beneath the ice was just a few steps ahead of them, like a carpet unfurling.

"Answer my question!" Zoe shouted.

But he wouldn't. He wouldn't even look at her. He had to finish his story—he had to purge himself of it—just as he had to finish the hole that was opening at his feet.

"Stan had a couple of ideas for making money," her father said. "They weren't dangerous, they weren't going to hurt anybody, but—I'm not gonna lie—they weren't exactly legal. The first one worked and then the second one worked. Having a little money was amazing. *Thrilling.* I can't even describe it. I bought Jonah that ladybug bed, even though he was too old for the thing. Remember? Then, the third time around, somebody *did* get hurt. An innocent person, I mean. She didn't get hurt bad, but still. Stan called it 'acceptable collateral damage.'"

Her father was still crying. He twisted the auger so hard it was as if he were punishing himself.

Zoe was crying now, too.

"Answer my question," she said.

"Stan eventually ran out of ideas for making money," her father said. "He told me it was *my* turn to think of something."

Zoe was shaking again. She couldn't control it. It was taking over her body like the red stain was taking over the ice.

She finally understood what her father was about to say, and she didn't know if she could stand to hear it.

"I didn't have any ideas," he said. "But Stan had gotten—he'd gotten rabid, almost. He demanded I come up with something."

The hole was deepening, widening. Sweat trickled down her father's neck.

"I told him there was an old couple who lived on the lake," he said.

The ice was changing faster, the red crawling toward them like a tide. Zoe's phone was buzzing. Her father *still* wouldn't look at her.

"I told him I thought they might have some money," he said.

Her father dropped his head to the top of the auger, sobbing. He was oblivious to everything but his own misery.

"I feared for those people, I swear to god," he said. "I told Stan I wanted no part of hurting Bert and Betty. But he went crazy on me—went absolutely ape-shit. You don't say no to somebody like that. He threatened to tell your mother everything. Threatened to hurt you kids. Threatened to tell the world who I really was. I didn't care if the world knew—the world never gave a *crap* about me—but I couldn't let your mom and you kids down again. I figured I'd rather die than do that." He paused. "So I started looking for a way to die."

Her father straightened up now, and resumed drilling.

The hole was nearly finished.

"Bert and Betty didn't have any money," said Zoe. "Stan killed them for nothing! He killed them because of *you*!"

Her father gave the auger one last twist, then fell backward, bewildered.

Red water surged up through the hole, like blood.

TWENTY-ONE

X STRODE TOWARD THEM, Ripper at his side. He was so close to his bounty that the Trembling had all but taken over his body and begun breathing for him. He never felt more inhuman, more monstrous, than in these moments. He was ashamed that Zoe would see him like this a second time. She'd see him shake and scream and spit vile oaths, all the tenderness she'd awoken in him suffocated by rage.

Could she really choose him? Over her own father?

X looked to her for a sign that she was still committed to their plan, but she was turned away. He couldn't make himself believe that he deserved her. The sensation of being loved was still too alien and new. He wanted to trust it, wanted to wrap himself in it, wanted to give himself up to it entirely. But this anger coursing through him made him feel polluted. Unworthy. Undeserving of even the name she'd given him. Love felt like a blanket someone was bound to yank away. The warmer he got now, the colder he would be later.

He needed to see Zoe's face. He needed to be sure she hadn't changed her mind.

X turned to her father, and found that he was gaping at him in shock. He held a strange, twisted piece of metal in his hands. Dark water was pooling at his feet.

He seemed to recognize X from their moment on the beach the day before. X could see him replaying the conversation in his head:

"Is this your first time in Canada?"

"Is this Canada?"

X motioned for Ripper to stay behind. She made a small, pouty sound, and stopped walking, the hem of her dress waving above her boots. X went ahead alone.

Yet again he looked to Zoe—and finally she turned.

Her face was aflame with anger. X had never seen her features so distorted. She looked ready to kill her father herself.

She rushed toward X.

She embraced him, but for the first time she felt cold and stiff. Utterly unlike herself. She gripped his arm so hard he could feel her nails even through his coat.

She gestured toward her father.

"He's the reason Stan killed Bert and Betty," she said.

"Yes," said X grimly. "He is."

"*Take* him," said Zoe.

X was startled by her fury. Had he done this to her? While she had been teaching him about kindness, had he been teaching her about rage? He tried to banish this new fear—tried to unthink the thought—but it had taken hold. Its roots were spreading.

Nonetheless, he nodded.

"Go to Ripper," he said. "Walk to the woods. Do not look back."

Ripper stepped forward. X did not know how she would greet Zoe—he prayed she would not be sarcastic or manic or dance in some outlandish way—nor how Zoe would respond in her present state.

They were tentative at first, but seemed to recognize something in each other. X could not stop studying them. It occurred to him that they were the only two people who had ever held him, had ever praised him, had ever *loved* him. He could see his entire life— everything that was decent and humane—in their faces. When X was young, he hadn't understood that Ripper cared for him as if he were one of her own lost children. He understood it now. He watched as Zoe's rage began to melt in her presence. He watched as Ripper put an arm around her shoulder, like a great, warm wing.

"I feel as if we are already well acquainted, dear girl," she said. "Perhaps it is because X made me read your letter aloud twenty-five times."

Zoe smiled weakly.

X watched as they crossed the lake, their arms linked, their heads touching gently. He heard Ripper tell Zoe that the lords were on their way.

"But they'll leave us alone once X takes my dad?" said Zoe. "Right?"

"Perhaps they will," said Ripper.

"What if he decides he *can't* take him?" said Zoe.

"I suspect they will make X watch as they murder you in some colorful way," said Ripper in an incongruously sweet voice. "But perhaps that is too obvious? The lords are a mystery, I confess. One never knows when they will feel the need to be creative."

X TURNED AT LAST toward his bounty, who was cowering against the shed and gripping the weird piece of metal as if it might protect him. X tried to tell himself that the man meant nothing to him, that his fate was of his own making, that his only name was 16th Soul.

But when he gazed at him, all he saw was Zoe's father.

All he saw were Jonah's eyes.

X pulled the metal out of the man's hands. He flung it across the ice. It skidded to the far edge of the lake before coming to rest in a clump of dead reeds.

"Have you any other toys we should dispose of?" said X.

The father was too frightened to speak. He looked pleadingly at X—and then he ran.

Why did they *always* run? Every one of them had run! What made them imagine they could get away?

X watched as Zoe's father raced for the shore, stumbling and slipping as he went. It was a pathetic spectacle. He remembered telling Zoe that her father was not evil, just weak. Had she not believed him? Could she really hate such a pitiful person, or was she just reeling from the shock and rage? Would she blame X tomorrow—and forever after—for what she'd told him to do today?

With a flick of his hand, X yanked the man back—it was as if he were on an invisible tether—and dashed him against the wooden shed. He left him suspended there, his feet dangling above the ground. With a few more gestures, he sent ice crawling like murderous ivy toward the man's hands and feet. Zoe's father watched helplessly as it bound him to the shed.

"What do you want from me?" he said miserably. "You can take anything I have. You can take anything you want."

"Yes," said X darkly. "I know."

"So what *do* you want?" said Zoe's father.

X unbuttoned his coat and let it fall to the ice in a heap.

"Just your soul," he said, "which you have made poor use of."

X cast his eyes around the lake.

"Which of these holes do you choose for your grave?"

Zoe's father flailed wildly, but the ice held him fast.

X ignored his exertions—he had seen such desperation many times—and pulled his shirt over his head. The man's sins were so eager to show themselves that X's back was burning.

He had to turn off his mind, had to shut out the man's questions, had to stop looking at his eyes.

X's body knew what to do. He just had to let his body do it.

He dropped his shirt. It mushroomed briefly as it fell.

He turned away from Zoe's father, and stretched out his arms. The muscles in his back and shoulders were aching. The cold air stung his skin.

He summoned up the man's sins. He could feel the terrible images starting to crawl across his back.

Zoe's father let out a sob.

"I know what I did!" he shouted through his tears. "You don't have to show me. I know *everything* I did!"

X was in such turmoil that the words cut through him. He felt more keenly than ever that—whether or not he was only doing what the lords had commanded, whether or not the punishment was just—he was piercing another human being's heart. Ripper said they were dustmen, but that was a kindly lie. She knew better, and so did he. He was a killer. And worse: he was a torturer.

He lowered his arms before the movie was over.

His back went white.

Behind him, Zoe's father gave a grateful sob. He tried to stop crying but couldn't.

When X turned, the man's chest was heaving and his face was a storm of tears. He looked raw and terrified. A helpless bird.

"Wait, stop, *please*," he said. "Talk to me for a second. Just for a second, okay? You love my daughter, right? I can see that. I saw the way you hugged her. I saw the way you looked at her. It's the way— it's the way I used to look at her mother."

X refused to listen. This man was nothing to him. He was just the 16th soul.

"Stop your mouth," he told Zoe's father, just as he had once told Stan. "Or I will plug it with my fist."

Zoe's father ignored the threat. He knew this was his last chance to speak.

"But if you love Zoe—why do this?" he said. "Why murder her own father?"

X knew he shouldn't answer, but the words rushed out of him.

"I do it because she asks me to!" he shouted. "I do it because you have hurt her who is dearest to me! I do it because either you or I must be banished to the Lowlands, and I have endured that darkness long enough!" It was as if X were defending the monstrous act not just to Zoe's father, but to himself. He could not stop. "If I do not take your soul, I will never see Zoe again—never feel her touch, never hear her voice, never curl her hair around my fingers. My heart was born in winter, sir, and I *will not* go back to the cold."

Zoe's father said nothing.

He had run out of words, as they always did.

But just as X was about to take the 16th soul down from the shed and plunge him into the lake, the 16th soul started screaming Zoe's name.

His voice was startling. It tore the air open.

"Zoe!" he screamed. "Zoe! Please!"

X turned frantically, and saw that Zoe and Ripper were still ascending the hill to the woods. They stopped now. Ripper held Zoe tightly, urging her not to turn.

"Zoe!" her father shouted. "Listen to me! Zoe!"

X leaped at him, and struck him hard across the face.

"I showed you a kindness, damn you!" he said. "I could have forced you to behold all your sins, but I did not! And yet you beg your daughter for sympathy? She will not save you. She is not your daughter anymore!"

"I don't *want* her to save me," said Zoe's father, and again he began screaming: "Zoe! Zoe! You don't have to look at me, just— just listen. Zoe, I'm sorry! Please, please, *please* know that I'm sorry. I was a disgrace as a father. As a man. As everything. I disgust myself. I don't deserve to live. And life without you and Jonah and your mom—it's not really *living*, anyway. I love you, okay? I absolutely freakin' love you. If you don't believe anything else I ever said, please, please, *please* believe that."

He was breathing so hard now that he had to collect himself before he could say more.

"If me dying helps you somehow, then I'll do it," he shouted with what energy he had left. "I mean, I already died once. It's gotta be easier the second time, right? I know you don't have any reason to believe me, but I think you're awesome, Zoe—and you'll always be my girl."

Zoe's father turned to X now.

"If you want my soul, just take it," he said. "*Take* it."

X was closing in on him, when, up on the hill, Zoe finally turned toward them. She walked back down to the lake, her steps heavy

332

and trancelike. Ripper could not stop her. Together, they descended and stepped on the dead reeds, which crackled under their feet.

Zoe was not looking at her father, but at X.

Nearby, a cluster of wild turkeys, black and red against the snow, raised their heads to X now, too. Even *they* seemed to be waiting.

X took the man's slender neck in his hand. Zoe's father gasped, but he did not resist, did not speak, did not look away.

He just stared at X—stared at him with Jonah's eyes.

X began closing his fist around his windpipe.

And then he stopped, not knowing why.

He felt a kind of stirring in his brain—a wind almost, as if someone had cracked a window or pushed open a door.

It was Zoe. She was searching his thoughts.

She'd told him that he was never to search hers. "There will be no mind-melding—or whatever that is!" she'd said. Yet here she was trying to figure out what he was thinking, why he was hesitating.

She was walking toward him across the lake, with Ripper following close behind. She was stepping around the holes. She seemed to know where they lay even without looking. And all the while, she was delving deeper and deeper into X. She was unfolding him—gently, like he was a piece of paper that might come apart in her hands. Surely, she knew what she would find? She'd taught him the word herself.

Mercy.

As suddenly as it had begun, the movement in his mind ceased. The wind retreated. The window closed. The door shut.

X looked to Zoe. She'd stopped 20 feet away. She was weeping. Her hair was white with snow.

She nodded to X. She seemed to want to reassure him, to soothe him, to make him feel loved.

Her eyes said, *It's okay, it's okay, it's okay. Let him go.*

X ripped Zoe's father from the shed by his neck—the ice shattered, the plywood groaned and splintered—then threw him to the ground.

Zoe drew closer.

She knelt beside her father.

X saw hope kindle in the man's eyes, as if he expected his daughter to throw herself into his arms.

X knew that she wouldn't.

"We're letting you go," Zoe told her father calmly, "because we don't want to turn *into* you."

Her father began to speak, but she shook her head.

"You don't get to talk," she said. "Remember?" She paused. "I was going to have X drown you in this lake, but I love him too much to make him do that. So I'm going to let you keep running and hiding and *ice fishing* or whatever, although—honestly?—it seems like you're really bad at it." Zoe looked at the auger, the fishing rods, the holes. Her father had caught nothing at all. "I never want to see you again, Dad," she said. "I mean it. And that's the last time I'm ever gonna call you 'Dad.' I'm going to try to forgive you—not because you deserve it, but because I don't want you to mess up *my* heart the way Stan messed up yours. I'm going to try to remember the good stuff. There *was* some good stuff." Zoe stopped, and stood. "Okay, that's enough. I'm done talking to you. I'm gonna go and . . . I'm gonna go and have a *life*. I'm going to have a life with X and Mom and Jonah. X and I won't give up until we figure out how. It's going to be a good life—and you won't get to watch."

Zoe went to X. He put his arm around her shoulder, pulled her to his chest, and spoke to her quietly.

Ripper approached Zoe's father.

"I would advise you to run, little rabbit," she said. "X may not be hungry for your soul, but my own stomach is rumbling."

Zoe's father got to his feet. He was sobbing, but he must have known Zoe wouldn't listen to another word.

He scrambled into the woods without looking back. The trees quaked and shed some snow, then settled once more.

X HAD FELT NO joy when Zoe said she would make a life with him, for he knew how unlikely it was. He had let her father go free, so the lords would almost certainly haul him back to the Lowlands. He suspected Dervish was lurking in the forest even now. He could picture him gouging the bark of a tree with his nails, barely able to contain his glee.

X listened. He waited. He looked to Zoe and Ripper, and saw that they were waiting, too. But everything was silent. There was nothing but the sound of their breathing and the tiny puffs of smoke it made, like steam from a train.

He stooped to collect his clothes, and began pulling them on.

No one spoke, for fear it would unleash something. Their eyes scanned the blackening woods.

Nothing.

Maybe the lords wouldn't come? Maybe Regent had convinced them that X had been punished enough? With each moment that passed, X became more and more convinced that it was possible. He was still in the grip of the Trembling. He was still feverish, still dizzy. His body was not his own. But Zoe had nursed him before, and he felt sure that if he could just lay his head against her—if he could just feel her cool breath settling over him—they could defeat the Trembling forever. Her father would be free. So would X. The lords would not own him any longer.

But then the buzzing began. They all heard it. It was faint but insistent. It sounded like a blackfly circling closer and closer.

X whirled toward it.

It was coming from Zoe.

She searched her pockets. It was her phone.

It was only her phone!

Zoe and Ripper stared down to read what was written there. Their faces looked eerie in the screen's yellow light.

X was about to look away when Zoe gasped.

The noise hit him like a punch.

She seemed unable to speak, so Ripper spoke for her.

"The lords are striking," she said.

X had known Ripper virtually his whole life. He had seen her fight and curse and flirt and sing. He had seen her tear out her fingernails and beg to be beaten. He had literally seen her in hell— but he'd never seen her afraid.

She was afraid now.

X wheeled around. The sky, the woods, the lake—they all spun before his eyes. But he found nothing to fear. The world was empty. He was certain of it.

"I see no threat," he said.

Zoe held out her phone, as if he could read it.

Her palm was shaking.

"I d-don't think they're coming after us," she said haltingly. "I th-think they're going after Jonah."

TWENTY-TWO

X AND RIPPER DOVE into holes in the ice. Zoe had begged them to take her with them but they left her standing on the lake—she would only have slowed them down.

They rushed toward Jonah through water, then earth, then water again as they joined the stream that ran behind the Bissells' house. X was a powerful swimmer. Ripper matched him stroke for stroke. Her hair had come loose. X could see it fanning out under the water—floating above her for a moment, then sinking down again. He didn't know what they'd find at Zoe's house, but he was glad to have Ripper with him. He felt there was nothing she wouldn't do for him. Nor he for her. As they neared the surface, light began to leak down and glint off her dress. She shimmered like an iridescent fish.

The cold water gummed up their muscles. It felt nearly solid. It seemed not to want to let them through. X had promised Zoe three things: that he would save Jonah, that neither he nor her mother would ever discover that her father was still alive, and that he himself would return to her one more time. But X felt no certainty now. He pictured Jonah in his room, surrounded by figurines of animals and elves. He pictured him on his ladybug bed, hugging Spock and Uhura to his chest, and trying to gentle them down with that quavering voice that seemed to run in the family: *D-don't be scared, guys. Because—because* I'm *n-not scared.*

As X and Ripper reached the pocket of air beneath the ice, their lungs were bursting. He nodded to her. Together they raised their fists and punched through the translucent ceiling. Ice fell into their eyes. It rained down around them in splinters.

Ripper climbed out of the river first, her hair flat against her skull, her dress twisted and wrinkled as tissue paper. She helped X out of the water. The moon was already up.

For a moment, they stood shivering and stamping. X felt a presence behind them. It seemed enormous. It was breathing and pulsing—and watching them. He wished with his whole being that he didn't have to turn. But he did.

A hundred lords stood in a chain around Zoe's house.

The house itself was so thickly coated with ice that X could hardly make out the windows, the roof, the doors. The land around it was ravaged and scarred. Trees had been pulled out of the ground and hurled like sticks. What was more, everything was frozen and glittering so that there was an awful beauty to the devastation: it was a wasteland strung with diamonds. The willow where Jonah had buried the Ninja Dad T-shirt lay on its side, broken and contorted as if its neck had been snapped.

The lords glowered at X and Ripper across the upturned earth. They seemed to be daring them to step forward and engage. Their silky garments—purple and green and yellow and red—were sickeningly vivid against the desolation of the hill. Their golden bands shone in the moonlight.

"Apparently," said Ripper, "we will not be taking them by surprise."

X gave a grim laugh.

"You have been a fine teacher to me," he said quietly. "Might I ask you to recommend a strategy one last time? If it would help, I would trade myself for the boy a thousand times."

"Well, we could ask them nicely," said Ripper. "But the fact that the lords have not already descended upon you and pulled you back to the Lowlands by your handsome hair suggests that they want more than merely to bring you home. They want to boil your heart. They want to watch as you listen to that poor boy scream."

Ripper paused. She seemed to regret speaking so bluntly, for X's face was clouded with pain.

"That being the case," she continued, "I propose a simple, unornamented fight to the death. I have always rather enjoyed them—though they're never quite as satisfying when no one can actually die."

Together, they circled the house at a safe distance, looking for weaknesses in the chain of bodies. There were none. The lords remained still, but even their stillness was full of menace. They were coiled and ready to strike. X peered into every face. Some were handsome, some ancient. Some were lovely, some desiccated or burned. No one regarded him with anything but disgust. X had questioned their authority. He had shamed them. He'd been offered an unheard-of chance to leave the Lowlands forever—a chance perhaps even the lords themselves had prayed for—and made a mockery of it. He'd refused to collect even one more soul. Now it was as if X and the lords were opposing magnets: the air between them vibrated with hatred.

As the chain of lords snaked by the front door, he saw Regent in his deep blue robe.

He was staring down at the snow.

X felt a tiny flutter of hope, but almost immediately it escaped his body like one of those clouds of breath, for Regent would not speak to him. He would not so much as raise his head. He stood with his arms clasped behind his back, as if they'd been bound together—as if even his body was saying, *This is beyond my control.*

A voice, high and nasal, called out from farther down the chain: "Not even your faithful kitten will help you now—you have betrayed him too many times!"

It was Dervish.

He grinned at X, his pointy, ratlike countenance all aglow.

"You even struck him in the face, or have you forgotten?" he continued. "Goodness, that was sweet comedy!"

X ignored him. Ripper snarled in the lord's direction.

The ice on the house cracked and contracted, each spasm as loud as a rifle shot. Jonah was in there somewhere.

X put a hand on Regent's shoulder.

"There is a boy in the house," he said.

Regent clenched his teeth, but did not reply.

"You *must* spare him," X pleaded.

Again, there was no answer, though the muscles in the lord's neck and jaw twitched violently.

"*Please*, Tariq," said X.

At this, a gasp of shock went up among the lords and traveled down the chain like a lit fuse. Regent closed his eyes as a wave of dread passed through him. Even Ripper was struck dumb. She pulled X away from Regent just as Dervish hooted with glee and came scampering toward them.

"The kitten TOLD YOU HIS TRUE NAME, did he?" he said. "My, what a grand romance you have had! Did you sit by a river and feed each other figs?"

Dervish puffed out his chest, and looked down the line of lords, expecting laughter. There was none.

Ripper, enjoying his humiliation, sneered at him.

"Will you not shut your mouth just this once?" she said. "*No one likes you.*"

Dervish's face flushed and his wormy lips quivered as he tried to think of a clever response. Finally, he turned to X.

"What absurd friends you have," he said. "Yet I suppose only a lunatic would join you on an errand such as this. She shall be punished, too—as will the dim piece of meat you call Banger, for serving as your messenger boy."

There was another sound like a gunshot. The ice had contracted again. It was strangling the house.

Jonah was in there somewhere.

X remembered how they'd all huddled together during the first ice storm. He remembered how it felt to be trapped in a groaning house. He hoped Jonah was looking out at him now—he wanted him to know that he'd come for him. But X couldn't see a thing through the ice. Jonah might have been banging on the glass with a little dinosaur in his hand. He might have been screaming. X would never hear him.

"You must spare Jonah," X said again, this time to Dervish. "He has no part in this."

"Ha!" shouted Dervish. "You have refused to bring me the father—so I will take the son! It seems a fair trade, does it not? I regret snuffing out the life of such a sweet boy—it is not the way of the Lowlands, just as it is not our way to parade about in the Overworld like this—but you yourself have driven me to it. It is you, not me, who is the cause of all this pain. It is YOU who laid waste to this mountain—YOU who imprisoned that boy in his tomb. Had you not been so insolent, none of this would have come to pass! But you believed yourself too fine for the Lowlands— just as your vile mother did. You are better than NO ONE and NOTHING, I assure you. Because you ARE no one and nothing. The foolish letter you call a name will not alter that. Your beloved *Tariq* should never have trusted you. He dealt you so much rope that you strangled not only yourself but a family of innocents besides!"

The words struck X hard. He knew there was truth in them.

"Release the boy," he said, "and I will follow you home."

No word had ever tasted more sour on his tongue than the word "home" did now.

"I will NOT release the boy, and you will come regardless," said Dervish. "If you tarry even an instant, we will return for your play-thing, Zoe. How much blood will you see spilled before you simply do as you are commanded? I am curious to find out. Now, please, I am weary of words. Let us watch this house die together, shall we? If you do not misbehave, I will let you pick the boy's bones from the ruins and make a gift of them to his mother."

Dervish turned away, twirling his cloak like a dancer. The house began shuddering. Spidery cracks spread through the ice. Wood buckled. Windows burst. Neither X nor Ripper had the power to

342

undo what the lords had done. They stood there watching as the roof split apart like a burst seam. The noise ricocheted down the mountain and echoed back endlessly, growing softer and softer but never quite disappearing.

The lords stared menacingly at X and Ripper, still hoping they'd be foolish enough to fight.

"Are you ready?" said Ripper, jolting X out of his shocked silence.

He gazed at her desperately.

"Do we really stand a chance against a hundred lords?" he said.

"Heavens no," she said, smiling the fearless smile that made so many in the Lowlands believe she was insane.

With that, Ripper raced forward. She struck a lord square in the face, then leaped over him—she was a golden blur in the moonlight—and landed on the roof of Zoe's house. Almost immediately, her boots gave way on the ice. She tumbled halfway down the shingles before regaining her footing. X watched as she crawled back up—her useless fingernails struggling to hold on—then lowered herself into the crevice in the roof.

"Jonah! Are you there?" she shouted. "My name is Olivia Leah Popplewell-Heath, and I once had a boy just like you!"

The lords stood stunned, their heads craned upward. Finally, two of them sprang into the air, alighted on the roof, and stalked after Ripper.

"They will cripple her in an instant," Dervish told X with a sneer. "But at least she is enterprising—unlike yourself, you quivering lamb."

X nodded, almost respectfully.

And then he punched Dervish in the throat.

The lord fell backward.

A clutch of lords rushed at X. He lashed out in every direction, but even the slightest of them was many times more powerful than he was. For every lord he struck, another five seemed to materialize from nowhere, as if reinforcements were pouring in from the Lowlands. X was kicked and buffeted and pushed to the ground. Someone had his hand over his face—it was impossible to breathe. X's chest heaved. Regent stood motionless just a few feet away, still glaring at the snow.

X tore the hand from his face, bending the fingers back till the bones popped and their owner cursed. He gulped in air. But more lords kept coming. He couldn't stand. The weight on top of him grew greater and greater. He felt as if he was not just being held down but actually pushed into the earth.

Behind him, he could hear the house screeching, bursting, imploding. He could hear Ripper—she was still shouting for Jonah. Hadn't she found him yet? How long could he last? Through the tangle of limbs above him, X could see shards of the moon. It was like a cold eye staring down—reminding him that he had failed. He heard the lords cursing at him in a dozen languages.

But he also heard a new sound now: a sort of dark purring. It rose up from the base of the mountain. It grew louder, grew closer. In the craziness of the moment, it took X a long time to realize what it was.

THE CAR CAME UP the drive like a bullet.

X was still pinned to the ground, his body so broken that some of the lords had grown bored with beating him and drifted away. He managed to turn his head. He saw Zoe's mother drive toward them. At the sight of her, he felt a wave of shame that eclipsed even the pain. She had *told* him to stay away from her family. Then he felt a second wave—a wave of fear for her. The lords would not scatter now simply because a mortal had appeared. The tragedy was in motion. It could not be halted.

X knew what would happen next: Zoe's mother would stop the car. She'd come rushing out of it. She would scream at the lords. When that failed, she would plead. The lords would descend on her. They'd push her back and forth, spin her around. They'd laugh at her uselessness. If they were feeling merciful, they would kill her quickly. If they weren't, they'd sit her next to X and Ripper, and make the three of them watch Jonah die. Either way, the tragedy would swallow everyone it could.

But Zoe's mother didn't stop the car. She didn't even slow down. She came roaring toward the lords. Some of them had never seen a car before—and all of them were startled by the woman's audacity—so for a moment she had the advantage.

X watched as she slammed into one of the lords and flattened him against the house. He watched as she backed up—her tires spinning madly, blackening the snow—and knocked a second down. He listened as the car *thump-thumped* over the body.

The lords left X where he lay, and swarmed the car. He stood, feeling useless and ashamed. He looked toward the house. The façade had been torn away. It looked like a dollhouse now. He could see furniture, toys, dresses, boots, and picture frames—all of it sliding and crashing into crazy heaps.

He could see Ripper, too. She'd been captured by the lords. They forced her to the edge of the house and flung her off. Her golden dress was torn, her arms and legs bloodied. But she landed like a cat.

"I could not find the boy," she told X.

Tears began to spill down her face. X had never seen her cry, and the sight of it made his own eyes sting.

"Either he was too frightened to answer when I called out," Ripper said, "or his little lungs have already been crushed."

They turned toward the car. A lord had immobilized it with just the palm of his hand. A half dozen others circled it now, their robes billowing. They shattered the windows with their fists. They reached for Zoe's mother, their arms like the tentacles of a beast. Still, she would not surrender. She gunned the engine, hammered on the horn, even set the windshield wipers flapping crazily.

Ripper dried her eyes.

"Oh, I *like* her," she said.

X stumbled to Zoe's mother. He knew the fight was lost. He begged her to come out of the car. He begged the lords not to harm her. Dervish was back on his feet now, a dark bruise spreading on his throat. When he saw X debasing himself, his rage dissipated and the glow returned to his face. He nodded for the other lords to unhand Zoe's mother.

She opened the car door. Like Regent, she would not even look at X. She pushed past the lords, and darted toward the house, screaming Jonah's name. But the house was in its death throes. Every wall, every joint, every nail was aching to give way. It screamed back even louder.

X LURCHED TOWARD THE house now, too. No one made a move to stop him, for they knew he was too late. Every time he took a step, another wall crumbled, another ceiling fell. The bedroom where he had slept, the living room where he had answered

346

questions from the silver bowl: everything was crushed, unrecognizable, gone.

In his mind, he saw only Zoe. He remembered how she looked on the lake where her father had been fishing—the way her eyes went wide with fear. *I don't think they're coming after us. I think they're going after Jonah.* He saw her reach up to embrace him. He felt it so clearly that it was as if she were right there in front of him. He remembered the things they said to each other in those last moments. He remembered the way her heart had hovered over his own for a fraction of a second before touching down gently, as if docking there. He had pressed his lips to hers for so long she'd finally pulled away in alarm.

"You're kissing me like I'm never going to see you again," she'd said. "*Stop* it."

She'd looked at him sternly.

"If you don't come back, I'll commit some horrible crime just so I get sent to the Lowlands," she said. She was trying to be funny, but she'd begun to cry. "Ripper will come get me—won't you, Ripper? And when I get there, I will find you, X. I will find you wherever you are, and I will act really obnoxious and dress really inappropriately, and I will tell *everyone* that I'm your girlfriend."

She paused. Tried to pull herself together. Couldn't.

"Promise me again that you'll come back," she said. "Promise me the way you promised me before. I want to hear the 'two worlds' thing."

X leaned forward to kiss her once more. His face was so feverish it felt like a lantern.

"I will come back," said X. "If I do not return, it is only because not one but *two* worlds conspired to stop me."

Only then could she let him go.

Zoe's mother lay doubled over in the snow, wailing. X tried to block out the sound—his heart couldn't bear it.

"Jonah! Jonah! Jonah! Mommy's here, baby! Mommy's here!"

Ripper knelt beside her. She put an arm around her and pulled her close, as if trying to share the pain. X looked away. Even the tenderness was too much. He hated himself for what he had done. There had been a wall separating two worlds—a wall that stood there for a reason. He had burned it down.

He was innocent once. He was not innocent anymore. He'd finally made himself worthy of his cell.

The house gave a last shriek and sank into itself. The screeching and rumbling was terrifying, but the silence that followed was worse. Zoe's mother stood and rushed into the rubble, desperate to find her son's body—desperate to hold it in her arms.

Dervish strutted toward her.

"Tell me, woman," he called out, "are you aware of who it is that caused you all this pain? Are you aware of who savaged your family and brought down your house?"

Zoe's mother was searching frantically through the wreckage. She stopped for a moment. She straightened up, and turned.

"*He* did," she said.

She was pointing at X.

Dervish smiled, his tiny rodent's teeth flashing.

"A wise answer," he said. "Perhaps you can convince him to return to the Lowlands before I must extinguish *your* heartbeat, too."

"Why don't you just take him yourself?" cried Zoe's mother. "Why don't you take him right now instead of—instead of *all this*?"

"A superlative question!" said Dervish. "FINALLY I meet someone intelligent! Our friend X must come willingly so that I know he has learned his lesson well—and truly been brought to heel. Also, madam, I will not lie to you: '*all this,*' as you call it, is more fun."

Dervish motioned to the other lords. They swirled toward him in unison. They raced over the snow toward the decimated sea of trees that used to be a forest—Zoe would have said they *zoomed*—and vanished one by one.

X drew close to Ripper, his face a picture of agony.

"I will not be the cause of more savagery," he said. "I will return to the Lowlands as the lords demand, but first I must ask a final kindness of you."

"I will do anything you ask, even if it involves mayhem or murder," said Ripper. She thought for a second, then added, "*Especially* if it does."

"I ask only that you carry a message to Zoe," said X. "Tell her the Lowlands will not hold me long. Tell her that, even as I grovel at the lords' feet, I will secretly do the very things I am promised are impossible. I will find my parents—and I will find a way back to her. Whatever portion of 'forever' I am allowed, I mean to spend with her."

X spoke a few more words, and then Ripper pulled him into a sorrowful hug.

Behind them, Zoe's mother continued to search for Jonah's body. They joined her without speaking, picking miserably through the rubble. Every minute that passed without finding him was torture. Zoe's mother moaned in an almost animal way. Once again, X tried to block out the sound. He listened for something, anything else. He heard grouse flapping around a shattered stump. He heard deer politely crunching through the snow.

And then, listening harder, listening deeper, he heard a sort of rustling beneath the ruins. It was so soft that Zoe's mother had not noticed it.

The noise was coming from belowground—from where the basement used to be.

X staggered toward the sound.

Ripper followed. She heard it now, too.

Finally, Zoe's mother turned, as well. In her daze, she'd picked up a twisted hanger and a shattered skateboard. She seemed not to know why she was holding them.

She dropped them and waded through the wreckage to what was left of the basement stairs. They were blocked with crumbling plaster, mangled kitchen chairs, a ruined floor lamp, and a hundred other fragments of the Bissells' lives.

She and X and Ripper hurled everything to the side. They cleared a path down. They were in the middle of what used to be the basement—it was just a concrete pit now, open to the sky—when they found the source of the noise.

It was coming from the empty old freezer that lay on the floor.

They watched as the lid creaked open. They watched as three trembling beings emerged in exactly this order: two black dogs and the pale little boy who had saved them.

TWENTY-THREE

ZOE EMERGED FROM THE WOODS and hiked the twisting ribbon of road back toward the beach. She was so numb she didn't feel the cold. She was so shell-shocked she couldn't think, beyond wishing—as she had since she was younger than Jonah even—that the cold months weren't always so snowy and so long. After Bert had gotten senile and absolutely everything seemed to tick him off, he'd liked to say that winter just didn't know when to shut up.

She passed the spot where the truck had been parked on the shoulder of the road. It was gone now, the only evidence of its existence two muddy ruts in the snow. The truck must have been her father's. As she walked, she said a silent prayer that she'd never see him again. She remembered what Banger had said to her at the hot springs: "You can't do what I did to my family and expect them to forgive you . . . Best thing would be if they decided I was just a bad dream."

Jonah and their mother deserved to heal.

So did she.

When Zoe got to the beach, she stood awhile and stared down at the row of huts on their stilts: yellow, red, blue. The tide was out, which gave the beach a desolate look. The birds were gone, too. They'd pulled the plastic bags out of the red hut, down the white ladder, and onto the rocks, where they'd torn them apart and feasted on the remains of Zoe and X's breakfast: French toast, onion rings, chocolate cake.

A raw wind curled in from the ocean. Zoe zipped her coat up to her throat, and headed down to the water in the dark, her feet click-clacking over the loose bed of stones. She rounded up the garbage at the base of the hut. It was gross and cold and scattered every-where. The plastic bags had filled with air and sailed down the beach. She managed to catch one and stuff it into a pocket. The second one floated out over the water before she could get to it. She didn't feel like walking into the surf, even in her boots. She watched it go.

It was strange climbing up to the red hut again. It was just a tiny, rickety box, but it felt like her and X's home somehow. She knew that was stupid. Still, he had brought her breakfast here—breakfast in bed, kind of. And she'd kissed him as he slept. Just ducking into the hut now made her crazy with longing. And there was a surprise, because X's presence—his magic, or whatever it was—hadn't yet faded. The place was still warm.

Zoe sat in the hut with her back to the wall. She listened for footsteps on the rocks. She waited. Once, X had told her that he tried not to turn his memories of her over and over in his head because he was afraid they'd fray and fade if he did—and then he couldn't keep them forever. It was excruciating not to think of him, but she tried. She focused all her energy on listening. In the end, it wasn't much different from thinking of X because what she was listening for was him. The warmth in the room was like his breath somehow. It made her feel loved. It made her certain that he'd return from her house with Ripper, even if it was only to say good-bye.

Sleep took her by surprise, and she had an intense dream about watching X bathe in the stream.

She woke up an hour later to the sound of barking.

The hut was deathly cold.

All evidence of X was gone. Zoe tried to remember her dream—she grabbed at its receding tendrils—and held it close for a second before letting it go.

SHE SAW HER MOTHER and brother trekking down the dimly lit beach with Ripper, Spock, and Uhura leading the way. Her mother ran to her the moment she saw her standing by the hut. Ripper was in no rush. She was carrying Jonah. His arms and legs were wrapped around her like a koala bear, and she was whispering in his ear and making him squeal with laughter.

Zoe scanned the darkness for X—and *kept* looking for him long past the point where it was clear that he wasn't there. She felt as if she were watching his absence walk toward her. She felt sadness hollowing out her heart so it could lie down for a while.

Within moments, everyone had fallen into everyone else's arms. Jonah asked if they could stay for five minutes so he could throw rocks into the ocean. His mother said, "Okay, but *just* five minutes," and Jonah said, "I can have five? What about ten? No? What about seven—what about *eight*?"

He hadn't been outside in so long.

Ripper ran ahead with Jonah, and Zoe and her mother drifted behind, walking arm in arm. There was too much to say. Where would they even start?

Zoe could barely see her mother's face in the dark, but it seemed like she didn't know the truth about her father. Should she tell her that he was alive—that he had abandoned them all? She didn't want to. She wanted to protect her mother from the facts.

But the truth rose up out of her. She couldn't keep it in.

"Dad didn't kill himself like you thought," she blurted. "That's not what happened."

Her mother stared at her, confused and waiting.

And there on the beach, as quietly as she could so that Jonah couldn't hear, she told her mother everything. The ocean was noisy and black. It nearly swallowed the words.

Up ahead, Jonah was looking at Ripper's hands and saying, "You chew your fingernails like I do!" Ripper was saying, "Something like that, yes. But *I* will stop if *you* will stop. Have we a bargain?"

FINALLY, THEY LEFT THE beach, and walked off in search of somewhere warm to make a plan for getting back to Montana. Spock whimpered the whole way. Uhura looked back and barked at him, as if to say, *Man up!* Zoe's mother was so shocked that her dead husband was still alive, so lost in her own head, that Zoe had to walk beside her and steer her around the bends in the road.

Zoe's own head felt clearer somehow, like the box at the back of her brain had sprung open and a lot of old, unhappy thoughts had drifted out over the ocean, like that plastic bag.

After two cold, meandering miles through the woods, they

found a diner glowing in the darkness. It must have been the place where X had bought breakfast. On the door, there was a laminated picture of cinnamon French toast and bacon. Zoe touched it with her fingertips as everybody else rushed inside.

While they waited for a table, diners began noticing Ripper— her shredded golden dress, her bloodied arms and legs, her tall black leather boots. A ripple of curiosity, then alarm, went through the place. Ripper announced quietly that it was time for her to leave.

Zoe walked outside with her and hugged her a long time. Somehow, saying good-bye to the only person who understood X the way she herself did was too much. She started crying, and couldn't stop.

"He said he'd come back," she sobbed. "He said he'd come back unless—unless two worlds conspired against him."

Ripper held her.

"But two worlds *did* conspire, dear girl," she said. "Two worlds threw *everything they had* between you. The Lowlands cannot keep X from you for long, however. He bid me tell you that he will find his parents and then return to you. And I believe he will, for I taught him myself and I am a marvelous teacher. The last thing he said to me was that he wants to be worthy of you, Zoe—because you have taught him what worthiness is."

Zoe smiled.

"Well, *that's* a little over-the-top," she said.

Ripper released her from her arms, and dried a tear coursing down Zoe's face.

"When you see him," said Zoe, "please tell him that I love him, and that I remember every, every, *every* time he touched me."

"I will," said Ripper.

"Also?" said Zoe. "Help him figure out where his parents are? He's right—he needs to know who they were. He deserves to, even if it hurts him like finding out about my dad hurt me."

"I will," said Ripper.

"And *please* tell him to clean his clothes," said Zoe. "They're getting gross."

Ripper laughed.

"I will tell him everything you ask when I return to the Lowlands," she said. "Yet I must tell you that I am in no hurry to see that fetid place again." She paused, and her eyes shone mischievously. "I have decided not to return just yet. I have decided to run."

"Really?" said Zoe. She had stopped crying and was staring at Ripper with wonder. "You are *so* badass."

"I suppose I am," said Ripper. "X once asked if I had ever visited my children when I was a bounty hunter—if I had ever stood across the street just to gaze at them."

"I asked Banger the same thing," said Zoe.

"I am ashamed to say that I never did," said Ripper. "The pain kept me from it. But Jonah has put me in mind of Alfie and Belinda, my own little boy and girl. They were so, so lovely, and deserved so much better than me. I should like to go to New England and find their graves. It might heal me a little to lay some flowers there, and water the grass with my tears."

"I think that's a cool idea," said Zoe.

"Thank you," said Ripper. "The lords no doubt expect me to flee—and they'll find a way to haul me back soon enough—but at least there's no one left on earth they can punish for my misbehavior. It appears there are advantages to having been dead since 1832."

Ripper was quiet now. She slipped a hand down the neckline of her dress, and withdrew a tightly folded piece of paper she had hidden there.

"X wanted to write you a letter," she said, "just as you wrote one to him."

She handed it to Zoe. It was written on a blank page torn from a book in Zoe's house.

"He begs your forgiveness for the letter being so brief," said Ripper. "He says that you taught him how to write it—and that you taught him what it means."

Zoe knew then exactly what the letter would say. She stared at the ratty piece of folded paper. To her eyes, it looked like a flower preparing to open. Her hand trembled just holding it.

She didn't want to read the letter in front of Ripper. She wanted to be alone. So they said their good-byes, and she watched her new friend stroll down the road in her torn but still glittering dress. There was a light rain falling now, although Zoe couldn't detect any clouds overhead—the drops seemed to leak down out of the stars.

She didn't see the exact moment when Ripper disappeared. Suddenly, she was just gone. She must have vanished while walking between one streetlight and the next.

Zoe unfolded the letter, and felt her heart unfold with it.

It was written in pencil, and the point had been pressed down so hard it had nearly torn through the paper.

It was a beautiful letter, as she knew it would be.

It just said: "X."

Acknowledgments

I would like to thank Jodi Reamer, who's a truly singular badass—a literary agent with a law degree *and* a black belt. The fact that she championed this novel was thrilling, humbling, and then thrilling again. Her instincts have been invaluable, as has her unflappable personality. I myself have been known to get kinda flapped.

I'd also like to thank Cindy Loh, who's an inspiring publisher and editor, as well as an excellent person to have on your team when you need to think up a title and/or order wine. Cindy's a triathlete who competes in those insane obstacle courses where you throw javelins and scale giant walls of mud. I would say she's a great multitasker, but I think everything she does is part of the same task: to fully live.

Jodi's right hand is Alec Shane. Cindy's is Hali Baumstein. Alec, Hali: they say really nice stuff about you behind your backs.

Thank you to the whole shrewd, funny, welcoming Bloomsbury team. Cristina Gilbert, who runs marketing, publicity, and sales in the U.S., is incredible and surrounds herself with other incredibles. Thank you to Lizzy Mason and Erica Barmash for introducing me to the YA community with such a sunburst of warmth and patience. (Erica: Dallas says he likes you back!) Thank you to Courtney Griffin, Emily Ritter, Beth Eller, Linette Kim, Shae McDaniel, Eshani Agrawal, Alona Fryman, and Ashley Poston. Thank you to the life-saving folks in managing editorial: Melissa Kavonic, Diane Aronson, Chandra Wohleber, and Patricia McHugh. Thank you to the inspired designers Donna Mark and Colleen Andrews and to the fantastic sales team, with whom I had my favorite meeting of 2016.

Bloomsbury's global team has been a crucial part of this journey. Thank you to Emma Hopkin, the managing director of Bloomsbury Children's Books worldwide; to Rebecca McNally, the publishing director of Bloomsbury Children's Books UK; and to Kate Cubitt, the managing director for Australia.

Thank you to Cecilia de la Campa, the director of foreign rights at Writers House, and to Kassie Evashevski, of UTA, for their ingenuity and dedication.

While I was writing this book, many friends gave me places to work and moral support during difficult times, and I love them for it: Missy Schwartz, Carla Sacks, John Morris, Michael & Sonja O'Donnell, Valerie Van Galder (& Bella!), Stephen Garrett, Maureen Buckley, James Wirth, Chris Mundy, and Nilou Panahpour.

I'm also immensely grateful to my elite team of first readers: Darin Strauss, Susannah Meadows, Radhika Jones, Melissa Maerz, Sara Vilkomerson, and Anthony Breznican.

For conspicuous acts of kindness in support of this book, sincere thanks to Tina Jordan, Kami Garcia, Breia Brissey, Andrew Long, Bonnie Siegler, Jessica Shaw, Kerry Kletter, and Kathleen Glasgow.

Thank you to Erin Berger and Jennifer Besser, who read the earliest chapters and gave me vital encouragement. Erin and Jen are cool in too many ways for me to enumerate, but their generosity floors me.

Thank you to Hans Bodenhamer, a Montana science teacher who answered all my questions about caving and took me on a conservation trip with the Bigfork High School Cave Club. Hans and a fellow explorer, Jason Ballenksy, challenged me to be as accurate about caving—and as respectful of nature—as I could. Any and all mistakes are on me.

Thank you to the loyal friends who've always been there for me: Jill Bernstein, Meeta Agrawal, Kristen Baldwin, Sara Boilen, Sabrina Calley, Veronica Chambers, Betsy Gleick, Devin Gordon, Barrie Gruner, Chris Heath, Carrie Levy, Rick Porras, Brian & Lyndsay Schott, Lou Vogel, and my fellow YA authors in the Sweet Sixteens and the Swanky Seventeens. A special hat-tip to Karen Valby, who suggested the name Zoe for my main character back when other people were insisting that I name her after *them*. (A note from my friend Kate Ward: "I would settle for the villain.")

I'm indebted to two gripping articles: Peter Stark's examination of what it feels like to freeze to death (*Outside* magazine) and Ray Kershaw's account of the Mossdale caving tragedy (*The Independent*).

My family and I moved to Montana in 2014 to be closer to my father-in-law, Dick Bevill. This book was written largely at a thrift-store desk overlooking Dick's ranch, and it is, I hope, animated with a bit of his own questing spirit and his reverence for the natural world.

Thanks also to my intrepid brother-in-law, James Peterson, who went caving with me so I wouldn't wuss out, and my nephew, Max McFarland, who coined the term "Struggle Buggy," which I have borrowed for Zoe's Taurus. Max uses it to describe his friend Nick's junky Toyota Corolla, which resembles a car only insofar as it is car-shaped and has tires.

Finally, I would like to thank my awesome, weird-in-a-good-way children, Lily and Theo, and my sister, Susan Heger, who is the most openhearted person I've ever known.

X and Zoe will return in

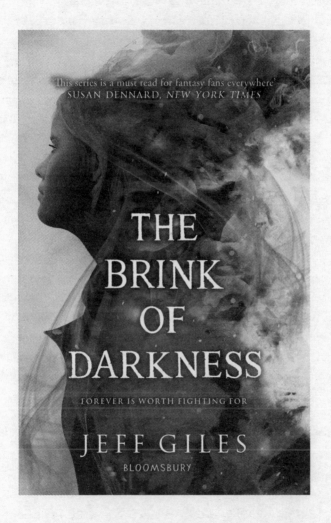

'This series is a must read for fantasy fans everywhere'
SUSAN DENNARD, *NEW YORK TIMES*

THE BRINK OF DARKNESS

FOREVER IS WORTH FIGHTING FOR

JEFF GILES

BLOOMSBURY

Coming July 2019